Maxen's ire gentled as he saw the fire leap higher in her eyes. Odd, he thought, but there was something so appealing about her daring. Something that went beyond bedding her, though it certainly did not exclude it.

"You do not hate me, Rhiannyn. You told me so yourself."

"I lied," she retorted.

He shrugged. "Then at least I can console myself with one thing."

"And what is that?"

He leaned near her. "That which you refused my brother."

She frowned.

"You desire me," he stated. "Hate me . . . very well . . . but you also want me."

She gasped. "You fantasize."

"Should I prove it to you?"

Defiantly, she tossed her head back. "Try, oh mighty Norman," she dared, "and know the truth."

Though Maxen knew they were only words spoken out of anger, not the invitation they sounded once they passed her lips, he took up the challenge. Gripping her arms, he lifted her slight figure.

"What are you doing?" she cried, straining back.

"Seeking the truth," he said, then ____ hand to the back of her he_____ And true to his seeking, li_____ nnyn flowered in his ha___

_____on Bride

Saxon Bride

Tamara Leigh

FANFARE™

BANTAM BOOKS
NEW YORK TORONTO LONDON SYDNEY AUCKLAND

Saxon Bride
A Bantam Fanfare Book/January 1996

ISBN 0-553-56534-6

Published simultaneously in the United States and Canada

PRINTED IN THE UNITED STATES OF AMERICA
RAD 0 9 8 7 6 5 4 3 2

To Skyler Hunt on his second birthday—a bundle of a miracle, and the littlest hero I've ever known. May you grow to one day become hero to a wonderful heroine.

Saxon Bride

Chapter One

"A thousand times I curse you!" the fallen knight shouted at the woman who cradled his head in her lap, her blue skirts turned purple with his blood.

Lifting an arm, he closed his fingers around the dagger protruding from his chest, dragged it from his body, and let it fall to the road where he lay. Splaying his hand over the mortal wound, he turned his glazed eyes back to the woman.

"To eternity I curse you, Rhiannyn of Etcheverry," he rasped, his accusing stare unwavering from her pale face. "If you will not belong to a Pendery, you will belong to no man—your days and nights yawning pits of deepest despair. Never again to know the love of a man."

With fingers that trembled, Rhiannyn brushed the tawny hair back from his damp brow. "Forgive me, Thomas," she whispered. "Pray, forgive me."

"The Devil forgive you!" Jerking his head back, he lifted his bloodied hand to her throat and encircled it.

Though approaching death weakened him, his grip was cruel, strangling. Rhiannyn did not draw back, telling herself it would be no less than she deserved if he ended her life. For a fleeting moment, she even wished he would. Then the torment of these past years, which had seen so many dead, would also end.

Too late, she wished she could relive the past few hours. Given a second chance, Thomas would not be dying in her arms. If only she had not run from him. . . . If only he had not come after her. . . .

Her tears brimmed over and coursed a slow path down her dirt-smudged face. "I never wanted this," she said, a sob catching her voice.

"Curse you," Thomas choked, then dragged his hand down her bodice, leaving a scarlet trail. Letting his arm fall back to his side, he shifted his gaze to the gray sky above.

"Avenge me, brother," he cried to the heavens with his last breath. His body spasmed, and though his eyelids did not fall, death took him.

"Nay!" Rhiannyn wailed, staring into sightless eyes that would never again darken with annoyance at her defiance, nor smile at her.

Thrusting clenched fists into the air, she stared up at the God who had allowed this terrible thing to happen. "Why?" she cried. "It did not have to be!"

Her cry was answered by the rolling thunder of an approaching storm.

"Now more will die," Rhiannyn screamed. "Is that your will?"

Chill droplets sputtered from the clouds, spotting her fair hair and mingling with her tears. A moment later, the rain was loosed in sheets that drenched her to the skin.

Rhiannyn did not turn at the sound of approaching horses, did not flee as she ought to. Instead, uncaring whether those who came were her kin or Thomas's avenging men, she bent over the man who lay silent in her lap.

"I will belong to none," she whispered, the salt of tears bitter on her tongue. " 'Twill be a burden I will carry the rest of my days." No husband, no children, only the great emptiness Thomas had banished her to—an emptiness complete now that she had lost not only her entire family to the conquering Normans, but the family she would some day have made with another.

She heard voices. Raised in anger, they shouted foreign words—the French of the Normans.

First fear, then relief swept her. She would not be made to carry her burden of guilt for long. With the coming of the Pendery knights, she was assured her own death was not far off.

Though she thought herself prepared for the fury, she cried out when merciless hands wrenched her upright, causing Thomas's body to roll off her.

"Saxon bitch!" Sir Ancel snarled at her. "What have you done to our lord?"

Rain pelting her upturned face, she met the livid gaze of the man who had been Thomas's friend. "He is dead." She spoke in French so he might understand. "I—"

The back of his hand struck her hard, sending her to her knees amidst the sludge of the muddy road. She expected him to come at her again, but instead he turned to the prone figure of his liege, around which the others had gathered.

"Thomas," he groaned as he turned him face up. "Thomas."

She could run, Rhiannyn knew, the bordering woods only a short sprint away. However, though the survivor in her urged her to do just that, she found herself curiously resigned to the fate awaiting her. Lifting her head, she looked past Thomas's men to the lone rider who had not dismounted.

His countenance mirroring disbelief, Thomas's fourteen-year-old brother stared at her a long moment before shifting his stricken gaze to the man Sir Ancel had pulled into his arms. The youth's name was Christophe, and he had always been kind to Rhiannyn. Lame from birth, he was a gentle soul destined to know books and healing, rather than weapons. And now he would certainly hate her, would cheer her demise when all was done, but he would not avenge his brother's death as Thomas had bid him to. He was incapable of such violence.

More than anything, Rhiannyn wanted to defend herself to Christophe, to explain what had happened, but she knew it would be a terrible mistake. Never would she be believed, and even if she were, naught would be gained from the telling of her story. These angry Normans would still avenge Thomas's death with further carnage of her people. Nay, let them think this her doing, and hers alone. As Thomas had died because of her, it was fitting justice that she be the one to shoulder his death.

"Lady Rhiannyn, rise," Sir Ancel commanded.

Lady only because Thomas had named her one, Rhiannyn mused. Intent on wedding her, though she had shamed him with her public refusal, Thomas had bestowed the title on her. After all, it would not have done for a favorite of the bastard Norman king to take a Saxon commoner to wife.

Imagining her blood would soon soak the same ground as Thomas's did, Rhiannyn rose and faced those who would stand in judgment of her.

"Who did this?" Sir Ancel demanded, his face contorted with loathing, his short-cropped hair plastered to his head.

Rhiannyn lowered her eyes so the lie could be more easily told. "It was I who killed him."

Sir Ancel grabbed her shoulders, his grip punishing. "No more of your Saxon lies," he said, shaking her so hard she thought the end was surely upon her. "Tell me the truth!"

"I have told it," she gasped. "It was I who did it."

"Do you think me a fool?" he snapped. "It was your lover who put the dagger to him, wasn't it?"

He spoke of Edwin, the second son of the Saxon thane

who had ruled Etcheverry before the coming of the Normans. Edwin, whose bitterness kept the enmity alive between the conquering Normans and the vanquished Saxons. Edwin, who had never been her lover, though he would have been her husband had the Normans not conquered a land they had no right to.

Though Rhiannyn would never admit it, it was Edwin who had aided in her escape that morn, he who had fought Thomas such a short time ago and been wounded by his opponent's blade. But it was not Edwin who had landed the death blow.

Some other person, unseen and surely of Saxon blood, had done the deed. He had thrown his dagger from the concealing woods a bare moment after Thomas had sliced through Edwin's sword arm.

Thomas's pained cry, mingled with Edwin's angry shout, echoed in Rhiannyn's head as she stared unseeingly at Sir Ancel. She saw instead Thomas falling, driving the dagger deeper into his chest. She ran forward to take him in her arms, and he stared up at her in disbelief as Edwin grabbed her arm and urged her to her feet. She heard Edwin's angry words, when she refused to leave the dying Thomas, and saw again his useless injured arm as he awkwardly mounted his steed. Then Thomas's sightless eyes staring past her. . . .

Gathering her courage, Rhiannyn met Sir Ancel's gaze. "Nay," she answered him, "it was I who killed him."

He sneered at her, not believing her. "And where is your weapon?"

The dagger. What had become of it? Blinking, Rhiannyn lowered her head and searched for a glint of blade. It hid itself well, and only by going down on hands and knees was she able to find it. Grasping its intricately carved hilt, she stumbled back to her feet and raised it for Sir Ancel to see. Though the nasty weapon had also drawn the blood of the earth—mud—Thomas's blood was still visible.

"This," she said. "This is what I used."

Still, disbelief showed on Sir Ancel's face and those behind him.

Was it that they did not believe her capable of such an atrocity? Rhiannyn wondered. Or that they did not believe she possessed the strength required to kill a man, especially one the size of Thomas?

Desperate, she stepped forward. "God is my witness," she lied, promising herself she would repent later. "It was I who killed your lord."

Rage replaced Sir Ancel's disbelief. Knocking her hand aside, he sent the dagger into the rain-beaten grass alongside the road. "Lying whore," he spat. "It was the Saxon coward who did it—Edwin!"

As Rhiannyn nursed her pained wrist, wondering if he had broken it, she saw another knight, Sir Guy, step forward and take up the dagger. For a long moment, he stared at it, then met Rhiannyn's gaze over the blade.

She looked away.

"It was Edwin, wasn't it?" Sir Ancel demanded.

She shook her head. "You are wrong. I hated Thomas. I—"

"*Non!*" Christophe shouted. Dismounting, he hobbled to where she and Sir Ancel stood. "You do not speak true, Lady Rhiannyn. You did not hate my brother. Never could you have done this."

Finding it impossible to hold his gaze, which begged her to say otherwise, Rhiannyn looked away. "I am responsible," she said, which was true whether it was she who had wielded the weapon or that other who had slipped away unseen.

Grabbing a handful of her wet hair, Sir Ancel forced her head back. "Fear not, young Christophe," he said. "Either way, justice will be done."

Rhiannyn quelled the impulse to struggle against the pain. After the death she had just witnessed, it shamed her to feel anything other than a twinge of discomfort.

"Do it now," she pleaded. "Be done with it."

Sir Ancel bared his teeth. "I am tempted," he said, "but it would be too good for the likes of you. Nay, when it is time, you will suffer as Thomas did. A slow and painful death."

For the first time, Rhiannyn felt the cold of wet clothes soaked through—or was it simply fear? Though she tried to suppress the answering shudder, it racked her body.

"I am resigned to my fate," she said through teeth that had begun to chatter. "Do with me as you will."

"Such brave words from a Saxon," Sir Ancel said. "We will see how well you fare in the dungeon." He thrust her from him.

Caught off balance, Rhiannyn stumbled and fell. Unmoving, she lay on the ground, arms splayed in the mud. Dear God, she prayed, be merciful.

It was Christophe who assisted her to her feet. "Lady Rhiannyn—"

"Do not call her that, boy!" Sir Ancel snapped. "She has never been, and will never be, a lady."

"She was to have been my brother's bride," Christophe reminded him.

"Aye, and Thomas was a fool to think he could trust her. Look at him." Sir Ancel jabbed a finger to where two of the knights had draped Thomas's body over the back of a horse. "He is dead, boy. Dead."

Turning his back to him, Christophe squeezed his eyes tightly closed, his lower jaw trembling as he fought emotions that endeavored to unman him before knights who would scorn him for showing a woman's weakness.

He must be strong—had to be strong. With Thomas gone, the estates would now fall to him, a boy who had never trained for knighthood, whose single aspiration had been to one day serve as his brother's steward. He wanted none of it, most especially not the struggle for power that would ensue, but what other course was there? Of the four sons born to Lydia Pendery, only two survived, himself and the eldest.

"Maxen," he murmured. Maxen, to whom all that was the Penderys' should have belonged had he not shunned it in favor of a different life.

Would he come out? Christophe wondered. And once out, would he stay?

• • •

His demons quieted, the tension finally drained from him, the lone figure rose from before the high altar and lifted his tonsured head to stare at the array of holy relics, the only witnesses to the fervent prayers he had offered.

"Answer them, Lord," he said quietly. He waited, as he did each time he prostrated himself in the chapel, and again he was denied deliverance from the memories that had brought him to this place.

Defeated by a God who was not yet ready to forgive him his atrocities, he turned and walked from the chapel. He would try again on the morrow, and the morrow after that. And one day there would be peace for his soul, a place for it other than perdition.

Paying no heed to the chill wind that cried the coming of winter, he left his head uncovered and crossed to the cloister where his studies awaited him.

It was Brother Aelfred who stopped him. "There is a messenger come from Etcheverry to speak with you, Brother Maxen," he said, his voice muffled by his hood.

Maxen frowned. What ill had befallen the house of Pendery that Thomas would call upon him now? For the past two years there had been only silence, as he had directed upon entering the monastery. Why had Thomas broken his vow to leave him be?

"He awaits you in the outer house," Brother Aelfred continued.

Maxen nodded.

At the outer house, the messenger stood without, his back to Maxen. The wind sifting through his short black hair and tugging at his clothes, the man stared at the walls surrounding the monastery. Then, as if sensing he was no longer alone, he slowly turned and met Maxen's questioning gaze.

Maxen drew to an abrupt halt, his heavy clerical gown eddying about his feet. "Guy," he said, recognizing the man who had fought beside him at Hastings.

Guy's lip whipped into a grin. "No other," he said.

Stepping forward, he clapped a hand to Maxen's shoulder. "It is good to see you again."

His demons roused, his body grown tense, Maxen pulled back. "Why have you come?" he asked.

Clearly, Guy was taken aback by the chilly reception, but he quickly assumed an impassive face. "Let us go inside and we will talk."

Maxen narrowed his gaze on him. "Something is wrong at Etcheverry?"

Guy nodded. "Very wrong, Maxen. Otherwise, I would not have come."

"Thomas sent you?"

"Nay, it was Christophe."

Christophe, Maxen thought, who must be . . . fourteen summers old? It could only mean something had happened to Thomas. An unbearable constriction in his chest, he asked, "What of Thomas?"

A silence ensued as Guy struggled with the words. In the end, though, he could find no way to soften them. "Thomas is dead."

Maxen stared at him. "Dead," he echoed. Another brother dead. The memories he had worked so diligently to put from his mind came surging back. As if there again, he saw the sloping meadow of Senlac that had been the battlefield. He saw the careless strew of ravaged bodies and heard the Norman battle cries of *"Dex aie"* and "God's help"; the Anglo-Saxon war cries of "Holy Cross" and "Out! Out!" He smelled the wasted blood and felt the heat of too many bodies pressing in around him. And he saw Nils. . . .

Maxen forced himself back to the present. Nils was dead, and now, too, was Thomas. There was only Christophe and himself.

So Guy would not see his torment, he turned his back to him and clenched a hand over his face. "How?" he demanded. "Saxons?"

"A Saxon woman. She whom he was going to wed."

Maxen swung back around. "A woman? His betrothed?"

Uncertain how to deal with this man of God who, at this moment, looked anything but, Guy took a cautious step back. "She claims to have been the one," he said, "but Sir Ancel believes it was her rebel lover who murdered Thomas."

Maxen knew he should distance himself immediately, that he should accept his brother's death and walk away, but he had to know. "Why did she turn on him?"

"Rhiannyn—that is her name—is the daughter of a villein who died at Hastings. She blames the Normans for the death of her family—her father and two brothers at Hastings, her mother during a raid on their village shortly before the battle. Foolish Thomas." Guy shook his head sadly. "He thought he could make her forget what she had lost by bringing her into the castle and grooming her to become his wife."

His hands hidden in the long sleeves of his robe, Maxen clenched them into fists in an attempt to control the emotions he had thought never again to experience. "It was Thomas who lost," he growled. "Lost everything."

"Aye. Rhiannyn refused to wed him, and though he could have forced her to marriage, he was determined that she would come to him willingly."

"And she did not?"

Guy issued a regretful sigh. "Over a sennight past she slipped free of the castle. When Thomas discovered her gone, he rode after her, would not wait for any to accompany him, though the woods are replete with Saxon rebels."

An old anger in his blood, Maxen inclined his head for Guy to continue.

"It was too late when we found them. Thomas was already dead, a dagger run through him."

"And the woman?"

"Rhiannyn was there. She claimed she had killed Thomas, but all knew it not likely. Though the murdering blood of the Saxons surely runs through her veins, she most assuredly has not the strength to do such a thing."

"Then she protects another."

"Aye, 'twould be Edwin Harwolfson, to whom she was betrothed ere William claimed England's throne."

"And who is this Edwin?"

"The second son of the thane who possessed those lands which King William awarded to Thomas. As the only survivor of his family, he claims right over Etcheverry, refuses to acknowledge any Norman as his overlord, and leads the Saxon rebels who abound in the woods of Andredeswald. It had to have been he who murdered your brother, Maxen."

"Revenge."

Guy nodded. "And he is more than qualified for it. A worthy adversary."

"Is the uprising limited to Etcheverry?"

"It was, but now it has grown beyond to other Pendery lands. Many are the villages that are dying as the young and strong go to join Edwin. There are not enough to work the land and tend—"

"Tell me more of this Edwin."

"He was a royal housecarle to King Edward before his death, and then later to the usurper, Harold."

Surprise shot through Maxen. A housecarle who had not died with his king? According to Saxon tradition, no housecarle should leave the battlefield alive if his lord was killed. There was no worse disgrace for a Saxon than to survive the death of one's lord.

"Now Edwin makes havoc on Normans he catches out in the open," Guy continued, "and those who dare pass through the woods. A half dozen times now he has led attacks against Etcheverry Castle, and several times against its sister castle, Blackspur. The first year he set fire to both castles so often that Thomas finally turned to using stone instead of wood."

Maxen briefly registered this last before voicing the pressing question. "How is it this Edwin did not die at Hastings?"

"The Saxons say that while William slept not a hundred feet away, an old witch pulled Edwin from beneath the dead and breathed life back into him—took him from the battlefield and healed up his wounds with magical words and herbs."

"And the Normans? What do they believe?"

Guy nearly pointed out that Maxen was also Norman. However, he captured the words before they could trip from his lips. "The Normans say Edwin is a coward. That he ran to the woods when his king fell."

"What think you?"

Guy blinked in surprise. "I?" He shook his head. "Word abounds of his ferocious bravery. And with mine own eyes I once saw the wound which he was said to have gained while fighting to protect his king. Though I dare not say it too loudly amongst others, methinks he did not take to flight."

Maxen wondered if he had ever met this Edwin. By invitation of the now deceased King Edward, who had had a particular fondness for Normans, the Penderys had resided on English soil for nearly a quarter century. It was for this reason the first language of the Pendery offspring was Anglo-Saxon, though they were equally fluent in Norman French. However, following King Edward's death, the Penderys had not supported Harold Godwinson's claim to the throne, siding instead with their liege, Duke William of Normandy, in overthrowing the usurper. So much bloodshed . . .

Maxen shook his head in an attempt to dispel the haunting images. With what he'd heard these last minutes, those images had grown sharper and more detailed, almost as if only yesterday he had pierced the blood-soaked soil of Senlac with his sword and walked away from the abomination.

Damn Thomas for his obsession with the deceitful Saxon wench. Damn him for dying and leaving none but Christophe to deal with the responsibility of the Pendery estates. Damn—

"There is only you." Guy broke through Maxen's silent cursing.

Maxen met his intense gaze. "What speak you of?" he demanded, knowing but not wanting to.

Guy shook his head. "Christophe cannot do it, Maxen—nor does he want to. If that which is the Penderys' is to remain theirs, you must come out of the monastery."

Leave the monastery, the refuge which, with prayer, might someday free him of his demons? "I cannot," Maxen said. "My vows have been spoken. My life is here."

"A petition has been dispatched to King William. If he agrees, which he would be a fool not to, you will be freed of your vows—at a price, of course."

Maxen stared at Guy, his insides madly churning emotions that would be better left undisturbed. With their arousal, he was viciously reminded of who he was and what he had done. Here were the reasons he had come to this place, never again to know the outside world that had made him bloodthirsty and merciless.

Incited, his monk's calm thrown to the four corners of the earth, he smote a fist into his palm. "Christophe sent the petition?"

Guy swallowed hard, then shook his head. "Nay, Maxen, it was I, though it was with Christophe's blessings that I did it."

Maxen stepped toward him. "You?"

Guy retreated. "Forgive me, but I had to."

Landing his hands on the smaller man's shoulders, Maxen shook him. "Why?" he snarled. "Who gave you the right to meddle in my life?"

Beneath the pressing weight, Guy squared his shoulders. "In the name of our friendship I did it. I could not bear to see all lost."

"But Christophe—"

"Nay, I have told you. Christophe is not fit to lord over Etcheverry and its environs, nor to lord over Trionne once your father passes on. If you do not come out, then it will be Sir Ancel Rogere who controls Pendery lands. Christophe will be naught but a figurehead."

"Rogere?"

"Aye, Thomas's friend whom he intended to make lord of Blackspur Castle. Surely you remember him?"

Vaguely. Thomas had first become acquainted with the

Norman prior to the Battle at Hastings. A landless noble, Rogere had sought his fortune fighting alongside Duke William in the quest for the English crown. However, he had fallen early in battle, and his only reward had been a handful of coins.

"Continue," Maxen ordered.

"It is he who sits at the high table in Christophe's stead. He who directs the household knights and to whom the steward answers. He whose intent it is to seal his power by petitioning your father for your sister, Elan, in marriage."

Guy's words sank in with finality. Loosing his grip on him, Maxen turned away. Lost. All was lost. Duty bound him to defend his family's holdings, even if it be at the cost of the very soul he'd worked so hard to save these past two years. He had no choice in the matter.

"How long ere the king's reply?" he asked, feeling suddenly weary.

"I would think the abbot should receive it within the next few days, no more than a sennight."

Maxen knew William would not dally long over the decision, nor did he have any delusions as to what that decision would be. After all, William had wanted to award the barony to Maxen, and had only grudgingly conferred it upon Thomas when Maxen refused and entered the monastery instead.

"Does Sir Ancel know what you do?" Maxen asked.

"He does not, my lord."

My lord. So, Guy also suffered no delusions as to what William's edict would be, Maxen thought, his anger flaring once more. Though it took every bit of resolve he had left, he forced the emotion down, letting it simmer just beneath the surface.

"I will ready myself," he said, and turned to go.

"Maxen?"

He looked over his shoulder. "Aye?"

Guy's regretful smile did not quite reach his eyes. "It is for the better."

Maxen's laugh was bitter. "Better for the house of Pendery," he said scornfully. "But me? Nay, Guy, this is where I belong." And she who had forced him from his sanctuary would pay dearly for what she had done.

"The woman, Guy. Does she yet live?"

"Aye, my lord, but only by the grace of your brother. Sir Ancel would have had her put to death, but it was the one thing Christophe would not allow."

"Why?"

"Regretfully, it would seem he is as enamored of her as was Thomas."

Foolish boy. Directly or not, the woman was as responsible for Thomas's death as her lover was. "Then she still dwells in the castle."

"Not ... exactly."

"Where, then?"

"The dungeons, my lord. Sir Ancel insisted."

Rightly so, Maxen thought, and realized the Maxen of old had edged out the Maxen he had struggled to shape these past two years. Suddenly, the vows he had taken seemed so hollow. They were never meant to be, and now they would be no more. All because of a treacherous woman.

So be it, Maxen thought. If he must give up the monastery, then damn compassion, charity, and forgiveness. Damn them all, every last one of those kindnesses he had been taught. And God help the Saxon wench.

Chapter Two

Rhiannyn sprang to her feet, but there was no refuge in the confines of her prison, and no escape past the man advancing on her.

"What do you want?" she demanded, pressing herself against the wall.

Stone-faced, his breath pungent, the guard caught hold of her and began dragging her from the cell.

She resisted, twisting side to side and lashing out with small fists and feet. Though the odds were against her, for she was too slight to make any impact on the burly guard, she refused to let go of her struggle—even when he heaved her onto his shoulder and carried her from the cell.

Cursing and pounding on his back, Rhiannyn watched through her tangle of hair as the cell receded and the passageway opened wide to swallow her into its frightening darkness.

Preferring her own darkness, she squeezed her eyes closed, and only when she was unceremoniously deposited on a stool did she open them again. Grabbing the splintered seat to keep her balance, she tossed her head back and stared at the guard's expressionless face.

"What is—" she began, but broke off when he stepped aside. She sat in the center of a dimly lit room, and straight ahead of her, mostly hidden in the shadows, was a dark figure.

The man swiped a hand across his face in a gesture that held no meaning for Rhiannyn until the guard produced a piece of soiled linen and began binding it about her eyes.

"Nay!" she protested, panicked at the prospect of being denied her vision. In the end, though, she had no choice in the matter.

Muttering foul words beneath his breath, the guard clasped her hands behind her, lashed them together with a length of coarse rope, then forced the blindfold on her.

Was this to be her end? Rhiannyn wondered as she teetered on the stool. Though she told herself it was as it should be, that she deserved no better, a part of her craved survival. Wait, she counseled. Wait and see.

She heard the sounds of retreat—the guard, no doubt—and waited with held breath to discover the reason she had been brought to this place.

There was quiet, long and bordering on the unbearable, then footsteps over the stone floor.

Her skin pricked as the air stirred with the man's coming, the sensation so strong she could not have said if he touched her.

"Comfortable?" he asked in Norman French, his hoarse voice close to her ear.

Jerking her head around, she felt the rasp of a lightly bearded jaw. However, the man did not draw back.

"Who are you?" she asked.

She felt his shrug. "Who do you want me to be, Rhiannyn of Etcheverry?"

Sensing the beast within the man, she swallowed hard on her fear. "It matters not what I want," she said, praying he did not detect the tremble in her voice. "You are Norman. Thus, my enemy."

"Norman or no, I have the power to be your judge . . . or your champion."

Wondering if it was a throat wound responsible for the rumbling whisper with which he spoke, she asked, "And which will you be?"

"That is up to you."

Her insides cringed. For certain, he wanted something from her. Likely, it was the same as Sir Ancel wanted—Edwin. Feeling like a mouse cornered by a cat, her life dangling before her, she awaited confirmation.

His hand closed over her lower jaw. "I would know where your lover dwells," he said, his thumb pressing into the hollow beneath her cheekbone.

Aye, the same as Sir Ancel. Her heartbeat quickened in anticipation of the brutality that was sure to follow, for each time Sir Ancel had come to her these past days, he had left her bruised and aching.

"As I have no lover, I know not whom you speak of," she said, pretending obtuseness. Stiffening, she readied herself for the blow—a blow that never came.

"I speak of Edwin," her tormentor growled, his hand tightening on her jaw.

More than a little addled by the fact he had not reacted as she'd expected, it took Rhiannyn a moment to formulate a reply. "I do not know where he is," she lied.

His breath upon her face was warm, smelling faintly of wine. "Don't you?"

She shook her head. "But if it is Thomas's murderer you seek, then it is not Edwin you want."

"Really?" he asked mockingly. "Then who?"

With a backward thrust, Rhiannyn wrenched out of his hold, and in the process, nearly toppled from the stool.

Catching her arm to steady her, the man pressed his fingers into the painful bruise Sir Ancel had inflicted the day before. Rhiannyn flinched, but bit back the cry of pain that would have betrayed her.

"I killed him," she declared, straining away from the vise of his hand. "It was I."

Silence, and then derisive laughter rumbled from his chest. "A wee Saxon wench downed a mighty knight of King William? You profane Thomas's memory with such tales, Rhiannyn."

Aye, but it was that or the massacre of her people.

"Surely it was Edwin who killed him," her tormentor said.

"He could not have," she said truthfully. "Thomas did serious injury to Edwin's sword arm and was about to slay him through when ... when I planted the dagger." She finished with a lie. "I had to do it."

"Do you think me a fool, Rhiannyn?"

Nay, for certain he was no fool, but why couldn't he just punish her and leave the others be? It was a useless debate she had undertaken, a waste of breath. "Why will you not let me see you?" she asked, attempting to turn the conversation.

His silence denied her an answer.

"Are you so unsightly that none can stand to look upon you?" she went on with reckless disregard.

Again, quiet.

"Are you Thomas's father?"

The silence stretched taut, almost to snapping, then he leaned close. His mouth brushing the sensitive lobe of her ear, he whispered, "Nay, Rhiannyn, I am brother to Thomas."

She started violently. "It cannot be. There is only Christophe now."

Pushing rough fingers through her hair, he caught a handful of it and forced her head back. Then he closed in on her, his leg riding alongside her thigh. "Though you may wish it otherwise," he said, "there is also Maxen Pendery. Maxen who now holds your pathetic fate in his avenging fist."

If that was so, why had there never been mention of another brother? Rhiannyn wondered, grateful the blindfold hid the quick tears his grasp caused to flow. Neither

Thomas nor Christophe had ever spoken of this Maxen, leading her to believe there were no others but their sister—

Suddenly, Rhiannyn's mind spun backward and recaptured Thomas's dying words. "Avenge me, brother." At the time she had thought it was Christophe he cried out to, but now it all made sense. It was Maxen he had summoned. And Maxen had come.

"I give you a choice, Rhiannyn," he said. "Deliver my brother's murderer to me or suffer the indignity of your people."

Then he would pursue and slay those who took refuge in Andredeswald, that which she had tried so hard to avoid by claiming to have been the one to kill Thomas. For some reason, she took this Maxen's warning more seriously than she had Sir Ancel's. Nevertheless, it would be useless to speak the truth, for even if he believed her story of the unseen person who had murdered his brother, he would still blame the Saxons and administer his revenge accordingly.

"I will hunt them down," he went on, enlarging on his threat, his hand clenching tighter in her hair and straining the roots. "All of them. And I will not rest until I have made certain the one who took Thomas's life is among those lives I take."

As if death had walked past her, a cold chill engulfed Rhiannyn. Wishing her arms free that she might hug them about her, she said, "Then it will be innocent lives you spoil." Innocent lives such as her mother's taken in the Norman raid upon their village. . . .

"The same as Thomas," Maxen Pendery reminded her.

He spoke true. Thomas had not been killed in battle. His life had been lost for no other reason than his desire to possess what she had refused him—herself. "Aye, Thomas," she agreed, her grief and mourning returning to her. "He should not have died."

Suddenly, Rhiannyn found herself released, the air agitated by Maxen's retreat, the stones echoing the long strides that carried him away from her. He had nearly struck her, she knew, but something in him that was not in

Sir Ancel had not allowed him the indulgence. Yet she feared him more. Why?

"Maxen," she called out.

Though he did not respond, she sensed him turn his regard on her. "I say again, do you seek revenge, 'tis against me it should be," she said, unknowingly slipping into the ease of the Anglo-Saxon language. "I am responsible for what befell Thomas. Not my people."

A strange stillness surrounded her, almost as if he had left the room, but she knew otherwise. She felt him straight through.

Finally, he spoke. "You will speak my language if you speak at all," he ordered in French. "Yours is dead."

For the first time, Rhiannyn puzzled over his accent, finding it so thick as to show little resemblance to either Thomas's or Christophe's. It was more like Sir Ancel's. "Do you not know our language, then?" she asked.

He drew near again. "Unlike my brothers, I was raised in Normandy. Thus, I do not embrace your vulgar tongue."

His feelings for a language not his own were echoed in Rhiannyn's past. She had known little French before Thomas Pendery had come to Etcheverry, and would have preferred it to have remained that way. However, Thomas had insisted that she learn, and she'd had little choice living amongst those who spoke only that language— excepting the Penderys, of course.

"Then you did not understand what I said?" she asked.

"I do not need to."

"But you do," she protested. "I take responsibility for Thomas's death. Your revenge should be against me." Though she tried to contain it, Rhiannyn could not prevent her startled reflex when his hand settled around her throat.

"Yes," he said, his fingers alternately compressing and loosing, "you are responsible, Rhiannyn, but I also want the one who drew final blood."

"You have the one," she said stubbornly.

His breath stirred the hair at her temples. "You will break," he warned her, "and when you do, I will have the one you protect."

Then he did not know her, Rhiannyn assured herself, for it had always been said of her that she was headstrong and more stubborn than any woman ought to be. In the face of such adversity, it was much to live up to, but she was determined she would. "I protect no one," she said, "not even myself."

His fingers stilled. "Which is what disturbs me," he said, "but then, you must desire this Edwin very much."

Wishing not to dignify his taunt with a response, Rhiannyn tried to seal her lips against a retort. But still it came. "He is not my lover!"

Maxen Pendery laughed. "Then you will not grieve overly much when I sever the life from him as he did Thomas."

Suddenly, Rhiannyn wanted very much to live, her flagging spirit drawing itself erect with the desire to undo this arrogant man. "Take care that he does not kill you first, Norman pig."

"His death or mine, Rhiannyn, I promise you we will see it together."

Teeth clenched, Rhiannyn stared into the darkness of the blindfold.

"One thing more," he said as he trailed fingers down her throat in what felt almost like a caress. "By your deceit, I am now lord of Etcheverry and beyond, and as such, I demand the respect due my station." Pushing aside the neck of her bliaut, he settled his hand to her bared shoulder.

Certain it was his intent to provoke words of maidenly outrage, Rhiannyn compressed her lips and tried hard not to think about the quickening of her flesh beneath his touch. Fear, she told herself, that was all it was.

"Henceforth," he continued, "you will address me as 'my lord'—for I am that—and never again will you speak my given name. Is that understood, *Rhiannyn*?"

She could not help the tart smile tugging at her lips. "Mayhap you ought understand something yourself, *Maxen Pendery*, and that is that I will never accept any Norman blackguard as my lord."

She felt the tension course from his hand to her shoulder, but still he did not strike her.

"Aye, you will," he growled. "That I promise." Then, to her surprise, he slid the bliaut back onto her shoulder and stepped away.

Uncertainly sitting on the stool, Rhiannyn listened to his footsteps diminish into silence. Then, despair gripping her, she slumped forward.

All had been for naught. As none believed her capable of murdering Thomas, she had given herself into the hands of her enemy only to become a pawn to a Norman bent on blood. She had been a fool, and now her people would pay for that foolishness with their lives.

Another's approach brought Rhiannyn's head up.

The guard. She knew it even before he touched her, for the powerful breath she felt on her was the same as when he had brought her from her cell.

"Come, wench," he snarled.

She was too fatigued to offer even a token resistance.

"Where are you taking me?" she asked as he guided her from the room.

"Depends."

"On?"

He laughed. "On whether or not you'd like a bit of company." He laid a hand to her buttocks.

Recoiling, Rhiannyn slammed against a dripping wall. "I would rather make company with the rats," she spat.

The guard grabbed her, wrenching her arm. "As you wish," he said, and pushed her forward.

Fool, Maxen chastised himself as he watched Rhiannyn disappear around a bend in the corridor. His misplaced sense of gallantry appearing, he had nearly gone to defend her against the perverted guard. But that would not have done, for the Saxon wench would have discovered his weakness—that the "blackguard" in him could sometimes be more gray than black. He must not forget who she was and what she had done.

But neither could he forget the livid bruises the torchlight had revealed, nor the scratches covering her. Odd, but he'd felt her pain when he had touched her, the tenderness of flesh that had refused to yield to the one who had beaten her. Sir Ancel?

Answering the question himself, Maxen nodded. It was Ancel, the man who had made bare effort to disguise his rancor when Maxen had arrived at Etcheverry a few hours earlier. His power over Christophe, hence the rule of the lands, wrested from him, the embittered knight would have to be watched closely.

His thoughts returning to Rhiannyn, Maxen wondered at the woman who had proved herself very different from the one he'd expected. A female expert at using seductive lies and the wiles of her body was what he'd expected. Instead, Rhiannyn had gained his grudging respect by employing her sharp tongue to do battle with him, rather than the weapons she might have used, and which he'd glimpsed beneath the ravages of dungeon life—voluptuous curves well-proportioned to her petite frame, the fragile beauty of her face, lips full and rosy, and curling gilt-tipped hair that fell well past her buttocks.

And then he'd touched her, and it had felt as if he'd touched that part of her that had been Thomas's. Had she lain with him? he wondered before throwing off his thoughts to ponder elsewhere. Though he better understood his brother's obsession with her, there was something else about Rhiannyn. Not only was she lovely, but she possessed a drawing light. It must have been the same for Thomas. . . .

Angry at himself for feeling what he felt, Maxen told himself Rhiannyn deserved the punishment Ancel had given her. And more. After all, what were bruises and scrapes compared to the sacrifice of life? When she, not Thomas, was alive? He had seen clearly the dark stain was spread across her bodice—blood. Undoubtedly Thomas's.

His enmity recaptured, Maxen smote a fist into his palm. From his teachings at the monastery he knew vengeance was not his, but God's, yet his growing impatience would not allow him to wait for however long God might take. And Rhiannyn would provide the means by which he satisfied his vengeance, he assured himself. She did not know it, but very soon she would lead him to the man who had slain Thomas. Then Edwin, his kith and kin, would know the full extent of the Pendery wrath.

A rhythmic scraping noise brought Rhiannyn's head up, its familiarity ruffling her memory. Squinting into the dimness, she waited to discover whether the sound was imagination or truth.

Truth. His boyish face uncertain, Christophe peered through the grate set high in the door. "Lady Rhiannyn?" he said in a low voice.

She sat upright. "Christophe. What do you here?"

"I've come to help."

Wincing at the unfolding of her stiff body, Rhiannyn pushed to her feet and took the two steps to the door of her prison. "Help?" she asked as she raised herself on tiptoe in order to see Christophe.

He lifted a hand, uncurled his fingers, and revealed a key. "I am going to free you," he said.

Rhiannyn's first thought was that it might be a trap he laid. However, she immediately gainsaid the preposterous idea, knowing in her heart he could never be so deceitful.

She gripped the bars. "Why? I was Thomas's downfall. How can you so easily forget?"

He shook his head. "Nay, I do not blame you as . . ." His voice trailing off, he lowered his gaze and sank his teeth into his bottom lip.

"As Maxen does," she finished for him.

His eyes sprang wide. "He has not hurt you, has he?"

"Nay, he has done me no harm." That was not exactly true, but neither could she define what it was he had done to her, and whether she had been injured.

Christophe's eyebrows gathered. "But he will," he said. "No matter how he may represent himself, Maxen is foremost a warrior. He has always been and will always be, no matter that he—"

"Then he does not know what you do."

Christophe shook his head. "Like Sir Ancel, he has forbidden me to see you."

Rhiannyn looked at the key and the freedom it offered. To see again the blue of the sky, the gray of a day filled with rain, the moon and stars, to breathe fresh air and smell the morning dew, to know the warmth of the sun—

Selfish thoughts, all of them, she chastised herself. In an England ruled by grasping Normans, freedom now meant little more than survival. For her, it would mean carrying a warning to Edwin and his followers about the coming of Maxen Pendery and the avenging fist he intended to smite them with.

"And when your brother discovers me gone," she said, "what punishment will be yours?"

"Maxen will not know it was I who released you."

She was not as confident. "But if he learns 'twas you?"

Though fear flashed in his eyes, Christophe pretended nonchalance. "I can take care of myself."

Unconvinced, Rhiannyn shook her head. One way or another, she would escape Maxen Pendery, but not Christophe's way. She would not have him risk his brother's wrath to help her achieve her end. Turning away, she rubbed her hands up and down her chilled arms. "I cannot," she murmured.

"But you must! The desire for vengeance eats at Maxen's insides." Christophe spoke with mounting urgency. "Are you prepared for what he will do to you?"

She glanced around at his serious face. "If the choice be me or you, then I must stay." She returned to her corner and lowered herself to the floor.

Christophe was silent a long moment, but then came the scrape of the key in the lock, followed by his appearance in the open doorway. His mind clearly made up, he crossed the cell and dropped the bundle he carried beside Rhiannyn. "Clothes to conceal your person," he informed her.

Grabbing the bundle, Rhiannyn scrambled to her feet

and held it out to him. "Nay, Christophe. Return these whence they came."

He crossed his arms over his chest. "You will need them to slip free of the castle."

Bewildered by a stubbornness she'd never before seen in the youth, Rhiannyn dropped the bundle at his feet. "Now take them and go," she said, "and do not concern yourself over me any longer."

"Think of your people," he urged. "Do you sacrifice yourself—"

"I will escape your brother," she interrupted, "but without your help."

He laid a hand to her shoulder. "Nay, lady, you will not. Many were the lives Maxen took at Hastings, and no mercy did he show any. No mercy will he show you."

"I will escape him."

"Do you not remember the ballads sung of the Bloodlust Warrior of Hastings?"

Well she remembered them—crude, triumphant songs that Thomas's men had sung many times in the hall while consuming wine and ale. Vivid and terrible they were in their accounts of the Norman warrior who had slain Saxon after Saxon, earning for himself Duke William's highest regard.

Rhiannyn nodded. "I remember," she said, then waited to hear what she dreaded Christophe would say next.

"It was Maxen," he confirmed. "The ballads are of him."

Fear cramped her belly. "They are only songs—"

"Nay, they are not. Don't you understand? It was hardly more than a game—albeit deadly—that Edwin and Thomas played. But now there is Maxen, and a more worthy opponent Edwin will never again have."

No choice, Rhiannyn realized. If she did not leave now and warn Edwin, there might never be another chance.

"End the bloodshed that has taken so many lives," Christophe pleaded. "Once you are returned to Edwin, surely he will take you far from this place."

Would he? she wondered. Would he accept her back

amongst their people? When she had refused to accompany him into the woods after Thomas had fallen, he had sat atop his horse and called her betrayer, accused her of siding with the Normans, and, like Thomas, he had cursed her.

"You will do it?" Christophe asked.

Regardless of what feelings Edwin now had for her, he must be warned, but dare she hope he would listen to her? Dare she believe he could be convinced to turn from his life of vengeance? There seemed only one way to find out.

Reluctantly, she nodded. "I will do it."

Christophe's sigh of relief echoed around the cell. "Then you must take leave now, whilst Maxen is behind doors with the steward."

"But the guard—"

"Is sleeping quite well."

"Sleeping?"

Christophe smiled sheepishly. "With a little help."

Which meant, Rhiannyn thought, that Christophe was dabbling in herbs again—and not their healing aspects. At another time and place, she would have shared his humor, but not here in the dungeon.

"In the grove I have tethered a horse that will speed your escape," he continued. "It is not very worthy, but neither is it likely to be missed for some time."

Sinking to her knees, Rhiannyn opened the bundle of clothes he had wrapped in a well-worn mantle, and drew forth a peasant's gown.

"I know—too large," Christophe said with apology, "but it was all I could mange."

She tried to smile. "It will be a fitting disguise."

"If you'd like, I will bring you some of your own garments to take with you. Once you are free of the castle, then—"

" 'Tis a wood to which I go, Christophe," she said gently, "not a castle."

"Surely there will be occasion someday."

Her smile was bitter. "As long as Normans rule England, it is not likely."

He looked away. "Still, you should have them. After all, they were made for you."

Wishing to console him, as she had so many times in the past, Rhiannyn stood and captured his hand. "I will never forget you, Christophe. You have been a good friend."

He colored, his eyes brightening with what might have been tears. "As have you," he said. Lifting her hand, he awkwardly pressed his mouth to it, then turned. However, in the doorway he paused and looked over his shoulder. "Was it your betrothed, lady?" he asked. "Was it Edwin who did it?"

Knowing it was useless to maintain that she had been the one to murder Thomas, and that there was nothing to be gained in allowing Christophe to think Edwin guilty, Rhiannyn shook her head. "Nay, Christophe, he did not."

He nodded, then walked from the cell.

"God be with you," she whispered as the shadows closed around the forlorn youth whose transition to manhood he had fought this past year. Then, her throat tight, she turned and readied herself for escape.

Chapter Three

As Andredeswald pulled her deeper into its embrace, Rhiannyn wondered for perhaps the hundredth time at the peculiar sense of being watched. Bringing her horse to a halt, she listened. Naught. Closing her eyes to better tune her hearing, she concentrated on the sounds around her—small animals scuttling for cover, the drone and buzz of insects, the air puffing at the leaves on the trees, the huffing of her horse, her own breathing. Though she did not believe the feeling of being watched was unfounded, she could detect nothing to attribute it to. Opening her eyes, she tipped her head back and searched the trees overhead for sight of one of the lookouts Edwin would surely have set about his camp.

She sighed. Wherever he was—if he even was—the man was not ready to show himself. Urging the horse forward, she worked the fingers of one hand through her snarled and filthy hair. Would any recognize her? she wondered, having earlier caught a glimpse of herself when she had stopped to take water at a stream.

It had not been her face that had stared back at her. Dark circles had traced lackluster eyes that had once shown warm brown; hollows beneath her cheekbones had made her face seem long, rather than softly rounded; her mouth had looked as if it would never smile again; and her hair . . . what had once been blonde was hidden beneath the dark of filth. Not quite eight and ten, yet she looked as if she approached thirty or more.

Just as well, she consoled herself as she guided the horse around thick bramble that threatened the animal's unprotected legs. Aye, just as well. If she had been old and unbecoming when Thomas first saw her, he would never have desired her. He would yet be alive, and Maxen Pendery would still be wherever he had come from.

Rhiannyn barely had time to acknowledge the whistle of a sling's missile before it struck her hard at the back of the neck and pitched her from the saddle. A moment later, amidst pain and a rushing in her ears, she hit the ground. The force with which she struck jolted every bone in her body, introducing her to another kind of pain, and then something—the horse's hoof?—struck her in the ribs.

Fighting to keep her senses, she dug her fingers into the dirt and tried to raise herself up. Though she managed to lift her chest, she held herself only a moment before collapsing. She must stay conscious. Must—

Voices. Jubilant and speaking the language of the Anglo-Saxons. Edwin's men, Rhiannyn reassured herself. They had to be. As their shabbily cross-gartered legs approached, she tried to see higher to know who had struck her down, but her vision blurred.

A leather shoe nudged her, then again, but still she found herself incapable of responding. Even when rough hands flipped her onto her back, she could give no words.

"Looks familiar," one of the two said.

Though her lids felt weighted, Rhiannyn forced them

open and focused on the gap-toothed, bearded face hovering above her.

"That she does," he agreed, his voice like the roll of thunder.

"Aethel?" she breathed.

Stunned silence, then, "Rhiannyn?"

His high-pitched cry of disbelief made her want to smile. She could not remember ever hearing him sound anything but gruff and surly. Dear, dear Aethel, who had been friend to her father, had undoubtedly thrown the stone. And it had hit precisely where he had intended. Just this once, it would have been nice had he been less accurate.

"It is she?" the other man asked.

"Aye, Peter. 'Tis Rhiannyn whom the Pendcry bastard stole from Edwin."

Ah, it was good to hear Anglo-Saxon spoken again, Rhiannyn mused. So wonderful—

"Traitor," Peter snarled, his bewildered face turning angry. "Norman whore."

Aethel's quick movement a blur to Rhiannyn, he straightened to his enormous height and seized Peter's tunic. "Keep your tongue, lad," he commanded, "else I will cut it from your ignorant mouth!"

Peter's stammered reply was undecipherable to Rhiannyn, then Aethel returned to her. "You have come alone?" he asked.

She nodded, the movement making her grimace. "Escaped."

He grunted and began probing the swelling at the back of her neck. "Had I known 'twas you who crept the woods," he said, "I would have received you far more kindly."

"I hurt," she whispered.

"I imagine you do."

"Edwin . . ."

"I am going to lift you now," he warned her, "then I will take you to him."

"He needs to know—" Pain racked Rhiannyn when his

arms came around her, and though she tried to bite back
the cry, it came.

"I've hardly touched you, little one," he said as he
straightened and eased her against his broad chest.

"My ribs," she gasped. "Broken?"

His concerned face dipped near hers. "Perhaps, but
we'll let Dora be the judge of that."

Dora. The old albino woman who, nearly two years
past, had appeared in the defeated and ravaged village of
Etcheverry, which had stood against the coming of the
Normans. Though the survivors had all feared her, a
handful—Rhiannyn among them—had come forward to
peer into the cart that bore their dead thane's son.

Although Edwin was barely alive, his torn and broken
body testament he would not be much longer among the
living, Dora had promised the villagers a miracle. She
would return Edwin to life, and in him they would have a
leader capable of reclaiming their land from the hated Normans.

None had believed her, for even if Edwin's body could
be mended, all knew his will would deny him life. As a
housecarle, it had been his duty to die alongside his king.
To live could only mean eternal disgrace. Still, Dora had
persisted, nursing an enraged and resistant Edwin back to
life during the days, and each night carting him out of the
village to where none were allowed to follow. And true to
Dora's promised miracle, though much against Edwin's
will, he had lived.

The steady thump of Aethel's gait lulled Rhiannyn into
a state of rest that was not quite sleep. Though she heard
the sporadic discourse between the two men, it was too
much effort to make out their words. The rare burst of
sunlight through thickening shadows teased her with its
warmth, but she knew neither comfort nor discomfort. Occasionally peering through narrowed eyes, she beheld
Aethel's wiry gray beard, and the sparsely leaved branches
above his head, but like the vaporous haze that swirled
about the floor of the inner wood, all melded into a confused blur.

It was Edwin's voice that roused Rhiannyn. Turning her head, she fixed her gaze on the unmoving visage of her betrothed, only vaguely aware of the press of men and women beyond him.

Normally a passably handsome man, he appeared less so at that moment. Sinister was what he looked. Though his face was shadowed by unkempt black hair that fell past his shoulders and a beard that had long been without benefit of clipping, it was the dark anger exuding from his features that most detracted from his looks. His mouth a compressed line, his hawkish nose flared, and higher, his green eyes narrowed to mere slits, he appeared hard and dispassionate. Frightful.

She had known he would be like this, but had fostered hope that with the passing of these last weeks he might come to understand why she had refused him. Not because she hadn't wanted to go with him, but because leaving Thomas to face death alone would have been cruel. But Edwin did not understand, and clearly had no intention of trying to.

"Rhiannyn," he said.

She swallowed past a dry throat. "Edwin."

He transferred his gaze to Aethel. "How did you come upon her?"

As if sensing Rhiannyn's trepidation, Aethel tightened his arms around her. "Nearly she came upon us," he answered. "Says she escaped the Normans."

Edwin stared at him a long moment, then nodded. "Set her down," he ordered.

"She is not well, Edwin. I threw my rock and struck—"

"She will stand, else she will lie where she falls," he snapped.

Aethel considered him a moment, then complied. "Hold steady, now," he bid Rhiannyn as he put her feet to the ground.

Knowing she faced condemnation if she plunged to her knees, Rhiannyn garnered all the strength she could and braced her feet apart. When Aethel's hand fell from her, she staggered, but stayed upright.

Sensing Edwin's raking gaze, she lifted her head. She saw the frayed sling that held the arm Thomas had wounded and put her chin up to brave his scrutiny.

"How did you know where to find me?" he demanded.

"A guess," she said, wishing her voice was stronger so it would not reflect her suffering. " 'Tis where I would have come." Where, as children, she and others had ventured to enjoy the warm pools of water that sprang from deep in the earth.

Stepping forward, Edwin clamped a fierce hand around her forearm. "Do you betray me again, Rhiannyn? Have you brought the Normans with you?"

"Nay," she said. "You know I would not do that."

"Do I?"

Though she tried, Rhiannyn could do nothing about the tears that filled her eyes. "I would never hurt you, nor my people."

Edwin sneered at her. "I know not whether you speak of the Normans or the Saxons."

Although Rhiannyn felt an intense yearning to pound her fists against his chest, she maintained her stance, knowing that not only would it be futile, but it would earn her further contempt.

"Of course I speak of the Saxons," she said. "Though the Normans stole me away, I am still one of you."

Edwin thrust her from him. "That you will have to prove."

Fortunate for Rhiannyn, Aethel was there to steady her. "I intend to," she retorted.

Edwin's gaze remained steely. "What changes have been wrought at Etcheverry since Thomas's death?"

Maxen. Her reason for coming. A chill pricking her skin, Rhiannyn said, "Another Pendery brother has come to claim Etcheverry. His name is Maxen, and he is dangerous."

Edwin's eyes lit with sudden interest. "Then the rumor is true. He has come."

Rhiannyn was surprised by his apparent lack of concern. If word had reached camp that Maxen Pendery had come to Etcheverry, then surely his reputation had also been spoken of.

"What know you of him?" Edwin asked.

She blinked aside her confusion. "He seeks Thomas's murderer, and says he will not rest until he is found. He told me—"

"Then you spoke with him."

"Aye, he came to me ere my escape."

"Why?"

"He wanted to know your whereabouts."

"Then he believes 'twas I who killed his brother."

She nodded. "Though I told him I had done it."

Laughter erupted from Edwin's throat. "Ever the martyr, aren't you, Rhiannyn?"

"But I feared he would—"

"Did he believe you?"

Her shoulders slumped. "Nay."

"Then your fears *are* founded, aren't they?"

"Not if we leave Andredeswald. Perhaps go north—"

"Run?" Edwin barked. He looked about him. "Did you hear that, men? The *lady* thinks us cowards."

Desperate to make him understand, Rhiannyn grasped his tunic. "Nay, Edwin, do not speak such things. 'Tis peace I seek. If you continue to fight, many will die—on both sides."

"I can think of no better cause than that of driving the Normans from our lands—of avenging the deaths of our men, women, and children."

He did not speak of Hastings, but of the village in which he had been returned to life. Nearly all of its buildings had been burnt to the ground and most of his people murdered—all because they had refused to hand over food supplies to the contingent Duke William had sent out prior to the deciding confrontation between himself and England's King Harold.

Defensively turning away from the haunting images that had risen before her, Rhiannyn pressed on. "This Maxen is said to have killed many men at Hastings. He—"

"And I did not?" Edwin snapped. "Hastings was about death, Rhiannyn. Everyone killed—some even their own."

"Listen to me," she pleaded. "Maxen Pendery is called the Bloodlust Warrior of Hastings. He did not just kill, he slaughtered. Don't you understand? This has to end!"

His face hard, Edwin reached up and pried her fingers loose, then pressed her palms together in a mockery of prayer. " 'Twill end," he assured her in an emotionless voice. "When the Normans are all dead it will be as it was before." No gentleness about him, he pushed her toward Aethel, then turned on his heel. However, he had taken barely two strides when he swung around.

"How did you escape?" he asked, suspicious.

It took effort for Rhiannyn to draw herself up from the despair she was quickly sinking into, but somehow she managed. "Christophe," she said. "He brought me the key."

Edwin considered this, then said, "It may have been a ruse."

"Nay, he would do no such thing."

His lips curled derisively. "Spineless whelp. By my troth, that child's heart of his will be the Penderys' undoing." Motioning for those gathered around to step aside, he strode away.

Though Rhiannyn would have liked to go back into Aethel's arms, she squared her shoulders and met the stares of the people she had grown up amongst—long-haired, bearded Saxons who refused to crop their hair or shave their faces as the Normans did. Some pegged her with accusatory gazes, others with suspicion, and yet others looked upon her with uncertainty. All because she'd shown heart for a dying man who was not of Saxon blood.

Was Thomas's murderer among them? she wondered, looking at each face anew. Or had Edwin already ferreted out the one responsible? She would have to ask him, but later—much later.

Dora broke the silence. Muttering beneath her breath, she pushed her way to the front, paused a moment to eye

Rhiannyn, then stepped up to her. Though Dora's body was bent, she moved with surprising speed.

"So, you're returned to us, child," she said, squinting up at Rhiannyn from the deep folds of a hood that protected her pink eyes from the light.

"She has been injured," Aethel said.

"Hmm," she grunted, raising a pale hand to worry at a lock of her white hair. "Looks fine to me. Nothing a good deal of scrubbing and a bit of food couldn't make right."

"She took a fine knock at the back of her neck, and says her ribs—"

Dora waved him to silence. "I do not remember Rhiannyn ever having trouble speaking for herself—quite the opposite. Let her tell me."

Rhiannyn had every intention of denying her ailments, of proving to all she was of good stock and fortitude. However, her body refused to corroborate the lie. Her knees buckled, pitching her forward.

Fortunately, Aethel was prepared, his bear's arms capturing her and saving her from another close look at the ground.

"I'm fine," Rhiannyn gasped, though she felt as if she had partaken of far too much wine.

Dora's cool, bony hands touched her neck, then felt up the sides of her face and pressed her brow. In the next instant, she jerked her hands away. "You've a curse upon you!" she screeched. "I feel it straight to my bones."

Thomas's curse—that if she would not belong to a Pendery, she would belong to no man, her days and nights . . . With the memory came the chill of that fateful day; a shiver rippled through Rhiannyn. " 'Tis true," she admitted. "I am cursed."

All around, a murmur arose, quieted only when Dora spoke. Her eyes sparkling out of the dark of her hood, she said, "Mayhap I can lift this curse."

Having accepted the curse as Thomas's due, Rhiannyn shook her head. " 'Tis done," she said.

"Done?" Issuing a shrill, broken laugh, Dora swung her

gaze to Aethel. "Bring her," she ordered. "I've much to do ere night falls."

"Weak," a caustic voice denounced.

Perspiration running into her eyes and salting her lips, Rhiannyn swung around to face her nemesis. The sword she had been practicing with hung heavy in her hands.

Edwin's own sword blade was propped easily upon his shoulder, the sling that had supported his injured arm long since abandoned. He swept her from head to foot with a look of distaste.

"Weak?" she repeated, finding it difficult to maintain the composure that had held her in good stead these past two weeks of trials and troubles, suspicion and ostracism.

"Aye, weak—like a woman."

"I *am* a woman."

"Perhaps I should clarify. What I should have said was that you are weak like a woman bred of Normans."

Rhiannyn knew she should not argue with him, that it only made things worse for her when she did, but she could not help herself. "And again, I remind you I am Saxon."

"It is what you say, but you have yet to prove it."

Letting her sword fall from her hand, Rhiannyn threw her palms up, baring her calluses. "This past sennight I have swung a sword half again as heavy as your own, and yet you say I have not proven fealty to my people?"

Though she knew he'd set her to learning the sword to punish her, in the camp there were several other women who also trained in the use of weaponry. It was not that there weren't enough men, Aethel had told her, but rather, it was thought women might be useful against unsuspecting Normans.

Stepping forward, Edwin grabbed Rhiannyn's hand and cursorily examined her palm. "Nay, you have not proven fealty," he said. Releasing her, he retrieved her sword and held it out to her. "Take it, and never again let me see it thrown carelessly to the ground. I will not tolerate such negligence."

Inwardly, Rhiannyn groaned at the prospect of taking its ungodly weight again. A smaller woman than most, she was taxed nearly beyond bearing to swing the thing. Her muscles and joints screamed, and her bruised ribs burned.

Made solely for training, the sword was more unwieldy than those used in battle. Aethel had explained that its purpose was to accustom a man to the weapon and develop his muscles. Thus, going into battle, the sword he carried would seem light and easily maneuverable.

Why, then, Rhiannyn had asked, did none of the others practice with such swords? His answer had been simple—no others had come into Edwin's disfavor.

Squaring her shoulders, Rhiannyn took the sword. Edwin motioned to the pel—the wooden post protruded straight up from the ground, displaying the marks Rhiannyn had made that day in her attempt to master the sword, as Edwin had ordered.

Garnering strength from the need to put him in his place, she stepped forward and struck the pel with all her might. Though the impact jolted every bone in her body and snapped her teeth together, she went at it again. The second blow fell short of the first by several inches, and the next by a few more. Still, she ignored Edwin's mutterings and persisted in proving him wrong.

Rhiannyn was beginning to wonder how much longer before she collapsed in a sweat-stained heap when shouts rose in an urgency she'd not heard before. Swinging around, she watched as a group of four riders burst upon the glade, all but one recognizable as a follower of Edwin.

On a horse whose better days were scarcely within memory, the stranger was conspicuously out of place. Wearing a shabby russet-colored mantle, under which the skirts of a robe were visible, the large man sat his horse with obvious unease. More than his garments and his awkward carriage, though, his tonsured head with its fringe of hair set him apart from Edwin's rebels. It was a monk the Saxons brought into their midst. But why?

Edwin wasted no time in striding across the glade to the riders.

Her own curiosity roused, Rhiannyn balanced the sword upon her shoulder as she had seen Edwin do, and followed him to where the horsemen had dismounted.

"Found him wandering through the woods," a stout Saxon informed Edwin. "Said the Normans were after him."

"Aye, and meant to kill him," another added.

Though it was not unusual for Saxons fleeing Norman oppression to seek refuge in Andredeswald and join with Edwin, swelling the ranks of the rebellion to more than ninety strong, Edwin was decidedly skeptical. Placing himself before the monk, he asked, "You are Saxon?"

The monk inclined his head.

"By what name are you called, Brother?"

"Justus," the man answered, his voice deep and resonant, and without hint of a foreign accent that might put lie to his claim of being a Saxon. "Brother Justus of St. Augustine."

A most peculiar sensation swept Rhiannyn, a stirring in her, a feeling she might have encountered this monk before. She swept her gaze up his great height, alighted upon broad shoulders, then peered into his rugged yet attractive face. There, a long nose, straight but for the slight bent that testified to its having been broken in the past, yielded to prominent cheekbones. Lower, lightly stubbled planes revealed a hard jaw, and in his chin was cut a cleft so deep its shadow appeared to be a dark smudge upon his skin.

Working her way back up, Rhiannyn picked out blue eyes fringed by lashes the same dark brown as his hair, hair that looked to be growing out of its severe tonsure cut. Aye, a handsome man, but not one she had met before, she concluded. She would surely have remembered a man of such size and countenance, most especially a monk.

"And you say the Normans make after you?" Edwin asked.

"Aye."

"Why?"

Sorrowful, the man shook his head. "The clergy arriving from Normandy think naught of impugning the reputation of the saints, of scattering the relics of centuries past, of . . ." Trailing off, he threw his hands into the air. "In my anger I challenged them, and have thus been marked a heretic."

"Then you run from them?"

Clasping his hands together, the monk nodded.

Large hands, Rhiannyn thought. Powerful hands that looked as if fashioned more for weapons than prayer. Were they, indeed, more familiar with weapons? Wondering if Edwin suffered the same doubts as she, she glanced at him. However, with his back to her, she could see naught of his expression.

"It is my shame that I run from them," the monk said, "but I had no other choice if I was to live."

"Why Andredeswald?"

He shrugged. "In the open, 'tis not difficult to spot a man of God. I thought only to take refuge a short time in the woods, but wandered astray, and could not find my way out."

"Which is how we came upon him," the stout Saxon said.

Edwin looked to each of the men who had brought the monk in. "Was he followed?"

In unison, they shook their heads.

"We waited to see if 'twas so," the stout one said, "but there was no sign of others. Still, I left Uric and Daniel behind to be certain."

Satisfied with this accounting, Edwin turned back to Brother Justus. "You say you are a man of God."

"I am."

Edwin swept a hand toward the gathering. "As you can see, we are outcasts ourselves—Saxons who would see our lands free of the heathens who have stolen them from us."

Brother Justus turned eyes that seemed curiously devoid of benevolence upon his audience, briefly fixing on each face before sweeping to the next.

When his fiery blue gaze touched Rhiannyn, she felt as

if scalded, but then he blinked and cooled her with eyes turned wintry. They lingered a moment on her face, looked higher to her hair straggling from its thick braid, then down the tarnished length of blade she held.

Reflexively, she tightened her grip on the sword, unaware she held her breath until he looked past her.

"Continue," Brother Justus said to Edwin.

Edwin widened his stance and clasped his hands behind him. "As we are without spiritual guidance, mayhap you would join with us."

"And minister to these good people?"

"Good?" Edwin scoffed. "Perhaps once, but now our days are filled with every manner of sin." He smiled. "Aye, minister to them, Brother Justus, hear their confessions and absolve them of their sins, but do not try to make them good—not yet."

Brother Justus's brow furrowed as he appeared to deliberate.

Impatient, Edwin shifted his weight and crossed his arms over his chest. "There is only one answer, Brother," he said.

The monk arched an eyebrow. "And what is that?"

"That you accept."

"And if I do not?"

Edwin turned a broad smile on those gathered around. "As I said, there is only one answer."

Meaning he would not allow him to leave, Rhiannyn thought. That he did not trust him.

Brother Justus shrugged. "Then I must needs accept."

Edwin clapped him on the shoulder. "Wise choice. Welcome to Andredeswald." Turning on his heel, he strode to where Rhiannyn and Aethel stood.

"What is your name?" Brother Justus called after him.

Halting, Edwin looked over his shoulder.

The monk shrugged an apology. "I must call you something."

"I am Edwin."

"Edwin," the man repeated, then lowered his gaze.

Rhiannyn's misgivings swelled—something about the monk did not ring true.

It seemed Edwin also felt it, for he drew Aethel aside and said, "Watch him . . . closely."

Though he had spoken low, Rhiannyn's pricked ears caught the words. Relieved that Edwin's good judgment held, she turned toward the camp with thoughts of the pallet that awaited her weary body.

"You are not finished," Edwin said shortly, his voice drawing her to a halt.

Trying to gain control over the quick anger he roused in her, Rhiannyn studied the ground a long moment. Damn him! she silently cursed. He was trying to break her— wanted her in tears and on her knees. Never! Drawing in a deep breath, she turned to him. "Lead on," she said.

Maxen, now Brother Justus to the Saxons, watched Rhiannyn cross the glade behind Edwin. At first sight he had been uncertain she was the same woman who had spent so many weeks in the castle dungeons, for her resemblance to that creature was distant.

But it was she, and even more lovely than he'd imagined she would be beneath the dirt, grime, and bruises. Hair that had only whispered of gold now gleamed that color, the cream of her skin was accented by the tint of roses in each cheek, and a shape that had promised much beneath her tattered bliaut had more than fulfilled its promise in the belted tunic and hose she wore to practice her swordskill. She was beautiful, almost angelic, and more than capable of luring spellbound men to their deaths.

Aye, it was Rhiannyn of Etcheverry, though stronger than before. Maxen had felt her resolve, seen it in her eyes, her carriage, and her stiffening when Edwin had called her back to task. A small woman with the strength of many.

But he would break her, Maxen vowed, his resentment over the hold she had on him lending him determination. Then the woman who was a scourge to the vows of his body—vows she had forced him to renounce—would be forever exorcised.

As the man called Aethel came toward him, Maxen

glanced one last time at Rhiannyn. Positioned before the pel, she assumed the proper stance and angled her sword in readiness for a mock attack. Though she did not look to Edwin, he spoke to her, gestured, then stepped back.

As Maxen had wondered whether Thomas had lain with Rhiannyn, he now wondered the same of Edwin, but then Rhiannyn dealt the wooden post an admirable blow and sped his thoughts elsewhere. He frowned. Perhaps she had spoken true, he reflected. Mayhap it was she who had murdered Thomas after all. Though he thought it, he still was not convinced. It had to be another.

With that in mind, Maxen swept his searching gaze over those who had returned to their intense training and, surprisingly, found that many appeared quite worthy. Their swings strong, their aim sure, they promised a well-matched battle when next they set themselves upon the castle to take back what they claimed was theirs. And it was theirs, a vexatious voice reminded him.

Had been theirs, he countered, but no more. Regardless, he must not forget his reason for coming into Edwin's grim world. It had been a difficult and restless two weeks he had waited since allowing Rhiannyn to escape to this place. He had followed her to the camp, thanking God often that none of Edwin's sentries spotted him, then had returned to Etcheverry. Knowing that to appear too suddenly after her arrival would have thrown more suspicion on him than he already shouldered, he had waited until this morn to finally ride out from the castle. True, it would have been less than difficult to ride with his men and stamp out Edwin's rebellion after Rhiannyn had shown him the way to the camp, but that would not necessarily have delivered Thomas's murderer to him—not directly.

Though Maxen had experienced doubt when he'd listened in on Rhiannyn's conversation with Christophe and heard her tell him that it was not Edwin who had killed Thomas, he had only believed it after following her to this place and seeing the injury to the man's fighting arm. As Rhiannyn had said, it would have been impossible for him to have thrown the dagger after receiving such a serious wound. Assuredly, it had not been Edwin, but who, then? Which one of these men had plunged his dagger into Thomas's heart and bled his life upon that field?

A fire growing in him, Maxen lowered his gaze so the great, hulking Aethel would not see the betraying depths of his eyes.

Aye, he told himself in an attempt to calm his blood, soon every last one of Edwin's rebels would know the yoke of Norman rule, including Rhiannyn. First, though, he must discover who had murdered Thomas and insure that the villain did not simply die, but that he suffered as Thomas had.

Chapter Four

"Some things simply do not fit."

Until he spoke, Rhiannyn had not known Edwin stood behind her. She, like all the others, had been too engrossed in the scene before the campfire to have heard his approach.

"What do you mean?" she asked without turning.

"There is something about him, this Brother Justus. I do not trust him."

"As you do not trust me?"

Laying a hand on her shoulder, Edwin began kneading the strained muscles there. "Perhaps," he murmured.

Having expected something quite different—scornful words, a reprimand, perhaps even rough handling—Rhiannyn was surprised by the gentleness of his touch, but also unnerved

by it. Did it mean the trials he had put her through were
at an end? Was this his forgiveness?

"He speaks the word well," she said, commenting on
the monk's delivery. Against her will she had discovered a
liking for Brother Justus's deep, cultured voice, and especially the power of his message.

"Aye," Edwin said, "he does speak it well."

"Yet you are still suspicious of him."

"Aren't you, Rhiannyn? I saw it in your eyes yesternoon
when first he came."

"I was, but now I am not so sure. He seems genuine
enough."

"He has been here not even two days," he reminded
her, "and yet you would throw caution aside and embrace
him?"

"Nay, not completely." She wished Edwin would take
his hand from her. Considering the day he had subjected
her to, this small intimacy made her uncomfortable, and
not a little resentful. However, in the next instant his touch
became more intimate. His breath brushed the side of her
neck, then his lips.

"Do not," she gasped, straining away.

He caught her about the waist and pulled her back
against him. "Do not? But none can see, Rhiannyn."

True, for she had chosen to watch Brother Justus's ora-
tion from a distance—in back of the others and from the
refuge of bordering trees—but that was not the reason she
protested. Simply, it felt wrong, especially since she had accepted Thomas's curse that she would never know marriage or motherhood.

" 'Tis improper," she said, attempting to pull free.

"But we are betrothed."

Forgetting she had no intention of ever wedding him,
she stilled. "Are we? That is the first I have heard of it
since I came."

He chuckled near her ear. "Of course. That has not
changed."

It had, she thought, but the time was not right to tell
him so. Rhiannyn turned to the one thing certain to arouse

his anger, hoping to distract him and douse his passions. "Have you yet discovered Thomas's murderer?" she asked. It was a question she had put to him several times since coming to Andredeswald.

Blessedly, he provided the expected reaction, his body tensing, an angry breath rushing from his chest. "Leave it be, Rhiannyn," he growled. "Whoever it was, 'tis done with."

Turning, she stared up into his hard, flushed face. "Nay, it is not. Were it, Maxen Pendery would not now be planning for our deaths."

She spoke of the bits and pieces she had overheard from those who spied on the Penderys. It was said the castle was being fortified, great blocks of stone arriving from Caen to replace the wooden palisades. The training of knights and men-at-arms lasted far into the night, and the steady ring of metal testified to the great number of weapons being forged in the smithy.

"My goal is no different," Edwin reminded her, the mouth that had tenderly touched her flesh now drawn into a thin line. "The Normans will leave England, and those who do not will possess only the soil in which their bodies rot."

Rhiannyn had no reply for the hate she heard in his every word. Her only thought was to remove herself as quickly as possible from his presence. Stepping back from him, she turned toward her tent. However, a high-pitched wail arrested her progress.

"There is a traitor amongst us!" old Dora screeched. "I have seen it! I have seen it!" Her wan hair flying out behind her, her hooked hands clawing the air, she swooped upon those assembled before the campfire.

Something ungodly crept beneath Rhiannyn's skin as she stared at the wildly gesticulating woman. Though she recognized it as a warning, she walked forward, unaware that Edwin did the same until he overtook her and swept past.

"A Judas," Dora cried, frantically searching the faces that had turned from the monk to her. "Our downfall."

Whispers of concern stirring the air, some of the Saxons rose to their feet, while others cowered and looked away as if fearful she might name them the one.

Swinging around, Dora strained her neck to stare up Brother Justus's length. "Where is she, oh man of a god that is not?" She spoke in a voice that did not sound her own.

"There is only one God," he replied, seemingly unmoved by her outburst. "The God of the Christians. And He *is*."

"Liar!" she screamed. Raising an arm, she set herself at him, but swiped only air when he stepped smoothly aside.

"Dora," Edwin called.

She started violently, then turned to face him. "I have seen it, Edwin," she said, spittle wending a slow path from one corner of her mouth to her chin. "So clear . . . Ooh," she moaned, her eyes glowing red as they rolled in their sockets. "The ruin of our people."

As if gentling a child, he put a hand to her shoulder. "No more," he said.

"But I have seen it!"

Taking her arm, Edwin urged her away from the campfire. "Come, you are not feeling well. That is all."

For a moment, Dora's shoulders slumped, but then she caught sight of Rhiannyn. Drawing herself upright, she leveled a bony, accusing finger on her. "She is the one!"

The sweat of fear breaking upon her brow, Rhiannyn knew the greatest desire to flee. However, her feet would not obey, even when Dora broke free of Edwin and rushed toward her.

Throwing herself upon Rhiannyn, Dora toppled them both to the ground, her raking nails scoring four stinging lines down Rhiannyn's neck before Edwin could pull her off.

"She has come to feed us more death," Dora shouted as she was hauled to her feet. "It is she who will betray us."

A hand to her neck, Rhiannyn struggled to sitting. "Nay," she gasped. "I would not betray you."

"Aye, 'tis you—your blood that will end our bid for the return of our lands and the ousting of the Normans."

A great murmur arose from those who had gathered around, their mutterings evidence of superstitions that no amount of Christianity would ever unseat.

"I will not allow you to destroy the future," Dora exclaimed. "This past is mine." She pounded a fist to her chest. "I have made it and I will change it."

What did she speak of? Rhiannyn wondered. Was this past she spoke of not the present? Was it not . . . She shook her head to clear it. Ah, but the woman was truly mad, she decided.

When Dora opened her mouth to continue her tirade, Edwin interrupted her. "I have told you before," he said from between clenched teeth, "your sorcery has no place here."

"But I speak true, Edwin," she protested, in her desperation taking hold of his tunic. " 'Tis Rhiannyn, though she is not alone."

"What do you mean?"

It was a small concession he made, but enough to spur her on. "I was given the sight of another who will betray us, a faceless one who will mate with Rhiannyn and—"

Edwin thrust her from him. "Rhiannyn will lie with me," he said angrily. "Dare you accuse me of being a traitor?"

Raising her hands in pleading, Dora shook her head. "Nay, Edwin. Though you may wish it so, Rhiannyn will never lie with you. 'Tis another she will fornicate with—I have seen it. She must die!"

Edwin shook his head. "I—"

"Did I not breathe life back into you after it had fled?" Dora reminded him. "Deny my sorcery you may, but without it there would be no more Edwin Harwolfson."

Her words, coupled with Edwin's hesitation, were the undoing of a handful of men. Rushing forward, they seized Rhiannyn and hauled her upright.

"Traitor," one spat.

"Whore," said another.

More men joined with them, and they began carrying her from the camp.

"Edwin," Rhiannyn cried, struggling against hands and fingers that grasped and pinched. "Edwin!" She saw him break free of his trancelike state and take a step toward her, but that was all. Again, he faltered.

Despairing of him, she cried to Aethel where he stood back from the others. He, though, appeared in more of a quandary than Edwin.

It was Brother Justus who finally answered Rhiannyn's plea. Placing himself before the ever-increasing swell of people intent on carrying out Dora's sentence, he held up a hand. "In the name of our Lord, I order you to release the woman!" he bellowed. "Now!"

That last gained their attention and brought them to a halt. Instantly, the babble of voices fell to hollow silence.

"Are you all pagans," Brother Justus said condemningly, "that you would believe in the ramblings of one who is of the Devil, rather than He whom I spoke of this eve? There is no place in Heaven for those who follow the beast. Are you, then, content with Hell?"

Rhiannyn was as awed by his vehement words and his austere countenance as the others. At that moment, there was something so terribly holy about him, something that would make one believe even if one had not before.

The silence that followed grew like a gathering storm, and then, suddenly, Rhiannyn found herself released. Tumbling to the ground, she cried out as pain returned to the ribs she had bruised weeks earlier.

"Nay!" Dora screeched. "Do not listen to him. He does not know as I do. Mayhap he be of the Devil, but not I. Not I!" When none returned to do her bidding, she darted to Rhiannyn, grasped her arm, and attempted to drag her upright. "She must die!"

Brother Justus stepped forward and uncurled her fingers from Rhiannyn's arm. "Away with you, witch," he said. "Be gone."

Dora pursed her mouth to spit in his face, but he thrust

her aside. Her saliva falling to the ground, she spun around to face Edwin.

"Look what he does—an outsider!" she said to him. "I warn you, Edwin, kill the betrayer and send this man away, else your battle is done with."

Weary, Edwin shook his head. "He is right, Dora. We are Christians."

Dora stared disbelievingly at him, then, issuing a primeval scream, fell to her knees. "Oh, death upon us!" she cried. "Death to the proud Saxon race. Death. Death. Death."

Skirting the tormented woman, Edwin strode to where Rhiannyn sat. "You are without injury?" he asked.

Was she? Rhiannyn wondered. Her tender ribs said otherwise. She touched a dirt-scuffed palm to her neck, then held it away and stared at the four crimson lines.

What would be her fate if Dora tried again to convince these people she was the betrayer? No matter that they were Christian, old superstitions were not so easily forgotten in the face of one who had worked miracles, and who still knew favor.

Swallowing hard, Rhiannyn looked up at Edwin. "I am well," she said.

He considered her, then reached down and cupped a hand beneath her jaw. "Betray me, Rhiannyn," he said, "lay with another, and your fate is decided. Understood?"

She nodded.

"Good." Releasing her, he strode to where the old woman writhed grotesquely on the ground. "Come, Dora," he said, a hand to her shoulder. "You must need sleep."

Leaping to her feet, Dora avoided his hands and ran to the cave where she spent most of her days and few of her nights. Where she went after dark, no one really knew, or dared ask. A shocked silence followed, then Edwin turned and went after her.

Fatigued, Rhiannyn dropped her head and squeezed her eyes closed, remaining thus until Brother Justus brought her back to reality.

"Give me your hand," he said.

Peering up through the veil of her hair, Rhiannyn looked from his outstretched hand to an unreadable face that might as well have shone condemnation for all the compassion she saw there. No more of the holiness he had exuded such a short time ago, only eyes that sparkled with something she found greatly disturbing.

Lowering her gaze, she looked beyond him to those who had dared to remain following Dora's fit. Their furtive glances revealing the misgivings they had toward her, they slowly withdrew.

Not until all were gone, leaving only Rhiannyn and Brother Justus, did she look back at him.

"Your hand," he repeated.

She hesitated, then placed hers in his much larger one. He raised her without visible strain or effort. Doubtless, beneath his robes his body was as solid as she had guessed from his appearance.

"Know that I believe you," he said, his fingers remaining clenched around hers.

At his touch, a strange sensation, at once stirring and startling, coursed through her. Again, that peculiar sense that she knew him teased her. Pulling her hand free, she stepped back and rubbed her sore ribs.

"Why?" she asked.

His blue gaze dark in the night, he said, "As I would not forsake my people, neither do I believe you would."

"But Dora—"

"Are you not Christian enough to believe in God, rather than in a crone who speaks heretical madness?"

But a crone who knew things others could not possibly know, Rhiannyn thought, who had brought Edwin back from death.

"I fear her," she murmured, though only after saying it did she discover she had spoken aloud.

"Then mayhap you are not right with God. Would you like to speak of it?" At her hesitation, he added, " 'Twill do your soul good."

Her soul. Memories of Thomas and her role in his death assailing her, Rhiannyn looked up into this man's face, which firelight danced upon. "Think you I still have one, Brother Justus?"

Fleetingly, a smile touched his lips. "And why would you not?"

Could she speak to this man of God? she wondered. Might he be able to ease her burden? Taking a chance she had thought she would never take, she met his steady gaze. "There is much that weighs upon my conscience," she said.

After lengthy consideration, he motioned for her to precede him. "Then we will talk of it."

Walking to where the fire burned, Rhiannyn lowered herself to the log positioned before it.

The monk followed suit, the folds of his robes the only thing between the touching of their thighs. "Now tell me about your soul," he said.

Hands clasped in her lap, Rhiannyn leaned forward and stared into the fire. "Methinks 'tis lost. That there is no saving it."

"You are wrong."

Although Dora had pronounced Thomas's curse lifted following an oft-repeated incantation and a drink so bitter Rhiannyn had feared her throat would swell closed, it remained with her. She peered into Brother Justus's probing eyes. "Though I know you do not believe in such things," she said, "I have been cursed."

"By whom?"

"By the man whose death I am responsible for."

Thomas. The anger that sprang from Maxen's depths demanded an outlet—now—but he held tight to it with the promise he would free it at a better time and place. At the moment he needed as much calm as his warring emotions would yield him. Otherwise, he might never know what she knew.

"Have I shocked you?" she asked.

He clenched his fists beneath the cover of his long sleeves. "Only in that you have staked your soul to this curse."

She nodded. "I have."

Tense, Maxen waited for her to continue. However, after several minutes passed and she spoke no more, he said, "Tell me of this man. How is it you are responsible for his death?"

She twisted her hands in her lap. "I ran from him. And when he came after me, I ..." Sinking her teeth into her bottom lip, she shook her head. "I should not have run."

A finger beneath her chin, Maxen lifted her head and looked into eyes bright with tears. It surprised him that, for a moment, those tears touched him as they ought not have. Hardening himself against them, he said, "Though you claim responsibility for his death, surely you did not kill him?"

Her eyes widened. "Oh, nay."

"Then who?"

"I ..." Nearly, Rhiannyn told him of the unseen person who had thrown the dagger, but something bade her otherwise—something in the burning depths of his eyes that had naught to do with the fire that crackled and breathed warmth upon them.

Rising quickly to her feet, she stepped away. "It does not matter," she said. "He is dead, and naught can change that."

Maxen forced an expression of puzzlement over his quick fury and rose. "But it does matter—if I am to help you."

She shook her head. "I thank you for coming to my aid, Brother Justus, and you have been very kind to listen to me, but I have no further need of assistance."

When she turned from him, Maxen's anger caused him to throw out an arm to detain her. However, he pulled it back, knowing that to allow her even a glimpse of the man beneath the robes would likely be his undoing.

"Good eve," he called to her.

Without reply, she hastened to her tent and disappeared within.

Seeking an outlet for his turbulent emotions, Maxen left the camp and strode to the glade where the pel stood. Taking up the sword Rhiannyn had left alongside it, he made his grip, stepped back, and in the light of a moon crossed by clouds, swung, again ... and again ... and again. ...

"The one."

The hoarsely spoken words barely had time to sink into Rhiannyn's sleepy consciousness before her mouth was forced open and something thick and smothering shoved inside.

Coming to full wakefulness, she began to struggle, ineffectually screaming against the gag and fighting hands that knew no gentleness as they bound her wrists together, then her ankles. Although it was too dark to identify her assailants, she knew who led them—she who had pronounced the sentence of death upon her. Dora.

Dear God, she prayed, let this be naught but a terrible dream. Let me awaken now.

She did not awaken, and the dream—if it was that—became more vivid. Rough hands closing around her ankles, she was dragged off her pallet and out into a moonlit night that was just beginning to pass into day. Frantically, she searched beyond the four shadowed figures surrounding her, but quickly saw that her struggle for life would be a solitary one unless she could alert others to her plight. With her bound hands, she reached to pull the gag from her mouth, but was prevented from doing so when her arms were forced above her head. She thrashed side to side and screamed into the wadded cloth, but it was not enough to awaken anyone—had someone wished to help her.

"Pick her up," Dora ordered, her voice a dark whisper.

Going down on his haunches, the largest of the shadows lifted Rhiannyn and slung her over his shoulder, effectively pinning her arms under the weight of her own body. Then he began a jarring walk out of the camp.

"Hurry," Dora urged.

Though she knew that all she did was in vain, Rhiannyn refused to give up the struggle, straining and bucking as she was carried deeper into the woods. When Thomas was dying in her arms, she would have welcomed death as an escape from all the pain and misery she had been dealt since the coming of the Normans, but no longer. Regardless of the daunting future that might be hers, she wanted to live.

After an interminable time, the jostling ended.

"Cast her in," Dora ordered.

In? Fear tightening about her, Rhiannyn tossed her head left and right in an attempt to discover what Dora referred to. She needn't have, for a moment later, the man swung her down and began lowering her into what was to be her grave.

She screamed against the gag, desperately grasping for a hold on his tunic. Mercifully, she caught a handful; however, the weight of her descending body tore it from her fingers and slammed her to the bottom of the deep trench. Amid the pain, the pungent smell and dampness of freshly cut earth assailed her senses. The soil loosened by her descent sprinkled down on her in a cruel mockery of what was to come.

The prospect of being buried alive lent Rhiannyn a presence of mind she would never have guessed herself capable of in such dreadful circumstances. Tearing her gaze from those hovering above, she lifted her joined hands and pulled the gag from her dry mouth, then let loose a scream so thin, it seemed to barely carry above her head.

As she frantically worked her tongue to return moisture to her mouth, she reached up, searching the walls on either side of her. It was not much, but a stubby, frayed root seemed her only hope. Latching onto it, she dragged herself to a sitting position and screamed again—this time louder.

"The stone," Dora hissed. "Bring it now!"

Rhiannyn did not understand the meaning of the witch's words. She struggled to her knees and was attempting to stand when a hand slammed into her chest and shoved her onto her back. Determinedly, she grasped the root again, but lost her hold as two men leaned into the pit and set a huge stone on her abdomen and hips.

"Nay!" she cried. She pushed at the stone, scraping her

knuckles until they bled, but to no avail. It was ungiving. "Dear God, please!" she pleaded. "Not this way. Please, not this way."

Dora's white hair and pale face were a blotch against the dark sky as she peered down into the grave. "He does not hear you, Rhiannyn, but I do," she said clearly, "and I say, death upon you." Straightening, she motioned to the faceless men, then began chanting strange words and moving in a macabre dance.

Hysteria edged out panic as dirt fell on Rhiannyn's legs. Filling her lungs, she emptied them with a long, high-pitched wail, followed by another, but still the dirt descended, settling death upon her as she called to one who could not hear her.

Chapter Five

In the haze of an uneasy sleep, Maxen had thought it a bird, but when it cried out again, he knew it to be human. And something deeper told him it was Rhiannyn.

Pushing away from the stub of the ravaged pel that he had dozed against, he surged to his feet with sword in hand, then turned in the direction of the cry and sprinted across the darkened glade.

Unfortunately, the monk's gown proved a hindrance, swirling around and between his feet and thus shortening his stride. Cursing profusely at the precious time he wasted, he paused to drop the sword and drag the garment over his head. Then, tossing it aside, he reclaimed the battered sword and thundered into the woods.

With the next scream, he corrected his course, veering to the left into thickening trees that reached out with gnarly branches to rake his exposed flesh. Single-minded, he felt none of it. Deeper and deeper he ran, until he heard voices—the murmur and grunting of men, the crackle of the old witch's voice as she recited words he had never heard, and another scream that ended on a whimper. . . .

Going into battle armored only in flesh and short braies, Maxen announced his coming with a bellow, then vaulted into the clearing. Instinct guiding him more than the dawning light of day, he struck the first man alongside the head with a blade so dull, it had naught but impact to prove itself worthy of being called a weapon. And it did prove itself worthy, the cracking of the man's skull echoing through the woods. For certain, he would never rise again.

" 'Tis the false monk," Dora screeched. He saw her poised at the edge of what looked to be a trench—nay, a grave. "Kill him!"

Immediately the large shadow beside her divided into two men, both bearing weapons as they advanced upon him.

Maxen's blood coursing strong and lusty as in days past, when he had first and foremost been a warrior, he lunged for the larger of the men, knocked aside the spade leveled at him, then countered with a blow to the man's midriff. Though it doubled his opponent over and caused him to cry pain, he did not fall.

Thinking to finish him off, Maxen raised the sword again, but in the next instant swung it to his side to turn away the thick branch the third man aimed at his head.

Though the man lost his weapon, he hurled himself at Maxen, and together they fell to the ground, Maxen landing on his back, the Saxon atop him.

Deeming the sword useless, Maxen released it and captured the man's descending fist in his palm, then he thrust his weight to the side and rolled his opponent beneath him. " 'Tis over," he growled. "Say your prayers." Placing his hand over the Saxon's face, he forced his head to the right, then wrenched it hard left and back. The snapping of the man's neck coincided with a cool burning in Maxen's side that instantly turned fiery.

Lurching back onto his knees, he stared in disbelief at the dagger protruding from his flesh, and which the dead man still gripped in his spasming fingers. However, there was no time to ponder it, for the shadow of the Saxon he had temporarily disabled fell over him. There was only one thing to do. Pulling the dagger from his side, Maxen twisted around and threw it. It was not likely a killing wound that pierced the man's shoulder, but it caused the man to drop his weapon and run.

A hand to his side to stem the outpouring of blood, Maxen stood and turned to search out the witch. There, on hands and knees beside the grave, she labored frantically to push dirt into the gaping hole.

Rhiannyn.

Forgetting the fire in his side, Maxen bolted forward, but not before the witch caught sight of him and sprang to her feet.

"The death of us!" she screeched, then turned and darted into the trees.

Though Maxen burned to pursue her, to put an end to the old hag, Rhiannyn was a more immediate concern. The grave being too narrow for him to go into, he flattened himself beside it and reached for the woman who lay still beneath the loosely piled dirt.

Had he come too late? he wondered. How long since that last scream? Telling himself the dread he felt was for the secret Rhiannyn might take with her into death, Maxen caught hold of her shoulders and managed to raise her several inches before he met resistance. It was as if she was wedged tightly, or . . .

Pushing aside the dirt, he slid his hands down her body and found the stone. It was awkward, positioned as he was above her, but he hefted it off her. Then, grasping her beneath the arms, he pulled her from the grave and rolled her onto her back.

"Rhiannyn," he called as he brushed the dirt from her face.

She remained motionless.

Too late? He pressed a hand between her breasts to

search out the beat of her heart. Naught—no rise and fall, no flutter beneath his fingers.

A different kind of anger gripped him. He had not killed two men to rescue a dead woman! "Rhiannyn!" he roared. Taking her by the shoulders, he shook her hard, then harder, but still nothing. Lord, let not the wickedness in him be without any good, he fiercely prayed. And then, from somewhere, the words Sir Guy had spoken at the monastery came back to him. "The old witch pulled Edwin from beneath the dead and breathed life back into him." Breathed life back into him . . .

Lowering Rhiannyn, Maxen knelt over her, pulled her jaw down, and placed his mouth over hers. He breathed once, twice, and again, but each time his breath returned to him. He grappled a moment with the dilemma, then pinched her nose closed. It took four more breaths before, miraculously, he captured her groan in his mouth.

Hardly able to believe he had succeeded in returning life to her, he held her head as she coughed—a graveled, labored sound that made him question whether or not she would live.

After a time, the coughing subsided, and a disoriented Rhiannyn blinked her eyes open. "What happened?" she whispered.

Maxen said gruffly, "The old witch tried to murder you," castigating himself for the sense of protectiveness assailing him. He watched as her eyes clouded with question, cleared with remembrance, then clouded anew with the horror of what had befallen her.

Her entire body trembling, she mumbled, "Buried me—alive." And then, softly, she began to cry.

Maxen fought the impulse, but against his will he smoothed the hair back from her brow—a comforting gesture made more so when he settled his palm against her cheek. "You live, Rhiannyn," he assured her as her tears wet his hand. "You are well and whole."

Was she? she wondered through her misery. Would her mind hold after the terror of this night? "I could not breathe," she said, feeling again the dirt slip through the hands she had held over her face. "And when I called, none came."

"I came," he said.

Aye, he had, but how? And why? A monk . . . Rhiannyn looked up at him and for the first time noticed his state of undress. No clerical gown, only a broad chest and shoulders half again as wide as her own.

Muddled by something she did not understand, she lifted her bound hands and lightly touched the shelf of muscles above his abdomen. Hard they were, and warm with the moisture of a man's perspiration.

"The false monk," she murmured. "I heard her call you that. Are you false, Brother Justus?"

His gaze narrowing, he pushed her hands off him. "I have killed as no man of God would ever do."

Turning her head, Rhiannyn saw the body that lay not ten feet from her, then another farther out. Two men dead, but what of the third? she wondered with renewed fear. Did he lurk in the trees waiting to kill? "There were three with Dora," she said. "I see only two."

"The third was wounded," Brother Justus explained. "Had he not run to save his life, I would have taken it as well."

The monk had killed to save her, and though Rhiannyn was grateful for her life, she felt even greater unease about this man. "Are you a man of God?" she asked.

He wavered a moment, then stood and looked down at her. "I was," he said, "but now no more."

"But—"

"We must flee," he interrupted harshly. "Soon Dora will return with others, and if we are still here, we shall both die."

"But where will we go?" she exclaimed. Where would a woman named a traitor and hated by Saxons and Normans alike, and a monk become a murderer, be welcome? She watched as Brother Justus, braies his only covering, strode to where one of the dead lay.

"I know a place," he said as he knelt beside the man. "We will go there."

The sound of tearing fabric startled Rhiannyn, but then she saw the reason for the destruction of the Saxon's tunic. Why she had not noticed the blood draining from Brother Justus's side when he had stood above her, she could not have said, but it was obviously a serious wound.

She gasped. "You've been hurt."

"I will live." Head bent, he wound the strip of material around his waist, tore off another, and wound it tighter yet. Then, going to where the other body lay crumpled—a man more his size—he quickly divested the unfortunate one of his clothes and donned them himself. "Your hands," he said, returning to tower over Rhiannyn once more.

Obediently, she raised them. She winced as the flat of a cool blade touched the inside of her wrists, and again when Brother Justus began sawing through the rope. A moment later, her fetters fell away. A strange relief washing over her, she rubbed the blood back to her hands while the rope around her ankles was also severed.

"There is no time to waste," Brother Justus said as he raised her to her feet.

Rhiannyn's head reeled and she staggered against him. "A moment, please," she beseeched.

"Do you want to live, Rhiannyn?" he asked roughly.

She nodded. "But—"

"Then move your feet," he ordered. "Now!"

Abruptly, she straightened from him, anger at his callous treatment lending her determination. "I am ready," she said.

"We can rest here a while," Brother Justus said.

Grateful, Rhiannyn turned and walked to the stream that had beckoned to her hours earlier when they had first begun following it. On her knees, she dipped her hands in the water, steeled herself for the sharp sting, then splashed it over her face and neck. Gasping and blinking, she paused to savor the wonderful cold trickling over her heated skin before scooping up another handful, and yet another, until the front of her tunic, damp with perspiration before, was now soaked with water.

Somewhat refreshed, though her heart still beat briskly from the quick pace Brother Justus had forced them to, Rhiannyn lifted the hem of her tunic to dry her face. However, a glimpse of her distorted reflection stopped her. There on the surface of the water was something of the young woman she had been, the layers of age and wear having peeled away to reveal herself to her again. Granted, she still looked older than her ten and seven years, but much fresher than the thirty she had looked upon escaping the castle's dungeon. And she was alive.

Shying away from remembrances of what had transpired only hours earlier, she buried her face in the tunic and rubbed vigorously—as if by doing so she might forever banish those memories. Still, they were there when she lifted her head, waiting to be turned over and over again in her head.

"Nay," she whispered. "Leave me be." It was not her pleading, but a movement on the water that put the memories behind her—at least for a while. Looking down, she saw the reflection of the one who stood behind her.

Brother Justus was unsmiling, his mouth hard and drawn, his eyes at once accusing and condemning.

A chill not in the air swept Rhiannyn, invisible fingers closing around her throat and beckoning her back in time. Panic gripping her, she leapt to her feet and stumbled back from him.

"Something is wrong?" he asked, reaching out to steady her.

She sidestepped him.

"What is it?" The face she had seen in the water had changed. His expression was one of concern now, and that did not fit with the man she'd just glimpsed, a man who, with the shedding of his clerical gown, appeared to have shed the last of his holiness as well.

"Naught. I . . ." Confused, she stared unaware down the front of her tunic. In the next instant, her churning thoughts gave way to embarrassment as she focused on the flawless mold of the wet material over her breasts.

Hoping that Brother Justus had not noticed, Rhiannyn looked up only to discover that the carelessness with which she had cooled herself a short time ago *had* captured his interest. Though modesty bade her to cover herself— immediately—she was momentarily paralyzed by his gaze. Slowly, like the feathering of fingers over flesh, it glided over the gentle rise of her breasts. There it lingered before ascending to the thrusting peaks.

Realizing that he looked at her not with monk's eyes, but with the eyes of a man, Rhiannyn broke free of her stupor, clapped a hand to her chest, and lifted the material from her skin.

"I—I have not thanked you for saving my life," she said quickly. "There is so much I owe you."

Instantly, his eyes cooled. "Aye, you do," he said.

His agreement jolted her—awakened her to something niggling at the back of her mind. Summoning it forth to examine it, she shivered as a foreboding crept beneath her skin.

"I know you," she whispered. This remembered feeling was the same she'd known as when Maxen Pendery had stood before her unseeing eyes. But could it be? Praying that it was only her imagination, she searched Brother Justus's face, then gazed higher to his dark hair.

Aye, the same feeling, but in no way did he resemble either Thomas or Christophe. The hair coloring was completely wrong, his features too sharply defined. And his voice—she detected none of the thick French accent, nor the strained, rasping quality with which Maxen Pendery had spoken. Too, Christophe had said his brother was a warrior, and this man was undoubtedly trained in the ways of the Church. But he had also killed as a warrior, she sharply reminded herself, something no man of God would ever do. He had admitted as much himself.

Uncertain, Rhiannyn hesitated a moment longer, but then she saw something in his eyes that cast all doubt aside—the predator.

Knowing herself to be the prey, she whirled and ran as if the Devil were in pursuit of her. The evil man had deceived her. He had carefully laid his deception by denying facility with the Anglo-Saxon language, by allowing her to escape. Then he had come to Edwin's camp to avenge his brother's death. And he would likely have achieved his end had he not come to her aid.

Why had he? Why had he not sacrificed her? What had he hoped to gain? Knowing these were futile questions, Rhiannyn turned her thoughts instead to those she had placed in jeopardy—Edwin and his followers. No matter that death would likely be hers if she returned to the camp, she had to warn them of the one who had come to destroy them. She must—

A heavy weight hurdled down upon her, knocking her to the ground. She was pinned beneath a man resolved to vengeance. Desperate, she swept her hands through the fallen leaves in search of something to defend herself with. As her assailant tried to tumble her onto her back, she strained to remove an embedded rock, resisting his efforts long enough to pull her weapon free, then fell onto her back and lifted the rock toward his head.

She missed her mark—and freedom—only by the breath of a moment.

Forcing Rhiannyn's arm above her head, Maxen Pendery pressed his thumb hard at the base of hers until her hand cramped and her fingers uncurled.

"Nay!" she cried as her hope rolled out of reach. Raising her free arm, she clenched a fist and struck him alongside the head where the rock should have landed. Unfortunately, her effort produced naught but a grunt, then he caught that arm and pinned it to the other.

As a last, futile attempt, she brought her knee up and into his side. Though she had not intentionally targeted his injury, she realized what she had done the moment a fierce curse rushed out on the air he expelled. Still, it did not move him off her, for he was too large a man, and too determined, to yield her anything.

"Enough!" he barked. His monkly pretense was abandoned entirely to reveal a savage bent in every harsh line of his face, in the cruel twist of his lips and eyes ablaze with contempt.

Stilling as she witnessed the terrible transformation, Rhiannyn said again, "I know you." This time, she added, "Maxen Pendery."

A smile, slight and cutting, turned his mouth. "Nay, Rhiannyn, you do not know me." Her wrists vised in one hand, he pushed back and straddled her hips. "Yet."

Dread rising, Rhiannyn watched as he felt down his side. A moment later he lifted his hand to scrutinize the amount of blood covering it. Not much—yet. He looked back at her, the hatred of enemies in his eyes.

Acknowledging that her destiny was the Devil's until she escaped him—if ever—Rhiannyn turned to the only defense she had against such a foe. Reaching deep inside herself, she dredged up enough of her own bitterness to disguise her fear.

"Know this, Norman," she said. "As you have killed, so will you be killed."

It was shocking the suddenness with which his eyes darkened—his pupils spreading wide to obliterate all color save a dark ring of iris that was more black than blue. Though it frightened Rhiannyn to the core, she was determined he would never know how much. "You will die, Maxen Pendery," she went on recklessly, "the same as . . ."

"Thomas," he supplied, nostrils flared, teeth clenched.

Fool, Rhiannyn chastised herself. She should never have drawn that parallel. But too late, and to back down now would only weaken her in his eyes. "And Nils," she added.

The vision conjured by her words swept Maxen back two years to Hastings. As if removed from his body, he saw himself straightening, pulling his sword from a Saxon's corpse, lifting his arm to wipe the spattered blood from his eyes, then turning to search out who would next die an unfortunate death. It was then he saw Nils—barely alive, yet treated as if already dead. Without honor, without glory, beyond deplorable. . . .

Realizing he had gone someplace—to a haunting of his

own—Rhiannyn was searching frantically to find advantage in it when he returned as abruptly as he'd left.

His eyes lit only by darkness, a flush of angry color beneath his skin, he lifted a hand and gripped her jaw. "Heed me well, Rhiannyn of Etcheverry," he said, his voice a cold, cold caress. "Your life is no longer your own. It belongs to me, to do with as I please, and to take if I so please. Give me no excuse and perhaps you will live to become a wretched old woman. Give me an excuse—just one—and I will do what Dora could not."

Pretending courage, Rhiannyn declared, "I am no man's possession. Imprison me you may, but never will I belong to you."

His harsh laughter echoed around the woods. "But you already do," he said. "Your tears are mine, the secret you hold so near you is mine, and your—"

"Secret?"

A bitter smile etching his lips, he leaned down and placed his mouth near her ear. "The one you will soon tell," he said.

Thomas's murderer—a Saxon without a face and a name. Rhiannyn shook her head.

Sitting back, Maxen repeated, "Soon." Then he smoothed his blood-tinged hand over her tunic, forming the damp material to her breasts. "And," he continued, "your body is mine."

Denying that the stirring in her was borne not of fear alone, Rhiannyn tossed her head back and leveled all of her hate on him. "I will not lie with you," she declared.

He removed his hand from her breast. "And I have not said you will."

But he had just laid claim to her. What else could he have meant? Rhiannyn frowned. "I don't understand."

"Later," he said, "but now we must go." He started to lift himself off her, then hesitated. "Are you going to resist?"

He expected her to go willingly? "All the way," she retorted.

His eyebrows arched. "Then you bring this on yourself." Removing the rope girded around his waist, he lifted her hands, and before she could protest, lashed them together.

"Come," he said as he rose to his feet, holding the excess of rope that was to be her lead. "Your prison awaits."

She lay unmoving. "You do not frighten me." Though she wished the saying of it could make it true, it was nowhere near the truth.

His gaze narrowed. "But I do, and that is good—very good." He jerked on the rope, causing it to dig into flesh already raw from her earlier plight.

Realizing that she had only succeeded in trading Dora for Maxen Pendery, Rhiannyn was swept with despair. She must not think of it, she told herself, must not dwell on the fact she was truly alone in this world turned hellish.

Knowing Maxen Pendery would drag her if he had to, or, worse, toss her over his shoulder, she struggled onto her knees, put a leg beneath her, and stood.

"Better and better," he said.

She could not stop the words that rushed to her lips. "You think so? Do not be so sure of yourself, Maxen Pendery, for Andredeswald still holds you, and it belongs to Edwin."

He reeled her near him. " 'My lord' to you, Rhiannyn, or have you so soon forgotten?"

Nay, she had not forgotten his coming to her in the dungeon. Never would she forget that, but neither would she allow him her fear. Tossing her head back, she braved his gaze. " 'Tis you who has forgotten, but again I say I will not accept you as my lord."

"And again, I say you will."

"Never."

His mouth quirked with dark humor. "By the morrow you will be addressing me properly. This, I vow."

Stubbornly, Rhiannyn refused to beg an explanation. This man would never be her lord, and never would she address him as such.

"Do you intend to reach the castle alive, Maxen," she

said, looked pointedly to the blood spreading along the side of his tunic, " 'twould be best we dally no longer."

An angry fire leaping in his eyes, he put her from him. Then he turned and led her in the direction of Etcheverry Castle and the trials awaiting her there.

The curious commoners, the workers on the wall, the men-at-arms positioned on the roof of the gatehouse, and the knights summoned from the donjon to witness the event, all stared as their injured lord led his prisoner over the drawbridge.

Head high, Rhiannyn stared at the back of Maxen's head, refusing anyone the pleasure of seeing her cower. It was not easy, for her fears were insistent, demanding she give in to them. She drew upon her anger and hate to overcome them.

Remember your father and brothers, their lives brutally taken at Hastings, she silently chanted as she passed beneath the great portal of the gatehouse. Forget not your mother's slow death when the roof of their stables, set fire to by the Normans, collapsed upon her. Feel again your terror and relive your flight into the woods when the Normans sought to defile you. Imprint this moment on your mind—the humiliation Maxen Pendery subjects you to, the raw chafing of your wrists, the hate of both Normans and Saxons that falls upon you. Remember.

Just inside the inner bailey, she was presented with another challenge in the form of Sir Ancel. One look into his eyes, cruel and glimmering with satisfaction, withered her resolve. Well she remembered his handling of her while he had overseen her stay in the dungeon, how he had beaten her and cursed her. Now, separating himself from the other knights, he stepped into her path and looked down his long nose at her.

Forced to a halt, Rhiannyn resisted the strain of her lead and met the knight's stare.

"Saxon whore," he proclaimed for all to hear.

Rhiannyn sucked in an angry breath. Saxon whore,

Norman whore. Continually, she was accused of being both, and yet she was neither. She was Saxon, and that was all, her virtue intact in spite of what any thought of her.

Though Maxen was blocked from her view, she felt his gaze boring through Sir Ancel's back. It did not deter her from doing what she did. Boldly, she leaned toward the knight and returned the insult. *"Nithing!"* she said.

Coward. It was one of the few Anglo-Saxon words he knew well. It had been shouted at the Normans during the battle of Hastings, and Rhiannyn had yelled it at him often during his visits to her cell.

Knowing the edge to which she pushed him, she steeled herself for the blow. It nearly came, his hand drawing back to deliver it, but it did not fall.

Catching Sir Ancel's arm, Maxen twisted it behind the knight's back and barked in his ear, "Stand down!"

Sir Ancel's jaw worked, broken words sputtered from his lips, and his face flushed purplish-red, but he was without any means of reprisal against his lord. His face a mask of suppressed rage, he relaxed taut muscles and, with a shove from Maxen, rejoined the ranks of the other knights.

For once the punishment was given elsewhere, and Rhiannyn was too stunned to react. What did it matter to Maxen if another struck her? she wondered. Was there a spark of humanity in him after all? Or was it simply that he reserved the pleasure of her suffering for himself?

"Ready yourselves," Maxen addressed his knights. "We ride within the hour."

Snapping her head back, Rhiannyn stared into his hard face. He intended to go after Edwin and his followers, she realized, hoping to catch them unawares and at last bring them to bay. During the past hour she had prayed it would not be so, that Maxen's injury would delay him from taking any such action, but it would seem otherwise.

"Nay," she breathed, shaking her head. "Pray, do not."

His gaze swept her face, then promptly dismissed her. No humanity, Rhiannyn concluded, her heart speeding with unease. Not even a spark.

Foregoing the rope, Maxen gripped her arm and pulled her toward the far tower of the gatehouse.

Immediately, confusion stirred Rhiannyn's insides. Tilting her head back, she looked up the soaring height of the great stonework structure. Though its primary function was to guard the entrance to the castle, the towers on either side of the portal also housed several small rooms intended for captives of higher status than those who were thrown into the cells below the donjon.

Surely Maxen would not imprison her here when the alternative would far better serve his revenge?

"Maxen!" a voice rang out.

Maxen turned Rhiannyn with him, and she watched Christophe's ungainly approach.

It had not struck Rhiannyn before, but now it did. Christophe had played an important role in Maxen's deception, allowing her to escape so his brother could follow and discover the location of Edwin's camp. But had he done it knowingly? Or had Maxen deceived him as well? Though his pleading, expressive eyes begged her to believe he had not known of his brother's plans, Rhiannyn could not be sure. Lowering her gaze, she stared at the ground.

"You wanted something, Christophe?" Maxen asked.

"You've been injured," he said, his brow wrinkling as he looked at the blood staining his brother's tunic. "Perhaps I—"

"You did not come to discuss my injury, did you?"

Nervous, Christophe scuffed the toe of his shoe in the dirt. "Nay, but . . ." He shook his head. "Would you allow it, I would speak with Lady Rhiannyn a moment. A—alone."

"She is a prisoner, Christophe, and no lady at that," Maxen snapped. "Now return to your books and squander no more time on her."

"But—"

"I have spoken."

Christophe hesitated, then turned away.

Indignant over Maxen's brusque treatment of his

brother, Rhiannyn lifted her chin. "He is not a child," she said to Maxen, "and should not be treated as one."

"Not a child," he repeated. "What then? A man?"

"Nay, but soon—do you show him respect and not beat down his voice."

Maxen opened his mouth to retort, but then, as if deeming her unworthy of such a discussion, snapped his teeth together and spun her around to enter the tower.

As the stairway was narrow, there was only one place for Rhiannyn—behind Maxen. In her attempt to keep pace with him, she stumbled twice during their ascent, but was kept from plunging headlong down the steps by his steely grip.

Reaching the uppermost floor, he threw open the door and pushed her inside. "Your prison," he announced.

Standing in the center of the small rectangular room, she noted that it was empty save for a pallet and a basin, its cold stone floor without benefit of rushes to warm it. Still, it was more livable than her dungeon cell had been. But why?

She turned to Maxen, and only just caught the light of pain and fatigue in his eyes before he hardened them. Though he played a good game of disguising the extent of his injury, it seemed that was all it was. He had been cut deep and lost an amount of blood that would have laid most men down by now . . . but not Maxen Pendery.

Rhiannyn nearly pitied him, but she pulled back before the emotion he was undeserving of could surface. "Why not the dungeon?" she asked.

A sardonic twist to his mouth, he thrust his chin at the opening in one wall that threw a wedge of light on the stone floor. "The dungeon has no windows," he said.

"And what do I need a window for?"

He smiled. "I would not want you to miss the sunrise. As you know, it can be quite spectacular when it is not hidden by English clouds." The smile flattened. "And it will be spectacular. This I promise you."

A chill wind swept Rhiannyn. He was toying with her, taking pleasure in her misgivings, but there was no point in asking what he meant. Nay, she would not, for soon enough she would know.

"How thoughtful of you," she murmured. Lifting her bound hands, she held them out to him. "And this?"

Striding forward, he began working the knot loose. "So simple, Rhiannyn," he said. "A name is all I ask."

She didn't have a name, though, and it would be futile to continue the lie that it had been she who had killed Thomas. However, she had to ask, "And if I gave you that name, would you leave the others be?"

"Edwin's followers?"

She nodded.

"Nay," he said. "The Saxon rebels cannot be allowed to continue their assaults. Be it by bloodshed or Norman rule, they will be stopped." Pulling the knot free, he unwound the rope. "The choice is yours which it will be."

Unfettered, Rhiannyn stepped back and rubbed her wrists.

"As I told you before," Maxen said as he bundled the rope, "keep your secret and scores will die. Tell me, and they may live."

She stilled. "I cannot."

He stared at her a long time before turning away. "So be it," he said at the door, then closed it behind him.

Rhiannyn listened as the bar fell into place, locking her in the tower room with naught but the long silence of solitude. "Run, Edwin," she said into the quiet. "Now, ere 'tis too late."

Chapter Six

Holding his shoulders broad, though they ached from the weakening in his side, Maxen approached the far end of the hall where his room was situated. It could hardly be called a chamber, he thought as he regarded the screen behind which the simple trappings lay. He'd had more privacy in the modest cell he'd occupied at the monastery. Granted, the lord's chamber at Etcheverry was of greater size than that cell had been, but all that separated it from the rest of the hall was this wooden, many-panelled screen held together by articulating leather hinges. What went on behind the screen could only be hidden from eyes, never prying ears.

Telling himself he must remember this—especially considering his knights had last served Sir Ancel—Maxen stepped around the screen, lifted the coarse Saxon tunic he had donned after the struggle with the witch's men, and began peeling back the crude bandages. However, the bloody flow having stemmed itself, the material was now stuck to the wound and refused to yield. He hesitated, then dropped the tunic and headed back out of the chamber to call for water and fresh bandages.

Christophe had anticipated the need. His lame leg forcing him to walk with an awkward sideways hitch, he approached with a wench at his elbow, her arms burdened with a basin of water and long strips of linen that fluttered to the rhythm of her swaying hips.

A Saxon woman whose face knew more expression than a brooding frown, Maxen mused as he received her inviting smile. It was a welcome change after the past hours with Rhiannyn, but not enough to make him want to bed the wench. Although two years of torturous celibacy made his body more than ready to know a woman again, *he* was not. But soon, for if he must live the sinful life of man, he was determined to live all of it. The same as before Hastings, though this time with memories. . . .

"Sit, and Theta and I will tend you," Christophe said.

"I did not know you had taken an interest in healing," Maxen said.

"Someone had to," Christophe muttered as he dropped the bag he carried to the bed.

"What mean you?"

Christophe shrugged. "With the ceaseless warring between the Saxons and Normans, it is much needed."

"There are others trained for such work."

"And there was one, but he is dead now."

"How?"

Christophe met his gaze. "Murdered," he said, then turned his attention to his bag and began spreading its contents.

"Continue," Maxen ordered, his anger piqued at having to rise to Christophe's bait. "I would know what it is you wish me to know."

Christophe turned back around. "The man was a Saxon, his name Josa. He was a good man. Much of what I know of healing I learned from him."

"And?"

"And he had the misfortune of continued loyalty to his own. In an attack upon the castle when it was first being raised, several Saxons fell. When all quieted, Josa, finished with tending Thomas's injured men, slipped outside the walls to see if any among his people lived. There was one, and Josa was attempting to help the man when Sir Ancel came upon him and struck him down with a blow to the head. Murdered, Maxen."

Though Maxen tried to harden himself against the injustice that had been done, he could not help but ask, "And Sir Ancel?"

"You ask if he was punished?"

In answer, Maxen raised his eyebrows.

"Thomas was angry with him, but naught else. Naught to prevent Ancel from doing the same in the future."

"Then you blame Thomas."

Christophe drew a deep breath. "Maxen, I am not saying Thomas was bad. All I am saying is that he was not good—and certainly not blameless for all the ill that has befallen the Penderys."

Opposing emotions warring within him, Maxen dragged the tunic over his head. "I have listened," he said as he tossed the garment aside, "and now I am finished." Sitting on the chest at the foot of the massive, curtained bed, he awaited Christophe's ministrations.

There was a long silence, then Christophe stepped forward. "You're a cold man, you know," he said as he began unwinding the dirty bandages.

Maxen was tempted to send him away, but quelled the impulse, for if the wound was to be cleansed of any infection that might have set in, he needed his younger brother. If he died later, fine, but not before he had done what he had come to Etcheverry to do.

The wound was cleansed, stitched closed, and puttied with a salve so pungent the wench looked near to retching. As Theta began to bandage the wound, Christophe broke the long quiet. "Rhiannyn is well?" he asked, his eyes luminous with a concern that made Maxen want to shake sense into him.

"As you saw, she lives," he answered curtly. Finding that Theta's fingers were more inclined to caress than help, he took the bandage from her and stood, then began winding it around his waist.

Christophe laid an arresting hand on his arm. "That is not what I asked."

Maxen was surprised by the boy's continued show of pluck, though he was still greatly displeased by whose cause Christophe had chosen to champion. "But that is your answer," he said, and secured the bandage.

Christophe's nostrils flared. "Then I will see for myself."

He swung away, but had barely taken a step before Maxen caught his arm. "I will not have her work any more deceit upon you," he growled, forgetting they were not alone—that the wench stood not two feet from him, and his retainers opposite the screen. "You are to stay away from her."

Christophe's attempt to pull out of Maxen's hold was unsuccessful. "Before I sent for you, it was I who was lord of Etcheverry," he reminded Maxen, "and I who ruled all you have come to claim."

"You? Nay, Christophe. Need I remind you that it was not of my choosing to shoulder the responsibilities of the heir? And that it was Sir Ancel who lorded Etcheverry in your stead, not you?"

Hurt flitted across Christophe's face. "I had thought you would be different after the monastery."

The words struck a chord in Maxen that would have best been left unplucked. Fighting an inner battle, he squeezed his eyes closed. "So had I."

"Then—"

The battle was lost. "Do you so soon forget Thomas lies cold beneath the earth?" Maxen exploded. "That the whore you call 'lady' is responsible for his death?"

Startled by his vehemence, Christophe took a step back.

Immediately, Maxen regretted the angry words he had been holding in for weeks. Though he had come near to speaking them to Christophe many times, until now he'd had enough presence of mind to hold them in. After all, it was his anger, his disappointment. . . .

Releasing Christophe, Maxen harkened back to his journey to Etcheverry. Throughout, he had allowed hope to build that Christophe might be groomed to become the lord of all that was the Penderys', thus freeing Maxen to one day return to the monastery. That, however, had proven to be a false hope. Within minutes of his reunion with the youngest Pendery, he'd seen clearly that Christophe was incapable of ever shouldering such immense responsibility. He was too gentle, too innocent, and too determined to remain that way. The bitterness that had come with that realization ran too deep for Maxen to keep it hidden forever, and now it was known.

Christophe's voice broke through Maxen's tormented thoughts. "It was a trick, wasn't it?"

Maxen knew what he referred to, though he'd told none of his plans for Rhiannyn. He'd allowed all to believe she'd escaped on her own, and when he'd gone from the castle three days earlier to put his plans in motion, he had told none of his destination. Now, though, they knew.

"Christophe—" Maxen looked around at the wench, having seen her out of the corner of his eye cock her head with interest. "Leave us!" he barked.

She jumped, her eyes growing wide in hesitation before she retreated.

"Harmless," Christophe said, dismissing her. "She speaks little French."

"No Saxon is harmless," Maxen retorted, "even those who wish to bed with a Norman."

Christophe pushed a hand through his hair, which was far too long to show any resemblance to the preferred Norman style. "You have not answered me," he said. "You tricked me, didn't you?"

Maxen had, but it did not absolve Christophe of what

he had done, nor of what he might do in the future if he was not corrected. "Aye," he said, "and you betrayed me."

"By assisting Rhiannyn?" He shook his head. "It cannot be called betrayal if I was doing something you wanted. In fact, it is just as well said that I was following orders."

"Then you would have done it if I'd asked?"

"No, I would not have."

Turning, Maxen threw open the chest containing the garments that had been Thomas's, and removed the quilted jerkin he would wear beneath his dead brother's hauberk. "Betrayal then," he concluded. "By my design or no, you acted to betray me."

"I acted to save a woman innocent of the crimes she is accused of."

Innocent. Always innocent. If Maxen could have grabbed the word from Christophe's mouth and thrown it to the floor, he would have ground it beneath his heel. "We have had this discussion before," he said, his patience threatening to let go again.

"Discussion?" Christophe exclaimed. "Nothing is discussion with you, Maxen. It either is or is not."

Maxen arched an eyebrow at him, then used the time to don the jerkin to cool his mounting anger. "As I am lord," he said, "that should come as no surprise to you."

"It does not, but still I would have my say."

Maxen nearly denied him, but Rhiannyn's words, that Christophe would become a man only if he was shown respect and his voice not beaten down, flew at him. Greatly it pained him to put any credence to what the deceitful woman said, but he conceded. "Then have your say, but be quick about it."

Christophe blinked in surprise, then jumped in. "You are wrong about Rhiannyn. Even though she tried to make Thomas think her bad, she is good of heart. Never would she knowingly do anyone harm."

The words glancing off him, Maxen stepped around the screen and called for a languishing squire to bring the great hauberk. "The Saxon witch has duped you, young Christophe," he said, coming back around, "the same as she did Thomas."

"I do not believe that."

"You fancy yourself in love with her?"

Christophe's head jerked on his slender neck. "Nay, Maxen," he said fiercely. "If anything, I think of her as a sister. Never a lover."

"A sister would not have betrayed you by leading your brother to his death."

"She wanted freedom, that is all. She could not know that because she ran from Thomas he would bring death upon himself."

"Then it is Thomas you blame?" Maxen exclaimed in disbelief and anger.

"Aye, had he allowed Rhiannyn to return to her people, he would not now be dead."

"If you think to convince me she is not responsible for his death, you had best do better than that."

"He caged her—imposed clothing, manners, and a title on her she wanted naught to do with."

"He would have made her his wife," Maxen said between clenched teeth, "not the bed warmer she deserved to be."

Christophe shook his head. "She did not want to become his wife. She did not love him."

"Love," Maxen said scornfully. "What fanciful notions have been put into your head, Christophe? Many are the marriages that are made without love. Such foolishness is not required to unite warring families and bring them to peace, to increase the family's holdings, to breed children of good stock that they may carry on the name."

"But it was not what she wanted."

Disgusted, Maxen growled, "And look what her selfishness has wrought. Another brother dead at the hands of the Saxons and my chosen life stolen from me."

Hands clenched at his sides, Christophe turned on his heel and limped away. "It is you who are selfish," he tossed over his shoulder. "You who could make all right, but will not let it be."

The hard truth of Christophe's words stole the rejoinder from Maxen's lips. At an impasse, he watched his brother go, then closed his eyes and prayed for guidance. In the end, though, there was naught . . . only growing enmity toward the woman who had disturbed all of his carefully laid plans.

From the narrow window of her tower room, Rhiannyn watched Maxen Pendery ride out from the castle with a garrison of what had to be more than a hundred men behind him. Probably a third of them were fully armored and mounted; the men-at-arms marched behind, carrying their weapons. As she riveted her gaze to the man who sat a horse far better in the raiments of a soldier than those of a monk, a tumult of emotions rose within her. Yet another of Maxen Pendery's deceptions . . . and there would be more.

Their destination the Andredeswald, their mission massacre, Maxen and his men grew ever more distant as Rhiannyn stared after them with eyes grown painfully dry. She could do naught to prevent the many deaths to come. Naught to prevent the warring between the conquered and the conquerors. But she would not weep, she promised herself. She would not shed useless tears over something that had not yet transpired—though it was very likely it would with one such as Maxen.

Though she did not weep, an anguished cry broke from her lips as she once again picked out among the distant riders the one who had deceived her.

"Nay," she cried over and over, even after Maxen Pendery had disappeared from view. She did not stop there. She pounded on the door, scattered the straw of her pallet, and when food was brought to her, flung it against the wall. Not until well past dark when exhaustion finally took her did she collapse upon the remains of her pallet and surrender to sleep—and then slept only fitfully as nightmares tormented her.

She lived again the burial, felt again the hard plunge to

the bottom of the grave, saw Dora's hideous dance, tasted the dirt heaped upon her, and each time awakened gasping for air and searching the dark for the one who had delivered her from death.

At the landing before the door to Rhiannyn's tower room, Maxen paused to unbuckle his chain mail hood. As he pushed it back off his head, each of the hundreds of links clamored as they settled at the base of his neck. He listened for other sounds, but there was only silence, almost as if Rhiannyn had gone. Had she? Or did she still sleep?

Although he did not believe escape possible, especially since Christophe had been given no choice in accompanying the war party into Andredeswald, and a sentry had been posted at the tower to insure no one else would attempt to free her, Maxen wasted no more time in lifting the bar and pushing the door open. On the threshold he hesitated, his gaze alighting on the slight figure curled on the pallet across the room.

Her tunic having ridden up around her waist, her hair spilled over her face and shoulders, she slept—no doubt exhaustion having carried her into slumber. Not surprising—in the short minutes that Maxen had spoken with the sentry, he'd heard of Rhiannyn's intermittent uprisings, and what Maxen had thought he'd only imagined was confirmed.

Two days past, riding from the castle with his mounted knights and men-at-arms, he had been uncertain whether he'd imagined hearing Rhiannyn's anguished scream, or feeling the hatred in her eyes boring into his back, but it seemed not to have been imagined after all. According to the sentry, with naught but her voice, pounding fists, and the hurling of the basin and food she was brought, she had managed to create endless hours of din that first day, but that had not been the end of it. The following day had seen a similar uprising, though it had lasted no more than an hour. Now she slept—but for not much longer.

Striding across the room, Maxen went down on one knee beside her and, ignoring the pain that shot through his side, reached out a hand to shake her awake. However, he left it in the air as another, warmer and brighter, laid its touch to her first. The sun. From the small window, it slanted its first rays of light upon her legs.

Something betraying and uninvited stirred within him as Maxen looked from tender-fleshed ankles to firm calves, then higher. The braies tucked into the top of Rhiannyn's hose molded themselves to softly rounded thighs that junctured at a place that, during monkhood, had been forbidden him. It was forbidden no longer, and his body knew it.

Though he ordered it to calm, Maxen's flesh responded as it had not for more than two years—kindling, igniting, then flaring to a burn that seared his resolve and left him erect and wanting. Why Rhiannyn? Why not that wench, Theta? Or another? Why this one who had been Thomas's downfall, the sight of whom ought to make his fingers convulse with deadly intent, rather than restrained desire?

At the stream, when he had gazed at her breasts beneath the wet tunic, and shortly thereafter when he had laid his hand to them, he had known his fallen brother's obsession, but now it was more than that. Hate her, certainly, but want her ... that too.

Cursing himself—and her—for the ache in his loins, and this insidious yearning for possession, Maxen searched Rhiannyn's visage beneath the silky throw of her hair. However, it was too well hidden, only the curve of her jaw and her small upturned nose visible. Lowering his hand, he swept the strands back and gazed at her, from lashes that shadowed the dark circles begot by a wakeful night, to a mouth full and waiting for the man who sold his soul to her. Guided by his body, though his mind condemned him for the weakness, he brushed his thumb across her lower lip, then trailed it down and curved his hand around her neck.

Innocent, Christophe maintained, but he was wrong—had to be wrong. Thinking to vanquish Rhiannyn and her allure from his thoughts, Maxen closed his eyes and silently moved his lips to prayers he had not spoken since before Guy had brought news of Thomas's death.

It was not a slow awakening, but an abrupt one that propelled Rhiannyn out of sleep. Wide-eyed, she stared at the man leaning over her, and barely suppressed a violent start when she saw who it was.

Maxen's eyes were closed. No words issuing from his mouth, though his lips moved, and his arm . . . it was outstretched to grasp her neck with steely fingers.

Believing he intended to strangle her, Rhiannyn battled with panic. However, she threw it off. Think, she urged herself. Think. Searching, she saw that Maxen wore chain mail, and lower, a sword and dagger. The sword was out of the question, but the dagger . . .

Throwing out an arm, she closed her fingers around the hilt and a moment later possessed the weapon. But only for a moment before Maxen stamped out her revolt with the speed of a seasoned warrior.

Releasing her throat, he swung his arm upward and encased her hand in his. "Give over," he demanded, angry color rushing into his face.

Rhiannyn strained back, futile in her efforts to come free with the dagger, but determined that if she must lose, thus forfeiting her life, it would be with a struggle worthy of this Norman beast.

"Nay!" she shouted. Pulling her knees up, she thrust her legs forward and slammed her feet into his chest. It served her poorly, though, for his body was as ungiving as a wall.

Knocking her legs aside, he surged to standing, the cruel clench of his hand over hers dragging her up with him and onto the tips of her toes.

"Accept your defeat gracefully, Rhiannyn," he said as he looked down at her.

"And die gracefully?" she spat, the burning in her strained shoulder almost enough to make her cry out in pain.

Stepping onto the pallet, Maxen pushed her back

against the cold stone wall and held her there with his body. "On my word, *you* will not die this day," he said.

There was more to that statement than on its face, but Rhiannyn was too agitated to contemplate it. "Not die? Then I am to believe it was not your intent to strangle the breath from me?"

Something flickered in his eyes, a shifting back in time, but then it cleared. "Though the temptation is ever-present, I assure you, you are quite safe."

"For how long?"

"For now."

Her laugh was bitter. "And I am to be reassured by that?"

"I offer no more." Cold and unfeeling, he smiled. "Now, do you give over the dagger, or must I take it from you?"

Tilting her head farther back, Rhiannyn stared at her childlike hand engulfed in his, then looked higher to the angled blade. In it she saw a distorted reflection of her small person beneath Maxen's towering shape. Clearly, she was no match for him; it would take less than the snapping of her wrist for him to defeat her.

Another time, another place, there would be a battle of minds rather than physical strength, she assured herself. That was what it would take to bring this man to his knees, not a token struggle that would only leave her broken and long in healing. Difficult as it was to accept yet another defeat at his hands, she yielded. "Take it."

Uncurling her fingers, Maxen took the dagger from her, then released her. "Wise," he said as he stepped back to resheath the weapon.

Unmoving against the wall, Rhiannyn looked to the open doorway which she had not noticed until that moment. How remote the possibility of escape if she ran? How many would she have to elude? Too many, she concluded, especially if the many included Maxen Pendery on her heels. She looked back at him and found him watching her.

"Again, wise," he said, as if reading her thoughts.

Disconcerted, she lowered her gaze, and for the first time noticed the dark streaks coloring his armor. Blood, and it could only be that of Saxons. "Why have you come?" she asked, hating herself for the tremor in her voice.

"There is something I wish to show you." Taking her arm, he pulled her toward the window.

Dreading what awaited her there, Rhiannyn momentarily escaped to reflections of two days earlier when she had watched Maxen ride out from the castle. Had he accomplished what she'd prayed he would not?

"Wait and watch," he said as he positioned her before the window, which was too narrow for them to stand side by side. At her back, he leaned forward to share the view.

Acutely aware of his breath stirring her hair, and of his muscled and mailed chest against her back, Rhiannyn gathered all that was in her to put him from her mind, but he would not budge—not until minutes later when the first sounds of a victorious clamor arose from the woods and echoed upon the castle's walls.

She sent desperate prayers to the heavens that what Maxen taunted her with would not be, but it was. Emerging onto the clearing that surrounded the castle, Maxen's soldiers rode on either side of scores of Saxons whose trudging feet hazed the air with the dust of their defeat.

"I always keep my word, Rhiannyn," Maxen said into her ear. "As promised, the sunrise is spectacular."

For Normans, she thought, but not for the Saxons whose land this was—whose children would be reared in the knowledge that they were born to a beaten people if the Normans were not soon put from England.

Her emotions gathering like a storm, Rhiannyn struggled to hold back the tears of desperation that burned her eyes. But one tear fell, then another. Convulsively, she swallowed, but still they came.

Maxen was beginning to wonder why Rhiannyn did not curse, weep, in some way demonstrate the impact of his conquest, when he felt the shudder of her shoulders and the tremble of her body. Unexpectedly, her anguish sieved through the barriers he had erected against compassion, and he cursed his weakness. When his curses failed to vanquish that weakness she roused in him, he turned to the only sure thing that would—Thomas.

Hardened once again, he pulled Rhiannyn around and lifted the chin she pressed to her chest. Again, his barriers trembled as he looked upon a face of abject misery, but they held. Touching a finger beneath her eye, he lifted a tear for her to see. "Mine," he said, reminding her of the possession he'd claimed over her.

For a long moment he stared into her moist, sparkling eyes, then the moment passed. The great tears drained away, loathing replaced anguish, and she swept her hand upward and soundly slapped his face.

"Villain!" she cried. "Naught is yours—naught but the death I wish upon you."

Drawing a deep breath, Maxen denied himself reaction to the sting of her hand and her cursing words. However, when she made to strike him a second time, he caught the wrist of her offending hand, then the other as she raised it. Clasping them together, he dragged her against him. "Let it be!" he ordered.

Angry huffs of breath issuing from her, she tossed her head back and met his gaze. "Or?" she asked boldly.

It rankled him that Rhiannyn would continue to provoke him when she might be so near death. After everything she had been through, her spirit ought to be broken, not thriving. "Or I will restrain you," he said. "Permanently."

What, exactly, he meant, Rhiannyn could only guess at, but his threat quieted her to seething. For now, her defiance was at an end.

"Good," he said, releasing her. "Now, we talk."

Stepping back from him, she clasped her hands before her and waited.

"Those men and women—your people," he began, "their destiny is in your hands, Rhiannyn. Tell me which of them murdered Thomas, and the rest will live. Hold to your secret, and their lives will be wiped clean from Norman lands."

She pretended to ignore his reference to the land of the Saxons. "You would take the lives of all for one?" She shook her head. "Though you are most inhuman, Maxen Pendery, I cannot believe you would welcome the slaughter of so many innocents upon whatever conscience dwells in the deepest of you."

His eyebrows soared. "Conscience. Innocents." He laughed. "Under Edwin's direction, they have pillaged and killed no better than those they accuse of doing the same."

"Who *have* done the same."

He conceded the point to her with a stretch of silence, then continued. "Regardless, by one or all, justice will be done. And do you think to test me, Rhiannyn," he warned, "the deaths will be upon your conscience, not mine."

Looking down, she stared sightlessly at her fingers. For all her talk, it would have been too great a risk, now that Maxen held the Saxon rebels, to continue withholding the name of who had killed Thomas. But what could she offer him? she sharply reminded herself. She did not know who had done it, and doubtless, Maxen would not believe her if she told him so.

"Who?" he asked, snatching her pained ponderings from her.

Slowly, she raised her eyes. "You will not believe me do I tell the truth. This, I know."

"If it is the truth, it will hold."

She shook her head. "Only a lie you are willing to believe will hold. Otherwise, you will not be satisfied."

"Tell me."

It was a waste of good breath, but she had no other course. Swallowing, she tilted her chin higher to brave his anger. "Who it was that killed your brother, I do not know," she said, her insides coiling as she witnessed the transformation of Maxen's face and bearing. "Thomas had only just wounded Edwin when the dagger came out of the trees. Whoever threw it was unseen."

"Better a lie I would be willing to believe than the pitiful one you have just told." Maxen ground the words out between clenched teeth. Then, with one long stride, he came forward and closed an unyielding hand around her arm. "Come see what you have this day wrought."

He pulled her out of the room and down the stairs, and her desperate pleas fell upon ears deafened to the truth—a truth she had made seem a lie by so long withholding it from him.

Between the gatehouse and the causeway leading up the motte to the inner bailey and its donjon, Maxen halted and yanked Rhiannyn in front of him so that she faced the drawbridge over which the Saxons would be led.

Only vaguely aware of the curious stares of those on the walls who had paused in their revelry to watch them, she tried to turn to Maxen, but his hands held her firm.

"Watch," he said.

"Maxen, I beseech you—"

"My lord," he corrected her.

It burned her to name him that, but if it meant she might reach him, then it would be the most worthy sacrifice she ever made. "My lord"—the words were strangled by a closed throat—"on my life, it is the truth I have told you."

His only response was a tightening of his hands on her arms.

Rhiannyn looked over her shoulder at the hard line of his jaw. "Listen to me," she pleaded. "I—"

"Even if it were the truth," he said, his gaze riveted to the drawbridge that had just taken the first footfall of the approaching party, "the end would be the same, for to allow Thomas's murder to go unavenged would be the downfall of all that is Pendery. That I cannot allow to happen. This day the Saxons will learn who is master and who is not. Now watch, Rhiannyn."

She had no choice, though it was with great shame that she turned back and saw the first of the captives step onto Norman ground. Obviously having discovered during the clash in Andredeswald that Maxen was not the monk he had represented himself to be, they dismissed him and focused all their attention on her. Displayed as she was before her people—as the traitor she was not—their eyes fell like killing daggers upon her. All went as her captor planned.

Quelling the impulse to cry out that she had not betrayed them, that she was also a prisoner, Rhiannyn clenched her fists as the Saxons, bound one to another, many clutching at wounds, entered the bailey. However, not until they were all within did her searching eyes tell her the unexpected. Edwin, Dora, and several others were not among those brought forth. Dead, then?

"Where is Edwin?" she asked.

"Escaped."

Rhiannyn jerked her head up and around to focus on Maxen's jaw again, the spasming of which was the only visible evidence of the anger roused by his admission. "You did not tell me," she said.

"I did not."

He did not because if she had known of Edwin's escape, she might have saved these lives by putting the blame on one Maxen could not lay hands to, she realized. He had known the workings of her mind . . . the desperation.

The Saxons herded before her made Rhiannyn want to crawl out of her skin and into another's—any other's—for even Aethel looked at her with everything opposite kindness. Not one among them was willing to believe her innocent. Aye, if the Normans did not kill her, her own surely would.

"Stay," Maxen said, then released her and stepped before the conquered.

Odd, though she ought to be grateful for the reprieve from his immediate presence, Rhiannyn felt more lost than ever. She felt exposed, vulnerable. . . .

"I seek the murderer of Thomas Pendery," Maxen said, raising his voice for all to hear. He paused to search each of the stony faces before continuing. "Deliver that man unto me and I will spare your lives. Deny me and all will suffer—men and women."

It seemed a very long time before he was given his answer, the silence thick with antagonism.

"Hell heap upon you, pretender of God," Aethel called, rending the quiet.

"Your dead brother will tell you who did it," an aged Saxon added, "when you meet him in hell!"

"Death to the murdering Normans!" another yelled.

A woman stepped forward to strain her bonds. "And the betrayer Rhiannyn," she spat.

Frenzied shouts rose from the others, and Rhiannyn was assailed with beastly imaginings of the death that awaited her at their hands. However, the men-at-arms reacted swiftly, closing around the prisoners and threatening their own deaths with the weapons they trained on them.

A hard twist to his mouth, Maxen returned to Rhiannyn's side. "It falls upon you, then," he said. "Which one?"

"I do not know."

"You lie." Taking her arm, he pulled her nearer the Saxons and made her suffer a closer look at their hate. "One last chance," he said in a low voice, "and then there is bloodshed."

Desperate, she looked from face to face, wondering if, perhaps, the sacrifice of one would be the greater for all. But whose death? Whose sacrifice must she decide? Knowing it was beyond her, that she could not make such a decision, she shook her head. "I cannot."

Lowering her gaze, she saw the fist Maxen clenched at his side, the knuckles turning white, and then his hand on her did the same, causing her to draw a sharp breath.

"That is your answer, then," he said, "and soon you will have mine." Looking around, he called to a knight who stood nearby. When the man stepped forward, he pushed Rhiannyn toward him. "Return her to the tower," he ordered, then swung around to face the Saxons.

"So it begins," he said.

As she was led away, Rhiannyn heard him call out his commands. The Saxons were to be divided, the young and unwounded incarcerated in the cells below the donjon, the others, made up of women, the aged, and the wounded, to be quartered in the outbuildings of the lower bailey. In the center of that bailey, a gallows was to be erected by noon on the morrow. Then it would truly begin.

Even when alone in her tower room, Rhiannyn refused her emotions the release they demanded. Sitting in the corner, her knees pulled to her chin, she closed her eyes and prayed with all that was in her for the lives that would be needlessly taken a day from now.

Amidst the commotion caused by the disbanding of the Saxons, Maxen called Sir Guy to his side.

"Aye, my lord?" the knight asked.

"I've a task for you."

Guy nodded. "Tell."

"There is one among the rebel Saxons I am looking for who bears a shoulder wound."

"Many are wounded," the knight reminded him, "and likely several bear such wounds."

"Aye, but this wound would not be fresh. It would be days old. Too, the man is much my size."

His task made tenfold easier, Guy swept a bow before his lord. "If he is among these Saxons, I will bring him to you myself."

If, Maxen thought, for the one who had escaped him when Dora had sought Rhiannyn's death might now be among the dead left at Edwin's camp, or have fled with Edwin. If he was here, though, he would certainly be the first to die. And not by hanging.

Chapter Seven

Damn Rhiannyn, and damn her closed mouth! Maxen silently cursed. Damn her for denying him the truth of Thomas's death. Damn her for testing him—forcing him to carry out a threat he had not thought he would have to. But more than anything, damn himself for the sins of his flesh that made him want hers.

However, it was not desire alone that wrung moisture from his heated body as he lay naked on the bed, the covers thrown to the floor. Nor was it desire that made his thoughts turn on senseless drivel. It was something else—that which had awakened him from the vision of Rhiannyn clothed in her golden hair and naught else. Something . . .

Once again, his thoughts slipped away from him and returned him to his dream. He saw Rhiannyn, her arms outstretched, her mouth smiling and ... tears. Tears? So strange. Still, she beckoned to him, laid back and invited him into her.

The heat turning fiery, Maxen sat straight up, jolting himself to an awakeness that seemed not of this world. What was wrong with him? he wondered as the shadows of night danced around the bed. Swaying, he put a hand out to steady himself and touched a mattress soaked through. What ... ? He lifted the other arm and slid his palm down his slick, feverish chest. Was this heat upon him, this malady, just another dream? Or as Christophe had warned, had the wound become infected?

The fever gripping him tighter, pulling him under, he searched along his side for the bandages Christophe had applied more than two days past. In all that time, they had not been tended to in spite of his brother's urgings, for Maxen had been too intent on one thing and one thing only. Now, though, would he pay the price of ungodly obsession? Would the Saxons—and Rhiannyn—have their wish and stand triumphant over his grave?

Anger rising from a mind fogged with heat, Maxen put his feet to the floor and stood. He must ... Grabbing the bedpost, he staggered against it, but managed to stay upright. Loudly, he cursed his weakness, then bellowed for Christophe.

Immediately, there was a stirring beyond the screen. He heard grunting and grumbling, the scraping of benches as men arose, and finally hurried footsteps over the rushes.

"My lord?" Guy asked as he stepped around the screen, a torch held before him.

"Where is Christophe?" Maxen demanded.

His brow furrowed, Guy drew to a halt before him. "Likely still tending the Saxons' injuries," he said. "Maxen, what has happened? Are you ill?"

Maxen's anger climaxed. Curse Christophe's soft heart! Curse his goodness that drew no lines between friend and enemy—that had forced Maxen to give his soul a second time to the Devil. "Send for him!" he shouted.

Although Guy's hesitation spoke clearly the question in his mind, Maxen did not answer him. Guy turned to the watchful knights who had abandoned their lumpy beds to peer at their lord in curiosity and repeated Maxen's command for Christophe to be summoned. Immediately, the gathering thinned by the two who went to carry it out, but quickly bulked with three more who moved in to take their places.

Knowing that he had already shown too much of the weakness of his ailing body to knights he had not yet brought fully under his control, Maxen attempted to level his gaze on their swimming faces. "Slaver elsewhere," he ordered. "All of you!"

Their hesitation was brief, then they all turned and made their way back to their benches and pallets.

"Not you, Guy," Maxen said, stopping the only one to have gained his trust. "Stay."

Gratitude reflected in his eyes, Guy turned back around. "I thank you, my lord," he said, then stepped to the wall sconce and set the torch in it.

Releasing his hold on the bedpost, Maxen stretched himself out on the bed to await his brother's coming.

Christophe must have run with all that was in his lame body, for he appeared far sooner than expected. The two knights who had gone for him were close on his heels—Sir Ancel and another Maxen could not put a name to—as well as the Saxon wench, Theta.

"Maxen?" Christophe said, his youthful face looking to have aged considerably since last Maxen had laid eyes upon him.

"There is infection," Maxen said.

His eyes reflecting alarm, Christophe laid his hand to his brother's arm, then quickly drew it back. "God's rood," he exclaimed. " 'Tis a fire that burns in you."

"Then put it out."

"I . . ." Christophe shook his head. "I can but try."

"Then do!"

Swallowing loudly, Christophe began removing the bandages, and a short time later probed Maxen's diseased flesh. "Aye, infection," he murmured in the language of the

Saxons, worry clear in his voice. "Some of the stitches are torn, and there is much—"

"What say you?" Sir Ancel demanded.

"Is he dying?" the other knight asked.

Christophe looked over his shoulder at them. "It—"

"Do not interpret for them," Maxen snapped, then turned on the two knights. "Be gone!"

Though the one complied immediately, Sir Ancel stood unmoving for a long moment, his gaze clashing with Maxen's. There was a challenge there, Maxen knew, one he had seen before, and which he would soon have to take up—but not before this ill was gone from his body.

"My lord," Ancel said, dipping his head in mock deference. A knowing smile curling his lips, he pivoted and made a leisurely exit.

"I may have to kill him," Maxen muttered.

"Theta," Christophe called, "bring forth the healing bag."

Theta darted a tongue over her lips, then reluctantly severed the stare she had lit upon Maxen's exposed body. Her hips swaying, she walked to the bed and placed the bag upon it.

"Guy," Maxen called.

Circling the bed to avoid interfering with Christophe's ministrations, the knight bent near Maxen. "Aye, my lord?"

"Did you find him?"

Confusion momentarily furrowed Guy's brow, but understanding smoothed it. "Regrets, but the Saxon you seek is not amongst those captured in Andredeswald."

Then the witch's man had either escaped him yet again, else he had already met his death, Maxen thought. Perhaps another day ... Closing his eyes, he began to drift out of consciousness. However, a nagging worry forced him back.

"Guy," he called to the knight again.

"What would you have me do, my lord?" his man asked.

"Rhiannyn. Bring her to me."

Christophe's head jerked up. "Whatever for?"

"And a chain," Maxen continued as if his brother had not spoken, "an iron at each end."

"What do you intend?" Christophe demanded.

"Do it now. Quickly."

Guy straightened and nodded. "I will bring her."

"Maxen, what are you doing?" Christophe asked again once Guy had gone.

Maxen pushed a hand up off his damp brow and plunged quavering fingers into his hair. "So hot," he said, squeezing his eyes closed. "Damned hot."

Christophe leaned over him. "You are not going to tell me?"

Maxen peered narrowly at him. "You will see."

"Damn you, Maxen! If you hurt her—"

Maxen bolted to sitting, forcing Christophe to step back to avoid collision. "You will do what?" he demanded. "Allow me to die?"

Christophe's eyes flew wide, his mouth working silently before the words finally emerged. "Nay, Maxen! You are my brother. I would but know your intentions."

Maxen stared at him, then collapsed back upon the mattress. "And you will," he muttered. "You will."

When the door opened, Rhiannyn did not turn from the window and the cloudy night she stared into. After all, Maxen's coming was of no surprise, for she'd heard the stirring within the bailey, the talk upon the walls, the scrape of boots over the steps, and the ring of metal on metal. No surprise at all that he was coming for her, though why he wore chain mail and what he wanted of her were questions she feared the answers to.

Her skin pricked as he stepped within the room, but that was all, for something told her it was not who she expected. Another had been sent in his stead.

"I am to bring you to my lord," a man said.

She turned and stared at the knight, whose face glowed yellow and orange in the light of a torch held by the squire who'd accompanied him. It was Sir Guy, and he wore only a tunic and hose—not the chain mail she had thought she'd heard. In Thomas's time the knight had never been friendly toward her, but neither had he been harsh as some of the others had been.

"What does he want of me?" she asked.

He frowned displeasure. "That is for him to tell. Now come."

Knowing it would be of no use to refuse him, Rhiannyn gathered herself from the window and walked to the door. "I will follow," she said.

"You will be led," he corrected her, then captured her arm.

As if escape was even a remote possibility, she thought. It nearly made her laugh.

Stepping aside to allow Sir Guy and Rhiannyn to descend ahead of him, the squire revealed that the ring of metal she had thought to be chain mail had not been her imagination after all, for over his arm was looped a length of chain. Her heart sped, but she did not falter in step, nor inquire into it. Soon enough she would know.

In silence, she was led to the donjon and into the hall where the knights had roused from their beds. Some sitting, others standing, they spoke in hushed tones until her presence came to their attention. They fell silent then, their gazes hard on her as she walked beside Sir Guy to the lord's sleeping chamber.

The sight that greeted Rhiannyn as she came around the screen made her falter, though Guy was quick to correct her stalled course and guide her to the far side of the bed, opposite where Christophe and Theta bent over Maxen Pendery's nude body.

Looking up, Christophe started, then swiftly yanked the coverlet over his brother's loins. However, it was not the man's flesh that had captured Rhiannyn's gaze, but the sheen of sweat covering Maxen's body, and more, the unsightly redness and swelling of the wound he had received in rescuing her from her ghastly sentence of death. It seemed that in saving her life, he might give his, for the infection looked well entrenched. Although Rhiannyn tried not to feel compassion for him, it tugged at her.

Maxen's eyes sprung open wide. "Off!" he roared, reaching to throw the cover away from him.

"My lord," Guy said quickly, "as you asked, I have brought the Saxon woman."

Maxen's hand convulsed on the cover, but he did not cast it off. Instead, he focused his bleary gaze first upon Rhiannyn, then upon Guy. "And the chain?" he asked.

"I have it."

Exhaustion dragging his eyelids closed, he nodded. "Good."

He spoke no more, his silence stretching until Guy was impelled to rouse him with the question not answered. "What am I to do, my lord?"

More silence, as if consciousness was lost, but then Maxen spoke. "One iron on her . . . the other on me."

Rhiannyn raised startled eyes to Christophe, who had frozen, hand midair, returning her stare. Though slow to recover, he was the first to speak. "What say you, Maxen?" he asked. "That you intend to chain Rhiannyn to you?"

"Now you know," Maxen mumbled, his eyes remaining closed against the astonished faces of those surrounding him. "Do it, Guy."

Guy waved the squire to him. Then, shaking his head, he lifted the chain and opened the iron to place it over Rhiannyn's wrist.

Rhiannyn was of an entirely different mind. Catching him unawares, she jerked free and turned to flee the insanity she had been delivered unto. Unfortunately, the squire, a man of good stature, caught her around the waist. Ignoring her yelp of distress, he threw her to the bed and pinned her writhing body while Guy clapped the iron on her. However, she was too fine-boned; the iron slipped off over her hand. Cursing beneath his breath, Guy dragged the chain lower and fastened it around her ankle instead.

A stunned Christophe finally found his voice. "Why?" he demanded, his voice breaking as the child in him overwhelmed the man.

"To be certain she is still here when I recover," Maxen said, seemingly unaware of her struggle, though it went on right beside him.

"The tower room would serve just as well."

Dry laughter. "Under whose watch? Yours, Christophe?" An uncomfortable silence followed before Maxen shattered it with the sharp command for Christophe to finish his ministrations.

Reluctant, tight-lipped, Christophe took the bandages held by Theta and began binding them around his brother's waist.

"My wrist," Maxen said, lifting it to receive his end of the chain.

Guy did as bid, then raised the key. "And this?"

If not for the squire still straddling her, Rhiannyn would have grabbed for it, regardless of the futility of such a gesture, but she could only look yearningly at the scrap of metal.

"I entrust it to you," Maxen said.

Nodding acceptance, Guy stood from the bed, spread the drawstring pouch at his waist, and deposited the key within. "I will keep it with my life."

"This I know." Reaching out, Maxen caught Rhiannyn's chin and lifted it. "Freedom is in the length of chain," he said, his gaze faltering as he strove to keep his lids from falling, "which is all I give you." He released her. "Let her up," he ordered the squire.

The moment the weight lifted from Rhiannyn, she scrambled off the bed and went down hard on her knees on the floor. With a rattle, the chain followed, snaking across the mattress and pooling its excess upon her thighs. She pushed it off her, then lunged to her feet and stepped back as far as the chain allowed her—perhaps an arm's length from the bed.

Never having known chains, not even when Sir Ancel had thrown her in the dungeon, she strained back, but Maxen, even in the grip of dire illness, refused to allow her any more freedom. Her flesh chaffing from the strain of the iron around it, and her mind reasoning that to resist would gain her naught but pain, she stepped forward and slackened the leash put on her.

Christophe's eyes, large and luminous in the torchlight, offered an apology, but Rhiannyn looked away. Defender or no, betrayer or his brother's unwilling pawn, the trust she had placed in him had proved beyond detrimental to the Saxons awaiting death on the morrow. She heard his pained sigh, felt it ripple through her heart, but looked again only when he began speaking to Maxen.

"You must not move overly much," he warned. "If there is any chance of preventing the infection from going to rot, these stitches must stay." No response. "Did you hear me, Maxen?"

"I heard," he mumbled.

"Good. Now I am going to give you an herbal that should ease the pain and heat. Can you lift your head?"

Maxen complied. His only reaction to the taste of the medicinal concoction was a frown.

"Now sleep," Christophe said. Crossing to the torch, he lifted it free of the sconce and motioned for Theta to precede him from the chamber.

"I will keep watch over him," Guy said.

Before Christophe could reply, Maxen did it for him. "I have no need of a keeper," he said. "Leave me to my rest."

"But Rhiannyn—"

"A mere woman," he harshly interrupted.

Abandoning the argument, Guy dipped his head in deference to his lord. "Of course." Throwing Rhiannyn a look replete with warning, he and the others took their leave.

For a long time Rhiannyn stood uncertain beside the bed. The dim light of the torches in the hall revealed the outline of Maxen's body, but denied her certainty as to whether he slept.

Shifting her weight, she winced at the rattle of the chain and held her breath in anticipation of Maxen's reaction. There was none, at least not until she relaxed. Then a clatter not of her making split the air and the chain grew taut again. Although she resisted Maxen's reeling, his strength in sickness was still greater than hers, and moments later she found herself sprawled upon the bed and being dragged across it.

She wanted to cry out, to call someone to her aid, but the realization that it would likely rouse only laughter from those without kept her mouth closed. The final pull of the chain rolled her against Maxen's side, and though she raised her hands to push him away, the dampness and heat of his body seeping through her thin garments stayed her. Lord, but he burned, she thought. What hope had he of living if the fever did not break—and soon? How long before the fire consumed him?

The effort Maxen had exerted to bring Rhiannyn to him had been almost too much for him, but now that he had her, he had no intention of letting her go—until, of course, the addition of her heat to his proved too much. He stared at the array of lights that played across his closed eyelids, and picked out the few coherent thoughts in his whirling mind.

Aye, if he was to die the death Rhiannyn had wished upon him, then she would witness it. Looping the chain around his fist, he pushed up onto an elbow and sought her shadow below him. "Your wish of death on me will not save your people," he said hoarsely. "Only I, and the life of the one you protect, will do that."

Remembrance of the angry words she had thrown at him jolted Rhiannyn. Was it possible . . . ? Nay, they had been words, naught else. No power did she possess to bring them to fruition. No Dora was she. If Maxen Pendery died, it was true the blame would rest with her, though not because she had wished it on him. It would rest with her because, no matter his purpose in rescuing her from Dora, he had taken a dagger to save her. Compassion stirred again, an almost painful ache in her, and she pressed her hand to his shoulder. "Sleep, Maxen," she whispered.

As if there was more he wished to say, he hovered over her, but then fell back. "Witch," he muttered. A short time later, his breathing deepened into sleep.

With no choice but to lie alongside him, Rhiannyn

eased onto her side and took his great heat against her back. Though she would have far preferred the cold and solitude of the tower room to sharing a bed with Maxen Pendery, to deny his welcome warmth would have been a lie, for it seemed so long since last she had known anything but cold.

Wide awake with awareness, she joined her palms before her face and began praying for something only God could give her—peace upon England and no more deaths upon her conscience.

The jerking of Maxen's body snatched Rhiannyn from sleep. Taking only a moment to orient herself, to acknowledge that the night past has been more than a terrible dream, she rolled onto her back and looked at the man she shared a bed with.

The bit of dawn filtering through the windows set high in the wall was enough to confirm that all was not well. The fever raged, flushing him red and beading moisture upon his skin.

Turning onto her knees, she bent over him and took his face between her hands. "Maxen," she called. "Maxen!"

His eyes squeezed closed, he shouted something she did not understand, then wrenched his head to the side. His body convulsed, his legs kicking at the coverlet that had ridden down about his ankles.

Desperate, Rhiannyn threw a leg over him and dropped to the floor. The chain following her across Maxen's body, she hurried to the screen and called for Christophe. Only just able to look around the screen, for the chain would go no farther, she was washed with relief to see Christophe running toward her.

" 'Tis worse," she said as he stepped around her to the bedside. "He convulses and throws himself about."

Pulling Maxen's head around, Christophe leaned over him and lifted each eyelid; the eyes were reddened, the pupils dilated. "Maxen," he said sharply, then again. Given no response, he grasped his brother's shoulders and shook him, but Maxen only shouted louder and rolled onto his stomach.

His face fearful, the betraying sparkle of tears in his eyes, Christophe looked around at where Rhiannyn stood forlorn behind him. "I will need assistance in getting him onto his back again. Will you help?"

Shedding the daze that had held her motionless, she stepped forward. "Of course."

"I will do it," Sir Guy said, halting her. Pushing her aside, he stepped over the chain and helped Christophe turn Maxen over.

Though Rhiannyn felt a twinge of hurt that she had been so thoughtlessly brushed aside, she was grateful that it was Sir Guy's jaw and not her own that took the blow of Maxen's fist.

"God's wrath!" Guy cursed, shifting his jaw side to side as he rubbed at the bruise soon to appear.

"Keep him still," Christophe directed once Maxen had settled down again. Pulling the coverlet over his brother's lower body, he stepped back. "I will return shortly with a draught to ease him." On his way out, he paused to press a reassuring hand to Rhiannyn's shoulder. "Not your fault," he said, then disappeared around the corner.

It surprised Rhiannyn that he still held her blameless even though Thomas was dead and Maxen well on his way. Odd, but it also hurt that he alone refused to show her any hate. It would be so much easier on her defenses if none showed her any kindness. Then, perhaps, she could harden herself as Maxen did—feeling naught for anyone, using deceit as a weapon and turning it on others without thought of the innocents taken by it. If only . . .

"If not your fault, then whose?" Guy asked, staring at her over his shoulder.

Though she knew his taunting was not without justification, she could not help her retort. "Look to Duke William for your answer."

His mouth tightened. "King William."

A sore point for certain, but unworthy of argument, she decided, especially under the circumstances. It took a very deep breath for her to back down, to give up the duel of wits Sir Guy called her to, but she managed.

Victory his, he smiled bitterly, then looked back to where Maxen was beginning to strain again. "I do not care to have you hovering at my back, Rhiannyn," he said. "Come around where I can better see you."

She straightened. "And what cause have I given you to fear me?"

Her words had exactly the effect on him that one expected of a prideful man—his body tensed, his fists clenched, and when he spoke again, his voice snapped with command. "Now!"

Drawing a deep breath, she dragged the chain with her to the foot of the bed.

Guy looked at her, opened his mouth to say something, but closed it when Maxen's body thrust up against his hands. Leaning all his weight on the bigger man, he managed to keep Maxen down long enough for the fit to pass. Then, calm come again, he put his mouth near Maxen's ear and spoke so low Rhiannyn had to strain to hear his words.

"Fight it, Maxen," he whispered. "Fight."

That Guy's loyalty to Maxen appeared more than mere fealty to his lord surprised Rhiannyn. Was Maxen capable of returning such friendship? Did he? "You are friends?" she asked.

Guy's expression told her she'd overstepped her bounds, and though he needn't have added words to it, he did. "Your deceitful voice is not welcome here. Let me hear no more of it."

Rhiannyn lapsed into silence.

Shortly thereafter, Christophe reappeared, and behind him came Theta and two other women whose arms were burdened with all manner of items. Though Theta met Rhiannyn's gaze, a smug smile playing about her lips, the other two—Mildreth and Lucilla—looked elsewhere. Both had been women of Rhiannyn's village, and had been taken by Thomas at the same time as she. They were as close to friends as Rhiannyn had come to having while living in this place, but now their uncertainty about her denied her the solace she might have found in their company.

As for Theta, Thomas has taken her from a village near Hastings and brought her with him to Etcheverry. For several months she had shared his bed, and though he refused to make her Lady Theta, still she greatly pretended the role. But that had all changed when Rhiannyn had been brought into the castle. Even though Rhiannyn had vehemently declared she would never wed Thomas, Theta had been displaced and had made no pretense of her hate for one she considered an interloper.

"Lady, the water and washcloth are for you," Christophe said, nodding to the items placed atop the chest, "and the garments." Startled, she raised questioning eyes to him. "Uncleanliness spreads disease," he explained. "If you are to share this place with Maxen, you must be clean."

Frowning, Rhiannyn glanced down her front and saw what Christophe had seen. Her trek through Andredeswald and two days in the tower had left her slovenly. Moreover, she still bore traces of the dirt from her early grave. She shuddered as those memories returned to her, but quickly pushed them back. How had she overlooked her present state? she wondered. It would seem the worry and pain of what was to become of her people had eclipsed all, even the cleanliness that had once been so important to her.

"I understand, Christophe," she said.

"All of you," he added.

Did he intend her to bathe in entirety before those present?

Reading her expression, he shook his head. "When we are gone."

Behind her hand, Theta snickered.

"Quiet thyself!" Christophe snapped.

Though she was slow to comply, Theta quieted.

Looking none too pleased, Christophe thrust a basin of water and a washcloth into the woman's hands. "Cool him," he ordered.

It was something Theta was more than willing to do. Her gaze flickering once more to Rhiannyn, she dipped the cloth and slowly circled it over Maxen's magnificent chest, then lower to an abdomen that even in rest seemed to ripple strength.

Tearing her gaze from the erotic dance of Theta's hands over Maxen, Rhiannyn sank down upon the edge of the chest.

"If you will raise him," Christophe said to Guy, "I will give him the draught."

Guy lifted Maxen and held him while Christophe forced the drink he'd concocted upon his brother. Though barely conscious, Maxen protested, but in the end downed what was given him.

Satisfied, Christophe turned his attention upon the bedding. Calling out orders to Mildreth and Lucilla as he worked, he created a flurry of activity that had Rhiannyn tucking her feet beneath her to avoid being swept away with the stagnant rushes. New rushes were spread, herbs sprinkled upon them, and surfaces wiped clean. The bedding was changed so completely that Maxen had to be lifted to accomplish the feat, and Rhiannyn had to look away to avoid once again gazing upon the nudity of his lower regions.

Glimpsing her embarrassment, Theta laughed. "Mayhap you would like to finish cooling our lord, Rhiannyn," she said, stepping around the bed to offer the saturated cloth to her. "Or yourself." Smiling, she swiped the cloth across Rhiannyn's blushing cheek.

It was the same as it had always been between them, though it would likely become worse now that Rhiannyn was relegated to a status beneath that of Theta. "As you enjoy it so much," Rhiannyn said evenly, "I would not wish to deny you the pleasure."

Wrinkling her nose and flashing teeth whose white contrasted starkly with blacker than night hair, Theta dipped the cloth again. "I had hoped you would say that," she murmured, then ran the cloth up Maxen's lightly haired legs.

Wishing herself anywhere but there, Rhiannyn fingered the garments Christophe had brought her. For the first time she noticed their fine material. They were ones Thomas had had made for her, presenting them to her the day before she had escaped from Etcheverry. Never worn, both gowns were as far from a commoner's clothing as could be.

Though unadorned, the ecru-colored chemise was fashioned of linen woven so tightly there was a sheen to it. Worn beneath the more lavish overgown of rose, it would glide smoothly over Rhiannyn's skin when she moved. In contrast, the overgown—the bliaut—was of heavier material, its V neckline, flared sleeves, and hemline ornately embroidered with threads that carried the glint of gold. Shorter than the undergown, the bliaut would fall to mid-calf when worn, leaving a length of chemise to skim the ground. Lastly, to complete the look of "lady," there was a sash of intertwined gold strands for defining the waist.

Nay, these garments were certainly not what Maxen would have chosen for her, Rhiannyn thought. Dare she don them, or should she send them back for something more appropriate?

"Rhiannyn."

She looked up to discover Christophe standing before her. Beyond, only Sir Guy and Theta remained. "Aye?" she asked.

"For now, there is naught else I can do for Maxen," he said, in that moment seeming more a man than a boy. "He should sleep, but does he awaken, he may wish something to drink. On the table is wine you can give him. I have added herbs to it for his pain."

The thought of trying to put drink to Maxen's lips was an unsettling one, and Rhiannyn prayed she would not have to do it. "Where are you going?" she asked.

"To tend the wounded."

"The Saxons?" Looking to Sir Guy, she saw from his face that he did not approve of the idea, but he did not speak against it.

"Aye," Christophe answered.

Though it was difficult to ask the question that had been hovering within her since she'd been brought to

Maxen on the night past, she had to. "And what of the hangings your brother ordered?"

Christophe looked over his shoulder to Sir Guy. "They will wait until he is well enough to witness them himself," he said.

Guy did not oppose him, though his mouth tightened.

A reprieve, but for how long? Rhiannyn wondered. For however long Maxen lay abed and unable to govern. Or until the fever took him and another—Sir Ancel—carried out the sentences of death.

"Do not forget," Christophe said, indicating the basin of water that awaited her.

She nodded, then watched as he and the others left. For a long time she stared at the screen around which they had disappeared, then she set about keeping her promise to Christophe.

Chapter Eight

"Maxen!" Rhiannyn called to him. "I cannot do this alone. You must help me."

Still he continued to thrash, throwing his head side to side and calling for drink in a voice so hoarse, it sounded as if his throat were filled with pebbles.

"Maxen," she called again.

His hand shot out, nearly sending the goblet flying from her fingers. "Burning," he said. "Accursed fire!" Then he thrust himself onto his side.

Remembering Christophe's warning against too much movement, Rhiannyn did the only thing she could think of. She returned the goblet to the table, lifted her hand, and slapped him—once, twice, and again. She would have continued had not his eyes sprung wide.

"Witch," he growled, his lips snarling,

his nostrils flared, his pupils wide and crazed with the illness gone to his head.

Were she of wax and not flesh, Rhiannyn thought she would surely have melted from the heat of his raging stare, but she was of flesh, as witnessed by the fear pricking across her skin. "I was trying to help," she said. "You were throwing yourself about and I feared the stitches might tear."

"Likely, you feared I might not die."

She shook her head. " 'Tis not true."

"Isn't it?"

She opened her mouth to continue the protest, but snapped it closed again. To argue with him in his present state of mind would be useless, though in his other state of mind it seemed little better. Tucking away the strand of freshly washed hair that had fallen into her eyes, she compressed her lips and met his gaze, only to discover it gone from her face. Until that moment, she had forgotten she wore naught but the chemise she'd hurriedly donned when Maxen's delirious thrashing had interrupting her bathing. Now, with his attention focused on it, she was more than aware of her breasts thrusting against the thin material. Self-consciously, she crossed her arms over them.

A sardonic smile curved Maxen's mouth, then his eyes fell closed. As Rhiannyn watched his chest rise and fall with shallow breaths, she wondered if he'd lost consciousness.

"Thirsty," he mumbled, his lids lifting once again. "So dry."

She retrieved the goblet she had earlier attempted to offer him. "I have drink," she said.

He looked at the vessel, then her. "Think you I would take it from your hand?"

At the unspoken accusation that she meant to poison him, Rhiannyn bridled. "My hand or not at all," she said.

To her great surprise, he acceded. "Then it must be." Lifting himself onto an elbow, he raised his head to accept the rim of the goblet against his lips. Then, eyes fixed to hers, he drained it.

Believing the worst past and that he would settle back to sleep now that his thirst had been quenched, Rhiannyn was surprised when he suddenly caught her arm, flung her to the bed, and rolled his length atop hers. The goblet clattered on the floor, and she stared wide-eyed as the man above her blotted out sight and feel of all but him.

Maxen held her gaze for interminable moments, then he took her face between his hands and lowered his head. So unexpected was the caress of his mouth upon hers that Rhiannyn was too shocked to react. Once the shock passed, though, something stronger than instinctual survival claimed her—something that delved emotions too long untouched. She fought it with a frantic litany of memories and pains, but it proved stronger than the past. It went beyond control. With a sigh of surrender, she opened her mouth to Maxen's urgings.

In the next instant, Rhiannyn discovered that his motives were far different from what he had led her to believe. Parting his lips, he trickled warm, heady wine onto her tongue. Though her natural reaction as it wended its way to the back of her throat was to expel it, he would not allow it. Still holding her face between his hands, he sealed his mouth over hers until she had no choice but to choke or swallow. She swallowed.

Maxen lifted his head. "Now if I fall, I do not fall alone," he murmured.

Indignation sparked by humiliation assailed Rhiannyn. "If you thought I meant to poison you," she snapped, "you had but to ask me to drink ere you."

A faint smile touched his lips. "I had thought of that, but this held far more appeal." His eyes, heavily lidded with the weight of malaise, strayed to her mouth. "And now would you like a proper kiss, Rhiannyn of Etcheverry?"

"I would not!" she exclaimed, frantic that he might drag her under his spell again. Lord, but she could not have such shame visited upon her twice in as many minutes.

When he returned his gaze to hers, she saw something

in his eyes that had not been there before. The predator—though not the one who had chased her through the woods and pounced upon her. This predator was one of want.

"You are mine, Rhiannyn," he said thickly, and slid a hand to the undercurve of her buttocks.

She jerked sideways to escape his searching fingers, but it was useless. "Maxen, please—"

"Not Edwin's," he continued, a slur now come into his voice, "not Thomas's ..." Lingeringly, he stroked his fingers up over her hip, her abdomen, her ribs, then inward to her breast. "Mine."

A mixture of panic and unfamiliar sensations assailing her, Rhiannyn began to struggle, but stilled a moment later for fear she might cause him further injury. "Release me, Maxen," she pleaded. "You are ill and—"

"And it has been a very long time," he said, moisture beading upon his brow. He curved his hand around her breast and stroked his thumb across her peaked nipple. "Too long."

Again, something happened to Rhiannyn as he touched her—something that transcended breathing and spiked frissons of pleasure to the forbidden region of her body, something deep and drawing that swayed the very passions she had thought herself barren of. A sweetness in her loins she had never known, a melting of flesh she had not thought possible ... Rhiannyn closed her eyes and felt what no man had ever made her feel. It was more than a kiss. More than a touch. It went far deeper and filled her more fully, and the promise ... the promise of a Norman! her mind sharply reminded her.

"Nay," she said. "You do not want this. You do not want me." Relief swept her as his hand left her breast. However, it was short-lived, for he caught the hem of her chemise and began pulling it up.

"Remember Thomas," she said with growing desperation.

His eyes sparked through the narrow slits of his lids, and a moment later, his crazed desire was cast out. "Never will I forget him," he said, "and neither will you." He rolled off her and onto his back.

As fast as her legs and the chain would allow, Rhiannyn scrambled across the mattress and off the bed. Distance her best ally—her only ally—she stepped back until the chain would give no more, then defensively crossed her arms over her chest.

Maxen stared at her, his face impassive but for the fatigue there. Then, turning his head opposite, he closed his eyes.

Immediately, Rhiannyn's gaze was drawn to his loins, which had come uncovered. Though she quickly looked away, it was too late not to have noticed all of him—the golden flesh nestled in dark, curling hair, the hard, muscled thighs that had moments ago trapped hers. However, Maxen's groan pulled her gaze back to him.

He did not speak it, yet she knew he was in pain. Had he done further injury to himself in his tussle with her? She warred with herself a long moment, part of her wanting to answer his need, another part fearful of the danger she would put herself in by going near him again. In the end, though, she stepped around the bed to the table. "Should I summon Christophe?" she asked.

He did not answer her, and a short time later his silence turned to sleep.

Uncertain, Rhiannyn stood motionless, her gaze fixed upon him. What was it he had caused to tremble inside her? she pondered. How was it that a man she believed she hated had the power to move her body as he'd done? Why had she felt what only Edwin should have made her feel? Why? She was still standing there minutes later when Sir Guy came around the screen.

Wordlessly, he flicked his gaze over her, wrinkled his brow as he took in her state of dress, then walked to where Maxen lay. "He is resting well?" he asked as he pulled the coverlet up over his lord.

Spurring herself to action, Rhiannyn hurried to where the bliaut lay upon the chest and pulled it over her head. Only when it had settled to just past her knees, leaving the longer chemise to cover her lower legs and drag its hem in the rushes, did she answer the knight. "He awoke a short time ago," she said as she knotted the sash around her waist. "I gave him the wine, and then he returned to sleeping."

"Was he in pain?"

She looked up to discover the knight watching her. "He did not speak of any, though I believe he was."

He nodded. "What did he speak of?"

She was taken aback by his question, but quickly recovered. "Little, though he was suspicious that I might have poisoned the wine."

"Understandable."

Rhiannyn took offense at that. "Why? Because I am Saxon?"

Stepping around the bed, Guy laid punishing hands to her shoulders. "Because one Pendery has already died because of you."

Accept the blame she did, but Rhiannyn was well and truly sick of hearing it spoken of so often by murdering Normans. "And how many of my people died because of him?" she retorted, tossing her head to where Maxen lay. "How many innocents did your almighty lord slay in the name of the bastard of Normandy?"

Guy's eyes turned flinty. "In battle, many were the Saxons who fell beneath his sword, for which he has spent the past two years in repentance."

"Repentance," Rhiannyn repeated scornfully. "The only repentance Maxen Pendery has ever known is his mockery of it when he donned monk's clothing had pretended holiness to deceive Edwin and his followers—and me! He does not know God, and never will he."

The knight frowned. "You are wrong. The monk is the truth of Maxen. Since Hastings, and prior to his being summoned to Etcheverry, he served in a monastery. If not for Thomas's death, he would still be there."

Rhiannyn was too stunned to respond. Upon discovering who Maxen was, never had she considered that he might truly be of the brotherhood of monks. She had thought it all a pretense, the tonsuring of his head an act of sacrifice in the name of revenge.

Now, though, reflecting back on the night he had

preached at the camp, and later when he had stood before the angry horde and pronounced them sinners for what they had meant to do to her, she realized Guy spoke the truth, not the lie she wanted to accuse him of. That night, Maxen—Brother Justus—had swept away her suspicions by presenting himself as a monk every bit worthy of his station. She had felt the power of God in his words, drawn strength from them, and known the touch of inner peace before Dora had shattered it with her accusations. Still, the man Rhiannyn had come to know these past days did not fit at all with the monk Guy proclaimed him to have been.

"I—I don't believe you," she said, though more of her believed than disbelieved. Then, as if to push her that little bit more she needed to acknowledge the truth, she remembered how Maxen had touched her breast earlier, and the words he had spoken. "It has been a very long time," he'd said. Surely only a man—a monk—long without the comfort of a woman would have expressed desire for one he hated. And there was no doubt he hated her.

She shook her head. "His anger is too great," she said, "his manner too vengeful for him to have been a monk."

Guy lowered his face near hers. "That surprises you? A second brother has died—needlessly—and now Maxen has been forced to renounce his chosen life to keep safe that which belongs to the Penderys. No, Rhiannyn, he is not a saint. No man truly of this earth is. Maxen is but a man who in one day lost two things very precious to him. And lost both to you."

The truth was a blow to Rhiannyn. Yet another lost life upon her conscience. Nay, Maxen was not dead—at least not yet—but the man he had chosen to be was no more, and all because she had chosen not to be Thomas's wife.

Her sorrows multiplying, Rhiannyn looked past Guy to Maxen, and for the first time since learning his true identity, realized that beneath his wrathful exterior there dwelt a human. A man who had known terrible remorse for the lives he had taken, and who had given his life to God in atonement for those sins. A man she had known as Brother

Justus, who had risked his life to save hers. Did he still exist, and if so, could he be reached?

"It is with awe that I look upon your life, Rhiannyn," Sir Guy said, forcing her back to the present, "awe that you yet live."

Rhiannyn sought his gaze. "Had I known ..." Her voice trailed off, and she realized she did not know what difference it would have made had she known the truth about Maxen.

"You would still be Saxon, and he Norman," Guy said. "You would still protect the one you refuse him, and he would still seek him."

In one thing only was Guy wrong. Regardless of who had killed Thomas, if she knew, she would now speak it to save the lives of the others. Wincing at the clattering chain, she turned from him.

"I warn you," Guy said, "I will seek your punishment if Maxen dies."

"This I know."

His tense silence was followed by the crunch of his booted feet over the rushes as he left.

Alone again with Maxen, Rhiannyn looked around at his still form. Where was the Maxen of mercy? she wondered. Where was the one with the power to bring peace to Etcheverry? And peace this Norman must bring, for to continue believing the Saxons would one day drive the Normans out was a lie she had too long fostered. It seemed that William the Bastard and his barons were in England to stay.

Acknowledging that hurt more than Rhiannyn would ever have believed, but it also gave her hope. "I will find you, Maxen," she whispered. "You will not die."

Rhiannyn was ready when, after the nooning meal that had been accompanied by raucous noise beyond the screen, Christophe and Theta came again. Standing, she looked to the other woman. "You will not be needed," she said.

Theta's smirk flattened as she straightened from the table she had emptied her armful of bandages upon. "What speak you of?" she demanded.

"I will assist Christophe in tending his brother."

"Truly?" Christophe exclaimed.

Bumping him aside, Theta walked forward and strategically placed herself so Rhiannyn was forced to look up at her. "As if any would trust you," she said, sneering. "Is it not enough that Thomas is dead because of you, and now mayhap Maxen as well?"

Rhiannyn longed to step back so she would not have to crane her neck to meet Theta's gaze, but knew that it would appear as if she was backing down. She tipped her chin up higher. "Maxen will live," she said, "and I will assist Christophe to that end."

Theta laughed. "Away with you. Take your chain and cower in the far corner there."

Rhiannyn shook her head. "Nay, Theta. 'Tis you who must leave."

The woman's smirk returned. "A bit high and mighty for a prisoner—a slave—wouldn't you say, Christophe?"

He stepped forward. "I think—"

" 'Tis time Theta took her leave," Rhiannyn finished for him.

Christophe hesitated, obviously uncertain as to what role he should play in this contest of wills.

"And I say 'tis time Rhiannyn took hers," Theta said darkly.

Rhiannyn stood her ground, but in the next moment found it slipping from beneath her as Theta gave her a great shove backward. Recovering her balance, though she nearly undid it when her heel caught upon the chain, she retook the ground she had lost. Although never one to give shove for shove, it took much for her to resist the temptation to do just that. Putting her hands on her hips, she met Theta's challenging stare. "I will not tell you again. Now go."

There would never be a better time for Christophe to intercede and prevent the fray coming on the air, and as if sensing that, he stepped forward. Taking Theta's arm, he pulled her back before she realized what was happening, then positioned himself before her. Unlike his brothers, who stood well above him, he came eye to eye with the woman.

"To tend my brother, I need only one pair of hands in addition to my own," he said. "As Rhiannyn is willing to be those hands, methinks your time would best be spent tending the Saxons, Theta."

Her face a mirror of surprise that quickly turned to anger, Theta demanded, "And why would I wish to do that? At your side is where I belong, not alone among filthy Saxons."

Had Rhiannyn not been separated from Theta by the block of Christophe's body, she would surely have lost control. It was insult enough to be called such names by the Normans, but by one who was also of Saxon birth . . .

Christophe squared his shoulders. "I have spoken. Henceforth, Rhiannyn will assist me with my brother."

A torrid argument was in Theta's eyes, but something kept it there. Looking past Christophe, she smiled a twisted smile at Rhiannyn. " 'Tis fine to know you are as much a whore as I," she said, "but when Maxen is done with you, know this—'tis me he will come back to. Just as Thomas would have had you not murdered him."

That Theta believed she offered to assist Christophe in order to gain Maxen's bed was almost laughable, but no laughter spilled from Rhiannyn's lips. The sly intimation that Theta had already bedded Maxen disturbed her too much, though why it should she had no desire to know.

With a flounce and a triumphant titter, Theta withdrew.

"My apologies," Christophe said as he turned to face Rhiannyn. "I should not have allowed her to say such things."

" 'Tis not your fault," she said, trying for a smile that felt tight. "Theta says what Theta wants, and it seems there is naught anyone can do about it."

"Were she not so unmoved by the sight of blood, I assure you I would have nothing to do with her. But she is the only one."

"I understand, Christophe. You needn't explain."

He pursed and unpursed his lips. "Then mayhap you will explain why you have offered to take her place.

Though it is understandable why you would not want to, it is beyond me why you would."

Disliking his intense scrutiny, Rhiannyn looked down at her hands. "Sir Guy told me the reason your brother is the way he is—what he gave up to succeed Thomas."

"You did not already know?"

She shook her head. "I thought it a disguise Maxen had taken for his deceit, and that was all. Now I better understand, and understanding, know that there must be some compassion in your brother, some way to reach him and end this terrible taking of lives."

Walking to her, Christophe tilted her chin up and looked into her eyes. "You are a dreamer, Rhiannyn. Maxen is the way he is, and not even your beauty, nor the goodness that shines from you, can change that."

Was he right? she wondered. Was there naught in Maxen that was decent? If that were so, why had he committed his life to God following the slaughter at Hastings? For what other reason would a man do such a selfless thing? Keeping the questions to herself, she offered Christophe her best effort at a teasing smile. "And you are becoming a terrible skeptic," she returned.

He shrugged. "Maxen tends to bring that out in people. But come, I will show you what needs to be done."

She followed him to the bedside and stood at his shoulder while he unwrapped Maxen's bandages.

" 'Tis not worsening," he said as he examined the unsightly wound, "but neither does it look to be improving."

"The stitches hold?" Rhiannyn asked, hopeful he would not confirm her fear that during her encounter with Maxen they had been torn.

"They hold," he said. Then, as Rhiannyn expelled her relief on a sigh, he launched into an explanation of how to cleanse the wound. As he spoke, he performed the task, and a short time later detailed his reasons for using the type of salve he had chosen.

"Now you," he said, placing fresh bandages in her hands. "When I raise him, pass these beneath."

They worked to accomplish the task quickly, though

more for the strain upon Christophe's arms than for the comfort of Maxen who slept unknowing through it all.

"Now secure them," Christophe instructed. Leaving her to it, he turned to the table and began picking through the items there.

Had it been any other but Maxen whom she passed her hands over, the task would have seemed meant for a simpleton. It was Maxen, though, and her fingers turned clumsy as they swept smooth muscle. She took an inordinate amount of time to accomplish what should have taken little, but finally it was done.

Christophe withheld comment, though he might certainly have commented on her ineptness. "Good," he said. "Now you must needs cool him as Theta did."

Even more daunting. Placing the basin of water upon the floor beside her, Rhiannyn wetted the cloth, then began swabbing it over Maxen, working from his moist brow downward.

"That is all for now," Christophe said as he plugged the bottle from which he had emptied powder into the wine Theta had brought. "Finish cooling him, and when he awakens, give him this to drink."

Reluctantly, Rhiannyn nodded. She would have far preferred that Christophe remain with her until she finished cooling Maxen, but knew his time would be best spent elsewhere. She had claimed the responsibility of caring for Maxen; he was in her hands now. "I will give it to him," she said, silently adding that this time there would be a different outcome to her offering drink to Maxen.

Quickly, Christophe gathered his things together. "I will return ere dark," he said. "Send for me if he worsens."

"I will."

He crossed to the screen, but there hesitated. "Rhiannyn?"

She looked over her shoulder. "Aye?"

"I had naught to do with Maxen's plans to follow you to Edwin's camp," he blurted out. "You believe that, don't you?"

She had been uncertain, fearful to trust anyone, but she

could no longer deny Christophe's innocence. True, he had played an important role, but for certain he'd had no knowledge of it. "Aye, Christophe," she said. "This I know."

His strained features awash with relief, he withdrew.

Wetting the cloth again, Rhiannyn wiped it over Maxen's powerful arms, then down his chest. Upon reaching the coverlet at his hips, she hesitated, then pulled the cloth upward from his feet. His male anatomy remaining covered, she proceeded to cool his legs and feet. It was a strange thing, the willing touch of her hands to a man who was her enemy, the knowing of his body that few but lovers would ever come to know, but necessary. So necessary.

Later, when Maxen came to partial consciousness, she cautiously offered the wine, bracing herself in the event he attempted to do the same as he'd done that morning. However, he was too delirious to question her intent, wordlessly drinking from the rim she held to his lips. The wine drained, she lowered him back to the mattress.

"Burning," he breathed, staring up at her through narrowed eyes.

Though the water in the basin was no longer chilled, Rhiannyn wet a cloth, folded it, and laid it upon his brow. "Try to sleep," she urged.

Unexpectedly, he dragged his arm up from the mattress and placed his palm against her cheek. "Angel," he said thickly. "Sweet, sweet angel."

Though she knew he spoke words formed by an incoherent mind, Rhiannyn's hope that Maxen Pendery might, indeed, be reachable, blossomed. "I am here," she said. "Now sleep."

He closed his eyes, then, like a caress, trailed his fingers down her neck to the V of her bliaut. A moment later, he dropped his arm back to his side and slept.

Denying what she had felt, Rhiannyn stepped back from the bed and rubbed her hands over the pricked flesh of her arms. Cold was what she was, she told herself. Only cold.

Chapter Nine

The days fell one upon the other, Maxen's illness taking him into an unconsciousness so deep he could not possibly have known who vigilantly tended his needs; who assisted Christophe in the cleansing and bandaging of his wound; who cooled his body and wet his parched mouth; who slept lightly beside him during the long nights, awakening to the slightest sound he made; who more than once coaxed him free of the terrible dreams in which he called out his brother's name—Nils; and who came to know by sight and touch every inch of his battle-battered flesh, including that which made him a man, when normal bodily functions necessitated she tend to them.

He did not know, but all others knew it was a determined Rhiannyn who refused him the peace of death, though at times it seemed the best end for him. Those who came and went—

Christophe, Sir Guy, the servants bearing viands, and occasionally Sir Ancel—all stared curiously at her. And to her surprise, Sir Guy began looking at her with uncertainty, his eyes absent of accusation and condemnation.

On the fifth day, as the night gave way to the dim of first morning, Rhiannyn awoke to cool flesh beneath her palm. With hope having waned that Maxen might ever recover, she at first feared the worst. However, the sudden spasming of his body told her it was not death come for him, but chills brought on by the sudden breaking of his fever.

In the bare light of a torch near to extinguishing, she looked into his face. "Maxen?" she breathed.

His lids fluttered, but remained closed. " 'Tis cold," he said. Shivering, he reached for the coverlet he had earlier kicked off.

Seeing it was too far out of his reach, Rhiannyn scrambled onto her knees and tugged it from beneath his feet. "I have it," she said, pulling it up over him.

As it settled on his chest, his strained face softened, but in the next instant creased as the chills gripped him more fiercely. Hoping it would be enough, Rhiannyn spread her own blanket over him and tucked it around his convulsing body. It was not enough, though, and there were no more blankets—naught to give him the warmth he sought.

Naught but her, she thought, bringing herself up short with memories of her childhood. Many were the biting winter nights when she and her brothers had crept off their pallets to share their mother and father's. The warmth of body cradling body had been unequalled by fire or blanket.

Of course, she could always awaken the others and call for more covering, she considered, then decided it would not be worth the great clamor when a better solution was at hand. Afraid to give too much thought to what she must do, for the implications of such intimacy would surely have turned her away, she lifted the covers and lay down beside Maxen.

Immediately, he turned onto his side, curved an arm

around her waist, and drew her back against him. Her chemise the only thing separating her flesh from his, Rhiannyn held her breath as he fit his hard contours to her softer ones. It was almost too much, this press of flesh made for lovers, not enemies, but she would not abandon him as the warning voice in her mind urged her to. She would give Maxen what he needed.

Letting her breath out on a long sigh, she tried to relax, to let her body flow into his and give him her heat. It was no easy feat, for twice more the chills racked him, each time thrusting his body more deeply against hers until, at last, he grew still.

Rhiannyn began to ease. Telling her fingers to unclench, her jaw to loosen, her back to unbind, and her legs to give, she closed her eyes and beckoned sleep to take her far from the disturbing feel of Maxen's body—though not to the grave again, she prayed. Since coming to Maxen's chamber, the nightmares had lessened, but still they came to her at least once a night.

She was still wide awake minutes later when he spoke, his breath moving through the hair at her crown. "I thank you," he murmured.

She jerked with surprise. Not only had he caught her unawares with his wakefulness, but the words of appreciation were disconcerting. Surely he spoke them out of incoherent thoughts still tainted by illness, without knowledge of whom he spoke to. However, she was not to know, for he soon fell back to sleep, leaving Rhiannyn to ponder his words.

The last time Maxen had laid with a woman, she'd smelled of smoke and sweat—smoke from tending the kitchen fires, sweat from too many hours spent there—so different from the creature whose womanly scent now wafted to his senses. The kitchen wench had been soft, but too soft, not like the woman curled into the arc of his body. She'd had hair so dark and straight, bearing not the slightest resemblance to the gilded tresses now curling around his fingers. He'd not known her name, but then, neither did he know this woman's. And he sent her away afterwards, declining to spend any more of the night with her—unlike this woman who had clearly spent the entire night with him. So why was his body not satisfied as it had been with the other woman? Why this deep, aching need as if he had not know satiation in years?

Because he had not known it, he reminded himself, his mind sloughing off the last of sleep. It was not a dream that he had given his life to God, nor that he had been forced to renounce that life. He was Maxen Pendery, reluctant lord of all of Etcheverry, and this woman was Rhiannyn. Rhiannyn who should have been lady of Etcheverry through marriage to Edwin had the Saxons not been defeated by the Normans; and then once again through marriage to Thomas when the conquering was done and the Normans victorious. Twice, she could have been a lady, and now she was reduced to a slave, a woman who had come into his bed like any other whore. Why? And had he taken what she'd offered? Or had he been too ill to claim it?

Searching backward, he fell into the darkness that had been his. He had been hot ... feverish ... burning. Gentle hands had touched him, eased his heat, spoken reassuringly to him, and put drink to his lips. Rhiannyn? Nay, it could not have been one who hated him as she did. More likely Theta. But last night ...

Determinedly, he delved until the haze thinned and showed him the unexpected, but also the only answer possible. Last night it had been Rhiannyn. Of that he was certain, for the woman who had given her heat to him still lay beside him. And that was all she had offered him, he realized. Not the use of her body for carnal pleasure, but something he'd needed far more. Why? The woman he thought she was, that he wanted her to be, should have left him to a cold that was more of the grave than anything he had ever known. Why hadn't she?

Frowning, he pushed up onto an elbow, which immediately caused daggers to stab at the backs of his eyes. With all that was in his ravaged body, he squeezed his eyes tight to fight the blackness sucking him toward its core. In the end he emerged triumphant, though more weakened than before. Calming his breath, he lifted a hand and smoothed back the hair falling over Rhiannyn's face. So angelic, as if she could never do anyone harm. So beautiful. So deceitful.

Again, why? Why had she not turned from him in his moment of need? Why did she refuse to stay where he had put her? Angered by the silence that was his only answer, Maxen rolled onto his back and stared at the ceiling high above.

Was it yesterday he had awakened to the slap of her hand? he wondered. Vaguely, he remembered calling her "witch," but more vividly he remembered claiming her as his—the kiss he had given her under the pretense of fearing she intended to poison him, her firm buttocks cupped in his hand, the breast which had peaked to his caress, the quivering thigh he had laid a hand to in his quest to know her more intimately. Whatever had possessed him? Why did he so desire her when Theta or any other would do just as well? A fleshly thing was all it was, he told himself, attempting to explain away his feelings, of this earth, and not of—

Rhiannyn's low moan swept his frustrated ponderings aside. She shifted her backside against his hip, settled as if to rest again, then suddenly twisted around amid a rattle of chain. Nestling her head upon his shoulder, she hugged herself to him and drew a bare leg up his thigh. Then, rippling a feline sound, she relaxed into him.

Damnation, Maxen silently cursed. Didn't she know what she risked? Of course she did, he concluded harshly. She knew better than he. Continuing to curse her for causing all of his energy to be channeled to that one place he had denied so long, he looked beyond the appeal of the face turned up to him and was not surprised to see that his man's flesh had tented the coverlet up from his hips. Not surprised at all considering the deep, aching pull of his loins.

He could push Rhiannyn away, he knew, sever the contact that roused his desire, but he was curiously loath to do so. Nay, let his mind drive her out, he challenged himself. Let *it* prove its strength.

Although it was difficult to maintain his belief after all the ill that had befallen him and his family, Maxen closed his eyes and turned to the prayers he and the other monks had used in times of carnal need. To a degree, they had served him well, though sometimes only as a result of fatigue from hours spent on his knees. The difference was that there had not been a warm, desirable body at his side when he had fought such desire.

How Rhiannyn wanted to sleep. To keep her eyes sealed against the light of day, to ignore the insistent feeling of being watched, to regain the hours of sleep lost to . . .

Opening her eyes just enough to see beyond her nose, she focused on her fingers from which dark, curling hair sprouted. Maxen's chest, she realized, and it was his body she was wantonly curled against. Shocked, she lifted her chin and looked into eyes she had not seen the color of for many days. Now, in the morning light, they shone their blue upon her. "You're awake," she said.

His eyebrows arched, but he remained silent.

Sitting up, she took the cover with her and pressed it to her chest. "The fever has passed," she said, offering him a tentative smile.

His mouth twisted. "Disappointed?"

She felt the smile slide straight off her face and fall to the pit of her stomach. She had put so much of her heart into these past days, to be confronted by the Maxen she had left off with was almost too much for her.

Fool, she flogged herself. What did you expect? That he would awaken with changed heart? That he would let your people go and make no more war upon them? All because you did what Theta could more easily have done? Still, it was a beginning, she reminded herself as she picked up her hope and brushed it off. There was much yet to do, but unfortunately, not much time to do it.

"Nay, I am not disappointed," she said. "I am most relieved."

"Then there must have been a greater threat to your person did I die rather than live. Guy, am I right?"

She was about to deny it when she recalled the knight's warning. He had indeed threatened her if Maxen died, but that was certainly not what fueled her relief. Though it was true she'd had an ulterior motive in wanting Maxen to live, it went beyond that. In fact, with each passing day it had become far more personal. She wanted Maxen to live simply that he might live—that the man who had so gently laid his hands to her and called her "angel," who had thanked her for her warmth, might someday show that same gentleness to others.

She shook her head. "You are wrong."

"And you lie." Abruptly, he sat up, grimacing as the sway of his body gave testament to his weakness.

"Maxen," she said, laying a hand to his arm, " 'tis too soon for you to rise. You have lain ill for five days now, and—"

"Five days!" he barked, his eyes springing wide.

"Aye, five days."

He looked to her hand resting on him, then pushed it into her lap. "I prefer your fear to your concern. 'Tis far more trustworthy."

The same Maxen—unchanged and ungiving. "You have much to be thankful for." She forced the words past stiff lips. "By God's will you live, and to him you must give thanks."

"God," he scoffed. " 'Tis Christophe who should be given credit." The chain he wore clattering, he tossed back the coverlet, swung his legs to the ground, and stood. However, he lay back down a moment later, his face ashen. "Accursed weakness," he muttered.

"If you are not to undo your healing, you need food and rest, Maxen," Rhiannyn said.

His gaze cold as the steel of a sword about to draw

blood, he looked back at her. "Do not pretend to know what I need," he said, his voice low and even, "and do not make me tell you again the proper way I am to be addressed."

She swallowed the retort that had no place in her plan of helping him to become human. "Aye, my lord," she said. Then, to keep from taking back words that had been painfully difficult to speak, she pulled the chain with her across the bed and lowered her feet to the floor. "I will call Christophe," she said as she patted the chemise down her legs. "He will wish to examine you."

Maxen made no reply, simply followed her around the bed with a gaze that pierced her through.

Self-consciously, Rhiannyn grabbed her bliaut from atop the chest, shook it out, and dragged it over her head. "Christophe, come quickly," she called around the screen, then began adjusting the sash.

"Fine clothes for a slave," Maxen commented.

She paused a moment, then knotted the sash. "They are what were brought me," she said. "If you prefer otherwise—"

"I *do* prefer otherwise."

She turned to face him. "Then I am sure you will see to it as soon as possible."

"That I will."

Rhiannyn was beyond grateful for Christophe's appearance, for it gave her respite from the battle Maxen was attempting to draw her into, and which she was sorely tempted to succumb to.

"Give praise," Christophe exclaimed as he crossed to the bed. "At last you have awakened. 'Twas feared you might not."

"You have much to learn about self-confidence, little brother," Maxen said, giving Christophe a smile Rhiannyn found herself wishing were for her. "It is by your hand I live."

"And in good spirits," Christophe added.

"You can thank Rhiannyn for that."

Confusion furrowing his brow, Christophe looked at her.

Having no answer for him, though she dreaded what Maxen's might be, Rhiannyn shrugged.

Christophe looked back at his brother. "Rhiannyn? How is that?"

The sparkle in Maxen's eyes told her that her fear of what his answer might be was not unfounded.

"You refer to her tending you these past days?" Christophe went on.

"Nay, I am sure 'tis Theta I have to thank for that."

"Theta?" Christophe shook his head. "Nay, it was Rhiannyn who cared for you when I could not. In fact, she insisted it be she, rather than Theta. Did she not tell you?"

The sparkle fled Maxen's eye. However, he asked for no explanation. Instead, he said, "Tell me how I fare, brother."

Reluctantly, Christophe granted Maxen the abrupt change of topic. " 'Twould seem quite well," he said as he turned the cover back to access the bandages. "But I will know better after examining the wound."

While he did so, Maxen brooded on Christophe's revelation. Though under different circumstances he would have been grateful, with Rhiannyn, he could not help but be both suspicious and angry, for it seemed she eluded him at every turn. If only she would stay in the role in which he had cast her.

Proclaiming Maxen well and truly healed, though he was adamant that a few days of rest were in order, Christophe finished with him. "I will tell the others," he said.

And end the speculation over who would succeed him, Maxen thought, though he did not say it. "I would entertain some food," he said. "I am quite hungry."

Christophe nodded, then was gone.

Alone again with Rhiannyn, Maxen sat up and propped himself against the headboard. "Why did you do it?" he asked.

"Tend you?"

"Aye."

Avoiding his gaze, she raked her fingers through the tangled web of curls that fell over her shoulders. "We may be enemies," she said, "but that does not mean I am without heart when one is in need."

"Theta could have tended me just as well."

"Nay, she could not have. I was here, she was not."

"She could have been."

Rhiannyn glanced at him, then away. "I wanted you to live, for it to be me who helped you back to life."

"Why? That I might be owing to you?"

"You could hardly be owing to me after saving my life," she reminded him. "Nay, Maxen—my lord," she hastily corrected herself, "not owing, but knowing."

"Knowing what?"

Sweeping her hair back, she stepped to the bed. "That all Saxons are not what you believe them to be. That we feel compassion, know pain . . . hurt. That we have only fought for what is rightfully ours."

It was something Maxen already knew. After all, had he not grown up amongst these people, been befriended by them, and friendly toward them before Duke William had called him and his brothers to prove their fealty by taking up swords against them? Caught up in the passion of a battle he had trained for since childhood, he had forsaken those he could more easily have called his own than the conquering Normans. Aye, it was something he knew too well, one of two reasons he had been sickened by the carnage he had been so much a part of. The other reason had been Nils, whose dying had opened Maxen's eyes to the unpardonable thing he had done, the atrocity for which he had spent two years in repentance. However, since learning of Thomas's death, he had repeatedly fought the memories, anger and revenge guiding him to the point at which he now found himself. But which way to go now? Toward the pleading in Rhiannyn's eyes, or the taking of more Saxon lives in payment for Thomas's?

Maxen felt as if he were being torn in two. Though he did not know which was the stronger in him—the good or the bad—he turned the way of compromise. "I want only the one who killed Thomas," he said.

Tears gathered in Rhiannyn's eyes, and the flare of her small nostrils attested to her struggle to keep her emotions down. She put out a hand to touch him, but then, as if fearing he might push her away, pulled it back. "If I knew," she said, "do you not think I would tell you? Give one life in exchange for so many?"

It made little sense that she would not, Maxen silently agreed, but still he found it difficult to believe she had not seen the one who had thrown the dagger. Even had she not, most certainly the one who had killed would have made himself known by bragging. Wouldn't he? "Nevertheless," he said, "there must be punishment, else there is naught to prevent it from happening again."

"Hanging innocents will not prevent it," she exclaimed. "It will only drive the Saxons to further warring, bringing more death upon Etcheverry."

Maxen knew he ought to waste no more breath upon the matter, that rest would serve him far better, but he found himself drawn into it. "And who will bring this war upon Etcheverry?" he asked. "Edwin is gone, Rhiannyn, his rebels under my control."

"Gone for now," she said, "but he will return. This I promise you."

"And I am to fear that?"

She shook her head. "Nay, but you should act upon it."

"Act upon it?"

"Aye. Give the rebels a reason to make peace with you. If ever Etcheverry is to prosper again, you will need them for planting and harvesting, for tending cattle and—"

"Need men more inclined to plant their scythes in my back than in the harvest?" Maxen harshly interrupted.

"Aye, that they are more inclined to do," she admitted, "but if you are fair with them, in time they could serve you well."

He laughed. "Your sense of reality is as poor as Christophe's. Never could Edwin's men be trusted."

"You do not know that."

"But I do, and I also know that I am done with this foolish conversation." Past done. So much that the thought of sleep held far more appeal than his need for the food that had yet to come. And where was it?

He saw in Rhiannyn's eyes that she wanted to continue the discussion, to convince him that what she spoke of was possible, but she turned away. "I suppose you will return me to the tower now," she said.

Maxen had not thought that far ahead. Indeed, even when he had sent her back to that place after bringing the vanquished Saxons into the castle, he had not known what he would do with her. And he still did not. "Perhaps in time," he said.

Puzzlement creasing her brow, she looked over her shoulder. "In time? Why not now?"

"I am not done with you."

Rhiannyn looked away again, the sudden surge of her heart echoing the fear of her mind. Maxen had claimed her, touched her, kissed her with wine, and made her feel things she had heretofore been innocent of. Did he now intend to violate her? Knowing she was only fooling herself to question the possibility, she acknowledged that he meant to take what no other man had, reducing her in all ways to the status of slave. Truly, though, it did not matter, she tried to convince herself. After all, it was not as if the loss of her virtue would have any impact on her future, not when she had accepted Thomas's curse that she would never wed. But what of children? What if Maxen put a bastard in her belly?

Sir Guy's appearance, along with Lucilla, who bore viands, brought a welcome interruption to Rhiannyn's thoughts. Sinking into a chair, she watched silently as Guy walked to the bed.

"You are well," he said to Maxen, relief in his voice.

"And hungry," Maxen added, his gaze devouring the food on the tray Lucilla had. A wry smile tugging at his lips, he looked back at his friend, then frowned. "Been brawling, eh?" he said of the bruise still visible along Guy's jaw.

Guy rubbed a hand over it. "Only with you," he said, then chuckled at Maxen's puzzled expression. " 'Twould seem you do not care to be moved about once you are abed."

Understanding coming quickly, Maxen grimaced, then swept his gaze to Rhiannyn before setting himself to the food.

Also understanding, though it was a different message Maxen's eyes had spoken to her, Rhiannyn clenched her hands in her lap. Would it be this night? she wondered. Or would he wait until he had fully recovered? Pray, not until he recovers, she pleaded. She needed time to become used to the idea of his possession, of his great body thrusting over hers as she knew would happen, for she had once come upon Thomas thrusting over Theta. Or perhaps, the sooner he took her, the better. Then it would be over with. . . .

"Rhiannyn."

She looked up at Lucilla, who, surprisingly, offered her a small smile. "Aye?" she asked.

"I've food for ye. Where would you have me set it?"

Rhiannyn peered at the selection, then back at Lucilla. "I am not really hungry."

"Then I will set it on the chest for later." The woman offered her another tentative smile, then turned away.

Drawing her knees to her chest, Rhiannyn winced at the noise made by the clashing links. How she hated the chain Maxen restrained her with, the symbol of her slavery. How she hated these past two years that had brought her to this place and time, this terrible conquering. Training her eyes on the floor, she blocked out Maxen's and Sir Guy's voices, and all those who came after.

Chapter Ten

Blood. Perfectly red as it spread outward through the mesh of linen. Staring in shock at the hilt of the dagger the linen had fallen back from, Rhiannyn wondered with amazement that only now she was beginning to feel the pain. When she'd picked up the napkin to wipe her mouth, she had not suspected that beneath it was hidden the keen weapon that had so easily sliced through her grasping fingers. But the pain was real, as was the blood flowing freely through her fingers, over the back of her hand, and down her wrist.

Turning her hand over, she swept her gaze down the length of blade, the edges of which shone more red than silver. So much blood . . .

She lifted the dagger from her injured hand and fisted her fingers into the napkin to stem the flow. How deeply she had cut herself, she had no idea, but the amount of blood told her it was not to be taken lightly.

Who had placed the weapon on her tray? she wondered. Not since returning to the castle had she been given so much as a meat knife with her meals, let alone a dagger of deadly intent. Why now? And who?

Her first thought was Lucilla. Had there been a message in the woman's smile? If so, what was the message? That she kill Maxen . . . or herself? Rhiannyn thought on it a moment longer, then discarded the idea that it could have been Lucilla. The woman was too gentle a soul. Wasn't she?

Too, Sir Ancel had come into the chamber. He was far more likely to have brought the dagger and slipped it beneath the napkin when he thought none were looking. In fact, Rhiannyn recalled having seen him nibbling at the foodstuffs on her tray while he'd conversed with Maxen. He could have done it then.

There had been others during the two hours Maxen had received them, but most of them were a blur, and none so likely to have left the dagger as Sir Ancel. Still, there was the question of who it was intended for. Was she being given the mercy of taking her own life ere another did, or was the hunger for power so strong that Maxen's death was the object?

"What in God's name!" Maxen's bellow broke into her wild speculations.

Starting violently, Rhiannyn looked to where he sat straight up in bed, having come out of the sleep he had fallen into less than an hour ago. Then, realizing the picture she presented standing at the foot of the bed, a dagger in one hand, the other drenched red from knuckles to wrist, she stumbled into explanation. "I—it—I cut . . ." Words failing her, she shook her head.

As if he'd never been ill, Maxen sprang from the bed wearing only the braies he had earlier donned, and gained her side in less than two strides. "Why?" he shouted, concern etching grooves alongside his mouth and turning his eyes a deep blue.

"Why?" she echoed, confused as to the answer he sought, and by the concern he showed.

With a string of blasphemous curses, he grabbed her arm, snatched the balled napkin from her hand, and began winding it around her wrist. "Naught is so bad that you must take your life over it," he growled, anger suffusing his face.

He thought she'd cut her wrist? To escape from this world into another that she was not sure would even receive her? "I was not trying to kill myself," she exclaimed. To prove it, she opened her hand and showed him her slashed fingers.

He stilled, the color slowly receding from his face as he stared at her hand. Then, a frown grooving his brow, he unwound the napkin and looked at the uncut flesh of her wrist. "Then you accidentally cut yourself ere you could use the dagger on me," he concluded, the concern wiped from his eyes.

Her jaw dropped, though she quickly snapped it closed again. "How can you believe that if you do not believe 'twas I who put a dagger through Thomas?" she asked, the pain of her injury much lessened by rising indignation.

Leaving her question unanswered, Maxen shifted his gaze to the dagger she yet held. "Are you going to do something with that?" he asked, his tone challenging.

She had forgotten about it. As if burnt, she dropped it to the floor. "You have not answered me," she said. "You refuse to believe I killed Thomas, but think me capable of killing you?"

"For certain, you could not have hated him as much as you do me," he answered, and began wrapping her hand in the bloodied linen.

But she did not hate him as she ought to, nor could she now that she knew what it was that drove him to seek such harsh revenge—now that she knew he was not the Devil, but only a man with years of hurt behind and before him. He was touchable. How, she did not know, but she could not give up hope. "I do not hate you," she said.

Maxen released her bandaged hand and settled his unfathomable gaze on her. "You should," he said.

"Why? Because of anger that is your due? Another brother dead, your calling stolen from you, your prayers unanswered?"

"You dare where you ought not to, Rhiannyn," he warned.

"I know."

"Then you ought know this as well—neither do I need nor welcome your understanding. Try as you might, no bearing will it have on the fate of the Saxon rebels, for I will do with them what I will."

"You will not kill them," she said, praying she was right. "This I know."

A muscle in his jaw spasmed. "You know nothing," he said, then pushed her down onto the chest. Pivoting around, he strode to the screen, pulling the chain between them taut, and called for Christophe.

Only then did Rhiannyn focus on his near nudity, having been blinded to it by the furor over her injury. Although she had seen his body many times these past days, there seemed something more powerful—and dangerous—about it.

"Where did you get it?" he asked.

She followed his gaze to the dagger near her feet and frowned. Something about the weapon struck her as peculiar. Nay, not peculiar, but familiar. The hilt—

"Answer me, Rhiannyn."

She nearly told Maxen the truth; however, fear for what he might do to Lucilla if he believed her to have been the one to bring the dagger forced her to lie. "I found it on the floor," she said. "One of your knights must have dropped it earlier."

"And how is it you cut yourself?"

"I—I saw its glint among the rushes, but did not know what it was until I picked it up—by the blade."

"Hmm. I thought it might have come to you on your meal tray."

How had he known? Rhiannyn wondered, trying to

keep her face impassive. But of course, she'd been standing over the tray when he'd risen from the bed to come to her aid. But was it possible he'd known of the dagger all along? That it was a test he had put her to?

" 'Twas on the floor I found it," she maintained.

Walking to where she sat cradling her injured hand, he went down on his haunches and lifted the dagger covered in blood and rushes. "For one who lies as often as you do," he mused as his gaze swept the weapon, "I would think you would be much better at it."

Her gaze also drawn to the dagger—specifically, its unusual hilt—Rhiannyn reflected that it was true she had lied to him, and often, but always to protect her people. However, what good was a lie not believed? Suddenly, her thoughts halted, her mind placing where she had seen the dagger.

"Thomas," she breathed, for that brief moment forgetting whose company she was in.

"Thomas?" Maxen latched onto his brother's name. "What about him?"

The urgency in his eyes, the need to know what she referred to, propelled Rhiannyn past caution. "The dagger," she said, her heart beating so furiously her head began to reel. " 'Tis the one."

"That killed him?"

She nodded.

"How do you know this?"

In her mind, she saw it again the day of Thomas's death. Unquestionably it was the same one that had protruded from his chest, the one she had desperately scrambled upon the muddy ground to retrieve, and which she had held up in proclamation that she had done the deed.

"I remember it," she answered. In silent explanation, she reached out to touch the hilt. However, the instant she laid a finger to it, she drew sharply back. It was as if evil dwelt in the intricately carved leaves that held the blade—a blade that had drawn not only Thomas's blood, but now hers, and might have drawn Maxen's had the one who'd left it not been so terribly wrong about her.

"Aye, it is the one," she whispered.

Maxen saw the fear in her, felt it in the air between them, and found himself drawn to offer her the comfort she seemed so badly in need of. He did not, though, for it would have shown heart he didn't have—or more precisely, could not afford to have. Looking away from her, he more closely examined the instrument of death. Although he knew his brother had been murdered with a dagger, never had he learned what had become of it, nor thought to ask. However, now he had it, though not in the way the one who had passed it to Rhiannyn would have wanted it.

"Was it Sir Ancel who took it from Thomas's body?" he asked, though he was certain he knew the answer. It had to have been the embittered knight who was responsible for its appearance this day.

Rhiannyn lowered her head into her hands. "Nay," she said, her voice muffled. "Thomas pulled it free."

Then he had not died immediately. . . . There were other questions Maxen would have asked, but he fixed himself to his course and held steady. "And Sir Ancel? Was it he who picked it up?"

She shook her head in her hands. "I did," she said, "but he knocked it from my hand."

Maxen's patience was waxing thin. Very thin. "And then he took it up?"

"Nay, it was another."

Pushing Rhiannyn's hands aside, Maxen lifted her chin and stared into eyes that looked suspiciously moist. "Who?"

Her answer, long in coming, surprised him when it was finally spoke. "Sir Guy."

It could not be, Maxen thought, denying the knight's role in attempting his death. This must be yet another lie Rhiannyn told, a falsehood to take from his side the only one among his men whom he trusted. Had to be.

"You do not believe me," she said softly. Sadly.

Refusing to be pulled into her eyes, he stood and called for Guy.

Christophe arrived first, though more than a bit disheveled from some interrupted task. He frowned with puzzlement as he looked from the dagger his brother held to the bloody napkin Rhiannyn grasped. Walking hurriedly to the chest, he knelt before Rhiannyn and uncurled her fingers. "How did this happen?" he asked.

"She cut herself," Maxen said.

"I see that, but how?"

When Maxen did not answer, Rhiannyn felt compelled to ease the young man's misgivings. "An accident," she said. "I picked it up not knowing what it was."

Christophe looked over his shoulder at his brother as if seeking confirmation that it had, indeed, been an accident.

" 'Tis the truth," Rhiannyn reassured him. "Will you need to stitch it?"

Suspicion still upon his face, he gently probed the tender flesh, then shook his head. "Nay, it will not require the needle. Bandages only."

While he set himself to tending her injury, Sir Guy appeared. "My lord?" he asked.

Maxen raised the dagger between them. "This was given Rhiannyn, by you, she would have me believe."

"I did not say he gave it to me," Rhiannyn protested.

Maxen sent her a silencing look. "She claims she does not know the one who left it for her, but that she saw you last possessing it."

The knight's face incredulous, he shook his head. "As God is my witness, Maxen, it was not I who gave her the dagger."

Maxen's sharp eyes searched Guy's. "Did you take it from the place Thomas died?"

"I did, but—"

"Then it was last in your possession."

"It was, but obviously no longer."

At least Rhiannyn had told him the truth, Maxen reflected. "Then you are saying it was stolen from you and given to her by another."

"There can be no other explanation but that it was taken from my belongings," Guy said, his eyes imploring Maxen to believe him. "Never would I betray you. Have I not proven by fealty many times over?"

"You have," Maxen agreed after a lengthy pause that beaded Guy's brow with perspiration. "But I would know who seeks my death."

"Not I, my lord."

In his mind, Maxen picked apart each of those who had come and gone that morn, finally settling on the two most likely—the Saxon wench, Lucilla, and Sir Ancel. Though it could very well be the wench, in the final examination, Sir Ancel seemed the most likely to have done it. If it was, the man would have to die.

"Have you the key, Guy?" Maxen asked. "I wish to be free of this chain."

His relief uncertain, the knight took it from his pouch and fit it into the iron. "It could have been one of the Saxons," he said.

"I have thought of that," Maxen said as the iron clattered to the floor, "and of another—a Norman."

Guy nodded with understanding. "Aye, it could have been him."

"Regardless, the punishment will be the same."

"And the punishment of Edwin's rebels?" Guy asked. "Does the sentence you pronounced upon them still hold?"

Maxen met Rhiannyn's eyes. Pray not, she silently beseeched.

"It holds," he said, then looked back at Guy. "And will be done on the morrow."

Rhiannyn did not want to believe he would execute the Saxons—could not believe he would do it—even though there had been nothing in his face to give her any hope.

Throughout, Christophe had remained silent, but now he stood and faced Maxen. "You are not my brother," he said, and walked stiffly past him and out of the chamber.

Some emotion crossed Maxen's face, but it was too fleeting to be read.

A short time later, Rhiannyn found herself no longer chained to a man, but to the frame of his bed and left to herself as Maxen went to join his men for the evening meal. Pushing aside her own meal, she curled up in the chair with a blanket and waited for what the night would bring. It brought hours of tortured thought, and nearing the middle of night, it brought Maxen back to her.

Striding across the rushes, he came to stand before her. He did not speak, nor touch her. He simply looked at her from that soaring height of his.

Rhiannyn was the first to break the uncomfortable silence. "Did you discover who left the dagger?" she asked.

His jaw shifted side to side. "Nay, I did not ... but I will."

She nodded, then the question she'd tossed over and over in her mind the last hours burst free. "What will it take?" she asked. "What to free the Saxons from your vengeance?"

Like a statue, he stood solid and unmoving, his eyes a glimmer in the muted light. And then he lifted her chin. "The truth, Rhiannyn," he said, his wine-scented breath warm upon her face. "Start telling me the truth, and perhaps I will start showing mercy."

Knowing that he referred to not only who had provided her the dagger, but also who had murdered Thomas, she said, "I do not know—just as I do not know Thomas's murderer. This I swear."

He searched her eyes, probing their vulnerable depths, then murmured, "I almost believe you."

His sincerity surprised her. "You do?"

"Almost."

Really, it was not much he offered, but it was more than she'd had. "Maxen," she began, in her desperation forgetting she was forbidden to call him by his name, "show your mercy."

Neither did he seem to notice her impropriety. Releasing her, he straightened. "I have already made my decision," he said, then turned to the bed and began throwing off his clothes.

His callousness was like oil upon the fire burning deep within Rhiannyn—a fire that Thomas had been singed by many times, but which had not vented from her with such intensity since he had died. In fact, she could not remember it ever having raged so mightily. Throwing back the blanket, she shot to her feet and dragged the chain with her to where Maxen stood.

"You think you are the only one who has lost?" she asked in a voice that trembled with fury.

Dropping his tunic to the chest, he turned to face her. "I warn you, Rhiannyn," he said harshly. "I have had too much drink this night and little enough food with which to take it up. Go back to your chair ere I make use of your misplaced anger in my bed."

"Misplaced?" she exploded, uncaring whether or not she awakened the entire hall. "You can be angry and I cannot?" Defiantly, she bridged the gap between them and peered up into his thunderous face. "You lost two brothers and your life of repentance for the atrocities you committed. And I am to feel owing to you for that?" Scornful laughter bubbled from her lips. "Still you have your parents, a sister, and even a country that does not belong to you. But what have I? Naught, Maxen Pendery. All that was dear to me is gone—two brothers, a father, a mother, and my country. I have naught, and less than naught, for you have made me a slave. I haven't even myself any longer."

She saw a shifting of emotions across his face, though she made no attempt to interpret them. "What vengeance mine?" she continued. "Should I have used the dagger as 'twas intended? Taken your life as you will take innocents on the morrow? Think you it would lessen the pain of what is already gone from me?"

"I have heard enough," he said in a voice that, for all its outward control, echoed something deeper.

"I am sure you have, but I am not finished."

"Aye, you are." Grabbing her arm, he propelled her to the chair and forced her down in it. "Do you rise again, or speak another word, by my troth you will regret it."

Too much of her anger yet to be expended, she ignored his threat and pushed up out of the chair. "I—"

He thrust her back down and held her shoulders against the chair back. "Think about it, Rhiannyn," he warned, his face so near hers that if she moved even slightly, their noses would touch. "Long and hard if you must, but think about it."

Her breathing shallow and quick, her teeth gnashed together with the words she held back, and her hands fisted with the desire to strike him, she stared into his eyes. For what seemed a lifetime, they remained thus, and then, as if the wind that had fanned the flames of her anger had suddenly stilled, she slumped in the chair. She wanted to cry, to let out her anguish, but not in Maxen's presence.

She watched him walk to the torch and extinguish it, then move as a shadow to the bed and lie down upon it. Alone, but not alone, she stared into the darkness and waited for the morning.

To Rhiannyn, standing on the wall-walk that spanned the top edge of the outer wall, the Saxons assembled below looked like a peasant's patchcloth mantle. There was no uniformity to them, no organization, and no hope against the many soldiers prepared to carry out Maxen Pendery's punishment. By nightfall, Rhiannyn thought, they would all be dead, their only victory escaping Norman rule.

Tearless, though her eyes burned with her refusal to be otherwise, she shifted her gaze to the gallows, then away. It was beyond cruel that Maxen was forcing her to witness the execution of her people, to stand in full sight of them at this highest point in the bailey where none could miss her presence, and alongside Maxen himself, who had pronounced his judgment upon them. But he had, and now, in the most terrible of ways, she had proof of how wrong she had been about him. As much as she had wanted to believe he was reachable, he was not.

So caught up in her tumult of emotions was she, she did not realize Maxen had leaned down and put his mouth near her ear until he spoke. "You are a brave woman, Rhiannyn of Etcheverry," he said. "Foolishly brave."

She glanced at him, briefly acknowledged that he still looked unwell, then said, "And you are a devil."

He took it in stride, a slight smile tugging at his lips as he straightened from her. "That is the least of things I have been called," he said, then swept his gaze back to the people below.

Believing she had nothing left to lose, Rhiannyn pushed her chin high in the air. "Very well," she said, "then perhaps something stronger. Perhaps . . . the Bloodlust Warrior of Etcheverry." Pretending pride in her choice, she nodded. "Aye, more appropriate."

If the daggers in his eyes could have leapt from them, they would surely have killed her where she stood. It frightened her, but she hid her fear.

Spreading his legs, he clasped his hands behind his back before returning his gaze to the Saxons. "Bloodlust Warrior," he murmured, then curled his lips in what could not possibly be mistaken for a smile. "Not in this instance, Rhiannyn. This is different."

Different how? she wanted to ask, the question igniting in her a spark of hope. In the next instant she extinguished it. Obviously, Maxen meant he was more justified in what he was about to do, than in what he had already done at Hastings. And perhaps he was, though it would not excuse him in the eyes of God. Once, perhaps, but surely not twice.

Steeling herself for what was to come, she thrust her shoulders back and assumed once again the foolish bravery Maxen had accused her of.

When all grew quiet, the Saxons having turned their full attention to where Maxen and Rhiannyn stood, Maxen spoke, his voice raised. "These past two years, many are the Normans you have killed, and yet the battle of Hastings has been done with for as long, England defeated, and King William crowned its ruler. You have left your families, your homes, and your crops, and all for the promise of something that will never happen—for Edwin Harwolfson, a man who has selfishly spent your lives to achieve his own end."

A murmur of dissent arose, followed by shouted curses that only died when Maxen's next words lit their ears.

"I offer you something different," he said.

Stepping forward, Aethel raised his fist and shook it. "And what be that, you Norman devil?" he shouted. "Dangling at the end of a rope rather than an honorable passing?"

"Death figures into it only by your choice," Maxen answered.

Rhiannyn frowned. Had she heard right? Nay, she could not have—unless Maxen was playing with words.

"Do you go the way of Edwin," he continued, "your fate is sealed. Do you pledge fealty to me, rebuild your homes, and put plough to the land again, I will give you back your lives."

Disbelief rippled through the Saxons, the same as it did Rhiannyn, who feared her knees might buckle beneath her. Looking to Maxen, she silently beckoned him to look at her so that she might see what was in his eyes and know for certain what was behind his words. However, he refused her all but his profile.

"But first," he went on, once again bringing an uncertain quiet to the Saxons, "those who come my way must prove themselves." He paused a long moment, then continued. "There are walls to be raised." He swept a hand to the vulnerable, unfinished stone rampart enclosing the outer bailey. "And buildings to be erected ere winter."

Rhiannyn swayed where she stood, only remembering to breathe when her lungs threatened to burst.

"Edwin's followers stand where you are," Maxen instructed. "Those wishing to live under the House of Pendery, gather left." At their hesitation, he added, "Make your choice. Now."

More hesitation, glances toward the nooses that dangled from the gallows, then a handful of Saxons, heads down, stepped around the others and to the left. Some of the men tried to block them, spoke angry words to them, but still they formed their small group.

More, Rhiannyn beseeched silently. Lord, show them the way. In answer to her prayer, a dozen more, including all of the women, stepped left. Another hesitation, then more followed until only five remained loyal to Edwin, Aethel among them.

Motioning for the men-at-arms to remove those who had chosen to stand with their absent leader, Maxen turned to Rhiannyn.

"I do not understand," she said, trying to glimpse his soul through the window of his eyes, but seeing no more than he allowed her to see. "Why have you done this?"

"I assure you it has naught to do with you," he said, then walked around and past her.

Of course it had nothing to do with her, but what? Had he done it for Christophe? "And the others?" she called after him. "What of them?"

He halted, but did not turn around. "They have made their choice," he said, his anger evident in his stiff posture, his deep and cutting voice, and his hands clenched into fists at his sides. "They are Edwin's men, and will be treated accordingly." Then he walked away.

Rhiannyn could not find any reason to argue it that might reach Maxen. She must be grateful for what he had given her in allowing most of the Saxons to live. Still, she was pained by the five who would die. But when? Why hadn't Maxen put them to the gallows straightaway and been done with it as he'd led her to believe he meant to do with all the Saxons?

She'd been awakened that morn by the feel of his hands around her ankle as he removed the iron and chain. He had informed her that she was to accompany him to the bailey, where she would witness the reckoning for herself. During the long walk, he had said naught of his true intentions, allowing her to believe the very worst. Allowing her to believe what he'd wanted her to believe.

Sudden anger swept aside Rhiannyn's relief. How dare he subject her to such unendurable pain. How dare he make pretense of a slaughter he'd had no intention of carrying out. How dare he. Though the insistent voice trailing her churning thoughts told he she was not thinking clearly, that she should not question him, but be thankful for what he had *not* done, Rhiannyn ignored it.

Hauling her skirts up much too high, she traversed the wall-walk and, in a flurry that nearly overturned her, descended the steps to the bailey. Behind, she heard one of the Saxon women call her a vile name, but she did not falter in her bid to gain the causeway leading up to the motte. Surprisingly, none tried to stop her. Soldiers stepped aside and raked curious glances over her, but naught else.

Chapter Eleven

Upon entering the hall, Rhiannyn immediately located Maxen. He stood behind a trestle table set with drink and food, his head bent, his arms outstretched, his palms laid flat upon the table. Before him were gathered a great number of his knights, and beside him sat the steward, who was passionately arguing something Rhiannyn wasted no time pondering.

Forgetting her station, forgetting propriety, forgetting all that would have served her well to remember, she advanced on Maxen. Halfway across the hall she was granted his regard.

Straightening, he narrowed his gaze on her—calculating, she knew, wondering what she intended. And what that was, she herself did not know until she stepped to the dais and acted on the first impulse that struck her.

Grasping the edge of the cloth that covered the table, she yanked hard and catapulted goblets, tankards, platters, and the books the steward guarded with his every breath. Harmless missiles, all of them, except the one that struck Sir Ancel in the temple and staggered him back a step.

Despite the commotion and harsh expletives of the knights, when all settled, Rhiannyn was left untouched. Holding the cloth, her lower jaw thrust determinedly forward, she stared into Maxen's steely blue eyes. "You are the lowliest of curs," she spat.

Splaying his palms on the bare wood tabletop, he leaned forward again. "Is that so?" he asked. So cool, as if completely unmoved by what she had done.

But he was not unmoved, Rhiannyn saw, for his eyes mirrored her own anger. For a moment, she was caught up in a fascination of the control he exercised, but she dragged free of it with the realization of the mistake she had made in confronting him—a grave mistake that shone in his eyes, the thin draw of his lips, and the bunching of his muscles beneath his tunic.

Retreat, her fear screamed. Stay, her anger countered. Obeying the latter, she threw the cloth aside, stepped to the table's edge, and threw her palm at his cheek.

Maxen caught it midair, denying her the stinging contact she sought. "I cannot allow you to do that—again," he said, looking from her bandaged hand to her flushed face.

Again. Aye, twice before she had struck him. Once out of anger, once to awaken him, and now again in anger— anger he was more than deserving of. "I have not asked your permission," she tossed back.

His left eyebrow arced. "As you should," he said, "and will." Looking past her to his men, he ordered them and the steward to take their leave.

Nasty laughter and crude comments spoken loudly enough to be heard accompanied the men from the hall.

"This is not at all what I expected," Maxen said when only he and Rhiannyn remained.

She braved his penetrating gaze. "And what did you expect? That I would fall to my knees before you? Embrace you? Worship you?" Though she knew it useless to try to escape his hold, she gave a show of resistance by jerking on her hand. Of course, he did not release her.

"I had thought you would at least be grateful," he said, his hand tightening.

"Grateful? You led me to believe it your intention to hang the Saxons, and all along you planned otherwise."

"Would you have preferred I take their lives?"

She blinked as reality crept back in on her. "Of course not," she said, "but neither did you need to be so cruel in allowing me to think you intended to slay them all. You could have told me."

How easy it would be to end her anger, and his, Maxen thought, or at least lessen it by explaining that what appeared to be cruelty had really been his final test of her story that she did not know who had killed Thomas. Now he believed her, for she had not broken when faced with the imminent death of her people, the nooses ready for their necks. But let her think him cruel, he decided. After all, wasn't he? Too, it would afford him more control over her, something mightily needed with one such as she.

"You were told," he said, "but in my time, not yours." His ire gentled as he saw the fire leap higher in her eyes. Odd, he thought, but there was something so appealing about her daring. Something that went beyond a desire to bed her, though it certainly did not exclude that.

"Though I tried to hate Thomas for who he was and what he had done,"she said evenly, "I could not. But you ... I do not even have to try."

For the first time in years, Maxen felt truly amused, the reference to his brother hardly needed. "You do not hate me, Rhiannyn. You told me so yourself."

"I lied," she retorted.

He shrugged. "Then at least I can console myself with one thing."

"And what is that?"

He leaned near her, liking the way his breath stirred the tendrils of hair that feathered her brow. "That which you refused Thomas," he said.

She frowned.

"You desire me," he stated. "Hate me . . . very well . . . but you also want me."

She gasped. "You suffer from the same delusions your brother did."

"I remember a kiss you did not object to days ago," he said. "You denied yourself the surrender, though you wanted it as badly as I."

Obviously, she remembered that wine-filled kiss, for color that could not be mistaken for anger flamed her cheeks. "You fantasize," she said.

"Should I prove it to you?"

Defiantly, she tossed her head back. "Try, oh mighty Norman, and know the truth."

Although Maxen knew they were only words spoken out of anger, not the invitation they sounded, he took up the challenge. Gripping her beneath the arms, he lifted her slight figure, and despite her protests, pulled her across the table. He positioned her on the table's edge, pushed a leg between her knees, and settled his hips in the cradle of her thighs.

"What think you are doing?" she cried, straining back.

"Seek the truth," he said, then cupped a hand to the back of her head and pulled her mouth to his. He took as he could not remember ever having taken, drank as he had never drunk, and tasted as he had never tasted. And true to his seeking, like a rose prickly with thorns, Rhiannyn flowered in his hands and beneath his mouth. Her resistance flung aside, her anger channeled into passions he had known lay beneath her Saxon pride, she merged with him.

Arching against Maxen, Rhiannyn slid her hands around his neck and into his hair. She ached. God, how she ached, every part of her sparking to the feel of this man against her. Groaning, she crushed her breasts to his chest and returned the stroke of his tongue. There was more she wanted, more she did not know of, but which her body was rapidly discovering and making known to her—and beyond that, there was what Maxen was preparing to teach her.

No longer holding her to him, for she clung of her own need, he glided his hands around her sides, over the tops of her thighs, and down her calves to the hem of her chemise. As he tugged it free from under her and raised it with her bliaut, trailing fingers over her legs encased in woolen hose, he deepened the kiss. Then his hands slid inside her braies and touched the bare flesh of her inner thighs.

The throbbing in her growing, Rhiannyn swept his mouth with her tongue, tasting the wine he had partaken of a short time ago. However, it was not that which intoxicated her, which made her whimper and jerk back from his kiss. It was his fingers brushing the bud of her femininity.

Head flung back, sensations bursting against the backs of her eyelids, she moaned as he drew circles over her flesh, then cried out as her awakening to womanhood stabbed her with pleasure she had heard spoken of, but never felt.

"More," she gasped.

"How much more?" he asked, his voice deeper than she had ever heard it.

Enough to end this aching need, to fulfill the promise, to crest the pinnacle rising up before her, she wanted to shout, but there was no breath for words, only for yearning. In silent answer, she thrust her hips against his seeking hand.

"Do you want me, Rhiannyn?" he asked.

"I want . . ." Her voice trailed off as waves of frustrated pleasure curled over her.

"Do you?"

She nodded.

His harsh sigh rolled upon the air, then he took his hands from her and lowered her back upon the table.

Her pleasure momentarily taken from her, Rhiannyn sought patience in the knowledge that soon she would know all of it, for surely Maxen would finish what he had started. Aye, soon she would know the way of man and woman. Opening her eyes, she glanced from the ceiling above to the man between her legs. His broad chest now bare, he looked up from hands that tugged at the string of his braies and met her gaze.

For Rhiannyn, the world seemed to stop in that moment. Her passions turned to ice as everything flooded back to her. Dear God, what was she doing? Whatever had possessed her to freely give herself to this man? To behave as if she were the whore Theta had gleefully accused her of being? Was she the same as that woman? Abruptly, she turned from the answers, though shame and humiliation still descended upon her.

Maxen must have seen the cooling in her eyes, for he stilled. "What is it?" he asked.

Swallowing hard, she reached to push her skirts down. "I cannot. 'Tis wrong."

He caught her wrists together. " 'Tis right," he said. "You belong to me, and very soon will be mine in every sense."

"Nay," she beseeched, appealing to that part of him that had sent him into the monastery in search of God's forgiveness. Still, she would fight him if he forced her to his will, even though she would undoubtedly lose such a battle.

Leaning forward, Maxen brushed his mouth across hers. "It is time for the taking, Rhiannyn," he murmured, then lifted his head and put his hands to his braies again.

"Please . . . don't," she whispered. "Don't do this."

The struggle that sprang up within him was visible, nearly touchable, in the unguarded emotions that flitted over his face.

Holding her breath, Rhiannyn waited to see which of him would win—the man who had become the monk, or the one who had earned himself the title of the Bloodlust Warrior of Hastings. Miraculously, it was the monk, the man she had vowed she would find beneath the warrior.

Straightening, Maxen stepped back, his body tense with the effort it took not to seize what she'd offered. "Be it today, tomorrow, or the day after, it will happen," he said, picking up the tunic he had discarded only minutes earlier. "Though not by rape." He pulled the tunic on.

Rhiannyn could not argue with what he said, for it would only be foolish to deny that her body wanted to know his. Admitting it only to herself, she acknowledged that what Maxen had set out to prove, he had proved beyond a doubt. She desired him. Nay, it would not have been rape with which he gained her virtue had her senses not returned. It would have been with her full consent.

Her shame going deeper, she sat up and pushed her skirts down her legs. Fearing that to linger might change Maxen's mind, she lowered her feet to the floor and turned to depart.

"Rhiannyn," he called.

Reluctantly, she turned back around. "Aye?"

"Henceforth, you will serve in the hall," he said, looking unapproachable with his great arms crossed over his chest. "You will serve at the meals and assist Mildreth with whatever else she assigns you."

Far less daunting a prospect than the days past when she had tended to his intimate needs, she thought, but still there would be contact with him. "And when night is come?" she asked.

"You will make your bed here with the others."

As she had when Thomas had been alive, though that was where the similarity ended. Now she was a slave to Maxen Pendery, and when he so desired, he would make her his leman, not his wife as Thomas would have if she had accepted him. If she had accepted him, he would still be alive. . . .

"And your clothes," Maxen said. "As you play the part, so will you dress it."

Meaning the finery she wore was inappropriate. "I will," she said, though how she was to obtain other garments was beyond her.

Walking to where one of the steward's books lay open on the floor, Maxen picked it up and carried it back to the table. "You may go now," he dismissed her, then turned his attention to the figures in the book he opened before him.

Only when she had gone from his sight, her footsteps fading amid the commotion of the courtyard, did Maxen give up his pretense of study. Slamming the book closed, he went in search of one willing and able to ease a need grown too intense to wait any longer.

"I've a bliaut I'll give you," Theta said.

Rhiannyn and Mildreth turned together to stare in astonishment at the woman they had not realized was listening in on their conversation. Rhiannyn had been on her way to the kitchen, a short walk from the donjon, when she'd run into Mildreth and told her about her clothing problem.

"Give me?" Rhiannyn repeated, knowing that Theta might be generous with words, but not with her belongings.

Her hips swaying, Theta stepped from the shadows. "Aye, yer a bit scrawny and short," she drawled, her snapping eyes saying what she left unsaid, "but my clothes'll do you well."

"And what price your generosity?" Mildreth asked.

"That," Theta said, indicating Rhiannyn's fine bliaut and chemise with a sweep of her hand.

A peasant's garments for a lady's? Rhiannyn thought. "I do not think so." Besides, for the bliaut and chemise to fit Theta, she would have to let out the seams and walk with bent knees. Though Theta was of good figure, her breasts were larger than Rhiannyn's, and she was taller by a good hand. Of course, did Theta use one of her own chemises beneath the bliaut, it would certainly improve the look.

Theta heaved an exaggerated sigh. "Then you will have to serve the tables dressed as you are," she said. "Of course, the lord will not approve. . . ."

It was that last bit that convinced Rhiannyn she must give her bliaut over—but not without concessions. "Very well," she said, "but I will require two of your bliauts for this one."

"Two?" Theta laughed. "I will give you one."

"And the chemise stays with me," Rhiannyn continued as if she had not been challenged.

"Then methinks you will have to look elsewhere. But do not forget that the nooning meal will be served an hour hence."

"I suppose I will just have to make this one a bit less fine," Rhiannyn said.

"And how's that?"

She shrugged. "A bit of dirt"—she looked to the ground—"grease"—she nodded to the kitchen across the courtyard—"and a tear here and there will serve the same purpose." Secretly, she delighted in the horror that rose to Theta's eyes. Then, to further her threat, she knelt and brushed a handful of dirt from the packed earth on her skirt.

"Two bliauts," Theta said quickly. "Aye, methinks I can manage that."

Rhiannyn cocked her head to the side. "You are sure? I would not want to leave you needful."

Clearly, Theta did not like the situation, but there was naught she could do if her desire for Rhiannyn's bliaut was to be fulfilled. "Two," she repeated, then turned away. "I will return in a moment."

"You can be a sly one," Mildreth said as Rhiannyn straightened from the ground.

"When I have to be," she agreed.

Mildreth offered her a smile she had kept from her since their reuniting, though it was tentative and lacking the warmth it had once held. "That is good," she said, "for you will need it with the new lord."

Deciding it best not to discuss Maxen with her, Rhiannyn asked Mildreth what her duties would be in the hall.

"He wants you to serve, eh?"

Rhiannyn nodded. "And assist you in whatever else might be needing."

"Ain't that kind of him," Mildreth said, "though 'tis probably more for his benefit than mine."

Silently, Rhiannyn agreed. Seeing her serving his men

would undoubtedly appease some of Maxen's need to avenge his brother's death.

"Ah well." Mildreth sighed. " 'Tis good, for I certainly could use the help."

"How?" Rhiannyn asked.

"Ere the meals, you can assist me in the kitchens. During them you can serve the wine and ale."

Although Thomas would have considered it beneath Rhiannyn, she did not. After all, she had been raised modestly, helping her mother with all the household chores, which had included cooking and serving her father and brothers. Still, serving Normans was not something she looked forward to.

"Ah, me!" Mildreth gasped. "I forgot about the lord's bath."

"Bath?"

"Aye, when he returned from the bailey he ordered that hot water be brought to his tub." She looked across the yard to the cauldrons that fogged the air with their heat. "And 'tis well and boiling now." Clamping her large teeth onto her bottom lip, she looked down at her burden of laundry, then back at Rhiannyn. "You could help by carrying the water," she said.

Carry water to Maxen's chamber that he might bathe? That she might suffer more humiliation from her near giving of herself to him?

"Of course, with your hand injured as 'tis," Mildreth went on, "it would be difficult."

More than anything, Rhiannyn wanted to avail herself of the excuse Mildreth offered, but knew she could not. "I will do it," she said.

"You're sure?"

She nodded.

Theta's reappearance, two well-worn bliauts over her arm, halted their progress to the kitchens. "Here," she said, thrusting them into Rhiannyn's arms. "Now out of that." She indicated the fine bliaut with a thrust of her chin.

Though Rhiannyn would have preferred a more private

place to make the exchange, there were few about to prevent her from stepping into the shadows and changing. Too, it was not as if she would be without the cover of her chemise. Acquiescing, she went into the shade of the donjon, quickly removed the bliaut, and replaced it with the least offensive of Theta's. It was too large, too coarse, smelled, and was woven of unattractive dun-colored thread, but she told herself she didn't care. It hung too long on her, falling nearly to her ankles, and the sash was so badly frayed, she doubted it would stay tied, but again, she told herself she didn't care. It would serve her far better than the other she traded, for in this she appeared to be without shape that might catch a man's eye.

When Rhiannyn exited the shadows, feeling as if she wore a shroud, Theta greedily snatched the finer bliaut from her, then turned and hastened toward the donjon. As she ascended the steps, Sir Guy arrested her progress and spoke something to her that did not carry past Theta's ears. However, it made her smile quite broadly and carried her to the hall more quickly.

Wondering what news the woman had been borne, Rhiannyn looked to Mildreth.

Mildreth shrugged, then grimaced at the picture Rhiannyn presented. "A shame." She clucked. "Now even I look better than you." Sighing, she swung toward the kitchens. "Come, I will show you where the buckets are."

Wishing Mildreth had not said anything, Rhiannyn followed her.

Perhaps he could have done it if she had not pranced into his chamber wearing the bliaut he had last seen on Rhiannyn, reminding him of what he had given up. Perhaps if she had shown some modesty, rather than wantonly baring herself and going down on her knees to bare him. But Maxen could not do it. The lust Rhiannyn had roused in him extinguished itself as Theta smoothed her hands down his abdomen and began working the knot from the tie of his braies.

"Damn!" he muttered. What hold was it Rhiannyn had over him that he could not slake his thirst for her with another? In a dark way, Theta was more beautiful, the curves of her woman's body more voluptuous than Rhiannyn's, yet she left him unmoved—worse, impotent. Mayhap the ill that remained in his blood was responsible for his lack of response.

"Something is the matter, milord?" Theta asked, tilting her head back while her fingers continued their work.

Vising her wrists together, Maxen stilled her. "Perhaps later," he said, then released her and turned to the bed where he'd thrown his tunic. Behind him, he heard Theta rise to her feet, then the crackle of rushes as she approached his back.

"But milord," she said, sliding her arms around his waist, "I am ready for you." Her hair falling over his shoulder, she leaned forward and put her mouth to the side of his neck.

"Later," he growled.

Disregarding his rejection, she slipped a hand into the waistband of his braies and snaked it downward to the crisp hair curling around his manhood. "I can make you ready for me," she whispered into his ear, then splayed her fingers over him.

Wrenching her hand from his braies, Maxen turned and pushed her back. "You may leave. Now."

He glimpsed her resentment a moment before she covered it with a seductive smile. "Later, then," she said, and bent to her discarded chemise and bliaut.

Trying to feel something for her, Maxen watched as she dressed herself, intimating with her hands over her body what she would have done for him, but still he was unmoved. As he'd noticed when she had first come to him, Rhiannyn's bliaut was too small for her, though it certainly emphasized her large breasts and plentiful hips to good advantage. He did not have to wonder how it was she had obtained the garment, for he was certain it had been traded for the clothing he had ordered Rhiannyn to wear for her new duties. Regret came upon him, but he quickly turned it back.

Theta's slippers in one hand, the bliaut off one shoulder, and its skirt askew, she sauntered to where Maxen stood. "Tonight?" she asked, coyly fluttering her lashes as she traced his right nipple with the tip of her finger.

"When I send for you," he said.

She smiled widely. "Do not be too long, milord, for if 'tis not you, 'twill be another."

Which, perhaps, was the reason he did not desire to possess her. The minuscule leavings of the other men she had lain with, including Thomas, held no appeal for him, though before he had become a monk, he had thought nothing of taking the pleasures of used women.

"So be it," he said.

Again, resentment sparked her eyes, but this time she did not turn it into a smile. Instead, she pivoted away and stepped around the screen.

Blowing a sigh above his head, Maxen raised his tunic to pull it on, but tossed it aside with the next thought. Where was his bath? The tub had been brought, but the water was yet missing from it.

Chapter Twelve

The water sloshed over Rhiannyn's bandaged hand as she drew to an abrupt halt. Thankfully, it was only hot, no longer boiling as when she'd first taken up the buckets. Barely noticing the heat, she stared in disbelief at the disheveled woman coming from Maxen's chamber.

Theta looked angry, but upon noticing Rhiannyn, feline satisfaction spread over her face. Her smile slightly crooked, her tongue darting out to taste her bottom lip, she changed course and headed straight for Rhiannyn.

"Better than Thomas," she purred when she came to stand before Rhiannyn. Smoothing a hand down her hip and inward, she laid it against her woman's place. "Ah, but how would you know, hmm?" she asked with mock sympathy. "Thomas wanted you as only his wife. It was me he bedded."

Emotions Rhiannyn would never have guessed she possessed coursed through her—hurt, sorrow, and even jealousy that Maxen might have lain with Theta. Nay, he *had* lain with her, she forced herself to acknowledge. Sir Guy his messenger, he had sent for the woman for no other purpose than to copulate with her.

But why should she care? she castigated herself. She had not cared when Thomas had continued to take Theta into his bed after proclaiming Rhiannyn would be his wife. In fact, she had been grateful he had channelled his desire into another. But not so with Maxen. Why?

A movement past Theta's shoulder caught Rhiannyn's eye. There at the edge of the screen, his chest bare, his braies his only covering, Maxen appeared, confirming what she already knew. He had done to Theta what he would have done to her had she not stopped him.

Though it had obviously been his intent to come farther into the hall, no modesty for his state of dress, he stopped the moment his gaze fell upon Rhiannyn.

She swallowed hard as he engulfed her with a stare that sent her emotions soaring where they had no right to spread their wings. Not hurt, but relief; not sorrow, but joy; and certainly not jealousy. Still, she was awash with shame for what had occurred between them such a short time ago. That she could not deny.

Following Rhiannyn's gaze, Theta looked around at Maxen. With a little laugh, she turned back and whispered, "Do not fear. He will not bother you, for he is well and truly sated."

What possessed Rhiannyn, she did not know, but she pulled back and smiled at the woman. "I would think so," she said in a voice meant only for Theta's ears, "now that he has lain with two women in less than an hour." Where the words came from, she could not have said. "In fact, I'm surprised he had anything left for you."

Theta jerked back a step, her eyes wide, her mouth a perfect circle that became a perfect line a moment later. She stared at Rhiannyn for what seemed interminable minutes, her mouth opening not once, but twice to spout a response she never found. Then, with a huff, she tramped away.

Squaring her shoulders, lifting her chin, and staring at a point past Maxen, Rhiannyn advanced on the chamber where the tub stood empty. To her great relief, she was allowed to pass without comment. However, after she emptied her buckets into the tub and turned to go for more, Maxen stepped into her path.

"And what is this?" he asked, distastefully flicking the sleeve of her ill-fitting bliaut.

She pinned her eyes to his chest. "More appropriate attire, my lord. Exactly what you ordered."

"Not exactly, though I suppose it will have to do."

"It does just fine. Now do you step aside I will bring more water for your bath."

"Or you could step around me," he proposed.

Impelled to meet his gaze, she looked up. "I could," she agreed, "if you allowed me to."

"You've my permission," he said, his eyes searching hers for what she tried so hard to hide.

"And you've my thanks," she said. The empty buckets swinging from her hands, she skirted him and breathed a sigh of relief upon gaining freedom from the chamber. Outside the hall, away from the eyes of the many gathering there for the approaching meal, Rhiannyn slipped into the shadows, dropped her buckets, and leaned back against the donjon.

She needed only a moment, she assured herself, a moment to compose herself and rein in her churning emotions. However, the moment grew long as she fought the undoing of her anger and hurt. She closed her eyes, but the tears squeezed through. She swallowed hard, but the lump in her throat lodged itself again. She clenched and unclenched her fists, but the tension remained. All because Maxen Pendery had pulled back when she had pleaded with him, and had instead turned to Theta.

"Rhiannyn?"

She opened her eyes, surprised to see Christophe standing before her, concern on his face. "Aye?" she answered, hoping he could not see her shadowed misery.

"Something is wrong?"

She shook her head. "I am not feeling well. That is all."

"Your hand?"

True, it pained her some to carry the water, but it seemed insignificant compared with this other thing she was feeling. "Nay, my hand is fine. 'Tis my head that fares poorly."

"Perhaps I've something to help you—"

" 'Twill pass," she interrupted. "Really." Stooping to retrieve her buckets, she swept past him.

"You should not be hauling water with your hand as it is," he called after her.

Ignoring him, she continued on to the kitchens.

Five more times she came and went, in silence emptying her burden of water while Maxen watched from the chair he reclined in. However, the last time she rounded the screen, she was greeted with a sight that made her halt. His head laid back against the rim, his eyes closed, Maxen sat in the tub.

How Rhiannyn wanted to retreat, to flee before he saw that she had returned, to suffer no more humiliation at his hands, but another part of her would not allow it. Her arms aching, the cut fingers of her right hand burning, she carried the buckets to the tub. She set one down, lifted the other, and stared straight ahead as she poured water into the tub. She did the same with the second, then turned away.

"You are not going to assist me with my bath?" Maxen asked.

Her back to him, she shook her head. " 'Tis not among my duties, my lord, but if you'd like, I could send a squire to you."

"Or Theta."

Though pained by his suggestion, she nodded agreement. "Or Theta."

"Of course, I could make it one of your duties."

She glanced around at him, but quickly averted her

gaze from his wet flesh. "Aye, you could, but I would ask that you do not."

"I can see no harm in it."

Certainly not for him, but for her. . . . "I would prefer not to, my lord."

"Rhiannyn."

Something in his voice made her look around, though she was careful to keep her gaze level with his. "Aye?"

Catching her wrist, he tugged so that she could either join him in the tub or go down on her knees beside it. She chose the latter.

"Do not believe everything you see—or are told," he said, transferring his hand to the curve of her jaw.

Trying not to feel the stirring in her, she stared into his eyes. "I fear I do not know what you speak of, my lord," she said. In truth, she was afraid to decipher his words.

"Nay? Then I will show you." Giving her no time for retreat, he pulled her to him and crossed his mouth over hers.

Aye, there was the fire, the longing, Maxen discovered at the first touch of his lips to hers. As he had known, it was not the illness that had sent Theta untouched from him, but desire for one woman, and one woman only. Rhiannyn. But she was not ready for him, and his point had yet to be made. With great reluctance, he released her.

Springing back onto her heels, Rhiannyn overturned the buckets in her haste to put distance between them. Then, gaining her feet, she dragged the back of her hand across her mouth as if to wipe away his branding of her—and traces of Theta.

Capturing her furious gaze, Maxen settled back in the tub. "As I said," he murmured, "do not believe everything you are told or think you see. 'Twas not Theta who last knew my touch, but you." Why he felt the need to reassure her he didn't know, but something moved him to.

"You think it matters to me who you lay with?" she asked. "I care not who you take into your bed so long as 'tis not me."

Closing his eyes, Maxen attempted to savor the warmth

of the bath he'd been denied far too long. "I warned you about that lying of yours. Either better it, or be done with it."

He felt her silence, then heard her retreat. Wondering at himself—and her—and the disturbing mess he had made of things, Maxen pushed a hand through his hair and settled it at the back of his tonsured head, which really was tonsured no longer. In place of the smooth scalp he had oft shaved at the monastery had grown hair—short, but before long it would wipe from him the last vestiges of the monk, leaving him no more a man of God, but the lord he had not wanted to become. The lord Rhiannyn had made him. Her lord.

It was worse than Rhiannyn had expected, especially with Maxen's eyes boring into her throughout the meal. It seemed there was no hiding from his sight, nowhere in the hall to retreat from the weight of his stare. And to worsen matters, many of the knights looked at her with open speculation as to what had occurred between her and Maxen when they had been ordered from the hall that morn.

Let them speculate, she thought, and if they believed what she had led Theta to believe, perhaps that was not so bad. After all, while Thomas had lived, his claim upon her had prevented the knights from bothering her as they did the other wenches. If they believed Maxen also claimed her, then mayhap it would serve the same purpose—unless they thought her status no better than Theta's. Praying otherwise, Rhiannyn lifted one of the two vessels she carried and poured ale into the tankard thrust before her.

"Ale!" another farther down the table called.

Feeling as if already pulled in too many directions, Rhiannyn hurried to him only to discover it was Sir Ancel who had summoned her. She looked from his satisfied expression to his tankard, which was already full with ale. She stepped back and started to turn from him, but he grabbed her arm and foiled her attempt at retreat.

"Where think you are going, wench?" he demanded,

though not so loudly that he drew more than cursory attention to himself.

"There are others waiting for drink," she said. "Others whose needs are real."

"And mine is not?" He lifted his tankard to his grinning lips, pulled long on it, then set it back to the table to reveal that it was half empty. "My tankard is not full."

Biting back the retort she would have liked to give, Rhiannyn tilted the vessel and filled his tankard back to full. "Now it is brimming," she said.

He did not release her. Instead, he drank the ale half down again and set it to the table for refilling.

With great restraint, Rhiannyn complied, then tugged to free her arm.

His fingers bruising her through her sleeve, Ancel lifted his tankard. "You cut yourself?" he asked, looking to her bandaged hand.

"A mishap," she said.

"With a dagger, I presume?"

A chill crept over her limbs. It had to have been he who had left her the dagger, the intended instrument of Maxen's death. Knowing an even greater need to be away from him, she tugged again to free herself, but to no avail.

Behind and beside her, calls for more ale went unanswered. "It is not only you I serve," she reminded him.

"Not yet," Ancel said. "But it will be."

"Wench! Bring me more wine," Maxen shouted from the high seat.

His grin grotesque, Ancel released her.

Rhiannyn whirled around, her heart beating so hard she thought it might burst from her chest. However, in the time it took to cross to the dais, she collected enough of herself to pour Maxen's drink.

"You are slow," he said as she drew back.

"My apologies. I was detained."

Lifting his goblet, Maxen leveled his gaze on her. "Sir Ancel?"

She was surprised he had noticed. "Aye."

"For what reason?"

Believing it would be useless to lodge complaint against the knight for his taunting of her, she shrugged. "It seems he was quite thirsty."

"For?"

"Ale, of course."

Maxen leaned forward. "You will tell me if ever he grows thirsty for anything other than drink, won't you?"

She knew, with her entire body, exactly to what he referred. Blood rushing to her face, she nodded.

Satisfied, Maxen reclined in his chair. "Finish with your duties, then."

Rhiannyn needed no more prodding. Moving down the table, she filled tankards and goblets as she went, and when she had emptied her last drop, she hastened to the barrels set against the wall to replenish her supply. There she crossed paths with Lucilla, whom she had not had an opportunity to speak with since the day before when the dagger had appeared on her tray. "I need to speak with you," she said.

A frown on her pretty face, Lucilla shifted her tray of viands to the opposite hand. "Now?"

"Nay, later. When the meal is finished."

The woman nodded, then continued on her way.

Refilling both vessels, Rhiannyn turned back around to find Maxen's gaze upon her. Quickly, she looked away.

Unfortunately, the nooning meal stretched into the evening meal without break for Rhiannyn, then expanded further into a night of drinking that left her feeling haggard and overheated.

Although it took her a while to catch on, she finally realized what motivated Maxen to allow and even encourage such indolence. Drinking very little himself, he watched and listened as those around him relaxed under the effects of alcohol, their tongues growing loose, their manners careless. He was studying them, she realized, measuring them for loyalty and integrity while he searched for the betrayer, or one who could tell him who the betrayer was. Still, it seemed as if he knew, for his gaze always returned to Sir Ancel.

Finally, to Rhiannyn's immense relief, Maxen rose and pronounced the night at an end. There was some grumbling, but all began readying for bedding down.

Using the opportunity created by the commotion of tables and benches being pushed against the walls in readiness for the night's sleep, Rhiannyn slipped out of the hall, crossed the courtyard, and entered the kitchen. There she found who she was looking for. Sitting on a stool, her head laid down upon a table, Lucilla slept in the solitude and quiet offered by this place far removed from the raucous hall.

Rhiannyn nearly turned away. Certain as she was that Sir Ancel had been the one to leave the dagger, the question she had wanted to put to the woman seemed hardly worth awakening her for. However, she found herself shaking Lucilla's shoulder. "Lucilla," she called.

The woman shifted and murmured something unintelligible, but did not awaken.

Rhiannyn shook her again. "Lucilla, awaken."

Groaning, the Saxon woman lifted her head and looked bleary-eyed at her. " 'Tis finished with?" she mumbled.

"Aye, they are gaining their beds now."

"Too drunk to bother with me, I hope."

"I think so."

Lucilla sat back. "And now, when I have the chance for a night's uninterrupted sleep, ye awaken me for our talk, hmm?"

"I'm sorry, but there is something I need to know."

"I was wondering on that. 'Tis about the dagger you wish to talk, is it not?"

Rhiannyn felt as if she'd been punched in the stomach. Was it possible it had been this woman and not Sir Ancel who had placed it? "How did you know?" she asked.

Lucilla rubbed a hand over her face, then cleared sleep from the corners of her eyes. "I've been questioned by the lord himself," she said. "He wanted to know if it was I who was responsible."

Of course. "Then you did not put it on my tray? Beneath the napkin?" Lord, please let her speak the truth, Rhiannyn prayed, and let it be this.

Lucilla smiled wryly. "Two years ago I would have done it when I was still abrew with foolish pride and hate for the Normans, but now . . ." She shook her head. "Nay, Rhiannyn, such a senseless risk I would not take. Though it has not been easy, I have come to accept these new masters, just as I accepted Edwin's father when he held these lands."

When all that was Etcheverry belonged to the Harwolfsons, Rhiannyn mused. When the fields had run with the water of irrigation, rather than the blood of men. . . .

In an unguarded moment, Lucilla reached forward and clasped her hand over Rhiannyn's. "They are not leaving, Rhiannyn. If only for yourself, you must accept this . . . and live with it."

Rhiannyn's smile was forced. "I *am* learning," she said. Turning her palm into Lucilla's, she squeezed the woman's hand, then pulled free and stepped back from the table. "Thank you," she said. "I am owing to you."

Lucilla shrugged. " 'Tis the way of friends."

Rhiannyn's sagging heart took notice. Then Lucilla no longer suspected her of having betrayed the Saxons? "Truly?" she asked.

"Truly."

With one shining star to light the night of this miserable day, Rhiannyn smiled, then turned to leave.

"What is it between you?" Lucilla asked.

The cryptic question pulled Rhiannyn back around. "Between us?"

"Aye. Between you and Maxen Pendery that was not between you and Thomas."

Rhiannyn's confusion was short-lived. "I do not know what you speak of," she said.

Lucilla fanned a yawn from her mouth. "I felt the air between you when I came to his lord's chamber. I saw how you watched each other this night. And now, at only the mention of his name, you flush like a girl about to know her first lover."

Rhiannyn gasped. "You are wrong."

"Am I?"

"What would I want with him? And he with me? He has Theta."

"Does he?"

"He took her to his bed this morn."

Lucilla frowned. "You are sure?"

"He denied it, but I saw with mine own eyes her coming from his chamber with her clothes well and truly mussed, and he with naught but braies to cover him."

Standing, Lucilla crossed to where Rhiannyn stood. "He denied it?" she asked, suspicion crossing her sleepy-eyed countenance.

Odd, but Rhiannyn felt as if cornered, as if her next words could determine whether she became a meal for Lucilla. "Aye," she said, "but I know different. As Thomas took Theta to his bed, so does his brother now take her."

"And that bothers you?" Lucilla said.

"Not at all!" Rhiannyn exclaimed. "Why are you doing this, Lucilla?"

"We are friends, are we not?"

"I begin to wonder."

She laid a hand to Rhiannyn's shoulder. "We are friends, which is why I do this. If only to yourself, you must admit what is in you—what you are feeling for his lord—then perhaps you can use it to your advantage."

"I want naught from him," Rhiannyn declared.

"Then for certain you will become his leman when 'tis his wife you should seek to be."

"Never would I wish to become his wife," Rhiannyn said vehemently. "I would more be Thomas's wife than his brother's, and that I most certainly did not want. Nay, Lucilla, I detest Maxen Pendery."

Lucilla nodded. "Aye, part of you does, but part of you aches at the thought of him taking pleasure with another."

It was on Rhiannyn's tongue to continue her protest, but she knew it a useless lie. "I do not understand it," she said. "How can I feel this when it mattered not that Thomas did the same?"

"The body is a strange thing. In most other matters it serves the mind, but not so when it is taken with desire. Then it rules."

What Lucilla said was true, Rhiannyn admitted to herself. She desired Maxen, her insides stirring at the remembrance of his kisses and caresses, but there was something more. Something in her heart that should not be there.

"Listen to me," Lucilla said, her voice urgent. "Do you give yourself to Pendery without benefit of vows, you are lost, your destiny that of a slave's, and the children you bear him bastards. However, do you deny him—give a little, then pull back—methinks he will wed you to gain your favors."

She, wed? What of the vow she had made herself to belong to none—no husband, no children, only the emptiness Thomas had banished her to? Her thoughts churned to a halt. Never would Maxen wed her. True, he might give her a child, but that was all. "And what makes you think he will not simply take what he wants?" she asked.

"I may know naught of lettering and numbers, of books and such," Lucilla said, "but I know men, and I know this. Though Maxen Pendery is a man unto himself, he shares one thing in common with Thomas."

"Which is?"

"He will not take a woman unless she gives herself."

As he had not taken her when he could easily have done so, Rhiannyn grudgingly acknowledged. "Your words are wise, Lucilla, but I cannot do what you suggest. Aye, I will deny him, but not that I might become his wife."

Lucilla dropped her hand from Rhiannyn, the sigh she heaved turning into a yawn. "Then I pray you will be strong."

"I will."

Looking doubtful, Lucilla walked past her. "Fare thee good eve," she said.

"And you," Rhiannyn called after her.

Were it not for Rhiannyn's empty belly and its painful rumble, she would have gone to the hall as well, but first she must have something to eat. Carrying a stool across the kitchen, she stepped onto it and quickly found the key hidden atop the pantry—fortunately, the same place it had been kept when Thomas was alive. When she had first been brought to the castle, many were the nights she had ventured to the kitchens for a bite to eat. In her anger she would refuse to partake of anything put before her in the company of Normans. Eventually, that had changed, but the hiding place for the key had not.

Trying not to think about her disturbing conversation with Lucilla, Rhiannyn cut a chunk of hard cheese, several pieces of dried meat, and a crust of bread to ease the hunger of a day. Then, locking the pantry and replacing the key, she turned with her platter of filched viands to the table where Lucilla had slept.

And there stood Maxen.

Rhiannyn nearly dropped her food. "You frightened me," she exclaimed, making no attempt to soften her irritation at being come upon without warning.

"My apologies," he said. "I thought you heard me."

Heard him? How could she have? In the silence of night he had come as if upon the padded feet of a wild cat—and he wore boots! "Nay, I did not hear you," she said, wondering when, exactly, he had come. Pray, after Lucilla's departure and not before. . . .

Maxen arched an eyebrow, then put his elbows on the high table and leaned forward. "Do you intend to eat?" he asked, nodding to the viands. "Or simply stand there looking as if you'd like to?"

Only then did it strike Rhiannyn that she'd been caught sneaking food—a terrible offense for one no longer the lady of the castle. What punishment would Maxen dole out for her trespass? she wondered. "I . . ." She looked at the viands and found they held far less appeal than they had a short time ago. She could eat come morn, she decided. Aye, lose her hunger in sleep and avoid whatever it was Maxen had tracked her to the kitchens for.

Walking to the table, she set the platter there. "For you, my lord," she said, and started for the door.

Maxen stepped into her path. "For me? But I have already eaten."

And she had not. "I would like to take myself to bed now," she said.

"While still hungry?"

"If needs be."

"Sit, Rhiannyn"—he motioned to the tall stool—"and eat."

What mood was he in? she wondered as she searched his steady gaze. What did he want with her? Nothing he was yet willing to make known to her, it seemed. With suspicion and dread, she seated herself and pulled the food before her. Then, nervous with the silence that settled around her, she asked what was most heavily upon her mind. "What is to become of those Saxons who refused you?"

"They have chosen death over life," Maxen answered. "That is what will become of them."

"But then why did you not simply have done with them this morn?"

He leaned near her. "In my time, Rhiannyn. Always my time."

His words chilled her, but still she pressed on. "I would ask that you allow me to speak with them," she said tentatively, hoping that she might be able to sway Aethel and the four others the way of the majority.

There was not even the hint of consideration before Maxen responded. "You may not," he said.

She tried to hold his gaze, but in the end looked elsewhere.

"Eat," he ordered.

She complied, all the while wishing him away, but without result, for he was still standing beside her when she finished her meal. Determined to bid him good eve and make for the hall, she stood.

"So, another of your lies found out," he said.

Dear Lord, which one? Rhiannyn wondered. Was it possible he had heard her tell Lucilla she had found the dagger on her tray, rather than on the floor as she'd told him? Perhaps he had heard her admission that it mattered to her if he made love to Theta. Or was it another lie he referred to?

"I fear I do not know what you speak of," she said, taking a step back from him.

He allowed it. "Why did you lie about the dagger?" he asked. "What gain in telling me you picked it off the floor when it was on your tray you found it?"

Lord, if he had overheard her speak of the dagger, then he had most certainly heard the last of her conversation with Lucilla. . . . Everything in her groaned, but she put a brave face over her distress. "I feared for Lucilla if I told you the truth," she admitted.

His expression hardened. "As you fear for her now?"

"She did not do it, my lord. I give you my word she is blameless."

His eyebrows shot high, mockingly displaying what he thought of her word. "If not her, then who?"

Dare she tell him her suspicion? If she did not, then who else but Lucilla to carry the blame? "Methinks 'twas Sir Ancel."

"And why do you think that?"

"He ate from my tray yestermorn when he and the others came to call. Too, he . . ."

"What?"

"This eve he inquired about my hand. He asked if it was a dagger I cut myself with."

Maxen appeared unmoved by the revelation. "Mayhap 'tis a lie you tell again, Rhiannyn. A lie to put Lucilla's punishment on a Norman."

"Nay," she exclaimed. "I speak the truth—as I know it."

He moved in on her, turning his body so she was backed up against the table's edge with no retreat behind or before her. "As you spoke the truth when you told me it was you who killed Thomas?" he asked. "When you said you found the dagger on the floor? When this noon you said it mattered not to you who I lie with so long as it was not you? Those truths, Rhiannyn?"

Never had she felt so deep a humiliation as she did with that last lie he threw at her. "Believe what you like," she said, forcing the words past a constricted throat, "but 'tis on you do you believe wrong." Then, feeling as if she were suffocating, she jumped to the side and hurried toward the doorway.

"Rhiannyn," he called after her, though his footsteps did not follow.

She faltered, then glanced over her shoulder.

"Do not think to play games with me," he said. "If you do, you will only discover how very wrong Lucilla is. You will come to my bed," he continued, "but not as my wife. Never as my wife."

Shame on her heels, Rhiannyn hastened from the kitchens on legs that longed to run, but which she forced to a walk.

Beaten with the fatigue of a body still struggling to heal itself, and with emotions wearing themselves thin in their war with one another, Maxen sat on the stool and began kneading the back of his neck.

Aye, it was Sir Ancel, the same as he had concluded long before he had followed Rhiannyn to the kitchens and stumbled upon a conversation he had felt little remorse in listening to. Trivial as it had been to learn where the dagger had been placed, he had been angered at the confirmation yet again that Rhiannyn had lied.

Still, his anger had had little chance to take hold, for Rhiannyn's admission of her attraction toward him had almost made him forget the lie. Too, he was armed now—with the knowledge of the advice Lucilla had given her, but which Rhiannyn had been curiously averse to. Not that he would marry her, but it was good to know how she might attempt to bring about such a union.

With a ragged sigh, Maxen stood. There would be a union, he assured himself, but not one of a respectable nature. "Soon," he said to the empty room. "Soon we will put an end to this chase."

Chapter Thirteen

Rubbing a hand across his unshaven jaw, Maxen stood atop the wall-walk, scanning all that was now his. The donjon, the stables, the granary, the smithy, the chapel, and beyond the rising walls, land as far as the eye could see.

The chapel. He swung his gaze back to the small whitewashed building. Not since his coming had he attended mass, nor gone down on his knees and spoken prayers that for nearly two years had been more familiar to him than his own name. The closest he had come these past weeks had been prayers in passing, their only purpose the easing of his flesh, the dousing of his desire for one he should not want. . . .

Trying to shed the vision of Rhiannyn that rose before him, he lit an all-encompassing gaze upon the castle. But again, he slipped into thoughts best left alone. If only this was what he wanted, he reflected. If he could take it all in with the pride and arrogance of a landed noble. If there was someone at his side with whom he could share it and rear a son to pass it on to. However, it hung around his neck like the weight of the dead—a burden that he could see no way clear of.

A shout below and to the left brought Maxen's head around and moved his hand from where it rested upon his sword hilt to the dagger of Thomas's death. Narrowing his eyes against the risen sun, he easily picked out the dust-billowed fight of two Saxons who, up until a sennight past, had been loyal to Edwin Harwolfson. Now, though, they struggled to give up the spent past and accept Norman rule. Knowing that whether or not they succeeded would likely determine the fate of Pendery lands, Maxen allowed them their quarrels, but that was all.

By day, the Saxons toiled under the weight of stone they raised to the walls, and of eyes that marked their every passing. By night, they slept under the close watch of men-at-arms given the license to strike first, then ask questions. Fortunately, thus far there had been no incidents of any consequence.

Of course, there was always Rhiannyn, an incident unto herself. Ever elusive, she ran a fine chase, though it was only because he allowed her to. The closest he had gotten to her since that night in the kitchens was during those times her wine pitcher settled upon the rim of his goblet. But he'd achieved naught but the further strain of soaring needs. For now, though, that was enough—or so he told himself—for every day brought more and more responsibilities to bear upon him.

As Etcheverry's harvest had been paltry, there was the issue of food for the winter, then the matter of wood for fires that would be badly needed to ward off the coming cold, not to mention clothing, blankets, and shelter for the Saxons who were numbered too many for their cramped quarters within the castle's walls, and now Blackspur Castle. . . .

Aye, his flesh could wait, he told himself. Rhiannyn

would be his, but when the time was right. Feeling like the martyr he had once so despised in other men, Maxen descended the steps to the wall-walk at a leisurely tread, and by the time he set foot to the inner bailey, the clash between the Saxons had ended. Amid grunting and cursing, the task of raising the walls was taken up again.

Turning toward the stables and those preparing to ride with him, Maxen came face to face with his brother. "Christophe," he said.

As if uncomfortable, Christophe shifted foot to foot before finally deciding to bear the greater of his weight on the lame leg. "I have not yet had the opportunity to thank you," he said.

"Thank me? For what?"

"The Saxons."

Of course. "Ah ... yes," Maxen said. Uncomfortable himself, he started to step around Christophe. However, his brother laid an arresting hand to his arm.

" 'Twas good of you," he said.

"Good," Maxen echoed the odd word.

No longer able to bear so much of his weight on his impaired leg, Christophe shifted to the solid one. "It would also seem I owe you an apology. I had believed the worst of you, and now am proven wrong."

For some reason, it irritated Maxen that good was thought of him. Weak, the warrior in him denounced. Not so, the monk countered. "Do not be so quick to give your apology," he said gruffly, "for 'tis yet to be seen whether the Saxons are true in their loyalty to me."

Disappointment was momentarily reflected in Christophe's eyes, then cleared with his next words. "If you would allow it, I would like to accompany you to Blackspur," he said.

"For what reason?"

"It has been a long time since last we talked as brothers. Methinks it would be a good opportunity."

Then they were brothers once again, Maxen reflected, it having weighed heavy on his mind that Christophe had rejected him as such. "Aye," he said, "I would like your company."

Christophe's face lit. "I must make ready, then," he said, and hurried toward the stables.

Maxen watched him disappear within, then turned his attention to the others. Everywhere squires scurried to meet the demands of their masters, many of whom grumbled mightily over matters that could be naught but trivial—among them, Sir Ancel. Others gabbed and laughed, while only a handful attended to the ride ahead.

Yet for all the commotion, Maxen knew they could ride within the minute—or the hour, he mused as his thoughts turned again to Rhiannyn. Aye, an hour. Such a small amount of time, considering the full day's ride to Blackspur. And to ride to that place in the peace that would be his once he took what he so badly needed. . . .

Damn martyrdom! he decided. Pivoting on his heel, he strode to the causeway.

Thinking herself fortunate to have avoided Maxen since the evening meal on the night past, Rhiannyn knelt on the stripped mattress of Maxen's bed, reached forward, and grasped the far edge. Throwing her weight backward, she pulled the mattress free. Her objective that much nearer, she searched a foot to the ground, balanced herself, and heaved again.

In her bid to remove the mattress that it might be skaken and turned, all went as planned until the seam beneath her fingers rended. She stumbled, nearly righted herself, then fell backward. The mattress and sprung feathers followed her to the floor, and she could not help the screech of surprise mingled with pain as she landed hard upon her buttocks. And then darkness enveloped her.

Glad there was none around to make her feel the fool for what she had done, she turned onto her hands and knees and crawled out from beneath the mattress. As her head emerged, she swiped at the feathers tickling her face and noisily expelled one that had invaded her mouth. "Ugh," she muttered.

Laughter, deep and heartfelt, preceded the booted legs that appeared before her a moment later.

Rhiannyn's first thought was to duck back beneath the mattress, but it would be a ridiculous gesture. Pushing the mattress off her, she stood and looked up at Maxen.

Amazing, she thought. It was a man she did not know who stood before her with laughing eyes, a mouth full of flashing teeth, and lips that had forsaken their downward turn for the human smile of laughter. He looked younger, more handsome, and reachable—suddenly so reachable. Ignoring the indignity that she ought to feel, she savored the man before her. Here was the Maxen Pendery she sought. Here was the one beneath the anger of loss and vengeance.

Although his laughter subsided, the sparkle in his eyes did not. "You are quite a sight, Rhiannyn of Etcheverry," he said finally.

She looked down at herself, and only then realized the extent of her feathering. Ah well, a small price to pay, she concluded. Gladly she would pay it ten times over to be afforded a glimpse of this side of Maxen. "I thought you had gone," she said.

Reaching forward, he picked a half dozen feathers from her hair, the gesture more intimate than Rhiannyn would ever have imagined.

"I also thought I had gone," he said, still smiling, "but something called me back."

"And what was that?"

He trailed a feather down the curve of her jaw to that thrilling place where neck met shoulder. "You," he said.

"I . . . don't understand," she breathed, though she was certain she did.

"Aye, you do. I returned for what you have too long denied us." He swept his ardent gaze over her, then chuckled. "Though now I fear the time might be better spent plucking you."

Something moved within Rhiannyn, something warm

and hopeful. Impulsively, she reached up and cupped her hand to his jaw. "I like this Maxen," she said.

His eyes flickered, then, like the shifting of day into night, darkened. "As opposed to?"

Her heart sinking, Rhiannyn lowered her hand back to her side. "As opposed to the cruelty of the one who allowed me to believe it was a hanging I accompanied him to a sennight past."

Maxen could not have said what was responsible for his admission, but he knew it went beyond desire for this woman. Mingled with that was a need to reassure her that he was not the beast he had led her to believe him to be. "A test," he said. "That is all it was, Rhiannyn."

She frowned. "A test?"

"Thomas's murderer. I had thought that faced with the deaths of your people, you might finally give me what I need."

"But what you need I do not possess," she protested.

He nodded. "This I know—now."

Then it was not cruelty he had shown her? Rhiannyn thought as she looked into eyes that knew light again. Only a test? Aye, a test—also deserving of her anger, but anger which she could not find it in her to give. By far, his distrust was preferable to what she had deemed cruelty. Though perhaps Maxen did not know it, she was reaching him, and as long as she was reaching him, there was hope. "I thank you," she said.

"For?"

"Telling me—and allowing the Saxons to live."

He came a step nearer. "A mistake I am sure to regret."

She felt as if he had stolen her air by bridging the space between them. "I will pray you do not," she said.

He stared at her a long moment, his eyes speaking to her of things they had spoken before, and which she had responded to. Nervous, she looked away. "I must return to my chores," she said.

He pulled her chin back around. "Will you yield to me, Rhiannyn?" he asked softly.

He spoke as if theirs was a battle of life and death, that

if she did not yield to him she might suffer the same as a knight who refused the one whose sword lay against his neck. Rhiannyn slid her gaze to Maxen's mouth and found herself wanting very much to give him the answer he sought. She did want him, but to yield any more than she already had would be a mistake she would regret the rest of her days. "Nay, my lord. I will not."

He touched his thumb to the corner of her mouth. "I could change your mind."

That he could, but to yield with her mind, as well as her body, was something she could not do. "My mind is decided," she said.

His jaw clenched hard, then he drew a deep breath and raggedly spent it. He looked to have accepted defeat, and surprised Rhiannyn by pulling her to him and capturing her mouth.

It was a deep kiss, and well explored before Rhiannyn grasped the presence of mind to struggle against it. "Nay," she gasped against his mouth, lifting her hands to his shoulders to push him away. "Release me."

Maxen strained her against him, hardened the kiss, then abruptly set her away. "To speed my journey," he said, grateful for the disguising chain mail that was as hard as he beneath it.

As he watched, Rhiannyn touched her fingers to her lips, curled them into her palm, then lifted a defiant chin. "God speed it," she said, her sincerity questionable.

Smiling wryly, Maxen turned and left her to her chores. Arriving at the stables a few minutes later, he was pleased to discover the men waiting and his great destrier ready, Guy standing by it.

As if fearing he might be trampled to the ground, the squire holding the destrier's reins jumped back, and only when Maxen was mounted did he draw near again. "The reins, milord," he said as he passed them into Maxen's waiting hands.

Nodding, Maxen looked to Guy. "Etcheverry is in your hands," he said, "and Rhiannyn. Keep them both for me." Without awaiting reply, he spurred the horse forward and beneath the portcullis. He felt the twenty-odd pairs of eyes that bored into his back, knew the questions running through their minds as they followed his reckless ride, and found it oddly amusing that his men likely thought him mad. And perhaps he was.

At last, Rhiannyn thought, none to prevent her from doing what she must to become one again with her people—if that was even possible. Though she had not ventured out amongst them for fear Maxen would forbid her doing so, she had watched from a distance these past days as the Saxons built him his wall. Long were the hours and strenuous the work they put out, and with only the promise of their reward to carry them.

As she descended the causeway, a bucket in each hand, the three kitchen wenches following her bearing equal burdens, Rhiannyn reflected on Aethel and the four others still imprisoned below the donjon. Twice now she had attempted to slip past the guard to go to them, but both times had been forced to turn back to avoid being discovered. Perhaps with Maxen gone the guard would ease his watch and she would be able to get past him. . . .

Despite the number of men Maxen had taken with him, he had left behind a great many to keep watch over Etcheverry and the Saxons did they think to take advantage of the absence of their lord. And all of those men seemed to be following her progress across the bailey. Truly, though, it was not they who caused a shiver of apprehension to course through Rhiannyn as she neared the workers, but anticipation of the reception that was only moments away.

Perhaps she ought to have heeded Lucilla's warning, she reflected. Lucilla who, with the help of these three women, regularly carried food and drink to the Saxons, and who had protested mightily when Rhiannyn had asked that she stand in for her this day. But too late now.

"Well, look who has come down from her fine perch," a Saxon man atop the wall called out.

Rhiannyn recognized him as Peter, who, with Aethel, had come upon her when she had fled into Andredeswald. He had not liked her then, and clearly liked her even less now.

The men on the scaffolding, those on the ramps up which the stone was conveyed, the handful working the hoists and pulleys, and the women whose job it was to mix the mortar, all paused in their labors to search out who had caught Peter's attention. None appeared any more welcoming than he when they saw it was Rhiannyn.

Setting her buckets on the ground, she pressed her shoulders back, lifted her chin, and looked at each in turn. Behind her, the three wenches noisily let down their own burdens. A moment later, the footsteps of their retreat told her she would stand alone before her people. "I have brought you drink," she said, "and midday bread and cheese."

"Aye?" one Saxon woman, Meghan, asked as she straightened. Her gaze suspicious, she wiped a forearm across her sweaty brow. "And what be a Norman whore doing among lowly Saxons?"

"A Saxon among Saxons," Rhiannyn corrected her, refusing to succumb to the anger roused by the vile thing she had again been named. "And as I am not a Norman, neither am I the whore you make me to be."

"Ha!" Peter laughed. "Even were ye not, which you most certainly are, you would still be a betrayer."

"I did not betray you."

"Nay?" a surly Saxon growled. "Then why do we build a wall against our own people when 'tis on the other side we ought to be?"

"It is true I led Maxen Pendery to Edwin's camp," she admitted, "but I did so unknowingly. As you were deceived, so was I."

"And we're to believe you?" Peter asked skeptically.

It was far more difficult than Rhiannyn had anticipated, but to back down now and flee to the mock safety of the donjon would only make matters worse. "No doubt you will believe what you like," she said, "but still I would have you know the truth."

"A traitor's truth," another woman snapped.

"Many of you I grew up amongst," she continued. "You know me, and do you search your hearts you will know that never would I betray you."

"Ah, but for the bed of the handsome monk, methinks many a whore would turn," Meghan said mockingly.

Rhiannyn ignored her. "There is food and drink aplenty," she said, knowing she had more than outworn the argument of her innocence. If ever these people were to come around, it would take time and patience. One day— one meal—was not enough. "Come and partake."

Throwing down her mortar hoe, Meghan made a leisurely advance while the others watched and waited. "Hmm," she grunted, looking from bucket to bucket. "From the hand of the enemy we are fed."

"An enemy you have accepted that you might know peace again," Rhiannyn pointed out.

"You think so?"

Fear coursed through Rhiannyn. Then was it a lie they had given Maxen? Did they intend rebellion? Not even if she went willingly into Maxen's bed would it save the Saxons a second time. Pray, let it not be. Let it be only anger this woman spoke. "Nay, I believe so," Rhiannyn said with a surety she was sadly lacking.

Smirking, Meghan fisted her hands upon her hips, stepped wide, and jutted her chin at Rhiannyn. "The lord is a bit stingy, is he?" she said, referring to Rhiannyn's garments. "But then, he is only concerned with what is beneath, isn't he?"

Not only did the Saxons snicker, but also those Normans who followed the conversation from their posts.

Self-consciously, Rhiannyn lifted a hand to smooth the bliaut, but hurriedly checked the gesture and clasped her hands before her. It would have been so easy to explain the bliaut, to tell these people that she was less than they, that when the wall was finished and they were released to the land, she would still be a slave to Maxen Pendery; but she could not. Even were they capable of pitying her, she wanted none of it. "The garments suit me fine," she said.

"Easy in, easy out, hmm?" Meghan taunted.

The snickering grew louder, stirring a resentment in Rhiannyn's blood that she had come to expect only during her encounters with Maxen. Linking her hands more tightly, she asked, "Are you going to eat?"

Meghan's answer came as a great surprise. One moment she was sneering, and in the next she had set herself upon Rhiannyn. Together they collapsed to the ground, Meghan rolling atop her as they came up against the great tub of mortar.

Rhiannyn had barely gotten her bearings when Meghan's fist slammed into her left eye. In spite of the bursting pain, she gathered enough of herself together to defend against the next blow. Furious, she knocked Meghan's descending arm aside, then countered with a punch of her own. It was poorly executed, for never had she come to fists with anyone, but still she made her mark—Meghan's nose.

With a yelp of pain, the woman fell to the side, blood streaming around the hand she clapped over her face.

Having gained the advantage, Rhiannyn turned onto her knees, threw a leg over Meghan, and straddled her. "Do you wish more?" she demanded.

Removing her hand to reveal bared teeth turned red, Meghan peered up at her. "Aye," she said, "much more." Then she reached with both hands and grabbed Rhiannyn's hair.

Rhiannyn cried out, and that weakness lost her the advantage. With a great heave, Meghan threw her off and jumped to her feet.

Somewhat winded, her scalp burning, Rhiannyn stared up at the woman who gestured for her to stand.

Clearly, Meghan had had training beyond the sword, for there was fight in her stance, confidence in the thrust of her jaw, and challenge in her eyes. And beyond her she had the support of the Saxons who had left their work to more closely follow the confrontation. Too, there were the Norman guards who seemed more interested in bettering their view than putting an end to the fight.

Knowing she could not back down, Rhiannyn stood. At least she and Meghan were well matched, she reassured herself, neither one the taller, nor the heavier. "Very well," she said, "let us put an end to this."

Eagerly, the Saxon woman breached the space separating them and fell upon Rhiannyn, her fists flailing as she grunted with exertion.

Instinct guided Rhiannyn in the defense of her person, and the offense she was surprisingly allowed. Several times she found herself laid flat upon the ground, her body the recipient of painful blows, but more often than she had believed herself capable, she gave back what she was given. Though it could not have been more than the spit of an hour that they fought, it seemed far longer.

At last, the tub of mortar proved the deciding factor. Slammed back against its rim, Rhiannyn evaded Meghan's attack by jumping to the side. Unfortunately for the other woman, she was unable to check her headlong rush and doubled over the tub. The wind knocked from her, she was easy prey—prey that Rhiannyn was quick to take advantage of. Stepping behind Meghan, she twisted both of the woman's arms up and behind her back until she cried out.

"Would you like a closer look?" Rhiannyn asked, pushing Meghan down toward the mortar bath.

Saxons and Normans alike muttered surprise at the turn of events, for though Rhiannyn had fought well, Meghan had clearly been the better of the two.

"I give! I give!" Meghan cried. "Lord bless it, but I give!"

Feeling as if someone else had stepped into her skin, and that she herself now stood outside it, Rhiannyn bent to the woman's ear. "Ah," she breathed, "but that would be too easy. I require more."

"More?" Meghan gasped. "Speak!"

"No more will you call me 'whore,' for that I am not. Nor will you seek to engage me in any further scraps. Agreed?"

When Meghan did not immediately concede, Rhiannyn

inched her arms farther up her back and pressed her nearer the mortar. "What is your answer?" she demanded.

Meghan groaned her pain, then grudgingly acquiesced. "Agreed."

Rhiannyn had only just released her when John, the master mason, strode briskly to where she and a muttering Meghan stood. "What goes?" he demanded in his poor Anglo-Saxon.

Though Rhiannyn knew she must look a terrible mess, her clothing begrimed, dirt a mask upon her face, and her eye swelling closed, she stepped before the man whose job it was to supervise work on the wall. "A disagreement only," she said, "and one that is now settled."

"Is that right?" He looked from her to Meghan, then back again. "I have no need of any more trouble than I've already been given with this lot of griping Saxons," he said. "Return to your kitchen duties and vex me no more, woman."

Rhiannyn shook her head. "Nay, I would stay to work alongside my own."

"Your duties are elsewhere. Now be gone."

"I—"

"One more pair of hands might serve you well, Master John," an unexpected voice interrupted.

All turned and shaded their eyes to see who it was that stood atop the wall. Sir Guy. Looking every bit the lord but for the droll smile that curved his usually flat mouth, he stood with legs spread and arms crossed over his chest.

Rhiannyn was surprised that the knight spoke Anglo-Saxon, for never before had she heard him utter a word of it.

"But Sir Guy," John protested, "look what this one has already wrought. Truly she will prove more a hindrance than a help."

"Has she not said the dispute is settled?" Guy asked.

"Aye, but—"

"Then you have naught to worry about."

"I do not think Lord Pendery would approve," John argued.

"You need not worry. If there is question, I will answer to him when he returns. Upon my head will his displeasure fall."

The man threw his hands in the air. "Upon your head, then." He turned back to the Saxons. "Be quick about your bread and drink. There is much to do ere dark."

Even after the others had turned away, Rhiannyn continued to stare at Sir Guy, who should have been the first to send her back to the kitchens. But he hadn't. Why?

His own gaze fixed on her, he lifted his hand and planed it out before him in silent invitation for her to join the others.

She held his gaze a moment longer, then turned to the simple meal that would have to sustain her throughout what would undoubtedly prove a taxing day for both body and mind.

Chapter Fourteen

"Then you will not **make Sir Ancel** lord of Blackspur as Thomas intended?" Christophe asked.

Pleased with all that **he had seen**, though it was really less than he had **expected** considering the construction on Blackspur **Castle** had commenced shortly after that at Etcheverry, Maxen turned from the wall and settled his gaze upon his brother. "Nay, 'twill be Guy's reward," he said, "unless you would like it for yourself."

Without hesitation, Christophe shook his head. "It is not for me, Maxen. You know that."

"Aye, but I would have it otherwise."

"And I would not."

What a useless exercise to have even suggested it, Maxen told himself scornfully. "Then Guy it is."

"And what of Sir Ancel?"

Looking down into the bailey, Maxen searched the man out and easily located him where he lay stretched out to receive the uncommon warmth of an autumn sun come out from behind the clouds. "As I have said, he cannot be trusted. For certain, it was he who left the dagger for Rhiannyn, and he who will continue to seek my death."

"Then you will kill him?"

Maxen eyed Christophe, as always trying to assess who it was beneath the young man's awkward exterior. "You do not sound disappointed," he said.

"I am not."

"For one as gentle of heart as you, brother, it surprises me that you would approve of such means of ridding one's self of an adversary."

In answer, Christophe spoke the bit of wisdom Maxen was more and more coming to expect from him. "There are some of whom you can be free only by their death."

"And you believe Ancel to be one of those?"

"I do."

"As do I."

Christophe stepped nearer him. "Knowing what you know about him, why have you not yet acted?"

Again Maxen paused to contemplate his brother. Was it only Christophe's lameness that had shaped him? Or did it go deeper than that? Nils's death? The horror of Hastings which he had undoubtedly heard much about, though he had not seen it with his own eyes? Thomas? Frustrated, Maxen gave Christophe the answer he awaited. "The time is not right."

"And when will it be right?"

"I am waiting on Ancel—when he says 'tis right."

Christophe's eyes looked near to popping from his head. "Explain," he beseeched.

Maxen rolled his shoulders in an attempt to break up the tension that had settled there during the journey from Etcheverry. "If naught else, a dying man ought to be able to choose when he dies."

Christophe shook his head. "Then you will allow him to get closer to you? To try again?"

"Aye, that is the plan."

"The next time he might succeed."

Maxen nodded. "Perhaps. But tell me, would that disappoint you so much?"

Christophe's placid expression turned to outrage. "I have lost two brothers already," he said, his voice rising. "Think you I care to lose another?"

"Think you on who that brother is," Maxen said. Then, something strange taking him, he began to list the terrible attributes that were his. "Cold-hearted, single-minded, merciless Maxen Pendery—the Bloodlust Warrior of Hastings. All used to describe me, and all well deserved. It would be only half a truth, if that, to defend what I did at Hastings by calling it duty to my liege. Nay, I, like so many others, was taken with bloodlust, a frenzied need to prove myself a warrior and a man. Aye, Christophe, I am despicable—such that two years with God did naught to cleanse me of the sins of my past."

Instantly, Christophe's ire transformed itself into empathy. "You are wrong, Maxen," he said. He laid a hand to his brother's shoulder. "No longer are you that man. You proved it with the Saxons—in allowing them to live."

A long pause. "Did I? Or was it only the needs of my flesh I proved?" As soon as the words were out, Maxen wished he could drag them back. Whatever had possessed him to speak such to his brother, to open to Christophe what was in the deepest of him?

"Rhiannyn?" Christophe guessed.

Disgusted with himself, Maxen pushed Christophe's hand off him and stepped away. "Aye," he said grudgingly. "She haunts me."

"Then 'tis true she had something to do with your decision."

How Maxen wanted to deny it. But he needed to speak it out, and who better to listen than one of his own blood? "Aye," he admitted. "She asked that I have mercy on them, put them back to the land. And God," he exclaimed, slamming a fist into his palm, "I have provided to do exactly that. It will serve me right do they all turn on me."

"You think they will?"

"I do not trust them not to, especially while Edwin still prowls the woods."

Christophe considered that a moment, then said, "Likely he has gone, brother."

Maxen shook his head. "Nay, he is still there. I feel it. He wants what is his."

"The land."

"And Rhiannyn."

"Would you give him either to end this?"

The land? Rhiannyn? "Nay, the land is Pendery only through King William, not mine to give, Christophe. Even if it meant peace, I could not confer it upon the Saxon rebel."

"But you could give him Rhiannyn."

He would more readily give Edwin the land, Maxen thought, surprising himself with the admission. Nay, it was preposterous. One night with her was all it would take, then he would return her to Edwin if that was what she wanted. Of course, that might mean death for her if Edwin still kept at his side the old crone who had nearly succeeded in murdering Rhiannyn.

"Maxen, do you love her?" Christophe broke into his madly churning thoughts.

"Love her?" he barked. "As Thomas wanted her, so do I. And that is all."

"He loved her," Christophe said. "'Tis true she did not return his affections, but still he loved her—in his own selfish way."

"Which got him killed."

"Aye, it did, but do not mistake that it was Rhiannyn responsible for what befell him."

"As you have already pointed out," Maxen grumbled.

"And will continue to until you finally concede it."

Maxen let out a harsh sigh. "Is it not enough that there is finally peace between you and me, Christophe? Content yourself with that and make good cheer of it, but do not ask me to call Rhiannyn blameless. She played no small role in Thomas's death."

"A similar role to the one I played for you in assisting in her escape, yet I was innocent of betraying her."

Exasperated, Maxen backhanded the air. "Enough," he snapped. "I like this new peace of ours far too much to destroy it with petty arguments."

Surprisingly, Christophe yielded. "Very well. But there is still much unsaid that could be said."

"I am sure," Maxen said. Then, motioning for Christophe to follow him, he descended the steps to the bailey.

Only in her untimely grave had Rhiannyn ever been so filthy. Now, though, it was not dirt that clung to her, but the mortar of a wall raised against Saxons.

The accumulation of five days' fatigue dragging her steps, she stopped and leaned against the stable fence to look at the wall she had worked so hard on. Side by side with people determined to keep her out, she had mixed mortar, lugged great buckets of it to the ramps, and even assisted in hoisting loads of rubble up the scaffolds. Never before had she worked so hard, not even when Edwin had forced her to learn the sword. But it was worth what it cost her.

Little as it was, she had made enough progress with her people to reward the aches and pains. No more did her ears fill with the malicious words the first three days had heaped upon her. Though generally ignored now, there were moments when she was almost one with the Saxons, such as on the previous day when she had gone for water to thin the mortar and lost her footing. Doused through to the skin, she had joined in their laughter at her. And then there was the pulley that had let go in the midst of lifting a basket of rubble to the top of the wall. She had seen it coming and jumped out of the way, only to be struck by an errant stone. Immediately, several Saxons had rushed to where she lay, their faces showing concern until they saw she was only bruised. Then they had grumbled all the way back to their labors. Although Rhiannyn knew the mishap may not have been an accident, she had been comforted by the knowledge that at least some of her people cared—even if they did not wish to.

"Pray, Maxen, stay away just a while longer," she whispered into the coming night which had cleared the bailey of nearly all but the guards stationed atop the walls. Why Sir Guy had allowed her to work on the wall she still did not know, but for certain Maxen would not allow it once he returned. And if he returned too soon, then all she had toiled for might be lost. "A few more days. . . ."

"My lady is saddened?" a hoarse voice behind her asked.

Rhiannyn jumped. She had thought herself alone, utterly alone. Swinging around, she opened her mouth to voice displeasure at being sneaked upon, but something prevented her from doing so, something familiar within the shadows of the hood draped low over the man's face, something that caused fear to leap through her every nerve. Warily, she reached to push the hood back from the man's face, but his voice froze her hand midair.

"Do not!"

"Edwin?" she whispered.

He lifted his head just enough to raise the shadows from his face. "You were expecting another?" he asked with a twisted smile. "Perhaps Maxen Pendery?"

Nervous, Rhiannyn shot her gaze to the men-at-arms within sight and saw that none looked their way. "Certainly not you," she said in a low voice.

"Obviously not."

"How did you come within?"

"Ah, me," he said sarcastically, "as there was no portal open to welcome me, I had to make my passage by wall. But come." He slipped a hand out from beneath his tattered mantle and grasped her arm. "We have much to speak of."

Fearing his intentions, Rhiannyn did not want to go with him, but she knew that to refuse him would only draw attention to them. Resignedly, she yielded to Edwin's pull and a short time later faced him in the deserted stables he had chosen for their talk.

"You are looking poorly, Rhiannyn," he said, brushing a thumb beneath her eye that was now yellowed from the bruise Meghan had given her. "Not quite the fair maiden I remember."

Indignant, Rhiannyn drew back from him. "I have been helping to build the wall."

"And brawling."

"When I must. But tell me, why have you come?"

He pushed back the hood, unveiling the harsh set of a face that was hardly familiar anymore. "What an odd question."

"Aye, I suppose 'tis," she agreed. "You have come for your rebels."

"And?"

She shook her head. "Nay, Edwin, do not ask them to challenge the Normans. No good will come of it. Surely they will die."

"What? You do not believe in the superiority of Saxons over Normans?"

"There are more Normans than Saxons, and heavily armed. Pray leave your people be that they might live and rear children and raise crops upon which to feed them. Maxen Pendery has promised them this. Do not take it from them."

"The promise of a Norman," Edwin spat. "Nay, Rhiannyn, they are my people. I trained them, and they will join with me against the Norman dog you fornicate with."

"I have not laid with him!" she protested.

"Think me a fool?" he growled. "You left with him—betrayed me."

"I did not! It was from Dora I ran. Maxen Pendery saved me from the death she tried to put upon me."

"What lie do you tell now? That Dora tried to kill you?"

"No lie, Edwin. You saw her that night. She wanted me dead—drew blood from me. When all slept, she and three others took me from my tent and tried to bury me alive. That is the truth!"

"And my truth to you, Rhiannyn, is that Pendery murdered three of my men before you left with him, not to mention those whose lives he took when he attacked our camp. He—"

"Three?" Rhiannyn gasped. "It cannot be. There were only two dead when I came to consciousness. The third was wounded and ran with Dora."

"I do not understand your part in this, Rhiannyn, but it was three that died—three whom I buried."

Rhiannyn could think of no reason why Maxen would have lied to her when he had so readily admitted to the taking of two lives. "Mayhap it was Dora who killed the third," she mused, knowing it was true the moment she said it. "Aye, so the man could not be made to tell the truth of what she tried to do to me."

"Dora is a healer," Edwin said, "not a murderer."

"Are you so blind, Edwin? Did you not see the grave she put me into?"

"Grave?"

Then Dora had moved the bodies to hide the truth from Edwin. "She is evil, Edwin. If only for your soul, you must send her from you."

Unreadable emotions crossed his face before it fell back to an expression of contempt. "It is exactly as she foretold," he said. "That you would betray your own people, take another to your bed. All Dora said has come to pass, and yet you wish me to believe lies that fall from your mouth like venom?"

"They are not lies," Rhiannyn said, appealing to him. "Believe me in this."

"As you would have me believe you did not lead Pendery to us?"

"I know now that in fleeing Etcheverry I led him to you, but I did not know it then. This I swear. And upon my soul, I have not laid with him."

Grasping her chin, Edwin lifted her face near his. "Even were it true," he said, "you *will* lay with him."

Which she could not swear upon her soul she would not do, Rhiannyn realized.

"What? No denial?" he taunted. "Tell me you will not

lay with him—put that upon your soul, Rhiannyn—and mayhap I will believe all your other untruths."

Her heart felt as if it might burst, her eyes to shed tears too long in keeping. "I ... cannot," she whispered.

Disgusted, Edwin shoved her back and strode away. "You may give yourself to the Norman dog," he said over his shoulder, "but you will not give my people." Pulling the hood back over his head, he eased the stable door open and slipped out into the engulfing dark, leaving behind only the creak of the door as it settled back into place.

Her emotions clamoring for release, Rhiannyn leaned against the stall wall and looked up toward heaven. "What am I to do?" she asked the unseen. "How to end this?"

Her only answer was another creaking of the door that should have made no more sound now that Edwin was gone. Had he returned? "Edwin?" she whispered, peering through the shadows. No one, only the door settling a second time.

Dear God, had there been someone else in the stables? she wondered frantically. Someone who might this moment be hurrying to alert the Normans to Edwin's presence?

Fearful, Rhiannyn spurred her feet from the stables to the outbuildings where the Saxons were quartered. In her flight she nearly stepped upon not one, but two of the men Maxen had set to watch over the Saxons. Pausing briefly to verify that both still lived, and finding that they were only unconscious—a wonder, considering Edwin's hatred of Normans—Rhiannyn ran the rest of the way to the larger of the buildings where the Saxons took their evening meal. It was there she found Edwin.

"Do we stand together?" he was asking from atop a table. "Take the castle and all who defend it?" He waited for an answer as his followers took note of Rhiannyn's appearance.

"Nay, Edwin," she shouted as she pushed her way through the melee. "You must leave—now!"

"You are not welcome here," he said. "Go."

"Heed me," she pleaded. "Methinks the Normans may this moment be coming for you."

His eyes narrowed. "You told them?"

A path opening for her to the table upon which Edwin stood, she placed herself before him and strained her neck back to meet his gaze. "Nay, but another may have," she said.

"And how would you know that?"

Desperate for the minutes already lost to argument, she cried, "Edwin, there is not much time. Do not question me, just leave."

Nervous, the Saxons began muttering amongst themselves, looking from Edwin to Rhiannyn with question and concern in their eyes, no doubt weighing the wisdom of what their leader asked them to do.

Ignoring Rhiannyn's imploring gaze, Edwin looked out across his rebels. "What is your answer?" he demanded.

An older Saxon stepped forward. "Were I not of forty-three summers, I would, Edwin," he said. "Were I still willing to die no matter the cost, indeed I would, but I am neither any longer. I cannot." He stepped back to his place.

"Pendery has promised to return us to the land," another of significantly less age said. "I am a simple man, and would like to sow the seed of children and crops ere I die."

"And you believe Pendery?" Edwin asked, his fists clenching and unclenching at his sides.

"With each day, there is less and less to believe in," another said, "but the Norman's promise is the best we have."

"Aye," a Saxon barely more than a boy agreed. "The Pendery provides well. There is food aplenty, clothing, and fuel for night fires to warm us."

Stunned by what she was hearing, far from what she had expected, Rhiannyn could only stare and wonder who would speak next.

"And what when winter comes and this raped land has provided only enough for the Normans?" Edwin asked. "Then you will either starve or meet your death of cold."

A murmur arose as all considered what they had not before.

What *would* winter bring? Rhiannyn wondered, for it was true what Edwin spoke. Near to bare was the harvest after another year of Saxon rebellion, and Thomas hardly had managed to feed his own during the winter past, leaving many of the Saxons who had taken him as their new master to fend for themselves. And there had been deaths. . . .

"Are there none who will follow me?" Edwin asked, his gaze momentarily lighting upon Rhiannyn with an anger all could see. "Who will take back what is ours?"

"What is yours," Meghan said bravely. "Aye, we are all Saxons, Edwin, but we are of the simple folk whereas you are of the noble. Be it Norman or Saxon who possesses Etcheverry, still we will answer to a master. For what should we give our lives in exchanging one for the other?"

Ready agreement stirred among the Saxons.

"I will follow you," Peter said. Pushing his way past the others, he jumped onto the table to stand beside Edwin, then issued a challenge. "Who will stand with the betrayer"—he pointed to Rhiannyn—"and who will remain loyal to the rightful lord of Etcheverry?"

Inwardly, Rhiannyn cringed, but a moment later her prayers were answered—or nearly—when only two more took up places alongside Edwin.

"Is Aethel not among you?" Edwin called out, his gaze searching for the height and breadth of a man who would have been conspicuous among those present.

"He and four others are imprisoned 'neath the donjon," Peter said.

"For?" Edwin asked.

"Loyalty to you, of course. Though they do not yet hang, 'tis certain they will."

Rhiannyn saw by the look in Edwin's eyes that he had set himself to devising a way of releasing them. However, it was not to be, for in the next instant all was thrown into chaos as the Normans swelled into the building with weapons drawn and ready for blood, Sir Guy at the fore.

Everything that followed appeared as a terrible blur to Rhiannyn. Tossing Peter a dagger, Edwin put his sword before him and leapt from the table to hurl himself straight at the advancing Normans. The air was filled with wrathful shouts, curses, the clashing of weapons, and the anguished cries of Saxons fearing for their lives.

Though those who had turned from Edwin were quick to lay themselves upon the ground in surrender, Rhiannyn remained standing—and praying.

"Your neck if they escape!" she heard Sir Guy shout.

Looking around, she saw Edwin and two others fight their way to the door and make a triumphant exit, with a contingent of no less than a dozen men-at-arms rushing after them. But where was the third man who had joined with Edwin? Dear God, was he dead?

"If you wish to live," Sir Guy shouted across the building, "you will remain where you are. Upon my vow, any who rise up will meet their immediate death." He turned his gaze upon Rhiannyn.

She looked away. The fury in his eyes chilled her through, warning her of a terrible retribution. Taking up her prayers again, Rhiannyn did not stop until, finally, the end was announced by the return of the men-at-arms who had gone after Edwin.

"Regrets, Sir Guy," one said, "but two escaped."

"And the other?"

"Wounded, but death nears him."

Guy walked over to the man and looked him in the eye. "Tell me it was Harwolfson."

The man cast his eyes down. "I cannot," he said. "He and the Saxon named Peter went over the wall. We followed, but could find naught of them before Andredeswald."

It must have taken near-inhuman control, but Guy did not strike him, nor look to have any intention of carrying out his threat of having the man's neck for allowing the escape. Instead, he turned and stared at Rhiannyn. He did not have to speak his summons, for it was in his eyes.

Her feet feeling as if encased in stone, she wove her way around and between the ones who had laid themselves at the mercy of the Normans, faltering only when she came upon one of the three Saxons who had chosen Edwin's way. For certain he was dead, his tunic darkened with blood from neck to hips. Shuddering, she continued past the unfortunate man to where Sir Guy awaited her.

"Will you allow me to speak first?" she asked.

To her surprise, he agreed. "Aye," he said against teeth clamped in fury. "Speak and be done with it that we might begin the fettering."

Then he had already come to his own conclusion, she realized, that all the Saxons had joined in the uprising. For that their punishment would be bondage until Maxen returned to pronounce his dread judgment upon them.

"It is not what it looks," Rhiannyn began. "Edwin asked these people to join with him, but they chose to stay under the house of Pendery, as was their promise to your lord—now their lord. Only three did Edwin convince to join with him."

Angry color flushed Sir Guy's face scarlet.

"She speaks true," Meghan said, having come up onto her knees.

From the ground came murmurs of agreement.

"She speaks a lie," another said. Theta. Skirting the men-at-arms, she sidled up to Guy, put an arm through his, then looked at Rhiannyn, who was staring at the other woman in shock. "With my own ears did I hear Rhiannyn and Edwin make plans with these people to take the castle while his lordship is absent. Had I not brought news to you, they would now be overrunning Etcheverry, slaughtering us."

So it had been Theta in the stables with her and Edwin, Rhiannyn realized. She who, by her own admission, had alerted Guy to what was barely a half-truth, and she who had this moment renounced her own to include herself among the Normans. " 'Tis Theta who lies," Rhiannyn countered. "None of these people plotted any such thing with Edwin. They are innocents."

"Aye, 'tis the Norman whore who lies," Meghan agreed, "not Rhiannyn."

"If you wish to live, wench," Sir Guy snapped, "you will lie down. Now."

Meghan hesitated, her teeth worrying her bottom lip, then she complied.

Guy turned his attention back to Rhiannyn. "I trusted you," he said. "I allowed you to join the work upon the wall that you might know your people again. It was what you wanted, though your place was in the hall, yet I conceded to your wishes. Now I see how wrong I was."

"Listen to me—" Rhiannyn began.

"I have listened enough, and now you will lie down too."

"But they have done naught wrong. Theta—"

"Down, Rhiannyn!"

Defeated, she lowered herself to the ground and lay between two Saxons.

"You tried," the man to her left whispered, his sad smile welcoming her back.

If only such were not the circumstances under which she gained acceptance, Rhiannyn silently mourned. Tears pricking the backs of her eyes, she squeezed them closed.

"You . . . you . . . and you," Sir Guy said to three men-at-arms. "Carry word to the baron of what has transpired at Etcheverry. He must needs return at once."

Calm, Rhiannyn urged herself. She must think calmly, prepare herself for the confrontation with Maxen, for within a day and night he would return. She must be ready.

The missive was delivered, but Maxen asked no questions, uttered not a word, before sending the messengers away.

"It cannot be," Christophe said as soon as the men had departed the hall.

Maxen remained silent, and for just a moment, closed his eyes and felt the pain behind the rage. Rhiannyn had deceived him again. With her people she had plotted to take Etcheverry. Lord, if only she had not been at the heart of the uprising.

"Maxen, wait until you have spoken with her," Christophe urged, reading his brother far too well for one he had been long without knowing.

"I warned you about being so quick with your apologies," Maxen finally said. "As Rhiannyn and her people have not fulfilled their end of the bargain, I need not fulfill mine. I am done with them all." Ignoring Christophe's outburst, he strode from the hall. Within the half hour he and his men rode out from Blackspur Castle.

Chapter Fifteen

She was ready, Rhiannyn assured herself when Maxen returned late the following day. From the great clamor without, she and the others knew the precise moment he rode through the portcullis. Yet he did not come immediately to the outbuilding that was their prison. For some, it might have seemed a reprieve, but for her, it made his coming that much more terrible.

They were bound one to another by the ankles, though now the silence of waiting had fallen over them and, for the first time, the chains were eerily silent.

Then approaching footsteps were heard.

Though Rhiannyn felt the beckon of Meghan's gaze upon her, she did not look that way. Instead, she stared straight ahead, and when Maxen threw open the door and strode into the midst of those he believed to have betrayed him, once again she told herself she was ready. But she wasn't, for the moment his searching gaze picked her out from beneath the layers of dust and mortar she'd worn since the day before, a part of her folded. Nay, never would she be ready for one such as Maxen Pendery, but neither did that mean she would simply throw up her hands in surrender.

Rage was visible everywhere in him—in the flare of his nostrils and the hard line of his mouth, the set of his shoulders and his fisted hands, and, of course, his eyes.

With a silent smiting of all that was in her that might prove detrimental to her people, with a healthy measure of docility that was not her, and with a rattle of chain, Rhiannyn stood. "My lord, will you hear us?" she asked.

He walked forward, the weight of his stare growing heavier with each footfall. "No more, Rhiannyn," he said, halting before her. "I have heard enough of your lies to last me an eternity."

The retort that sprang to her lips came easily, but was not so easily pushed back down. Burying it, Rhiannyn said, "They are not lies. What I must needs tell you, what you need to hear, is the truth."

As swift as the lightning of winter's first rainstorm, Maxen caught her arm and dragged her up against him. "I have said *no more*," he hissed.

She swallowed hard. "But there is more. What you've been told is not true. These people denied Edwin for their new master—you, my lord. Pray, do not punish them for giving themselves to you."

He looked near to bursting with all that was in him, but as if realizing it, released her before he could do her harm. Turning, Maxen swept his gaze over the expectant faces of men and women whose only champion was a filthy, infuriating woman whom the weak part of him wanted to believe, but whom his mind rejected. Could it be Theta who had lied? Of course she could have lied, he told himself. But so could Rhiannyn have lied—be lying to him now.

"Only three joined with Edwin," she continued, defying him, "two of them dead now. All the others stood down. You must believe me."

He swung back around to face her. "You were plotting while you worked on the wall with them," he said, "though why Guy would allow it is quite beyond me."

"You are wrong. Does it not tell you something that these people immediately surrendered when they were come upon? Ask Sir Guy." She looked past Maxen to where the knight stood near the door—and beside him, Christophe. "Did they not go to the ground when you and the others rushed in?" she asked Guy. "Was there one among them who resisted?"

Before the knight could answer, Maxen retorted, "Fearing for their lives, no doubt."

"Nay. Keeping their word to you."

It only angered Maxen further how much he wanted to believe her, but still he held to his control, though with only a single thread grown taut. "You will not convince me, Rhiannyn," he said, "so waste no more of your words upon my ears." What was done was done, and now he must do what he should have in the beginning. Pivoting around, he headed for the door, but had taken only a few steps when Rhiannyn spoke again, her voice turned doubly desperate.

"What do you intend?" she called after him.

"You know the answer to that," he tossed over his shoulder.

Silence followed him halfway across the building before it was split with Rhiannyn's cry. "I yield!"

He drew to an abrupt halt, then turned around for what he swore would be the last time. Though he knew exactly to what she referred, he arched an eyebrow in silent question.

She lowered her gaze. "I yield," she repeated so softly he had to strain to catch it.

She yielded, that this night he might finally know her body. Of course, her surrender was not unconditional—that much was clear. Attached to it were the strings of her people. For them, she would give the only thing she possessed which he desired—but he should not even be considering it. He cursed himself. He ought to throw her yielding back at her. Simply do what needed to be done to insure Etcheverry's future. Forget that it might be Theta who lied, and be done with these Saxons forever.

Vacillating between two emotions equally potent, he stared long and hard at Rhiannyn, knowing that beneath the filthy, pitiful figure she made was a woman he wanted more than any other he had ever known—in spite of the likelihood she had deceived him. Ah Lord, but anger was a powerful aphrodisiac, turning that destructive emotion so thoroughly in on itself there was only one end to it—desire.

"Bring her to my chamber," he ordered one of the guards, then he stalked from the building.

Guy followed him, his silence more irritating than the scratching of cat claws upon a door.

Past the stables, Maxen swung around to face the knight. "I want every one of them questioned," he ordered. "Singly."

Guy frowned. "But I had thought . . . Rhiannyn . . ."

"If punishment is due, it will be done, regardless of what is yielded me."

Relief shined out of Guy's face. "Wise, my lord," he said, then turned back to the outbuilding.

Wise. At least not all of him was in his braies, Maxen consoled himself. Aye, he would ascertain for certain, or reasonably certain, whether the Saxons had rebelled against him, and if it proved so, then this time he would not waver from his punishment of them.

Rhiannyn stared straight ahead—beyond the guard who was stepping around the Saxons to gain her side, and past Christophe to a point of emptiness.

She had just given herself to Maxen Pendery in word, but more, he would soon take her in body. Not a surprise really, the only surprise being that it had not happened earlier, but at least she would gain something from the giving of herself. Had she already surrendered to Maxen, she would have naught to bargain with.

For a weak moment, she closed her eyes, then opened them and looked out over the Saxons, nearly all of whom watched her with degrees of pity. They knew exactly what she had surrendered, and those who had thought her already given to Maxen Pendery—having been most vocal in branding her a Norman whore—looked at once surprised and contrite. Most especially Meghan.

Rhiannyn offered the woman a tight smile meant to reassure, then looked down at the guard who had sunk to his haunches at her feet. He was rough in removing the manacle; however, she hardly felt the scrape of the iron upon her skin, for over and over again the shrill voice of one who had known echoed through her head.

'Tis another she will fornicate with, old Dora had said, . . . *another she will fornicate with.*

It seemed Maxen waited a long time for Rhiannyn, though he knew it was only anticipation that dragged the minutes into hours they were not. He was restless, not only with waiting, but with irritation at Christophe's passionate plea that he behave the godly man and leave Rhiannyn untouched—that he give her yielding back to her and have faith in her word that the Saxons were innocent. To his own surprise, Maxen had managed to keep back his irate words and sent Christophe away. However, it was the youth who had had the last word, resolutely declaring Maxen's future with Rhiannyn damned if he took advantage of her sacrifice.

Future. Maxen silently spurned the thought. It was not as if there were any beyond the pleasure they would find in each other's bodies. Still, Christophe's words stayed with him. He sighed. At least he could credit his young brother with one thing—wisdom. Aye, he was wise, but only in that he declined a lordship of his own in knowing he would make a weak master. He simply had too much heart.

In the dark of Maxen's thoughts, Rhiannyn suddenly materialized before him. What a waif she appeared, her hair wild and unclean, her face smudged and unsmiling, her mortar-streaked clothes destined more for the burn pile than the wash.

"You may leave us," he told the guard, and a moment later he was alone with Rhiannyn as he had wanted to be ever since he had found her fallen beneath his mattress a sennight past.

Lifting his ride-weary body from the chair, he walked to her and lifted her chin. Only then did he notice beneath her eye the shadow of a bruise nearly healed. Thinking he must have been too taken with emotion, and the outbuilding of too little light not to have seen it before, he asked, "Someone struck you?"

She started to lift a hand to her eye, but pressed her arm back to her side. "A disagreement only," she said.

Wrath rising in him that someone had dared to mark her, he barked, "Who?"

Clearly, she was contemplating another lie, then she shrugged. " 'Twas the Saxon woman Meghan I fought, and Meghan I bettered."

A woman, and Rhiannyn had prevailed. A strange swell of pride for her small victory pushed through Maxen, but recognizing it, he threw it off and turned his thoughts instead to the Devil's bargain she had struck with him.

Staring into eyes that at first appeared vacant, but upon closer examination revealed a spark in their depths, he said, "The Saxons are this moment being questioned."

She blinked, the confusion upon her face giving rise to suspicion. "Why?" she asked. "I would think our arrangement precludes any such action."

He shrugged with a nonchalance he truly did not feel. "I must know."

She jerked her chin free of his hand. "And if 'tis determined they are still culpable?" she demanded, that spark in her eyes turning to a flame.

"Then it will be as it should have been," he said, watching her carefully, but making no move to take hold of her again. "They will hang on the morrow." In that moment he knew her loathing—felt it straight through—but she made no further retort. Instead, she spun around and headed from the chamber.

In two strides, Maxen caught her back to him. "And

where do you think you are going?" he asked. Lord, but she was beautiful, part of him exclaimed. Even in filth and deception it could not be hid.

She glared up at him. "My place is with my people. 'Tis quite beyond me why you have wasted my time and yours in bringing me here."

"Then you have changed your mind? You will not yield?"

"Yield?" she gasped. "Whatever for?"

"The Saxons."

Her laughter was scornful. "As I will have gained naught in yielding to you, there is naught I owe you."

"But you *have* gained."

Her expression was both confusion and fury. "You speak in riddles, Maxen Pendery. I yielded to you that my people might live. You are not keeping your end of the bargain."

"If the Saxons are shown to be guilty, their fate is the same as it would have been when I came to the outbuilding. If, however, they are innocent, all will be as it was when I rode for Blackspur. I give them an ear, Rhiannyn, a chance to convince me of their loyalty. 'Tis something they had not ere you called to yield, and something I had no intention of lending them a second time."

Now she understood, he saw. Though on the surface it did little to smooth her disposition, he sensed that beneath her tightly schooled face she was in the midst of concession.

" 'Tis not what you agreed to," she declared.

"I do not recall agreeing to anything. In fact, I know I did not."

"You knew exactly what I offered myself in exchange for," she snapped. "Absolution, not trial."

"Aye," he admitted, "but 'tis a fool who exchanges his life for naught but the pleasures of his body. Come, Rhiannyn, do you truly have so little faith in your people?"

She drew herself up to her full height, though his stature still eclipsed hers. "The Normans believe what they wish to believe," she said, speaking between clenched teeth, "not the truth."

Refusing to be drawn into a futile argument neither could convince the other of, Maxen asked, "Do you accept, Rhiannyn?"

He saw refusal in her eyes. She drew breath to speak it, then clenched her fists to keep it down. With grudging acceptance, she nodded.

Maxen waited her out only a short while before lowering his head and claiming her lips. She did not respond, but then, with as much resentment as there was in her, he knew it would take far more than a kiss to awaken her. But later. "You must feel the virgin about to be strapped to a stone and sacrificed," he said, drawing back. "But then, you're not a virgin, are you, Rhiannyn?"

Her only response was the shifting of her jaw beneath his hand. Releasing her, Maxen returned to his chair and dropped back into it. "You may undress," he said.

Her entire body started almost comically, but Maxen found little amusement in it. He had not intended to shock her with such blatant disregard for any modesty she might possess. It had just come out that way. "I've ordered you a bath," he explained, though why, for the love of God, he owed her an explanation he could not say. "You may use my robe for cover until the water arrives." He nodded to where the garment lay over the chest.

The distress upon her face easing, though not entirely, she walked to the robe and fingered the fine material. Then, glancing once more his way, she began untying the sash of her bliaut.

Maxen stared as she took off the outer gown, part of him deep in desire to see the chemise removed that was the only thing between his eyes and Rhiannyn's body. However, another part of him stood him up and carried him past her to the screen. "Have your bath and make ready for me," he said, "then I will come to you." Though he longed to look back at her, he did not. Instead, he went into the hall and called for ale.

Too confused to feel relief, Rhiannyn stared at the

blank screen. Why? she wondered. One moment he had seemed bent on furthering her shame, and the next he had ended it—though only temporarily, she reminded herself. He would be back, and then the virginity he believed her to be lacking would be his, and never another's. She would become precisely what Lucilla had warned her against. For her people she would give herself into Maxen Pendery's expert hands and by the morrow be named his leman and Dora proven right. And still her people might die ... and a child be born of her union with Maxen.

"No children, Lord," she whispered as her mind flashed images of the planting of Maxen's bastard seed. "Let me be barren."

The water for her bath arrived just as the first tear squeezed out from beneath her lashes. Flinging it away with the back of her hand, she faced away from the wenches who carried pail after pail to the waiting tub, then she was alone again.

Feeling outside of herself, she removed her chemise and stepped into the drawing warmth of the tub. Not since before she had fled Etcheverry with Thomas in quick pursuit had she had a proper bath. Even with the night looming menacingly before her, the warmth seeped past the barriers of her worry, feeling more wonderful than she could ever remember it having felt. She sighed as boiling water cooled by the many steps from the kitchens to Maxen's chamber closed around her like the arms of ...

Of what? she silently demanded. Of a lover? Of Maxen? Nay, she promptly refused the idea. Like the arms of her beloved father now dead. Like her mother's heavy bosom against which she had comforted her children. Never the arms of her enemy—and forever Maxen Pendery would be her enemy.

Cursing herself more than him, Rhiannyn first washed her hair, then began removing the layers of dirt that clogged her every pore and cast upon her skin a grayish tone. She scrubbed until she shone more pink than pale, until her flesh stung with raw awareness, and the water went from clear to cloudy. Then, her cleansing done and her minutes numbered before Maxen reappeared, she spared a moment to settle back against the smooth wall of the tub.

Closing her eyes, she tried to ready herself for the night ahead, so near now that she could clearly imagine the pain of awakening that would soon be hers. Aye, the pain of women which her mother had told her of two years ago when Rhiannyn's marriage to Edwin had been imminent. In that clear, reassuring voice of hers, she had spoken of the things that were done to a woman's body on the night of her wedding—invasion, pain, blood, then perhaps a bit of pleasure. Perhaps. . . .

Rhiannyn trembled, though not from water that had cooled, but from memories of the pleasure Maxen had elicited from her that day not so long ago when he had laid her back upon the trestle table in the hall. That he would this night give her both pain and pleasure she did not doubt, but that he would know of her surrender to all things pleasurable made her wish to seek a hole in which to bury herself and her shame.

Could a woman hide these things, she wondered, offer no response so that a man would never again wish to lay with her? As she dried herself and donned the robe that smelled of Maxen, she told herself she would try to remain unmoving beneath his ravishment, that she would put her mind elsewhere and deny him the satisfaction of knowing her desire. However, time passed and he did not return to take her as he had indicated he would. More time passed, during which food was brought to her, and still he did not come. Eventually, his voice came to her above the noises of feasting in the hall.

Wondering what announcement he was about to make, Rhiannyn crept to the far side of the screen. Peering around it, she could see most of the hall. As she watched, Maxen stood up from his high seat and awaited a quiet which came quickly for him.

"As I have this day returned from Blackspur Castle," he addressed his men, "and found it to be in a state near ready for settlement, I would announce the one I have chosen to install as its castellan."

Most eyes turned to Sir Ancel, who sat a half dozen men from Maxen, a smug, knowing smile on his face as he raised his goblet to drink from it. It never made it to his lips, though, for Maxen's next words froze it midair.

"Sir Guy Torquay, stand."

Confused mutterings echoed Guy's bewilderment as he slowly rose at the right hand of his lord.

"For having served me faithfully, I give you your reward," Maxen said. "Come the completion of Blackspur Castle, it and all of its lands I bestow upon you to protect and lord in my name."

The stunned silence ended with the slamming of Sir Ancel's goblet to the tabletop. Abruptly, the spurned knight stood and reached for his dagger.

Rhiannyn's heart leapt high, the warning she struggled to call out stopped by Maxen's next words. "Think on it carefully, Ancel," he said in a low and menacing voice. Though he now faced the knight, he did not meet threat with threat by pulling forth his own dagger. Instead, he laid his hands flat upon the table—silently confident he could fly his own dagger ere Ancel's ever reached him.

For a tense moment, the knight gripped the hilt of his dagger, measuring both risk and gain. In the end, risk prevailed. Opening his hand, he spread his fingers wide to show emptiness, then said darkly, "Blackspur is mine."

"It is Pendery," Maxen corrected him. "And I am Pendery."

"Thomas promised it to me."

"Thomas is dead."

Ancel's hand drifted back to the sheathed dagger, but with visible restraint he lowered it and pressed it hard against his thigh. "Then you will not honor your dead brother's wishes?"

"I will not."

The hall was cloaked in another long silence, Ancel's gaze hard upon Maxen. Then without further word he stepped over the bench, strode around the table, and traversed the hall to the doors that stood open to a deepening night. Immediately, the dark swallowed him.

Looking back to the high table, Rhiannyn barely caught the knowing look Maxen exchanged with Sir Guy the moment before he lifted his goblet in salute. There followed a murmur of agreement, then others lifted their vessels to join their lord in receiving Guy as castellan of Blackspur.

Slipping back around the screen, Rhiannyn lowered herself to the bed and clasped her hands between her knees as the worry in her loomed larger. Maxen knew, had to know, it was Ancel who had placed the dagger for her to slay him with, and if he had not believed it before this night, surely he must now. But why did he do nothing? Was he so fool to believe the knight was naught but threats? Or was he waiting—and for what?

Gradually, the din in the hall lulled to the quiet of sleep brought by night, and still Rhiannyn sat the edge of the bed alone, though now her worry over Ancel muddled itself with the bargain she had struck with Maxen.

Where was he? she wondered. Abruptly she stood, paced the chamber twice, then dropped back down upon the bed. Why did he not just come and have done with it? Why all this waiting that jangled every one of her nerves?

"Curse you, Maxen Pendery," she muttered as she lowered her chin to her chest and closed her eyelids for just a moment—or two. Though she fought the weight of exhaustion that came upon her, in the end she capitulated and lay back upon the mattress. No matter, she told herself. Maxen would awaken her when it was time.

Nay, he would not awaken her, Maxen decided as he looked down at the angel curled upon his bed, her glossy tresses golden even in the dim light afforded by a torch near to burning out.

It had been no oversight that he had not returned to her as he had intended. Instead, once free of his chamber, he had examined the situation with a mind clear of the smell, sight, sound, and touch of her, acknowledging that the bargain they had struck would never suffice. Some part of him warped by his years in the monastery had reached out and told him the mistake he would make in gaining Rhiannyn's body without her willingness. True, it would not be rape, but nearly. Patience and the right circumstances would bring her to him, of that he was certain. Not this—this sacrifice for the lives of her people. She must come to him, not he to her. Why it mattered, he had not so closely examined, but it did. If only she looked less inviting. . . .

Sighing past the quickening of his flesh, Maxen slid his arms beneath her and lifted her from his bed. Rhiannyn stirred, shifted, then pushed her face into his shoulder and resumed her deep breathing.

Knowing he must remove her completely from his chamber, else he might do what he so wanted to, Maxen carried her into the hall that had finally quietened to sleep and laid her on the bench that was hers. He knew it was hers only because he had, several nights before his journey to Blackspur Castle, abandoned his bed to seek her out. He had not so much as touched her, but he had stood for incalculable time looking upon her.

Ah, but he wanted to touch her now. . . . With a sound half-groan, half-sigh, Maxen gave in to the impulse and laid his hand to the curve of her cheek. It fit his hand perfectly. Going just a bit further, and then no more, he promised himself, he brushed his thumb down her lower lip.

In response, Rhiannyn groaned, then turned from her back to her side and curled her body in on itself. Perhaps she was cold, Maxen pondered. His robe was not nearly as thick as the layers of clothing she normally slept in. Searching to the side, he bent to a nearby knight, pulled his blanket from him, and was met with a moment of grumbling before the man returned to his drink-driven sleep. Too late castigating himself for playing the nurturer, Maxen draped the blanket over Rhiannyn and stepped back.

"My lord," murmured one who had come unannounced to his back.

Damn Rhiannyn! Maxen silently cursed as he turned to

face the man. Only she was capable of rendering his instincts and senses useless, for had he not been so immersed in her, he would certainly have heard Sir Guy's approach far in advance of his appearance. If it had been Ancel, his intent deadly, surely the knight would now be gloating over Maxen's figure lying at his feet, the rushes running red with his life. Lord, but he must do something about the man. And soon.

"What is it?" Maxen asked in a harsh whisper, unable to control his irritation even though Guy was not to blame.

"Your ear, my lord," the knight said. "May we speak in your chamber?"

"Can it not wait until morning?"

"It can, and would have had I not seen you here in the hall."

Maxen considered his shadowed face a moment, then turned on his heel and motioned for the man to follow.

Neither saw Christophe where he sat against the wall, for his pallet was well doused in shadows. It was from there he had watched his brother carry an untouched Rhiannyn from his chamber, and from there he now sent up a prayer of thanks. Knowing what Maxen had yet to acknowledge, he smiled, then lay down and plunged into sleep.

"The inquiries are finished?" Maxen asked his vassal once they had gained the privacy of his chamber.

"Aye, and all tell the same tale. As Rhiannyn said, they denied Edwin for you."

"Why?"

"In this it would seem most were honest, my lord."

Maxen nodded for him to continue.

"For what you provide them. They are tired of fighting, tired of cold, and most tired of hunger."

"A beginning," Maxen muttered, but now, more important, the question he so badly needed answered in only one way. "And what of Rhiannyn's role?"

The knight shook his head. "There is not one among the Saxons who does not say she also stood down from Edwin. They say she pleaded with him to leave."

She had pleaded with him to leave, Maxen mused, though she had done naught to alert the Normans of the enemy's presence within their walls. Too much to expect, he told himself. After all, she was still of Edwin's people—a Saxon no matter who made himself her master. Pushing a hand through the hair on his scalp that had grown just long enough to allow him the gesture, Maxen dropped into the chair and thrust his legs out before him. Could he believe the Saxons? he wondered, though the real question was whether he could believe Rhiannyn. And damnation, he wanted to! "What do you think?" he asked Guy.

"I think the Saxons are not to be trusted," he answered, "but also I think it more likely they chose to stay rather than go with Edwin."

"And Rhiannyn?"

Guy shook his head. "I had thought she betrayed, but perhaps not."

As Maxen wanted to believe himself. "What of Theta?"

"The wench has much to gain by lying—or at least thinks she does."

"Such as?"

"You, my lord."

Maxen's voice when it rolled past his lips sounded harsh even to his ears. "Is that so?"

Guy shrugged a shoulder. "You asked what I thought, and that is my answer."

At least the knight did not cower, nor change his mind as others might. For this, Maxen's spark of ire cooled. "On the morrow you will return the Saxons to their work upon the wall," he said.

Guy did not seem surprised. "What of punishment?" he asked. "A reminder of what awaits them *do* they turn from you."

What Guy spoke was wise, and would undoubtedly have appealed to the Maxen of Hastings, but this Maxen, wound up as he was with Rhiannyn, spoke from another side of his mouth. "No punishment," he said.

"And of their guard?"

Maxen was not a foolish man. "Double it."

"As you order." Guy turned to take his leave.

"Guy."

The knight turned back around. "Aye, my lord?"

"We have not yet spoken of your reason for allowing Rhiannyn to work on the wall."

He shifted his weight, though not awkwardly. "As she wished to, it seemed the easiest way to keep her under eye. There looked to be little threat to her person in the mixing of mortar."

"And that was your only reason—keeping watch over her?"

This time, the shifting of Guy's body showed unease. "I must admit that I pitied her desire to gain again the acceptance of her people," he said.

"And did she?"

"Aye, though more because of the stand she took for them following Edwin's flight."

Whether that was beneficial to Maxen or not had yet to be decided, but he nodded his approval. "You have served me well," he said.

Guy dipped his head in acceptance of the praise. "As is my desire."

"Is it also your desire to lord Blackspur?"

Striding the distance that separated them, Guy went down on a knee beside Maxen and bowed his head. "Assuredly, I am pleased and honored that you have chosen me. Upon my vow, you will not regret your decision."

"This I know," Maxen said, then grasped Guy's arm and brought the knight with him to standing. "We will talk more of it on the morrow."

Guy's face solemn, though behind it there surely clamored a hundred different emotions, the knight bid Maxen good eve and took his leave.

And what of Rhiannyn? Maxen turned again to the problem pressing most urgently upon his body. What was he to do with her, and how best to bring her quickly to his bed? Shedding his clothes, he stretched out upon the mattress to ponder the answer. However, fatigue immediately dragged him into sleep.

Chapter
Sixteen

Rhiannyn was not where she had thought she would be the morning after Maxen's taking of her—nor did she feel the pain of that taking. And as for the pleasure, she could not remember the giving of any. Uncertain, she sat up and let the blanket fall back to reveal the robe she still wore. Then she knew. She had no remembrances because there was naught to remember. She had fallen asleep on Maxen's bed, and without demanding payment for deliverance of her people, he had carried her from it to her place in the hall.

But why? Her bottom lip clamped between her teeth, she stood and stepped over and around the sleeping figures that the first light of morning revealed to her. Knowing they would be rising soon, and seeing from random vacant pallets that some already had, she hurried across the hall with hopes Maxen still lay abed.

He did, though his lids sprang wide the moment she stepped around the screen. "I had not thought yours would be the first face I saw this morn," he said. Sitting up, he propped himself against the headboard and nodded for her to come nearer. At her hesitation, he reminded her, "As I did not sample your fruit on the night past, 'tis hardly likely I will do so now."

True, and even if he did, it was not as if she weren't prepared for it, Rhiannyn reminded herself. A small price to pay for the lives it might save.

"Come into the light," he said.

Drawing a deep breath, she crossed the chamber and positioned herself an arm's reach from the bed. "What of our bargain?" she asked, hating the tremor in her voice. "It was not fulfilled."

"I know. 'Twas I who did not fulfill it."

"Why?"

With no concern for his nudity, he pushed back the covers and swung his legs to the floor. "Do not question it, Rhiannyn," he said, standing, "just be grateful I have decided not to take you up on your yielding."

Then he would not breach her? Now? Ever? But more important, what exactly did that bode for the Saxons? Confused, she looked past him to avoid staring upon his splendid frame, but it was too late to safeguard against the images her eyes had captured. "And my people?" she asked. "What of them?"

Maxen turned from her and began rummaging through the careless throw of clothes upon the floor. Out of the corner of her eye, Rhiannyn saw that whatever it was he searched for he was unable to find.

"Mayhap you should offer me my robe," he said, looking over his shoulder, his stare boring into her until she felt compelled to look at where he crouched.

Immediately, her gaze was drawn to a muscled back that melded into firm buttocks. Ignoring his suggestion of offering him the robe, she defensively grasped the lapels together and focused past him. "What of the Saxons?" she asked, trying not to feel things she ought not to.

With a ragged sigh, Maxen straightened and stepped around the bed to the chest. He lifted the lid which, to her immense relief, gave adequate cover to his lower extremities. "Be assured they are safe," he said as he began another search. "They will resume work on the wall today."

Truly, it was not what she had expected to hear, though her heart had hoped for just such words. And though she would have wished otherwise—to cloak herself in indifference—her emotions began unfolding. "Then you are not going to—"

"Nay, I am not."

Her relief soared, her breath caught, and her knees weakened, but somehow she avoided dropping to the floor. "You believe them, then?" she asked.

He made her wait. Removing braies from the chest, he stepped into them, pulled them up, and unhurriedly tied them. Then he came back to her. "Sir Guy has questioned them all," he said, "and 'twould seem to be as you claim. *Seem*," he emphasized.

Then he did not believe Theta's lies? Rhiannyn wondered amidst precarious emotions. Was this the reason he had not breached her maiden's passage as he had intended to? "Is that why you did not . . . come to me?" she asked.

Crooking a finger, Maxen lingeringly slid the back of it down her face before dropping his arm back to his side. "Nay, Rhiannyn, that is not the reason. Though I very much wished to, I had already decided against laying with you ere the news was brought me."

Instinct, trustworthy or not, told her he spoke the truth, and a door deep within Rhiannyn creaked open. In that unguarded moment, Maxen stepped inside. A mistake, and one she knew the moment he crossed to the other side of her. But once in, he would not be cast out. Leave now, she urged herself, while you are still unscathed and whole, but she had to ask, "Why?"

He considered her a long moment, his gaze like a touch. "I have said it before. I want you willing, Rhiannyn—not simply a body 'neath mine into which I might empty my seed. That I can get from the next wench who passes my chamber."

His words evoked imaginings Rhiannyn was powerless to ignore, and there was no imagination about the hot color warming her face. "You ask too much," she breathed.

This time Maxen touched her with more than his eyes, lightly feathering his hand down her neck to the cleft of her breasts between the robe's lapels. "Do I?" he asked huskily.

Nay, he did not, but she could not tell him that. "I—"

"Permit me a taste of that which I did not take last eve." At her expression of distress he smiled, the curving of his mouth softening every harsh line of his face. "A kiss," he said. "That is all."

As if their shared kisses had not more than once led beyond. . . .

"But a small yielding," he reminded her.

Though Rhiannyn knew she ought to take her cue from the memories of their past encounters, she could not deny Maxen. It was true he asked very little considering she might now be forever spoiled had he not changed his mind. But this time she would keep control of their kiss, she vowed. Aye, one kiss and then parting. Tilting her mouth up to his, she steeled herself for the touch of his lips.

"Nay," he said. "*You* must kiss me."

Surprised, she drew back a space, but with the next breath conceded. "Do you bend your head to me, I will accommodate."

An uncommon gleam leapt into his eyes, then he bent to her.

Rising onto the tips of her toes, Rhiannyn strained her neck back and softly put her mouth against his. Surprisingly, Maxen did not move, his lips yielding to hers, but naught else. Curiously emboldened, she pressed more firmly to him and breathed his breath. Enough, she told herself as something inside her stirred, and though she started to lower her heels back to the floor, the kiss demanded completion. She gripped Maxen's forearms to steady herself and turned a chaste kiss into one that should be reserved for lovers. When he opened his mouth, her hesitation was brief, then she dipped her tongue to his.

It was heady, this kiss he had given her control of— perhaps that was the reason it affected her so. Always before she had been the recipient, giving only when given to and best intentions had run awry, but this was different. This was fresh ... exciting ... most certainly wanton. And it was more her than she had ever been.

Seeking beyond the limits a small voice told her she ought not trespass, she glided her hands up over sinewed arms, across thick shoulders, then curved one around Maxen's neck and plunged the other into his hair. At last he responded, pulling her so tightly to him her breasts were crushed between them.

"Now you are learning," he said into her mouth, then began wresting control from her.

However, Rhiannyn was not ready to relinquish. This was her kiss, and her direction. "I am not finished learning," she whispered, then determinedly grasped either side of his face and slanted her mouth across his.

Maxen's reaction was immediate, rising up between them and pressing itself to her abdomen.

Her senses falling over themselves, Rhiannyn moaned, then instinctively began moving her hips against him. However, a moment later they stood apart. Baffled by their unexpected parting, she swayed where she stood while grasping at words that completely failed her.

Maxen knew what she was at a loss for. "You would not wish it to go any further, would you?" he asked, his lower jaw thrust forward, his eyes intense.

Words—staccato and barely intelligible—tumbled from her lips. "Of ... of course not." She had nearly surrendered exactly what he had given back to her. In fact, she had, for if he had lain her back upon the bed and pushed between her legs, she did not think she would have tried to stop him. Nay, she *knew* she would not have. Thankfully, he had taken back control.

Searching for a way out from beneath her shame, she

clasped her hands at her waist, filled her lungs deeply, and met his regard. "I thank you for sparing the Saxons' lives," she said. "For believing them."

He must have know exactly what she did, but for the moment he allowed her to grasp at talk she thought might veer him from what had just transpired. "For now, 'tis what I believe," he said. "Until they prove me wrong, of course."

"They will not," she said, the conviction in her voice strong even to her own ears. "They are yours now."

He quirked an eyebrow. "And you?" he asked, sweeping her back to the subject she had tried to put behind them. "Are you mine as well?"

"What of Theta?" Rhiannyn tried again. "Surely you must know she lied."

His patience obviously taxed, he muttered, "As I am not completely certain the Saxons tell the truth, neither am I certain she lied. Now your answer, Rhiannyn. Are you mine?"

The silence grew so awkward, her thoughts and emotions so churned, Rhiannyn conceded—somewhat. "As my people have accepted you as their lord, so have I."

"You know that is not what I ask."

She looked away, then back at him. "Only do you ask my yielding in payment for the lives of the Saxons will I lay me down for you, Maxen Pendery," she said.

Another silence, then his mouth twisted with humor he shared only with himself. Returning to the chest, he again rummaged through the contents. "How are you with a needle?" he asked without looking up.

"Proficient."

"That is good, for I am most short of garments."

Then he wished her to sew for him. The realization settled like lead in the pit of Rhiannyn's stomach, though it was not the stitching she minded, but the measurements and fittings it would take to produce clothing for him. Why could he not choose another? Because he wants you willing, her mind taunted, and 'tis only a matter of time ere you present him the opportunity again.

"And clippers?" he asked, interrupting her spiteful thoughts.

"Clippers?"

To demonstrate, he scissored his fingers across his brow. "As you can see, I am in dire need of a cut."

"I fear I am not very good." It was a half-lie, for many a time she had trimmed—just a bit—her father's wild beard and evened the ends of his long hair and that of both her brothers. Well, not so much a lie, really, she excused herself, for it was true she'd had no experience with the Norman hairstyle of the crown cropped close and the back of the head shaven down to the base of the neck.

"You will do," Maxen said.

She would? Only if he preferred jagged-shorn hair to the severity of his monk's tonsure. "I will do my best," she murmured.

The tunic and hose Maxen donned were of coarse woollen and well worn, proving he had not spoken false when he had said he was in need of new garments. Sitting on the edge of the bed, he pulled on boots equally worn, then stood and walked past her. "There is much to be done this day," he said over his shoulder. "Clothe yourself and attend to your duties."

Rhiannyn stared after him long after he disappeared, her mind warring with the opposing emotions of relief for the Saxons' fate, and what had transpired between her and Maxen this morn. Unthinking, she lifted a hand and laid three fingers to her lips. How vivid the remembrance of their kiss. How sweet still the taste of his tongue upon hers. Gliding her other hand to her abdomen, she laid her palm to where he had pressed his man's flesh. How real the impression his body had left in hers. . . .

"Rhiannyn." She heard her name upon his lips even now that he was gone. But he wasn't gone, for he had returned, and so stealthily she'd been given no warning. Her heart lurching, she dropped her arms back to her sides and raised her gaze to his. "Aye?"

From the narrowing of his eyes, she saw he had noticed the guilty withdrawal of her hands from the places he had so recently touched. "No more will you work upon the wall," he said. "Understood?"

Then he meant to keep her from her people? To seclude her? "But—"

"I have spoken. Now is it understood, Rhiannyn?"

Anger returning, she jerked her head up and down. "Of course."

He turned to go, but came back around in the next instant. "I have not said you cannot see them," he said, "simply that you are not to assist them. Your duties are in the hall."

As fast as it had risen, her anger drained. "Aye, my lord," she said. "I will comply."

He nodded, then for the second time left her.

Hoping she would not cross Maxen's path, Rhiannyn followed the meal from the inner to the outer bailey where the Saxons labored upon a wall that was growing near to completion. Did the weather only hold, another sennight would likely see it done. But what then for her people? she wondered. Of what use would they be come another winter of less than adequate food? Would Maxen turn them out as Thomas had done with the others the year before, only then granting them the mock freedom he had denied them in forcing them to Etcheverry?

Her concern too great, Rhiannyn put it away—for now—and turned her attention back to the path she walked just in time to avoid tripping over a dog that had found and claimed the only ray of sunshine cast over the entire castle. Lucky dog, she thought, realizing for the first time the chill upon the air. Wishing she had tossed a mantle over her shoulders, she rubbed her arms and quickened her step to keep up with the women ahead of her.

Although Rhiannyn had offered to help carry the food and drink, Mildreth had adamantly forbidden her doing so, her only explanation being that the "lord" was returned and would not look kindly upon it. It was an awkward thing for Rhiannyn to go amongst her people with empty hands and without offer of easing their burden just a bit by assisting them. However, as soon as word spread that she had come and all eyes were turned upon her, she forgot the awkwardness as she saw their looks of surprise and guilt. Undoubtedly, they thought her sacrificed to Maxen on the night past and wondered what she did out from the donjon.

Meghan was the first to approach her—hesitantly, then with a brisk stride. "How fare you, Rhiannyn?" she asked, her voice pitched low so that no others might hear the delicate question.

"Well," Rhiannyn answered.

"Did the bastard hurt you?"

She shook her head. "Nay, he did not."

Meghan glanced at someone on the wall behind her, then back at Rhiannyn. "I canna imagine he'd be a gentle one," she murmured, "but you say he did you no harm?"

It was not an easy thing to discuss, especially with so many onlookers, but Rhiannyn knew she had to set Meghan straight. And a double purpose it would serve, for then all would be apprised by the woman's penchant for gossip, and the guilt weighing on shoulders already far too burdened would be eased. "I did not lay with him, Meghan," she said. "He . . . decided otherwise and put me to my own bed."

The woman's head jerked back as if she'd been struck, but she quickly recovered. "You don't say!" she loudly exclaimed. "Imagine that."

Though Rhiannyn knew Meghan would eventually tell all, she was dismayed at the prospect of the woman doing so at that moment. "Please, Meghan," she beseeched, "speak not so loud."

She looked around, then at Rhiannyn again. "I understand," she said.

Rhiannyn was not so certain she did.

For a moment deep in thought, Meghan twisted her lips side to side, then she grinned. " 'Twould certainly explain why he's workin' so hard," she said.

Rhiannyn frowned. "Who?"

"Pendery, of course." With a toss of her head and an upward dart of her eyes, Meghan indicated the wall behind.

Dread rising, Rhiannyn looked up the scaffolding that held half a dozen men aloft, and there to the side stood Maxen. The clouded sky the backdrop against which his magnificent form was painted, he stood looking down upon her with hands on his hips and his tunic darkened with the perspiration of common man's work.

Though they were separated by many feet, it felt to Rhiannyn as if he stood as near her as he had that morn. However, there looked to be no anger in his gaze as she had feared there might be. Indeed, his eyes smiled even if his mouth did not.

"And here we were plotting how we might make him a permanent part of the wall," Meghan said.

Rhiannyn dragged her gaze from Maxen. "A permanent part of the wall?" she repeated.

"Aye, but that was when we thought . . . er, thought he did wrong by you." Meghan chuckled. "I suppose we'll just have to let him live a bit longer. What do you think?"

Passing over the woman's attempt at humor, Rhiannyn glanced again at Maxen. "I don't understand what he is doing here."

"Workin'."

Rhiannyn grimaced. "That I can see. I just do not understand his reason when 'tis not his place."

Meghan looked around at Maxen, then back at Rhiannyn. "Impatient is what he is," she said with a one-shoulder shrug. "Says he wants the wall done that building can begin on livin' quarters here in the bailey."

"For whom?"

"Us, of course, though I won't believe it 'til I see it."

Emotions churning, Rhiannyn watched Maxen motion for the others to precede him, then she followed his descent of the ramp to the bailey where food was being laid out. If he would only stay away from her heart and stop leaving footprints all over it, she wished. If only he would remain the cur, she would be safe.

"And if that ain't doubtful enough," Meghan continued, "he says come spring he will lay out a village before the castle where we might dwell and from which we can work the land."

"He did?" Rhiannyn asked, more to herself than Meghan. Would Maxen truly provide for these people as he said, or would he fold as Thomas had? Certainly he seemed of stronger resolve than his brother, but again there was the question of who would be sacrificed when the food supplies began running low. Certainly not his Normans.

"Aye, he said it," Meghan answered, "but the winter will tell."

Rhiannyn watched Maxen pause to take drink, then continue toward her. "He comes this way," she warned.

"Does he?" Meghan looked behind her again, then turned a slow grin upon Rhiannyn. "For all the Norman that's in him, he's a fine-lookin' man," she said a mite too loudly.

Amazed, Rhiannyn blinked. For as little time as Maxen had spent among the Saxons, it didn't seem possible he could have earned even the grudging admiration of a woman who ought still to look upon him as her enemy. But that was what Meghan revealed—a woman's appreciation for a man.

"Ah well, I'll be off to get my share of food ere the gluttons take it all," Meghan said. With a flounce, she skirted Rhiannyn.

Feeling awkward beneath the furtive glances of the Saxons and the unswerving stare of Maxen, Rhiannyn clasped her hands together and awaited him.

"Meghan?" he asked as he placed himself before her. "The one who darkened your eye?"

Unsettled by his question, but knowing he already knew the answer to it, she nodded. "Aye, but we are friends now."

"Hmm," he rumbled, glancing at the woman's retreating back. However, his next words introduced another topic. "You waste no time," he said.

She knew he referred to her having come to the bailey.

"As you have forbidden me, I did not come to work, only to show them that all is well."

Maxen assumed the increasingly familiar stance of hands on hips and legs braced apart. "And is it?" he asked, his gaze probing, though there was that peculiar sparkle in his eyes.

Rhiannyn tried to suppress the small smile tugging at her lips, but it came anyway. "Aye," she said, "it is quite well. But tell me, what do you laboring on the walls when 'tis the work of one not the lord?"

"It is hard work," he said, glancing behind him.

"Then why do you do it?"

He swung his gaze back to her. "To know these Saxons of yours better."

She shook her head. "But why? Is it not enough to know them from the high seat?"

"Not if I am to gain their loyalty." He swept his hand up to stop the words of denial she had been about to speak. "Though they may not have betrayed me as you have said, 'tis not by loyalty I hold them, Rhiannyn, but by fear."

He was right. Still, there was nothing unusual about that. "It is the way of the Normans," she reminded him.

"Aye, but not my way if this land is ever to be settled in lasting peace."

Hope surged through her. "You think it will be?"

He stared at her a long moment, then looked past her. "When Edwin Harwolfson is brought to heel," he said. "Only then can peace begin."

His honesty hurt, but at least he had not lied to her. Seeking another direction for their talk, Rhiannyn turned to the events of yestereve. "What of Sir Ancel?" she asked.

His eyes narrowed. "What of him?"

Knowing he guessed that she had eavesdropped, she held her chin high to counter any condemnation he might put upon her. "I saw what happened last night."

"Did you?"

She nodded. "I heard the commotion and looked around the screen. Why do you naught about him when you must surely know 'twas he who put the dagger on my tray? When yestereve he threatened to put a blade through you himself?"

There was no condemnation in the skewed smile Maxen showed her. "Are you concerned for my welfare, Rhiannyn, or for your Saxons should Ancel accomplish what he has twice now failed to attain?"

Though weeks ago she would have denied any concern for him, she found she no longer could. "Both," she said honestly.

"I am gladdened," he said, his secret smile widening. "And hungry." Abruptly, he swung away from her.

"But what will you do?" she called after him.

He stopped, looked over his shoulder, and spoke a single word. "Wait." Then he resumed his course.

Wondering what exactly he meant, Rhiannyn stared after him, but was without answer when she turned to the donjon several minutes later. As she approached the causeway, a feeling of menace drew her eyes to the wall-walk overhead. There stood Sir Ancel, his derisive smile widening as his eyes met hers.

Immediately, Rhiannyn's feet forgot the simplicity of walking, and in the righting of her footing she was forced to break eye contact with the knight. However, when she looked up again, his gaze had travelled beyond her to where the Saxons and Maxen were filling their bellies. Shivering from head to toe with a chill not of the wind, Rhiannyn continued up the causeway.

Chapter Seventeen

Rhiannyn was given ten days of reprieve before Maxen paid her any more attention other than probing glances and the odd brushing of their sleeves in passing. With the completion of the wall five days past, he now spent the daylight hours in the hall with the demesne books, the steward, and one or another of his knights—usually Sir Guy.

Whatever pressing business he had that was responsible for his disregard of her, Rhiannyn told herself she was thankful. It allowed her time with her people she might otherwise not have had, and an easing of spirit she had been too long without. But it was also difficult, for Theta took every opportunity to belittle her, taunt her, and in front of her, regale others with tales of Maxen's latest acts of sexual prowess. Rhiannyn tried not to believe her, but the little devil on her shoulder was vigilant with reminders of Maxen's loss of interest.

"Fine, fine," she muttered as she lifted the pry bar for the ale barrel from its hook. She didn't care. Really she didn't. Putting all her strength behind her, she worked the flat end of the bar beneath the lid of the barrel, then pressed her weight upon it. However, for all her effort, it gave very little. Grumbling, she tried again. Unfortunately, the bar slipped out of position and, catching her off balance, landed her upon her backside amid the dirt.

Exasperated, Rhiannyn looked over her shoulder to the butler whose job it was to dispense the castle's drink. Aldwin sat in the corner, perfectly oblivious after a night of too much ale—no different from the night before, or the night before that.

Sighing, Rhiannyn stood and brushed herself off. At least Aldwin was a kind sort, she thought, excusing the sorrowful old man his fondness for brew. Retrieving the bar, she determinedly approached the barrel again.

"Rhiannyn," Lucilla's voice drifted down the stairs of the cellar.

Rhiannyn peered up at the woman where she stood atop the step. "Aye?"

"Lord Pendery asks for you. He said to tell you 'tis time."

Time? Whatever could he mean? That he wished her in his bed was the first thought that came to her. But no, he had freed her of that obligation. Unless, of course, he had changed his mind. . . . "Did he say what it was time for?" she asked.

"Only that you would know, but dally not, for he seems on the impatient side."

Laying the bar atop the barrel, Rhiannyn mounted the steps, shared a questioning look with Lucilla, then proceeded to the hall.

Maxen stood alone behind the great table. To the right of him were his ever-present books, to the left, bolts of cloth ranging in color from white to a blue so deep it looked like the night sky of a full moon. He looked up only when she stood directly opposite him.

"Time, my lord?" she asked.

For the first time in days, he did more than glance at her, sweeping his gaze over her twice before answering. "You have forgotten," he finally said.

She frowned.

He smiled. Then he reached for the scissors that lay beside the books and held them out to her.

Understanding dawning on her, Rhiannyn took them from him. He meant her to cut his hair, which also meant the cloth was for the garments he wished her to sew for him. "I thought, perhaps, you had decided against it," she said.

"Nay, there just has not been enough time."

"And now there is?"

He lowered himself into his chair. "Not really, but the hair is in my eyes and ears and is become most annoying."

Resigned to the task, Rhiannyn walked around the table. "A bench would be better," she suggested, noting that the high-backed chair would prove a hindrance for her.

Maxen vacated the chair, seated himself upon the bench, and pulled the largest of the demesne books—the ledger—in front of him. "Shorten the fringe to the same length as the crown," he said referring to the halo of hair, "and the sides a bit, but leave the back long. I wish it to grow out."

"But 'tis not Norman," she said.

"I have always preferred the Saxon hairstyle, or lack of it. But as I have no choice in the matter of the hair atop my head, I must needs compromise."

As Rhiannyn had seen when Maxen's men were Thomas's, more and more of the Normans were adopting the Saxon hairstyle, but never had Thomas. Though he had allowed his men to do so, he had declared that a baron of King William's must maintain the face of Norman dominance. Maxen, however, seemed of a different mind, but then, he was very different from Thomas.

Lifting the scissors, Rhiannyn parted off a section of his hair and began cutting—at first with great indecision, but a short time later with vision. The silvered blades flashed, their meeting time and again a crisp hiss in the silence of her task and Maxen's attention upon his books.

"What a curiosity," she mused after a time. "A Saxon holding over a Norman what could truly be made a weapon against him." Not that she was of such a mind—certainly she was not—but still the thought came upon her. "Are you not worried I might do you harm?"

"I am not," Maxen said without looking up.

Rhiannyn paused mid-snip and waited for his gaze to turn upon her. However, even though he must have sensed it, he remained focused on the book before him. "How is it you trust me in this, but not in other things?" she asked.

Heaving a sigh, Maxen looked up from his figures. "You lie, Rhiannyn—granted, more for others than yourself—but still you lie. You are more willful than any woman I have ever known, and you test my patience so that I must constantly adjust the bounds, but you are not capable of murder."

"Yet you hold me responsible for Thomas's death," she unthinkingly reminded him. Damn it all! she silently cursed. Never should she have said it, especially in the face of the small peace they now managed. A peace about to explode into renewed hostility.

To her surprise, Maxen's eyes grew only a bit hard, his mouth a pinch tight, and when he spoke his voice was level and beset with only a trace of ire. "Responsibility and murder are two different things, Rhiannyn. We have already established that 'twas another who killed him—your faceless hider in the woods."

Leave the subject be, Rhiannyn told herself, but she could not. "But I am as guilty, am I not?" she asked.

Immediately, Maxen tossed the question back at her. "Are you?"

She blinked. Shouldn't he be ready to agree with her, rather than offer her room to defend herself? The willful part of her he had spoken of pressed for her to turn away from further talk of Thomas's death, but the other part badly wanted him to understand. "I only wanted to escape him," she said. "No harm did I wish him."

Maxen absorbed her pitiful defense, then said, "Though Edwin wished him harm, didn't he?"

Again set off-center by his seeming lack of enmity, Rhiannyn was slow in answering. "They fought, but by all I might swear upon, Edwin did not do it, Maxen. You must believe me."

"I do," he said without hesitation, then, in the midst of her wide-eyed surprise, asked, "Why did you not flee with him?"

"I—I should have," she said, trying not to see again that fateful day awash in crimson and gray, "but I could not leave Thomas to die alone."

"Why?"

How had her comment of scissors being made into a weapon come to this, Rhiannyn wondered, and why did she feel this pressing need for Maxen's acceptance of her accounting? "I may not have loved him as he wished me to," she said, "but I cared for him. Your brother was a good man."

"And foolish," Maxen said. "He should have let you go." Suddenly, he laughed. " 'Twould seem I am the same fool, though, for neither will I let you go, and do you think to flee me as you did Thomas, I would also come after you." His eyes serious—searching—he lifted a hand and laid it alongside her jaw. "I wonder, Rhiannyn, will you be the death of me?"

She shook her head. "Though I thought once to escape you, 'tis my vow to you that I will not. I have accepted my lot here at Etcheverry."

"And if Edwin comes for you again?"

"Do you not understand?" she pleaded. "As I did not go with him when he came, neither will I go with him does he return."

"Will he return?"

She frowned. "I do not know. There is only Aethel now, and the four others who would go with Edwin were he able to release them from the dungeons. 'Twould seem a great risk for so few."

Maxen dropped his hand from her. "Aye, but Saxons

are wont to taking great risks," he said, then sank into reflections he did not share with her.

However, Rhiannyn was certain she knew what he was
contemplating. "Maxen, pray do not use Aethel and the
others to your own end," she said. "They may not have
chosen your way, but still they are good men." At least
Aethel was, for of the four others there was not one she
knew well enough to pass judgment.

"What would you have me do?" Maxen asked. "Release
them?"

"I would," she said, though she knew she asked far too
much.

Disregarding her appeal, he thoughtfully rubbed a hand
across his shaven jaw. " 'Tis the gallows I ought to send
them to," he said.

"Why haven't you?"

He looked as if he might disregard her question, but
then he shrugged and gave her an answer quite unexpected. "Part of me admires them. Though it would serve
me better to ensure I need never again engage them in battle, 'tis not so easy to fault a man who stands for his be-
liefs."

Lord, but it was a day of revelations, Rhiannyn thought.
Never would she have guessed Maxen capable of such an
admission. Yet it made sense of why he had not yet dealt
with the Saxons. "Then what will you do?"

"They ought to have had plenty of time for thought,"
he said. "Mayhap now they will be more willing to accept
me as the others have."

"And if they do not?"

He pushed a hand through the hair she had clipped.
"As much as I admire them, Rhiannyn, I cannot say one
thing and do another."

Her heart sank a little, but not nearly so deep as it
would have had he not offered her any hope. "I know," she
said, for it was the way of things, and would always be the
way of things for those who dared step in the path of
might over right.

"Continue," Maxen ordered, bringing the discussion to an end.

Taking up the scissors again, Rhiannyn applied them to his hair while her mind spun back and forth over all they had spoken of. Why he had deigned to speak of such things with her was a mystery, for she would more have expected him to refuse talk beyond the complication of what still lay unresolved between them. But somehow they had avoided that. . . .

Clipping by clipping, Maxen's hair fell away until all that was left to cut was that above his brow. "Do you turn," she said to him, "I will finish."

Without a word, he swung his legs over the bench and faced her.

However, Rhiannyn was not prepared to stand between the thighs that came on either side of her. It was enough that she had spent so long a time in his immediate presence—sliding fingers over his scalp and pulling them through his hair—but this? Avoiding the watchful gaze he lifted to her, she stepped to the side, but he drew her back between his legs.

" 'Tis easier this way," he said when her startled eyes met his.

Easier for him, but not her, she thought, but no word of it would she speak. She would bear it and soon enough be done with his hair and him. Trying not to dwell on the straddle of his thighs, she lifted the scissors and set about her task again.

Though it did not take long to finish the cut, it seemed hours, for Maxen's presence and touch were deep-felt. "You are done," she said, stepping back to survey her work.

"Better?" he asked.

"Indeed." She was more pleased than she had thought she would be. The monk was completely gone from Maxen, the last of him scattered upon his shoulders, the bench, and the rushes. Before her was a man more handsome for it.

"Good," he said. Standing, he brushed the hair from

his tunic, stomped his legs to shake it from his hose, then swept it from the bench. When he was done, he regained the high seat and motioned to the cloth. "For my garments," he said.

Stepping beside him, Rhiannyn lifted the beautiful blue and rubbed it between her fingers. " 'Twill make a fine tunic," she said. "And the others." She touched each bolt in turn.

"The blue is for you."

She jerked her gaze back to the fine material, then to him. "Whatever for?" she exclaimed.

Distastefully, he plucked at the skirt of the old bliaut she wore. "I am most tired of seeing you clothed in such."

"But 'tis as you ordered."

"Never did I order you to sloven yourself."

It was true she was the most poorly clothed of the wenches, but it had suited her fine—especially as it kept eyes from her that she did not wish upon her. Still, if Maxen wished her finer clothes, there were always those Thomas had provided her. Nay, they were too fine, she remembered, their material of the same quality as the blue, but heavily embellished with embroidery, and one even set with gems about the neck.

"The blue is not at all suitable for a serving wench," she said. Pushing the material aside, she pulled forth another. "Mayhap the brown."

Maxen dragged the blue back over the brown. "This one," he said in a tone that made it abundantly clear he would suffer no argument on the matter. "And if there is any remaining after you are done with it, you may fashion me a tunic."

Knowing it would do her no good to breach his patience further that day, Rhiannyn shrugged. "Very well," she conceded. Deciding it past time she left him to his books, she began gathering the bolts into her arms.

"Leave them," he said. "Later I will have them delivered to my chamber."

She looked back at him. "Your chamber?"

"Aye, a quiet place to make stitches, don't you think?"

A dangerous place to make stitches. "I can just as well sew before the hearth," she pointed out.

One side of Maxen's mouth hitched into a smile. "If that is what you wish," he said, "but the cloth will be stored in my chest."

"Fine." She stepped away. "I will begin this eve after supper."

"Rhiannyn."

She looked back at him.

"As my need is not so great, attend to your bliaut first."

She had planned exactly the opposite, but if that was what he wanted . . .

"My lord," a voice interrupted.

Both looked to Guy's hurried entrance into the hall.

"What is it?" Maxen asked.

The knight lifted a thinly rolled parchment. "A reply from Trionne."

The Castle Trionne, Rhiannyn knew, home of Maxen and Christophe's parents. "I will take my leave now," she said, stepping from behind the table.

Maxen allowed her departure, his mind now fully upon the missive being passed into his hands.

As she crossed the hall, Rhiannyn heard him speak. " 'Tis good," he said. "The supplies are being amassed and should arrive ere the new month."

Rhiannyn made quick sense of his words. The stores badly needed to tide Etcheverry through the winter were on their way—and from Trionne, no less. During the winter past, Thomas's father had been able to assist very little, his own harvests scant, but this year a blessing must have been upon them. One great worry in her easing, Rhiannyn quickened her steps with the thought that she must tell Mildreth, for the woman's fretting was even greater than her own.

"So, it will not be such a chill winter after all," Guy's voice drifted to her.

The parchment crackled. "Only if the others—Sir Jeremy of Bronton and Darik of Westering—also provide."

Rhiannyn's step faltered. Then Trionne could not render all they needed . . . ?

"Think you they will?" Guy asked.

"If they are able to, for 'tis their lives they are owing to me."

Norman lives Maxen had saved at Hastings, Rhiannyn guessed. Oh pray, let them be able to send stores as well. Rounding the corner, she leaned back against the wall and listened. It was not good of her, she knew, but she had to know what might be said once it was thought she was no longer present.

"The Saxons will be a great burden upon the foodstuffs if there are no more stores forthcoming," Guy continued.

Rhiannyn held her breath for Maxen's reply.

"All will be a great burden," he said, "but none will be treated any different. If winter hunting is what is required to feed all, then that is what we shall do."

Rhiannyn slumped as if struck by the force of Maxen moving through her, burrowing a place just beneath her heart. He truly did care, and would provide for the Saxons even as he provided for his Normans.

"It will not be easy," Guy said.

"I do not expect it to be."

Pushing away from the wall, Rhiannyn hurried down the corridor and out into a cold, biting day that suddenly seemed tenfold warmer than when she had earlier passed beneath the same overcast sky.

A fortnight later, the awaited missives arrived in the wake of news of Edwin Harwolfson's plundering to the west. Few were the details gathered about the man, but much was the talk of the growing number of Saxons joining with him to form a larger, stronger rebellion than he had accumulated in the woods of Andredeswald. No doubt Edwin gathered into his fold many of those already touched by the coming winter—Saxons without any hope of surviving the season unless they joined with him to take what they were not given.

Grown weary of the talk that filled every corner of the hall, Maxen chose to open the missives in private. Turning from the nooning meal that had just been called, he strode to his chamber, dropped into the chair, and broke the first wax seal. A scan of the parchment was all it took for him to smile with relief. Darik of Westering would not fail him, the promised supplies to follow shortly. However, Jeremy of Bronton's missive wiped the smile away. The knight offered naught but sincere regrets, his anger over the loss of a great number of his winter's supplies to the "wolf"— Edwin Harwolfson—evident in every line.

Laying the parchment aside, Maxen ground the heels of his hands into his eyes. He knew exactly what must be done to curb a voracious Edwin, and that it was he whom King William would call upon to do it. Fortunately, he had all of winter in which to plan the Saxon's downfall, for it would be spring ere he was ordered to duty. And then there would be more killing. . . .

Abruptly, he stood from the chair. Nay, he would not think of it now. Instead, he would join his men for the meal and think of the woman whom he had yet to bring into his bed. Unfortunately, these past weeks had been too filled with the laying-in of winter to allow him the indulgence of pursuing Rhiannyn, but now there was time aplenty.

Chapter Eighteen

"The wolf!" Elan Pendery said scornfully into the wind she rode against. So much talk of a man—a mere man—and a Saxon at that. Well others might fear him, but not she. Why, if ever she came upon him, she would simply trample him beneath her horse. She giggled at the vision born of her fertile mind.

Aye, she would see him well dead for all he had put her through these past days. Only when her people had crossed the channel two years ago to claim a throne rightfully theirs had she ever been so confined to the boredom of castle walls, but at ten and four she hadn't minded so much, for she'd had Christophe to entertain her. But he was gone now to Etcheverry, and with him all the great fun they had made together. Now she must find amusement elsewhere—or, considering this day's turn of events, a place to more fully worry over her father's unwelcome pronouncement. The remembrance of it stole the smile from her face and blanked the scenery from before her eyes.

Six months ago she had been too indifferent to propriety and too overcome to be concerned for the future, but now it was upon her and it was the most terrible thing she had ever met with. That morn she had swallowed dismay with her bread and cheese when her father had announced he had finally made a suitable match for her. One Sir Arthur, a man of no less than forty years, three wives now passed on, four children, and a demesne equal to that of Trionne. But that was not what bothered Elan so, though it certainly invited no squeals of delight from her. It was that other thing, which would be discovered about her once she was wed. Ah, it had been a mistake for certain, the same recklessness that seemed to come in most things she set herself to, but naught could change the past. Nor the traces of it.

But no, she would not dwell too deeply upon it, not just yet, she told herself. Time aplenty lay ahead in the hours before last light.

He saw her long before she saw him, and that was just as it should be. But who was she, this fair maiden who, from the top of her head to her fine woollen mantle, and down to the toes of her slippers, looked to be all of a lady? And what was she doing unescorted away from the castle?

For all the anger that now seemed so much a part of him, Edwin could not help but smile. Aye, lovely, her ashen hair visible as the stirring air lifted her veil from it as she rode nearer and nearer the bordering woods. As she drew closer, Edwin saw she was not quite as dainty as she'd appeared from a distance, but neither was she uncommonly large. Of average form, he would say, but on the surface, that was the only thing average about her. Though he had yet to tell the color of her eyes, they snapped with light and life as she scanned the land before her. And then from that pretty mouth came exultant laughter. She recklessly spurred her horse across the threshold of the woods, and only when fully hidden from sight of the castle did she slow—not fifty feet from where Edwin stood, spying on the castle of Trionne.

"Once again, my dear," she said to herself, speaking aloud in perfect Anglo-Saxon, "you have done it—escaped them one and all!" Then she grimaced, an expression that might have turned any other's face unattractive, but not hers. "Not that any shall notice," she added, barely loud enough for Edwin to be certain he had heard right.

What a curious creature, he thought. And very likely useful. Aye, she was a lady and would no doubt be of good purpose to him.

Looking over his shoulder, Edwin sharply motioned for those hidden behind and to the side of him to remain unmoving. He would not have any one of them spoiling this opportunity that had unexpectedly fallen into his lap.

The men nodded, then sank more deeply into their hiding places.

Only when the lady clicked her tongue and prodded her horse to proceed more deeply into the woods did Edwin move, using the sounds of her movement to mask his. In this way he eventually overtook her and gained ground ahead of her, thus to arouse less suspicion in her than if he'd revealed himself at the edge of the woods.

Then the act began. "Testra!" he called as he backtracked where he had just tread. "Testra." He had but to call twice more for a horse nowhere near before the lady came upon him.

Her blue eyes opening wide, she reined her horse in and stared warily at Edwin, who was pretending his own surprise.

"Who are you?" she demanded in a voice still too young to hide the childishness it was leaving behind.

She could not be more than six and ten, Edwin realized. Not that sixteen was so young, but he had thought her older than she now showed herself to be.

"I fear I have lost my horse," Edwin said, "or rather, he has lost me."

She was not going to allow her question to go unanswered. Looking down from her mount, she asked, "Who are you to come onto my father's lands?"

Her father's lands . . . As the smile was just too difficult to hide, Edwin used it as a sign of friendliness and stepped forward. "Your father's lands?" he repeated.

"Aye, Baron Pendery, possessor of all you have no doubt tramped this day."

Maxen's sister, then, and a far more useful pawn than Edwin would ever have hoped for. But how to convince her to come down from her horse so he might ensure stealing her away? "I am Bacus," he said, using the name of his brother fallen at Hastings, "come from across the wood to seek winter shelter at yon castle."

For all her youth, something wise and measured showed in the lady's eyes. "Is that so?" she asked.

"'Tis so."

"Hmm," she murmured, her gaze swiftly gauging him from head to toe before returning to his face. "Of what village are you, Saxon?"

"I am of no village, which is the reason I seek to avail myself of Trionne."

"You and hundreds of others," she said. "Have you something to offer they have not?"

Edwin closed the distance between them by two steps made to appear casual, but still he would not be able to reach for her should she spur the horse away. "I am well fit with knowledge of horses—training and care," he answered. "But tell me, by what name are you called, daughter of Pendery?"

She hesitated, then smiled faintly and said, "I am Lady Elan."

"Ah, I should have guessed, for your beauty is exactly as I have heard it spoken of."

No stranger to flattery, she sat straighter in the saddle. "Is it?"

Edwin used her moment of vain unguardedness to bring himself half a dozen steps nearer her. Now but a lunge was all it would require to have her from the horse.

"Aye, Lady Elan, how my eyes ache just to look upon you," he said, feeding her what she so hungered for.

She batted her eyelashes, swept the tip of a very pink tongue across her bottom lip, then smiled fully enough to reveal two rows of even teeth. But there was something else about her that she unintentionally granted him a glimpse of—an assessing of him for some purpose she did not wish him to know of.

"And what do you hope to gain with such uncommon flattery, my good man?" she asked. "Is it truly winter shelter, or a tumble up my skirts?" Amidst the surprise he could not hide, she leaned forward and in a conspiratorial tone, added, "Or is it something else you seek, *Bacus*?"

Of vainglory and unladylike daring she was, but she was also astute, Edwin acknowledged. Had she guessed who he was? Nay, even she could not be so fool or so reckless as to engage him in such conversation did she know his true identity. For certain, she was suspicious, but she did not know, could not know, unless this was a clever trap laid for "the wolf." It seemed hardly possible that it might be, for he had advanced upon Trionne with the tightest control of his forces, and those he had left a short space behind had yet to call out a warning.

"And what do you think I seek, my lady?" he asked.

She shifted upon her saddle, made a show of inspecting her fingernails, then turned her gaze back to him. "I think you are neither named Bacus, nor come to seek shelter at Trionne," she said. "And Testra—that is your horse's name, is it not?—is likely tethered nearby."

If a trap, she played her part poorly by voicing her suspicion, but still Edwin was wary. He raised his eyebrows. "Ah, then who might I be, and what think you I am doing in your wood?" he asked.

Unexpectedly, she put out a hand and motioned him forward to assist in her alighting.

And now the trap would be sprung if it was indeed that, Edwin thought. Prepared for wherever it might descend from, his ears alert, his eyes watchful, and the dagger and sword beneath his mantle a hand away, he took the two strides to her mount. Then, raising his arms to her, he easily lifted her down to the ground.

Naught. Not even the whisper of a breeze begot by advancing soldiers, nor the vibration of their coming beneath his thin-soled boots. Nay, not a trap, but a woman filled with foolishness.

When Edwin released her, she took no step back as a lady ought to, but tipped her face up and smiled at him. "I think . . ." she murmured, playing at thoughts she no doubt already knew quite well.

Something raw and long unanswered strained within Edwin as he looked upon her comeliness and felt the warmth of her body cross the very small space between them. In her face were set eyes of blue framed by long lashes; beneath, a fine nose; and below, a mouth full and red. It was by no artifice she was made so lovely—God had made her so.

Lifting a hand, the lady Elan idly tapped a finger against her lips, then affected sudden revelation. "I think you are one of those Saxons who does not yet accept his Norman master."

Perceptive, Edwin granted her, but not in the safeguarding of her person. In this she was most unwise. "If that is your belief," he said, "why then do you stand unafraid before me?"

It hardly seemed possible she could come any nearer without making contact with him, but she did just that, causing a desire thoroughly unlike that of revenge to fill Edwin's loins. "Because, Bacus of no lord," she said in a husky voice, "I like what fills my eyes."

It was Edwin who stepped back. Good God, the brat was seducing him! And doing a fine job at that. Could she be lying when she called herself a lady, in claiming to be Elan Pendery? he wondered. No lady he had ever known had been so brash and provocative. Certainly Rhiannyn had never acted in such manner, and she had been a lady only by Thomas Pendery's decree. Only village whores behaved so, and many a skirt he had flung up on those willing wenches.

"I can see I have put you off," the woman-child said, remorse edging her voice, though it was not reflected upon her face.

Skeptical, Edwin stared at her. "It surprises me to hear a lady speak so," he said, "making me question if you are, indeed, that."

"There is a time to be a lady and a time to be a woman," she said, recovering the distance he had put between them, "and for the moment—nay, the afternoon—I prefer to be a woman."

Whoever she was, a fine tumble she would make, but Edwin was too taken aback to act on his man's instincts. But perhaps this was a dream and only that, he reasoned when all else failed to explain the oddity. Certainly it would explain the outlandishness of a woman who appeared to be a lady, but spoke and acted in a manner entirely opposite gentle breeding.

"How much more invitation would you like, Saxon?" she asked as she pulled the brooch from her mantle. A moment later, the garment slid down her body and pooled at her feet, revealing a jewel-encrusted bliaut and a figure as lovely as her face.

Damn, Edwin silently cursed, but this woman—or was she a girl?—made him feel like an untried boy. His pride in danger of being ground beneath her pretty slippers, he reacted as he ought to have ere she began this maddening banter of hers. Grasping her upper arms, he dragged her so fully against him her breasts flattened to his chest and her woman's place settled firmly below his man's. Then he claimed her mouth—or perhaps she claimed his. No matter, she tasted of honey and all that a woman should taste of. Lady or whore, Elan Pendery or pretender, she was his to do with as he pleased. And he pleased mightily.

He touched her, fondled her, probed, and in return was explored with an enthusiasm that heated his blood with a want he could not deny. Forgetting all but the hunger of his flesh for hers, he backed her against a tree, tugged her skirts high, lowered his braies, and took her—not gently as he would have a virgin, for his first thrust breached no flesh that had not been breached before, but with the savageness of a man not a gentleman with a woman not a lady. Though the thought flitted through his mind that she was not as experienced as she made out to be, it found no place to rest within his ardor and darted away in the next instant.

Elan—or whatever her name was—clung to him, sighed, moaned, tossed her head side to side, then affected a cry of culmination that nearly undid Edwin's very real response. She was a pretender through and through, he thought the moment before he emptied himself into her. His breathing ragged, his senses deluged, he slackened against her.

"Ah, Bacus," she sighed, squeezing herself around him. "I knew you would not disappoint me."

Liar, he wanted to call her, but was too pleasured to interrupt his downward spiral.

"Did I please you?" she asked.

He withheld his answer just long enough to savor the last of his body's tremors, then braced an arm against the tree, pushed himself back a space, and looked into her expectant eyes. "What do you think?" he asked.

She smiled. "I think you would have me again if you were able to."

What was she up to? he wondered. "And you think I am not?"

She shrugged. "Perhaps, but I have not yet met a man who could."

Though Edwin knew it would only be a short time before he could perform again, he suddenly had no desire to do so. She had fulfilled a need of his—one of the basest—but to play any more of her game was too distasteful to excite him further. "I am finished," he said. Stepping back, he pulled his braies up and left her to put order to herself.

She did so lingeringly, as if to entice him back to her, but when he did not bite, heaved a sigh and pushed off the tree. "That is it, then?" she asked.

"How is it you came alone into the woods?" he asked,

wishing to speak no more of what had transpired between them. "I would not think your *father* would allow it."

"He did not," she said, her act of a grown sexual woman falling away to reveal the genuine pleasure of the child that was still so much a part of her.

"Then who?" he prompted.

Looking quite pleased with herself, she said, "The guard at the postern gate. We have an understanding, he and I."

An understanding. Then they were lovers. "I am sure," Edwin said, making no attempt to keep derision from his voice.

She wagged a finger at him. "Ah, nay, Bacus, not that kind of an understanding."

"What, then?"

She made a play of patting her veil down her hair before answering. "As I am fond of freedom, so is he of fine drink. One for the other, you see."

The Norman greed, Edwin labeled the man's conduct. He put his pleasure before the safety of his lord's daughter—if she was that. "The man ought to be flogged and clapped into irons for making such a bargain," he said. "No Saxon would ever allow it."

She laughed. "But he *is* a Saxon," she said, reminding Edwin that the Penderys had resided on English soil when it had still been English, their association with the Saxons going back twenty or more years.

"A Saxon turned Norman, then," he said.

"One or the other, I don't understand what concern 'tis of yours. Unless . . ." Making a pretense of treading carefully, she picked her way over to Edwin, tossed her head back, and beamed a wide smile at him. "Can it be you have come to care for me in so short a time, Bacus?"

Such an enigma she was, he mused. Part of him fancied her, and the other spurned her. Mayhap it would be different when—and if—she left the child behind to become fully woman, but as she was, she could only mean trouble for him.

Forget that she might be Elan Pendery, unlikely as it

seemed, Edwin advised himself, forget that she might be a useful pawn against the Castle Trionne. Just content thyself with the taking of her. It was done now, and that was enough. Besides, if he wanted more of her, by the morrow he would hold all of Trionne, including her. Aye, best not to muddy the way now with such an impetuous one whose absence might alert old man Pendery to those in his woods.

"And now you are back to Trionne?" he asked as he walked her to her horse.

"I suppose I am," she said, "unless, of course, you'd like my aid in locating your mount."

He looked at her and saw a mixture of childish teasing and adult knowing in her eyes. Aye, she knew there was no missing horse to be found, knew he lied in everything the same as she, but still she showed no fear of him.

"Nay," he said. "I am sure the beast is not far off."

Thoughtfully, she stroked a hand across her horse's flank—once, twice, then again before her eyes returned to his. "As you will," she said, then offered him her arm. "Do you hand me up, I will be on my way."

He raised her back to her saddle with near as much ease as when he had lifted her down. "Fare thee well," he said, stepping back to allow her to turn her horse out of the woods.

She nodded and steered her mount around for leave-taking. However, little distance separated them when she pulled in the reins and looked back at him. "I know who you are, Edwin Harwolfson," she said, a bittersweet smile tugging at her lips. As he stared in shock, she added, "I knew the moment I came upon you."

He jerked free of his stupor. For what purpose had this woman come knowingly upon him, risking herself and giving her body to him? "What is your game?" he asked, in an instant determining that he might just be able to reach her ere she put heels to her horse and fled.

"Farewell, Edwin," she said, sounding just a bit sad. Then, with a snap of her wrist and a nudge of her heels, she spurred her horse forward through the trees.

Knowing that if he was to salvage any of his plans for

Trionne he must apprehend her, Edwin bolted after her with all that was in him. Over thicket, muddy ground, and stream he bounded, around trees and beneath low-hanging branches he raced. Although at times his reward seemed within reach, finally, his breath rasping from him, anger suffusing him, Edwin surrendered the chase. He stood at the edge of the wood staring out upon the meadow, into the midst of which sped horse and rider. Gradually the two diminished in size until they appeared but a speck against the looming castle, and then they disappeared altogether.

Aloud, Edwin cursed himself and his body's needs, but most especially his stupidity in allowing the vixen her freedom. Elan Pendery or not, she was of that place, and now he could not risk trying to obtain what was to have been his greatest triumph to date, and the cornerstone of the Saxon uprising—Trionne Castle.

"Accursed Penderys," he growled, then slammed his fist into the trunk of the nearest tree, bloodying his knuckles. Feeling no pain, only deepening rage and a desire for revenge that bordered on the obsessive, he drew his arm back a second time. However, he did not strike again, for Dora came suddenly to mind. Aye, she would know what to do. She always knew, just as she had known Rhiannyn would betray him and lay with another.

Chapter Nineteen

There was great cause to celebrate at Etcheverry, for this day the promised supplies had arrived from Trionne. However, though wine and ale flowed freely, the platters of viands were only slightly more generous than they had been the previous weeks.

Although many grumbled that they were allowed little taste of the windfall, Maxen stood firm, refusing them the gluttony that would unnecessarily diminish the foodstuffs that must sustain them through the winter—a winter that seemed to weigh heavily upon his mind.

Avoiding his gaze that lately seemed ever upon her, and most especially this night when she first wore the blue bliaut made of his cloth, Rhiannyn moved down the table filling tankards and goblets as she went. Too soon, the last drop of ale dripped from the lip of her pitcher, sending her once again to the barrel set against the wall. However, it proved as empty as her vessel.

Had the last wench who'd dipped into it called for another to be brought up from the cellar? she wondered. And if she had, was the butler arranging to have it brought up, or was he too deep in his cups to make any sense of the request?

Knowing it fell to her to investigate the situation, Rhiannyn hurriedly crossed the hall and descended the steps to the cellar. There she discovered Aldwin where he could be found most times—in the corner slumped upon a stool.

"Aldwin," she groaned, "now what am I to do?" No answer, not that she'd expected one, just the steady rise and fall of his chest.

With no other thought but to be quick about filling her pitcher, Rhiannyn retrieved the pry bar she had been unsuccessful with the last time she had tried to use it, and walked to the nearest ale barrel. However, she had only just slid the tool beneath the lip when a sound echoed to her from the dungeons where Aethel and the others remained imprisoned. She froze, wanting badly to go to them, but knowing she would never make it past the guard.

After minutes of unbroken silence during which she listened intently to discover the source of the noise, she returned to the task of opening the barrel. This time the lid gave to her efforts. Filled with triumph, she laid the lid aside and dipped her pitcher into the ale. It was then she heard it again, followed by the throaty laugh of a woman. Theta?

Rhiannyn's curiosity greater than her prudence, she set her pitcher atop an unopened barrel and crossed to the entrance of the dungeon. Poking her head around the door frame, she peered down the dimly lit corridor to where shadows convulsed upon the walls across from the guard's station. Almost immediately there came more laughter, then groaning as if someone were in pain. But it was not pain, Rhiannyn knew, for she had heard such sounds before—when her parents had thought she and her brothers slept, when Thomas had summoned Theta to his bed, when the knights took wenches to their pallets, and when Maxen had made love to her on the trestle table. . . .

Shunting that last memory aside, she put a foot forward, then hesitated. Ah, Lord, but she really shouldn't, she told herself as she vacillated between returning to the hall and taking advantage of an opportunity that might never come her way again. With all that stood between her and Maxen—the lies, the deceit, the accusations, and misunderstandings—and twice now his mercy upon the Saxons, she really shouldn't tempt fate. She really shouldn't.

But she did. Stepping lightly down the corridor, she watched as, ahead, the shadows heaved in the mating ritual she was less innocent of than she'd been before Maxen Pendery. Though she felt the heat of a blush brought on by the remembrance of her time with Maxen, she continued forward without misstep.

In the small alcove that was the guard's station, Rhiannyn came upon the lovers, though she was careful not to be seen herself. A glimpse was all it took for her to confirm it was Theta the guard had lured to his dreary world beneath the castle. Her black hair loosed and tumbling like a curtain down her back, her head thrown back, she sat on the man's lap facing him while he pushed up into her.

Quickly, Rhiannyn slipped past the station and headed for the cells that lay around the bend. However, upon turning the corner, she abruptly halted in the chilly, dark place, in which terrible memories had been made not so long ago. She shivered as those remembrances swelled within her— days and nights without end when a vengeful Ancel had come to her, and later when a faceless Maxen had put fear into her. It had been as she'd imagined Hell must be. Surely it was the same for Aethel and the others.

That thought jolting her back to action, Rhiannyn retraced her steps, retrieved a torch she prayed would not be missed, then ventured forth. When she came to the open cell in which Maxen had first presented himself to her, she faltered, but did not stop. Rounding the bend, she felt the cells ahead beckon to her, though no sounds issued from them.

Did Aethel and the others sleep? she wondered. The thought that they might no longer be there, and the implications therefrom, were too horrible to contemplate. Aye, they must be sleeping, for it was near on night—not that they would know the moon from the sun in this place.

"Who goes?" a voice boomed ahead of her, startling her. Aethel.

"'Tis I," she answered in a high whisper. "Rhiannyn."

"Rhiannyn," another's voice echoed.

"Whore," said another.

"I am here," Aethel said, pushing his large fingers through the door's grate to show her.

He was in the end cell—the same in which she had spent so many days.

Ignoring the faces that pressed to the other grates she passed, Rhiannyn lifted the torch and shined it on the small opening, which revealed a portion of Aethel's bearded face.

"Have you a key?" he asked.

She shook her head. "Nay, I—"

"Then why have you come?"

"I had to," she said.

"He sent you?"

Maxen. "Nay, I have come without his knowledge."

"Come to pay your last respects ere the bastard hoists us to our deaths, hmm?" one of the others sneered.

Although Rhiannyn wanted to deny it, she did not know Maxen's plans for them, for not since their discussion while she had cut his hair weeks past had he spoken of them. "Has he come to you?" she asked.

"He has," Aethel answered, "bringing with him his lies of food, shelter, and land for all who settle themselves peacefully beneath his rule."

And, of course, they had declined Maxen's offer. "Would you rather suffer death than the chance that he speaks true?" she asked.

"A Norman speak true?" the Saxon in the cell beside

Aethel's said scornfully. "Just because he beds you well, does not mean God speaks through him."

"He does not bed me!" Rhiannyn exclaimed just a bit too loudly.

" 'Tis not what the wench, Theta, tells us," another hissed through the grate.

"Keep your mouths about you," Aethel reprimanded them.

It should not have surprised her that Theta had come to the cells to work her worst upon Rhiannyn's name, but it did. "Theta lies," she said.

"Is that so?" Aethel said. "Then is it also a lie that you alerted the Normans when Edwin came for us?"

" 'Twas Theta who notified the Normans, not I," Rhiannyn said.

"And we are to believe you who led Maxen Pendery to our camp?" Aethel snapped. "Do you think us fools?"

" 'Tis true he followed me," Rhiannyn admitted, though her heart was sinking ever faster, "but I did not knowingly lead him."

"Nor knowingly follow him back to Etcheverry Castle after he murdered three of ours," he added with cutting sarcasm.

It was futile. Never would she be believed. "I will defend myself no more," she said, holding Aethel's gaze and wishing it were the gentle one she had so often encountered before the coming of the Normans. "But I ask that you not sacrifice yourself for a cause long lost."

"You are weak, Rhiannyn of Etcheverry," he said. "Keep your Norman company if that is what pleases you, but do not attempt to press the devils upon us. We stand with Edwin and no other."

The agreement of the others echoed around her like the closing of a door, but still she summoned one last pleading. "Aethel . . ."

A voice raised in anger—Maxen's—rumbled down the corridor, and a moment later was answered by the anxious voices of Theta and the guard.

"He is come," Rhiannyn gasped.

"Then go to him," Aethel said.

"Aye, and tell yer lover there'll be no more Saxons bendin' over fer him," one of the others spat.

Feeling attacked on all sides, and knowing it likely she would very soon be attacked by one who could lay hands to her, Rhiannyn sent Aethel a look of beseeching, then turned and hurried back down the corridor. Around the first bend, she realized she still carried the torch—a beacon to her presence in the dungeon. With hands that fumbled, she deposited it in the first sconce she came to, then crept along the wall toward the voices still speaking from the guard's station.

"Just having a little fun, milord." Theta's voice carried clearly to Rhiannyn. "Surely there's no harm in that."

"No harm?" Maxen growled. "And what of your duties, guard?"

"I—I've kept them, milord. There's none come or gone this eve. All is secure."

Pray, believe him, Rhiannyn silently pleaded. Later she would figure a way to slip past the man.

"None?" Maxen asked. "Not even Rhiannyn?"

"Ah, nay," the guard said hurriedly. "Had she, I would surely have seen her."

Maxen's silence loudly spoke his doubt.

"Mayhap milord is just a bit jealous?" Theta said, her words wrapped in a softly vibrant sound like that of a cat. "I did warn you, you know."

"Warn me?"

"Aye, that if 'twas not you, it would be another. So, 'tis no one's fault but your own that I had to seek elsewhere."

"Did I want you in my bed," Maxen said angrily, "you would have been there long ago. But as I do not, I care not whom you carry on with so long as it does not take my men from their duties. Now clothe yourself and be gone from here."

Rhiannyn's breath caught. Then Maxen had not lied to her when he'd denied having taken Theta into his bed? And Theta's later boasting of their lovemaking was grounded only in more of her falsehoods?

"Put your jealousy aside, milord, and I will accommodate you," the woman said daringly. "Here . . . now if you like."

"I will not tell you again, wench," Maxen said. "Be gone."

More silence, followed by rustling, as if Theta gathered her clothes, then her parting words. "When you grow tired of Rhiannyn—and you most certainly will—you have but to call and I will come."

Maxen did not choose to dignify her words with a response, and a short time later Rhiannyn heard the retreating patter of Theta's feet.

"Where are you going, milord?" the guard asked, alerting Rhiannyn to Maxen's movement.

"To search the dungeons, and I warn you, man, the consequences will be dire if I find one there who does not belong."

Frantically, Rhiannyn swept her gaze left and right for a place to conceal herself. The nearest refuge was not a refuge at all, but the open cell Maxen had first had her brought to. Resigning herself to it, she hurried down the corridor and entered it just as she heard Maxen round the corner.

Her heart beating so rapidly it was almost painful, she stepped into the darkest corner, pressed herself back against the wall, and slid down to huddle upon the floor. Over the arms she wrapped around her knees, she peered across to the corridor that was coming to light with the torch Maxen carried before him. And then he was there, turning back the shadows with the illuminating torch.

Blessedly, Rhiannyn's shadows held, though only because Maxen had yet to bring the light into the cell. Did he, he would certainly discover her hiding place.

He stood there for what seemed forever, perhaps also remembering the past—in his mind seeing her sitting upon the stool with her hands bound behind her back; hearing again her false declaration that it was she who had murdered Thomas, feeling the raging anger that he had barely kept from turning on her. . . .

"Rhiannyn, show yourself," he said, jolting her back to the present.

She was found out. Even though he could not possibly see her, he knew. It was useless to maintain a hiding place he would pull her from did she not comply, so Rhiannyn decided it best to surrender with dignity rather than suffer humiliation. Standing, she drew a deep breath, thrust her shoulders back, and walked into the light.

As she neared Maxen, she saw that his expression was grim, boding no good for her, but she did not falter. "I know what you are thinking," she said as she drew to a halt less than three feet from him.

"What am I thinking, Rhiannyn?" he asked, his tone less than friendly.

"That I have deceived you again, and though you will not believe me, I tell you now 'tis not true."

His face remained stone. "What was your purpose in coming down here?"

"To speak with Aethel."

"Which I forbade you to do."

"You did."

His eyes were the only thing moving about him, picking their way down her figure before sweeping again to her face. "And did you speak with him?"

She nodded.

"What was the result?"

That he was even interested surprised her. "The same as yours," she said. "He and the others stand firm with Edwin."

"A pity."

His meaning was clear—the end was near for them. They were of no use to Maxen locked in the dungeons, and not to be trusted out of them. "What will you do?" she asked, knowing but needing to hear it from him.

"What would you have me do?"

His question was completely unexpected. "It hardly matters what I would have you do," she said, wondering why he was baiting her.

"Doesn't it?"

She shook her head. "I don't understand. Why are you asking me these things?"

Maxen's answer was long in coming, his gaze drifting from her to the cell behind her, searching the walls, the floor, and lastly, the ceiling. "I'm not sure myself," he finally answered.

Perhaps that was good, perhaps it was not, but she would rather ponder it away from this place that was far too disturbing to linger in any longer. "I am ready to return to the hall now," she said. Better punishment there than here.

"I am not," Maxen said. Taking her arm, he turned her back into the cell. Immediately, the whole of it came to light, showing that it was barren but for the stool in the center and two sets of chains fastened to the far wall. Pulling Rhiannyn after him, Maxen crossed to the single sconce, set the torch in it, then strode back the way he had come.

Whatever did he intend? Rhiannyn frantically wondered. "Please, Maxen," she beseeched, straining from his hold. "Let us leave this place."

He pulled her around to face him. "Sit."

"What?" she gasped.

"Sit."

Following his gaze, she looked behind and down at the stool, then back at him. "Ah, nay, Maxen." She shook her head. "I do not wish to."

"Trust me."

Trust him? How could she when he meant to make her relive that dreadful day? And for what? Because she had defied him in venturing into the dungeons? What perversity dwelt in him that he would choose this rather than any other means?

" 'Tis not what you think, Rhiannyn," he said.

She searched his eyes, but they revealed nothing. Doubting him, but seeing no way around what he asked of her, she reluctantly lowered herself to the stool.

"Now close your eyes," he instructed.

"Why?"

"Trust me," he said again.

What other choice did she have? She closed her eyes, but immediately opened them wide again as the memories flooded her. "I do not like this place, Maxen," she said, hearing her own desperation. "Punish me however you wish, but not this way."

"As there is naught to punish you for, 'tis not what I intend," he said, his reassurance edged with impatience.

Nothing made sense anymore. But had it ever? "I did what you forbade me to do," she reminded him.

"And I understand why you did it," he said, bending near her. "Now close your eyes."

Rhiannyn was too surprised—and moved—by his admission to immediately comply. This was not at all what she expected from Maxen. What of the accusations, the anger, the distrust like a wall between them?

"Rhiannyn," he prompted.

Swallowing hard, she lowered her lids.

"Don't think, just feel," he said softly into her ear. Then, lingeringly, he slid his hands down her arms and drew them behind her back.

Not a rope this time, but his fingers which clasped her wrists in one hand. She shuddered. "Maxen—"

He stopped her words with the caress of his mouth against hers. "I am going to erase that memory," he said, drawing back just a little, "for both of us."

Then he also felt the ill of this place, she wondered, regretted what he had done? Opening her eyes, she saw that he had gone down on one knee beside her, his gaze now level with hers. "How?" she breathed, her heart pounding more furiously than was good for it. Even her mind turned weak.

Gently, he pushed back a strand of her hair, the gesture causing her to tremble. "By putting another in its place," he said. "Are you willing, Rhiannyn?"

What he was asking for was more than the remaking of a memory, she realized. He was asking for the giving of herself—asking her to surrender that they might both have what they had long wanted and she had denied them. But in this place? "Here?" she whispered.

He smiled a smile that held all the promise of the man beneath the avenger. "Though we will start here, 'twill end in my bed—if you agree. Do you?"

The last of her resistance offered very little. "I should not," she said so quietly that it hardly seemed as if she had spoken.

"But will you?"

As Rhiannyn looked into the eyes of the man she was about to yield all of herself to, she realized the awful truth of her feelings for him. Although she had more than once felt him moving about her heart, she knew now that somehow he had come into it. And though she had never before felt the intensity of this emotion, she knew it was love—not the love of a child for its parent, a sister for a brother, nor a friend for a friend. Far from it. This was the love of man and woman. She loved Maxen Pendery.

But he will never love you, a voice whispered, sneaking past her body's yearnings. Never. Rejecting this voice and the pain it brought, and putting from her mind where she was, Rhiannyn surrendered. "Love me, Maxen," she said, leaning toward him. "Love me."

She saw his hesitation over the words she had not meant to say, but in the next instant his lips claimed hers. Still holding her wrists behind her, he bent her back with the force of his kiss and the searching thrust of his tongue. Rhiannyn melted into him, thrilling to his touch as he glided his free hand from her thigh to her belly, up her ribs, then to her breast.

"Ah, yes," she breathed. "Yes."

Encouraged, Maxen deepened the kiss, and with his thumb, roused her nipple beneath the material of her bliaut and chemise.

Rhiannyn gasped at the wonderful sensations, wanting to shed her garments that she might feel his skin upon hers. God, how she ached. How she yearned to touch him as he touched her. To that end, she strained to free her hands from his hold, but when he would not release her, she slid her mouth off his and met his gaze. "Please Maxen," she said. "Release me that I might know you as you know me."

He stared at her, read the passion in her eyes, and set her wrists free.

Lifting her arms, Rhiannyn wrapped them around him.

"Touch me," he said, then lowered his head and put his mouth to her earlobe. Gently, he nipped at it, his warm breath filling her ear, causing an uncontrolled trembling to course through her.

With a boldness greater than that of the words she had spoken, Rhiannyn thrust one hand into his hair, and with the other explored his chest, down past his waist and hip, and lower, grasping the hem of his tunic. Dragging it up, she hungrily laid her palm to the hard swells of his stomach.

Maxen groaned against her throat. "This is how we should have started," he said hoarsely. Placing a hand over hers, he guided it to his manhood where it thrust against his braies and curled her fingers around it.

Rhiannyn had thought herself awakened, but now knew how very far she was from it. There was so much yet to be learned, and Maxen would be the one to show her. Through the material of his braies, she grasped him tightly, then inched her fingers up him.

A curious strangled sound came from his throat, then he scooped her from the stool. "Hold to me," he said.

She put her arms around his neck and hugged herself tightly to him as he carried her from the cell. There was no need to ask where he was taking her, for she knew well their destination. As he had promised, what they had started was to be finished in his bed.

As Maxen approached the guard's station, he pressed Rhiannyn's face into his chest, for he knew that did she look upon the man's stunned face, she might descend from the place they had both risen to and refuse him once again. Aye, he would deal with both the guard and the drunken one in the cellar on the morrow, but not a moment before. They could wait. He could not.

Ascending from the cellar and into the hall that still brimmed with his men, he continued to hold Rhiannyn's face against him. Still, there was naught he could do to shield her from the yammering of voices that immediately dropped low, only to rise again with the coarse comments that only a drunken man would speak in the presence of his lord.

Maxen felt Rhiannyn stiffen in shame. However, she did not attempt to lift her head and look upon those who stared at her, nor to clamber down from him as he feared she might. Instead, she clung more tightly to him.

It was on Maxen's tongue to order his men to their pallets, but the thought entered his mind that their revelry might mask the sounds of lovemaking that would otherwise carry to their ears. Knowing it would be easier for Rhiannyn to give all of herself to him amidst the din, he pressed his lips together and continued across the hall.

It was Christophe who nearly ended Maxen's quest to have Rhiannyn at last. Standing from the hearth, the youth waited to catch his brother's eyes and when Maxen glanced at him, Christophe glared condemnation. Christophe knew exactly what was about to happen, and though there was naught he could do about it, he wanted his brother to know his feelings.

Damnation! Maxen silently cursed as he turned his eyes forward again. Why should he care what Christophe thought of him? Why this sudden questioning of whether he should take what Rhiannyn was finally willing to yield? Nay, he would not give her up. Someday Christophe would understand—when his blood ran hot for a woman, when he grew hard just looking upon her, when he was so thoroughly denied that nothing could cool his need. But more, he would understand when desire for a woman came from above his belly rather than below it.

Aye, Maxen admitted to himself, he wanted Rhiannyn not only to ease his man's need, but to satisfy emotions that had somehow become entangled with desire. In the beginning he had thought one tumble with her was all it would take to exorcise her from him, but now he knew it would never be enough. What that meant he had yet to look closely upon, nor did he wish to, but he would. Later.

Though the hall was well illuminated, only a glimmer of light filtered through to his chamber, no torches having been lit this side of the screen. It would do, Maxen concluded as he carried Rhiannyn to the bed, for beyond this night there would be days in which he would savor every curve and hollow of her bewitching body. That thought sped him into the future he would make with her, and he abruptly quieted his mind. Later, he reminded himself.

Setting Rhiannyn on her feet alongside the bed, Maxen stepped back and waited for her to look at him.

She did so almost immediately, but there was uncertainty in her eyes that had not been there a few minutes ago.

Although the last thing Maxen wanted was to give her a chance to refuse him again, something dragged it from him. "You still wish to?" he asked.

A small hesitation, then she nodded.

Though a shout of relief rose to his throat, he suppressed it. "I want to do this right, Rhiannyn. Will you let me?"

Certainly she did not understand what he meant, but again nodded.

His hands sure, he quickly untied the sash around her waist and let it drop to the rushes. As she shuddered in anticipation, he turned her back to him and slid her bliaut and chemise off one shoulder. Then, pushing her hair aside, he laid his mouth to the tender flesh. She quivered at his touch, a little gasp of pleasure leaping down her throat and into her chest.

So responsive—just as he'd known she would be if ever she came willingly to him. He pushed the garments farther down her arm, little by little revealing the blossom of one breast until the material fell away from a golden nipple taut and ready for his mouth.

Not yet, Maxen schooled himself. It was too soon. Still,

he slid his hand over her ribs and closed aching fingers around her breast.

Her breath quickening, Rhiannyn dropped her head back against his shoulder. The soft moan she loosed upon the air drove him to explore further the handful that, as yet, was all he had of her. With weakening restraint, he squeezed his hand to the peak of her and took her nipple between thumb and forefinger.

Immediately, Rhiannyn arched, thrusting more fully into his palm.

It was almost too much for Maxen, his body's response nearly painful. Nay, he denied himself. He would do it right as he'd told her he would. As easy and immediately gratifying as it would be for him to simply press her back upon the bed, push up her skirts, and enter her, he must go slowly.

When he lifted his hand from her, she groaned and started to turn. Maxen grasped her shoulders and kept her back to him. "Patience," he said. " 'Twill happen soon enough."

She shuddered, then nodded.

Vowing that wherever her voice had gone to he would have it back when she cried out her pleasure beneath him, Maxen pushed her garments off the opposite shoulder and down her arm, then the sleeves over her hands. With a whisper, bliaut and chemise fell to the rushes.

Restraint, he reminded himself as he bent past the most exquisite buttocks he had ever seen. A hand on either side of her leg, he slid her hose downward, lifted her foot, then removed the hose with her slipper. He did the same with the other leg, then straightened.

"Turn to me, Rhiannyn," he said.

She came around, her pretty breasts tempting his hands. Clenching them into fists, Maxen looked lower to the pale down between her thighs, lingered a moment, then raised his gaze back to her face. "Beautiful," he said. "More than I ever imagined."

Still she did not speak, though he glimpsed apprehension in her eyes.

Determined to wipe it away, he tilted her chin up, kissed her long until she began to respond, then drew back. "There is naught to fear, Rhiannyn," he said. "I will not hurt you."

She searched his face, then nodded again.

Curse it! Maxen silently blasphemed. This quiet of hers was itself a distraction. Why did she not speak? He dragged his tunic over his head, tossed it aside, and reached for the cord of his braies.

"Nay." She spoke at last, her hands staying his. "I would do it."

Her brazen words, more than their unexpectedness, surprised Maxen, but when she pushed his hands aside, he offered no objection. Then, as he had unclothed her, she did the same to him. Lingeringly, she slid his braies down, her fingers grazing the hair that lightly covered his thighs, calves, and lastly, his ankles. When the last of his clothing had joined hers on the floor, she began the journey back up—a journey even more torturous than the first. Somehow Maxen held to himself, denying that part of him which had grown hard and jutting between them.

"I have seen you before," she whispered, her fingers coming to rest high on his thighs, "but never like this."

Nay, never like this. He could not remember himself ever having been so ready for a woman. But then, it had been years since last he had slaked his needs, and many weeks now since Rhiannyn had first stoked the fires, not just to life but to raging.

"I think I am ready," she said, tipping her face up to him.

Burning, Maxen closed his hands around her arms, lowered his head, and captured the lips she parted to him. For what seemed an unending moment, each breathed the other's breath, tangled tongues, and laid hands where they had never been before. But the merging of their bodies—her breasts to his chest, his member to her belly—demanded further exploration. Exploration that would best be done on the bed.

Leaving her lips, Maxen gently laid Rhiannyn back

upon the mattress, drew a knee up alongside her, then bent to her breast and took her nipple into his mouth.

"Maxen," she panted as he swirled his tongue around her. "Maxen." Pressing upward, she plunged a hand into his hair to hold him to her and glided the other down his back to his buttocks. Then, growing frantic, she sank her nails into him and raised her hips to take his flesh against her.

Still intending to do it right, though it took every bit of control he had left, Maxen fought down his body's desire to simply part her and drive straight to her depths. Trembling with restraint, he shifted and took her other nipple into his mouth.

Rhiannyn whimpered, rubbed herself against him, then dragged her nails across his hip and inward. Suddenly her hand held him, her fingers sheathing him so perfectly, it was almost as if he had joined with her.

Throwing his head back, Maxen struggled to curb his needs, but just as he caught the thread of control, Rhiannyn drew her fingers to the top of him.

His undoing.

Like the animal he had not wanted to be, he roughly pushed between her legs, parted her moist flesh, closed his hand over the hand she held him with, then guided himself to her and breached her maidenly flesh in a single stroke.

Her maidenly flesh . . .

"Ah, God," he groaned, turning back the animal that had possessed him. "I am the first." Though he'd had moments of doubt, he had been so sure there must have been at least one other—if not Thomas, then certainly Edwin. But there had been neither. So wrong about her. In so many ways he had been wrong.

Chapter Twenty

With Maxen's entrance Rhiannyn had felt discomfort, but little of the pain her mother had spoken of. Still, she knew there was more to come, for he had yet to fully penetrate her, her hand and his still upon him, preventing him from doing so.

Knowing she was on the brink of something wonderful, and wondering why she had yet to fully realize it, Rhiannyn lifted her lids and saw the indecision in Maxen's eyes—a battle between desire and control. The desire pulsed hard through him, most especially in that part filling her so warmly, but the control clenched his teeth, hardened his jaw, and trembled almost violently through him.

Why was he fighting it? she wondered through the haze of a passion unfulfilled. Why did he not complete what he had started? What they both wanted? In answer, the words he had spoken upon entering her played back through her head, though this time with meaning. *I am the first. . . .*

She should have told him, she realized. She should have set him right when he had accused her of being otherwise, but she hadn't, for she'd thought he would think her a liar in that as well. And now it seemed he suffered remorse at the taking of her virtue. That or else he had no liking for a woman untried, perhaps preferring one who could pleasure him as expertly as he did her.

"Do I displease you?" she asked, praying he would say otherwise.

He settled his gaze to hers. "You should have told me," he said. However, before she could defend herself, knowing came upon his face. "But then I would not have believed you. That is what you are thinking, is it not?"

She nodded. "Though more I am thinking I would like you to finish what you have started."

Her invitation lost on him, he started to pull back.

"Nay," she pleaded. "Do not." Tightening an arm around him, she arched her back to stay with him, then thrust her hips upward. She gained little, though, for the obstacle of their hands kept him from sinking more deeply into her.

"God, Rhiannyn, do not do that," he growled. Loosing her arm from around him, and her hand from beneath his, he fell back upon the mattress and laid his forearm across his eyes. "Had I known, 'twould have been different."

How different? she nearly asked, but stopped herself before she added to a discussion she did not wish to have with him. What was done was done . . . and with her consent. Now it ought to be completed, this ache of both body and heart eased. Though Maxen did not love her, she needed to have this part of him that might carry her through the life that lay ahead of her. Just once she wanted to feel the only love he was capable of giving her—physical love. Turning onto her knees, she dropped a leg over him and straddled him before he realized her intent.

"Rhiannyn!" he barked, thrusting up onto his elbows. Her hair falling between them, she pressed her hands to his shoulders to urge him back, but he was ungiving. "Finish it, Maxen," she said, "else I will."

It seemed a long time before he answered her, but when he did, it was not what she wished to hear. "Though a man can take a woman against her will, 'tis not possible for a woman to take a man."

"If it is against his will," she agreed, her voice grown husky. "But 'tis also what you want." To demonstrate, she slid her hand over him and recaptured his manhood. It was near as hard as when he'd left her, and a moment later surged solid again.

"You do not know what you're asking," he said between clenched teeth.

Perhaps not, but she knew what she wanted. Taking advantage of his wavering, she guided him to her as he had done, then lowered herself onto him.

Like the breaking of a storm, Maxen's resistance fell away, and a moment later he drove fully into her, touching her womb, withdrawing slightly, then touching it again.

Rhiannyn knew greater discomfort than before, but still it was not the terrible pain of which she'd been warned. Nay, it was not, and now there were waves cresting upon that discomfort, dragging it under and drowning it in sensations of such magnificent intensity she thought she might never breathe again.

"Follow me, Rhiannyn," Maxen said, breaking through the agitated stir of her body's motions. When she faltered, he put his hands to her buttocks and guided her to his rhythm—pulling her to him as he thrust upward, then easing her off him when he withdrew into the mattress.

Learning the cadence of his lovemaking, Rhiannyn was rewarded with the touch of his hands at other places. They seemed everywhere, yet only one place at a time. She thrilled at the kneading of her breasts, the feathering of his fingers down her ribs to the tops of her thighs, and drew a sharp breath when he slid a hand between them and touched the fiery bud just above where their bodies met.

Winding a hand into her hair, Maxen pulled her head down to his. "Do you feel it?" he asked into her ear, his voice tortured as if he held something in he would rather let out.

"I feel it," she said, knowing that he must be referring to her soaring.

"What color is it?" he asked.

"Color?" she repeated, confusion losing her the precious rhythm. Immediately, Maxen guided her back to it.

"Aye," he said. "What color do you see when you close your eyes?"

Only then did Rhiannyn understand what he referred to—against the insides of her eyelids the bright golden light rushing toward the white. "Gold," she gasped, ". . . and white."

Without warning, Maxen rolled to the side, and a moment later strained over her with increasing intensity until all Rhiannyn saw was the white light, and all she felt was the culmination her body strove for. "Maxen!" she cried. "I see it!"

Though they reached the pinnacle together, it was not his shout, but hers that carried beyond the screen to those in the hall. She didn't care. All that mattered were the sweet spasms of their bodies that were indistinguishable one from the other, and when the last spasm was done with, she clung to Maxen as she had never clung to another in her life.

I love you. She said the words over and over again, though it was only her mind that heard her. And only her mind that would ever hear her, for never would she be able to say it aloud. Desire Maxen, aye, she could admit that to him, but to give of her entire soul when her love would never be returned was the way of a pain deeper than she already felt.

Sudden tears sprang to her eyes as the echoes of Thomas's curse rolled through her head, followed closely by the screeching of a mad old woman. But perhaps Dora was not so mad, for she had foretold that Rhiannyn would take one other than Edwin as her lover—and now her ravings were made true. What else might Dora be right about? That Rhiannyn would be the downfall of her people?

"I feared you might cry," Maxen said, breaking into her churning thoughts. Rolling onto his side, he drew back a space, glided a thumb beneath both her eyes, and captured moisture on it. "Regrets?" he asked, looking from the sparkling tears into the eyes that had shed them.

She attempted a smile, but it quivered straight off her mouth. Did she regret her yielding? she wondered, though she knew the tears were not of that. Aye, some, but it was done now and in the past. However, this love aching from her heart was not done with, and might never be, but she could not tell him that. "'Twas what we both wanted," she said, evading his question.

"Aye, but you would wish it otherwise."

"There can be no pride in laying with one's enemy," she said.

The light in his eyes shifted. "Then you still think me your enemy."

Was he? Though Saxon pride wished her to believe so, she knew it was not true. He might be her lord, but he was not her enemy. He had proven that several times over now in his mercy upon her people, his generosity and fairness toward them, and in his waiting for her to be ready for him. "Nay, Maxen, I spoke wrong. You are not my enemy."

She had not realized the tension that had grown in him while he'd waited upon her answer, but she knew it now by the easing of his body against hers. "Then what am I?" he asked.

Uncomfortable with his question, she shrugged. "You are a Norman, but not the Norman I feared."

A faint smile touched his lips. "I am also your lover, Rhiannyn."

Evading his gaze, she stared at the rippling shadows cast over his muscled abdomen. "And I your leman," she murmured.

The word was like the foulest blow Maxen had ever been dealt. So coarse, so crude, so vulgar after what they had just shared, but also true, he forced himself to admit. At best others would call her his leman, at worst, his whore. Though none would dare speak it before him, plenty would be the whispers behind his back, and many the sly comments that would fall upon her ears. Damnation, he ought not to care—as he had not before the monastery, when he had chosen a favorite to spend his passion upon night after night.

Turning his back on such disturbing thoughts, he voiced the first thing that came to mind. "Tell me of your family."

Immediately, Rhiannyn's eyelids flew open to reveal large eyes, dark with dilated pupils, her body tensing as his had a short while ago. "Why?" she asked warily.

Aye. Why? "I know so little about you," he said, only mildly surprised at the realization that he truly did wish to know her better—to know who and what had shaped her into the woman he was ever drawn to. Though Guy had apprised him of the death of her father and brothers at Hastings, her mother in a raid upon their village, he knew no more.

"They are dead now," she said. "That is enough."

"At the hands of Normans."

"Of course." Her voice was carefully matter-of-fact, though Maxen was certain there was emotion just beneath the surface. Then, with a suddenness that nearly had her out of his hands and off the bed, she twisted around, sat up, and put her feet on the floor.

He caught her with one arm and pulled her around to face him. "Where do you think you're going?" he asked.

As if painfully conscious of her nudity, she closed her body to him—crossing her arms over her chest and pressing her thighs together. "To my bench," she said, refusing to meet his gaze. "The others are making ready and so too must I."

Maxen had missed the scrape and screech of benches and tables being moved into position for the night, but now the sounds came clearly to him. "I wish you in my bed," he said.

" 'Tis not where a leman usually passes the night," she reminded him, still looking anywhere but at him.

"Mayhap, but it is where you will most assuredly pass this night." And all others, he added to himself.

Confusion reflected upon the face she finally turned to him, and in her eyes beneath drawn brows, she asked, "Even do I wish otherwise?"

"Methinks you do not wish otherwise," he said, urging her closer to him. " 'Tis simply that I asked something of you which you long to run away from."

She strained to resist his pull, but lay alongside him a moment later. "I do not care to relive for your benefit that which ought to remain in the past," she said, anger in her voice.

He had struck a chord deep in her, Maxen knew, but it only made him that much more determined to learn the remains of her past. Searching behind him, he pulled the coverlet over them, then curved an arm around her waist. "Tell me," he said.

She shook her head. "As I would not ask you to speak of what haunts you, for certainly there is blood upon your hands that no amount of prayer has washed from them, neither should you ask it of me."

Hastings. She had struck at that place in him wherein torment lay. The screams of lingering death, the warm smell of blood a hundred times worse than the mass slaughter of pigs, the desperate mutterings of men calling to a God who had turned from them that day, the eyes of the dead and dying opened wide in disbelief, and then Nils descended upon by his own. . . .

"Forgive me." Rhiannyn's voice broke into memories that made him want to rage—to take more blood upon hands so thoroughly soaked that, as she had said, no amount of prayer might ever cleanse them.

Finger by finger Maxen unclenched his fists, then called his body back from the strain that caused every muscle in him to ache. "One day I will tell you of my past," he said, though he could not say whether he would keep such a promise, "but now is your time."

The extinguishing of nearly all the torches in the hall threw deep shadows over Rhiannyn's face, stealing from him the play of emotions that passed over it. But perhaps it would be easier for her, he reasoned. Perhaps the telling of it would come more readily.

It did. "My father and ... two brothers worked the land under Edwin's father," she began, her voice hardly more than a whisper. "Claye was the older of my brothers, Wynter a year younger than I."

When silence fell, Maxen crushed the impulse to prompt her and waited for her to continue.

"Did you know that Wynter was barely fifteen summers old when he marched to Hastings?" she said, pain filling her voice. However, in the next breath—one that stirred the hair at his brow—she shook it off. " 'Twas a one-room wattle and daub hut I was born and raised in. Though all I had of my own was a pallet away from my brothers, it was enough. My mother and I kept the home, tended to the land when we were needed, and now and then sewed for Lord and Lady Harwolfson. . . ." She trailed off, but a moment later took up again. "Claye and I quarrelled often, but Mother always knew how to soothe hurt feelings, and Father how to turn anger into laughter. It was not much, but we were happy." She sighed. "It must sound rather dismal to you, but they were lovely times. Often hard, but never short of love."

And all the while Maxen had been raised in the comfort of a great hall, the working of the land distant to him, his training for knighthood of paramount importance to a father whose contact with his sons was nearly exclusive to that end. Nay, not dismal. Enviable. "And Edwin?" he prompted as he had promised himself he would not. "How did you come to be betrothed to him?"

"Though he was not the eldest son, his gain was to be great in wedding a noblewoman from the north who was her father's only offspring. To that end, he rode from King Edward's court for the wedding, only to arrive at Etcheverry to the news that his intended had been taken by fever. It was then we first talked. You see, I had seen Edwin before, but never spoken with him."

"What happened?"

"I was gathering rushes at the river when he came upon me, and though I begged leave of him that he might be alone with his mourning, he was insistent that I stay and finish my task. After a time, he began talking about his betrothed, and though he had never met her, he seemed saddened by her loss, especially when he spoke of the son he had thought a year would bring him. When the rushes were finally bundled, I asked for my leave-taking, but again he denied me and bid me to come sit beside him. I knew I should not, but could hardly refuse the lord's son. Hours later, we were both holding tight to our bellies and laughing over one another's jests. Great friends, I thought. His wife, he decided, and told me so that day. Of course I did not believe him until his father came to mine the following morning to seal the betrothal."

Though he might call it anything but jealousy, that was exactly what crawled through Maxen's insides, twisting them as it went. "And did you wish to wed him?" he asked.

As if she sensed the maddening emotion, Rhiannyn reacted to soothe it. "Maxen, the Edwin you think you know is not the one who told me he was going to marry me that day. He is much changed, but still the true of him is hidden somewhere beneath these past two years. Norman or Saxon, such great loss, especially of ones you have loved, cannot be erased. 'Tis the same for all who live and breathe."

Her defense of Edwin wound Maxen's resentment even tighter. "Did you wish to wed him?" he asked again.

She hesitated before answering, then shrugged. "He was a man as any other, though I did have a great liking for him."

"Why did you not wed straightaway?"

"We were to have, but hardly had my father accepted the betrothal when Edwin was summoned back to London by King Edward's death. And then King Harold . . ."

It was just as well words failed her, for Maxen needed no further explanation. Harold Godwinson's reign, which had lasted less than ten months, had been rife with conflict, culminating with his defeat at Hastings. "Your father and brothers joined with Harold then," he said, knowing from Guy that it was so.

She drew a deep breath and nodded. "They followed Edwin's father into battle."

"And your mother and you?"

"We remained behind."

"What happened, Rhiannyn?"

"Maxen, I . . . I don't . . ."

He sensed the storm, but pressed on. "The Normans came, didn't they?"

She took a long moment to gather herself before continuing. "Aye, only days before the great battle they rode on our village."

"And?"

"And we resisted. There were so many more of them than us, and we were only women, children, and men of too great an age to stop them. When all was done, they had raped, pillaged, and gone on to set fire to nearly every one of the buildings."

"How did you escape?"

"When we realized we had lost, my mother and I hid ourselves in the stables, but they set fire to that as well." She shuddered, then whispered, "Only I escaped."

Sliding an arm under her, Maxen drew her toward him, and she came willingly to settle her head beneath his chin. "Your mother?" he asked.

She pressed nearer him. "My mother was behind me when the roof fell in. It burned only my skirts, but she . . . I tried to reach her, to pull her from beneath the timbers, but the fire burned too hot and high, and then the Normans came for me." A sob caught in her throat. "I can still hear my mother's screams as I fled into the trees."

Maxen felt the warm trail of Rhiannyn's tears slide onto his shoulder. "Yet you escaped them."

"In that, God was with me," she said, her voice catching as she fought not to cry aloud. "Only that. Day and night I prayed for my father and brothers' safe return, but they, like so many others, never came home. Hastings took them ... and holds them still."

It struck Maxen that he might have been the one to have slain one or more of her menfolk, but before he could sink into his own hell, Rhiannyn's storm unleashed itself. Turning her face into his shoulder to muffle the cries of her heart, she clung to him, growing ever tense until, finally, she loosed her torment in great sobs.

Not knowing what else to do, for always before when he'd been confronted with a woman's tears, he'd simply turned away, Maxen held her and murmured comforting words he had not known himself capable of—though he thought it unlikely she heard any of them. How long it was before the storm passed, he could not have said, but when it did, Rhiannyn lay slack in his arms, softly hiccoughing the last of her tattered emotions.

"I will make it right with you, Rhiannyn," he said, stroking her head as if she were a child. "Upon my vow, all will come right."

Rhiannyn awoke in a tangle—not of blankets, but of limbs that were not all her own. Opening eyes that yet burned from too much crying, she looked into Maxen's face and saw that he still slept, no doubt exhausted from a sleepless night. Several times his restlessness had roused her from her own troubled sleep. However, rested or not, she must rise, for though she was no longer chaste, she still served.

Carefully disentangling her arms and legs from Maxen's, she lowered her feet to the rushes, stood, and walked around the bed. There she found hers and Maxen's clothes exactly where they had fallen on the night past. The remembrance flushed her cheeks with warmth. She had been so bold, insistent, even when he had pulled back upon discovering her still a virgin.

Shaking her head as if the gesture would unburden her, she scooped up the garments, laid them on the bed, and pulled her chemise free. She had only just donned it when she heard the approach of familiar footsteps. Alarmed, she walked to the screen and looked around it.

Christophe faltered upon seeing her, sloshing water from the basin he carried upon the rushes. However, he quickly recovered. Offering a smile over the concern he could not disguise, he continued toward her.

As there was no one beyond Christophe, and she did not wish to awaken Maxen, Rhiannyn hugged her chemise to her and stepped around the screen. She saw that he carried water upon which rose petals floated. "For me?" she asked quickly to keep him from speaking words that might shame her.

"I thought you might need it," he said in a low voice.

Evading his gaze, she dipped her fingers into the water. "Hmm, and warm."

"Are you well?" Christophe asked.

She looked at him. "I am fine."

"I heard you—"

"I know," she blurted, embarrassment sweeping her as she recalled the cry that had broken from her when Maxen had taken her with him to a shattering climax. For certain, all in the hall had heard—and known.

"I heard you weeping." Christophe thus completed his words, though neither could he have missed that other cry. "Did Maxen do you harm? If he did—"

"Nay, Christophe he did not," she assured him. " 'Twas for another reason that I cried."

"I don't understand."

Though Rhiannyn did not wish to speak further of those memories, she knew she owed him an explanation. "I finally cried out the past."

Confusion flitted across his face before it settled with understanding. "Your family," he guessed.

Though she had never spoken at length of them, he knew she had lost all of them to the Norman invasion. "Aye," she said.

"You told Maxen?" he asked, his eyebrows arching so high, they disappeared beneath the hair falling over his brow.

She nodded. "And he offered great comfort."

"I find that hard to believe."

"As do I."

Clearly adrift in things he did not understand, Christophe passed the basin into Rhiannyn's hands and stepped back. "As my brother will offer no apology for what he did to you yestereve, I offer mine," he said. "Never should it have happened."

Like a shield, Rhiannyn balanced the basin before her. "No apologies are necessary, Christophe. Maxen did not take what he was not given."

Again Christophe appeared confused.

"I wish I could explain it better," Rhiannyn said, "but I cannot. You see, I do not understand it myself."

Of a sudden, Christophe did. "You love him, don't you?" he said more than asked.

It was Rhiannyn's turn to slosh water, though it fell not to the rushes, but down the front of her chemise. "I . . ." She did not want to lie to him, but neither was she willing to admit her deepest emotions.

"Nay," Christophe said. "You needn't answer."

Because he had guessed right and knew he had, Rhiannyn thought, but she did not deny the truth as she wanted to. As their friendship had always been one of truth, to now turn it into a lie was something she was unwilling to do.

"I take my leave," he said, then turned and hobbled away.

Found out and feeling it to the pit of her stomach, Rhiannyn slipped back around the screen, verified that Maxen still slept, then carried the basin to the chest and set it down.

I will not cry again, she told herself as she stared sightlessly at the petals like tears upon the water. *I am done with it.*

Chapter Twenty-one

A lovely scent, like the roses of summer past. Summer past when he had walked through the monastery gardens and tried to replace haunting memories with the smell bursting from unfolding petals. In the end, though, their crimson had only served to remind him of the blood upon his hands.

Dragging himself from the dream, Maxen lifted heavy lids and focused on the bed he lay in, then slid his gaze down his naked body to the coverlet slanted across his hips, and farther to the foot of the bed where bare shoulders peeked out from a curtain of fair hair. Rhiannyn, he realized, their night together now come to day. But why had she gone from him, and why had he not awakened when she'd slipped away? He was not usually so deep a sleeper—nor could he afford to be if he was to live to a respectable age.

Sitting up, he watched as Rhiannyn

reached to the side, dipped a cloth in water—rose water, he guessed from the smell that had entered his dream— and bent forward to wash herself. Though he felt terribly dry, his tongue cleaving to the roof of his mouth, he waited on her as time and again she returned to the basin. Finally, though, she laid the cloth down and turned sideways to retrieve her chemise, causing him to pull a long breath at the sight of creamy breasts tipped golden.

She must have heard him, for she hurriedly pressed the garment to her chest and glanced over her shoulder at him. Her eyes, still slightly swollen from her crying, opened wide, then she averted her gaze. "I did not mean to awaken you," she apologized.

"You did not," he said, wishing he could wish away the chemise she held before her.

She turned her back to him, stealing all from sight, and dragged the chemise over her head. Standing, she reached for the bliaut.

"Leave it," he said.

She hesitated before drawing her arm back to her side, but did not turn to face him as he silently beckoned her to.

The quiet stretched long and unbearable, then Rhiannyn heard the creak of the bed, followed a moment later by Maxen's footsteps. Too soon, his heat came up against her back and his hands settled on her shoulders.

"Now you are truly mine," he said.

Then one night was not all he intended to have of her? she thought. He would make her his leman in every sense of the word? She slid a hand up her abdomen and wondered how long before she carried his babe. A child without a name. A bastard. Nay, she decided, it must never happen. But how to turn away his seed?

When Maxen pulled her around, she jerked her hand from her belly, curled her fingers into her palms, and lifted her head.

"What happened?" he asked, his gaze settling upon the front of her chemise that was still damp.

Looking down, she saw that her nipples were pressed darkly against the thin material. "Clumsy," she said, nervously plucking the chemise from her skin. "I tipped water onto myself."

"Christophe?" he asked. " 'Twas he who brought it for you?"

She looked back at him. "He did."

"Thoughtful," Maxen said, though he looked anything but pleased by his brother's gesture.

"He meant well."

"I'm sure he did," Maxen said brusquely, then changed the subject. "How do you feel?"

Though she couldn't be sure whether he referred to the giving of her virginity or the tears she had shed over the loss of her family, she chose the latter to respond to. "I am well," she said, "though most sorry I burdened you with my weeping."

" 'Twas I who asked you to unburden yourself," he reminded her, his face softening, his hands caressing her shoulders.

" 'Tis just that I have never really cried. Not like that," she said, her breath thickening with a resurgence of the desire she had known in Maxen's arms. "But last night . . ." She shook her head. "Everyone dear to me is lost."

His hands stilled. "And now Edwin."

She blinked, surprised to find the Saxon still so heavy upon his mind. Had she not well enough explained her feelings for Edwin last night? Perhaps not. "Though I care for him," she said, "he is not dear to me, Maxen. We were to have been wed, and that is all."

He searched her face before pressing a kiss to her mouth. "I am pleased," he said, then stepped back from her.

Realizing it must be jealousy that had guided Maxen's words, Rhiannyn was overcome with a most peculiar sense of lightness, though she quickly scoffed it aside with the reminder that there was no future for her with this man she had come to love. Jealousy was a basic emotion—also among the basest. It was the same with animals whose mating was little more than answer to their body's urges.

"You may clothe yourself," Maxen said as he turned to

do the same, "but you will remain here until I send for you."

"But what of my duties? I must serve ale at the breaking of fast and—"

"Your duties are no more," he smoothly interrupted as he pulled his tunic over his head. "Sew if your hands are idle, but I do not wish to see you waiting upon my men any longer."

Perhaps she should have been grateful, she thought, for it was no pleasant task to tote drink for men whose eyes, if not their hands, seemed all over her at once, and who grew callous and crude when their cups had been filled one too many times—or not enough. Still, she was greatly unsettled by Maxen's decision. In fact, the more she thought on it, the more she took exception to it. What she had done with him was naught to be proud of, but neither would she be ashamed of it. Determined that she would not hide from staring eyes that would undoubtedly defile her with their knowing, she squared her shoulders and waited for Maxen to look up from the belt he secured about his waist. When he did, she was ready—or thought she was.

"I do not wish favoritism just because I . . ." she began, but her indignant declaration faded into nothingness as she searched for words other than those she'd nearly spoken.

"Because we have become lovers?" Maxen finished for her.

He could not have been more direct, but at least he had not called her his leman. "I will not be treated any differently," she said, putting her chin into the air.

Maxen propped his hands upon his hips and stared hard at her. "But you *will* be treated differently," he said. "Today is not the same as yesterday."

"I am not going to hide from what has happened."

"I have not asked you to."

"You have told me I may not leave your chamber."

"Until I summon you."

"And when will that be?"

He sighed. "Midday at the latest."

Wise or not, Rhiannyn pressed on. "And then I will resume my duties?"

"Resume? Nay." He shook his head. "As I have said, I will not have you serving my men any longer."

"If 'tis not good enough for me now, why was it good enough for me yesterday?"

Thinner and thinner his patience ran, his mouth drawing into a tight line. "I don't really need to answer that, Rhiannyn. You know the reason."

"Your reason," she tossed back, her anger running high, "not mine."

"Very well, my reason, and that is enough." He must have seen it was not enough for her, for he immediately followed with a warning that spoiled further argument. "I have chained you before, Rhiannyn. If needs be, I will chain you again."

She worked her mouth over words that would push Maxen to make good his threat, then prudently snapped it closed.

"Good," he said, then strode past her and out of the chamber.

Groaning aloud her frustration, Rhiannyn kicked a toe through the rushes, paced the room a dozen or more times, then sank into the chair.

"You have not won, Maxen Pendery," she muttered.

And neither have you, her mind retorted.

"I have not asked you," she replied aloud. Immediately, she felt the idiot for having this conversation with herself. Resigned to a long wait, she dropped her head back to stare at the ceiling.

It was Sir Guy who came for her following the nooning meal. Pushing away the tray of viands Lucilla had earlier brought her, Rhiannyn stood, and without a word, followed the knight into the hall where Maxen sat in the center of a dozen knights of high rank. Standing against the wall to the left and right of him were those of lesser rank, flanked by a handful of men-at-arms. And before the hearth stood Christophe—withdrawn, yet with eyes watchful and wary.

Though Rhiannyn was in little better mood than when Maxen had left her hours before, curiosity over this strange gathering took the edge off her emotions and her mind off the glancing looks she had known she would receive.

"Rhiannyn, come stand beside me," Maxen said as she neared the dais.

Head high, she skirted the table and walked to where he sat. "My lord?" she asked.

"A moment," he said, his eyes trained across the hall to the entrance of the cellar, which lay shrouded in shadows.

It was a long waiting moment, but when it ended, five Saxons came into the light, each led by a man-at-arms.

"What goes?" Rhiannyn whispered, unable to make sense of Maxen's summoning of Aethel and the others from their cells. Unless it was time to have done with them. . . . Nay, she thought, he would not bring them before her if that were the case. Or would he? He had forced her to accompany him to the hanging he had never intended, but then, as he had later explained, it had only been to see whether she spoke the truth or a lie.

She looked to Aethel first, for not only did she feel the strength of his stare, but the bond long ago forged between them—a bond that for him was broken. His many weeks below ground had paled him and grown his hair and beard long and wild, but the eyes with which he looked upon her were sharp, ready, and filled with accusation. Still, she braved them.

The five were forced to a halt ten feet from the table, their clattering chains a long time in falling to silence.

As all awaited Maxen's intent, he stared long at each of the prisoners. Only after thoroughly assessing them did he return his gaze to the one who towered in the middle—Aethel. "What is your decision?" he asked in their tongue.

The great man stood just a bit taller and grew just a bit wider. "The same as it was when last we spoke," he said.

Though she stood stock still, Rhiannyn's insides sagged with her heart. What other choice did Maxen have but to put them to death. No other choice, she answered herself. If they would not stand with him, then neither would they be allowed to stand against him.

To make his pronouncement, Maxen stood. However, it was not the Saxons he addressed, but Rhiannyn. "My gift to you," he said, his gaze intense on her.

"Gift?" she echoed, feeling as if she'd fallen into a deep well. "Whatever do you mean?"

"They are yours—to do with however you wish."

The few of Maxen's men who understood Anglo-Saxon muttered among themselves, their bewilderment nearly as great as her own. A moment later the Saxons awoke from their own shock to join the escalating din of translations and questions.

A gift. Why? Rhiannyn wondered. Because she had yielded to him? Though it hardly seemed likely, she could think of no other explanation. But nay, it could not be. Could it? "I fear I do not understand," she said.

Maxen turned his gaze from her to his men who were near to losing control of themselves. He did not need to speak a word to bring them back to their places, for one look at his reproving face sent a wave of warning through their ranks and brought them to silence. Satisfied, he looked again at Rhiannyn. "What is to be their fate?" he asked.

She glanced past him to the Saxons, then to the surrounding Normans—few of whom looked anything but provoked by the announcement. And of those most strongly opposed, stood Sir Ancel. She could see it in the high color that ran from his neck to hairline, the clenched jaw thrust forward, the flare of his large nostrils, and the dark eyes with the steely glint of a sharpened dagger. A moment later, those same eyes tripped from her to Maxen.

"Name it," Maxen urged her.

She looked back at him. There was only one thing that could be done with them, but would it be stretching Maxen's generosity too much to advance such an idea? "They will not serve you well here at Etcheverry," she said, laying the ground for a proposal he would undoubtedly reject.

"That I know."

"Neither would they serve you well at Blackspur."

He nodded agreement.

Briefly, she wondered what other alternative he might accept. However, unable to come up with any other but the impossible, she plunged forward. "Then I would ask that you release them."

"To Edwin," he said, seemingly unmoved by her proposal.

"If that is what they choose."

"Suffer no delusions that they will decide otherwise," he said, his voice level.

She nodded.

"On the morrow then," he pronounced, then motioned for the guards to lead the Saxons away.

He would release them? Allow them to go to his enemy that they might strengthen Edwin's ranks and, come spring, fight against him? Through her shock, Rhiannyn felt Aethel's gaze pull at her. Impelled to look at him, she caught the slight smile that turned his mouth before he was prodded back toward the dungeon.

"Return to your duties," Maxen ordered the standing Normans. "It is done with."

As the men began to disperse, a red-faced Sir Ancel stepped forward. "For this whore," he growled, leveling a finger at Rhiannyn, "you would unleash the very Saxons whose intent it is to murder our king?"

One moment the fractious knight was upright, and the next he lay flat upon his back. His lord standing over him and the other knights and men-at-arms fallen into a waiting quiet as they watched him, he cupped a hand over his gushing nose and struggled to regain his feet. However, Maxen dropped a booted foot to his chest and pinned him where he lay.

"Shall we end this now, Ancel?" Maxen demanded, the hand he had struck the knight with curling around the hilt of his sword.

For one endless minute, Ancel stared wordlessly up at Maxen, for certain considering the wisdom of accepting the challenge. In the end, though, he jerked his head side to side. "I am at your feet, my lord," he said, his voice muffled by his hand. "What else is there to end?"

Maxen looked long and hard at him, his hand alternately gripping and loosing the sword hilt. "We will see, won't we?" he finally said, then lifted his foot from the man's chest and ordered him to rise.

Ancel did so warily, as if waiting for a sword to be drawn on him. But Maxen was playing no game with him—at least not the kind the knight expected. Dropping his hand from his nose, Ancel squared himself, then dragged his bloodied palm down his tunic. "Your leave, my lord?" he requested, the red continuing to dribble from his nose.

Dismissingly, Maxen backhanded the air.

Looking most assured for a trampled and thoroughly disgraced knight, Ancel walked from the hall.

Talking amongst themselves and often glancing back at their lord, the others also withdrew. A short time later, only Sir Guy, Christophe, and Rhiannyn remained.

"Why?" Guy asked as he stepped to Maxen's side.

Studying his knuckles which were flecked with Ancel's easily won blood, Maxen asked, "Why the Saxons, or why Ancel?"

"Both."

Leaving the blood be, Maxen met his man's gaze. "The Saxons are only five," he said. "They hold not the sway of whether King William will remain or be overthrown. Besides, they are my gift to Rhiannyn. She has done with them what she thought best."

A gift you have not yet explained, Rhiannyn thought, though she held her tongue.

"As for Ancel," he continued, "the time is not right."

Guy threw up his hands. "When?"

"Soon."

"Mayhap not soon enough," Christophe said from the hearth. "You might see your own death before his."

"Such confidence, little brother," Maxen scoffed. "You do me great honor."

"And you underestimate Ancel," Christophe returned.

Rhiannyn watched the exchange with growing tension, feeling what was not said between the brothers, but which was most clear to her. It went beyond the Saxons, beyond Ancel. It was she, Christophe angered by Maxen's making her his leman, and Maxen incensed that his brother took exception to it—putting guilt upon him.

"This audience is at an end," Maxen said, then strode to the great doors and disappeared without.

A moment later, Rhiannyn followed, but Maxen had gone from sight by the time she stepped outside. With no answer to the question of why he had given her the fate of the Saxons, she started back inside. However, another question of a far different sort turned her feet elsewhere, carrying her to the kitchens where a gossiping Mildreth and Lucilla wielded sharp knives over unsuspecting vegetables while three other wenches pounded dough.

Catching sight of her, Mildreth ordered the three others to leave, then beckoned Rhiannyn forward. "You look a mite pale," she said.

Rhiannyn touched her cheek. "Do I?"

Lucilla nodded, her eyes expectant, though her lips remained sealed against whatever it was she wished to speak.

"Are you well, child?" Mildreth asked, her knowing eyes sweeping Rhiannyn crown to foot.

So Mildreth knew that on the night past she had lain with Maxen—as did Lucilla. Indeed, likely all knew it by now. Still, there had been no condemnation in the woman's voice, had there? "I am fine," Rhiannyn assured her.

"A bit sore?" Lucilla asked, no subtlety about her.

A bit, but that most certainly was not what she had come to discuss. "Fine," she repeated, the blush of embarrassment warming her face. Then, sidestepping her own question to first give the news, she said, "The Saxons held below ground will be released on the morrow."

Mildreth frowned. "To work upon the wall?"

"Nay, to make their way outside the castle walls."

"Go on with you!" Mildreth exclaimed. "Surely you can't mean the lord is just gonna let them go like that?"

Would he? Rhiannyn fleetingly wondered. Aye, he had said he would, and she believed him. " 'Tis what he says," she stated.

"Why?" Lucilla asked.

Rhiannyn shrugged. "He said only that it was a gift to me."

"Generous is he!" Lucilla exclaimed. "For but a night with him, five lives. Now I'm wonderin' what a full sennight might bring you."

"Lucilla!" Mildreth reprimanded.

"Lordy," the woman squawked, "but 'tis true, is it not?"

Rhiannyn certainly felt no pride in what had happened yestereve, but now she felt dirtied by it—a whore well paid.

" 'Course now that he's had you, he'll not ask you to wed him," Lucilla continued aloud. "That is not so good. Any child he might put you with will be called bastard. I told you—"

"Hush, Lucilla," Mildreth snapped.

"There may not be children," Rhiannyn said, though how she was to prevent it was still unknown to her—thus, the reason she had veered toward the kitchens.

"No children?" Lucilla snorted loudly. "Ye look fine and healthy to me, and as for Pendery . . ." She chuckled, her eyes alight with recollection. "No question a fine brood that man will make—of bastards, of course."

"I have no wish to birth any bastards," Rhiannyn said, "which is why I have come to speak with you."

Mildreth's eyes narrowed. "Aye?" she prompted.

"Surely there must be something that can keep a child from growing inside me."

In an instant, understanding showed on both women's faces, but though they warmed to the idea with all manner of advice, an hour later Rhiannyn was nowhere nearer a solution. That left only Christophe.

• • •

"I know I should not ask this of you," Rhiannyn began, speaking low so that any nearby could not listen in upon them, "but there is no one else I can turn to."

Christophe looked up from the leaved plants he had spread upon a table for sorting. "You know I would do anything within my power for you."

But how to broach so delicate a subject? Rhiannyn wondered. Directly, she told herself, then hurdled forth with her request. "I am in need of an herb—or a potion," she whispered, leaning nearer him. "One that will prevent me from being taken with child."

The stunned expression upon Christophe's face was almost comical. "I see," he said. "You do not wish to bear my brother any bastards."

She nodded. "Can you help me?"

He seemed disturbed by her request, and in the next breath she knew the reason. "There is a certain root which it is said will make a woman barren for as long as she takes it, but I understand it is not without risk."

"Risk?"

Christophe thought a moment on it, then said, "Dire illness if too much is taken at a time. Theta told me one woman even died when she consumed great quantities of it in trying to rid herself of a babe that already grew in her."

Rhiannyn was momentarily taken aback, but pressed on. "Is it that which Theta uses herself?"

"Aye, though not when she and Thomas were . . ." Uncomfortable, he shifted, folded and unfolded his hands, then shrugged. "As you can imagine, his child she did wish to conceive, though it was never the right time when he called her to him." He barked a short, bitter laugh. "Ah, in some things Thomas was truly wise."

He had known when to lay with a woman and when not to, Rhiannyn realized. Having proclaimed that she would be his wife, Thomas had not wished to make bastards on another. Aye, Christophe was right, in some things his brother had been wise. "Then in the right quantity there is no danger?" she asked.

"Safe enough, I suppose."

"Can you obtain it?"

"Perhaps, though I do not know that I wish to."

"Why ever not?" she exclaimed.

Keeping his answer to himself, Christophe returned to the sorting of his plants.

"Christophe," Rhiannyn said.

He looked up. "None of this would be necessary if you and Maxen would but see what is before you. Mayhap a child might make you see it more clearly."

She gasped. "What are you talking about?"

"That you ought to wed."

Wed? When Maxen had declared that never would he take her as his wife? Rhiannyn wondered in a fluster. When there was so much that stood between them? "Even did Maxen wish to wed me," she said, "I would not wish it—just as I did not wish to wed Thomas."

Christophe's eyes delved into hers. "But you did not love Thomas."

It was the same as he had guessed that morning. For certain he knew her feelings for Maxen.

"I know, Rhiannyn," he said, confirming her thoughts. "I know you, and I know what is in your eyes when you look at my brother. In fact, I likely knew ere you did. But you know now, don't you?"

So transparent, Rhiannyn thought. Was it possible Maxen also knew what should only be known to her?

"Do not lie to me," Christophe said, boyish pleading in his eyes.

She sighed. "Very well," she said, " 'tis true."

His shoulders slumped with relief.

"But why do you speak of wedding?" she asked. "Never would Maxen consent to wed me. A Saxon."

"Why do you think that?"

"For—for many reasons," she sputtered, wondering how she had come to be drawn into this ridiculous conversation. "Both parties must be willing, and as we both are not, and he does not love me in return, 'tis impossible what you suggest."

"Methinks you are wrong about him."

Rhiannyn was shocked. "He cannot possibly return my affections."

"Though he is not so easy to read as you, there is something about him . . ."

Nay, Rhiannyn thought immediately, Christophe was wrong. Else he only conjured emotions Maxen was incapable of in order to appease some part of him that so wanted to believe. "Now that you know my feelings," she said, attempting to conclude their conversation, "I would but ask that you keep my confidence in this."

Rising from the morass of his reflections, Christophe studied her a time, then nodded. "I will."

Relieved, she asked again what she had yet to know. "Can you obtain the root?"

His face clouded. "Though I can make you no promises, I will try."

"I understand." Wishing to ease his troubled mind, she stepped forward and hugged him. "It is really for the best," she said as she drew back.

In the heavy silence that followed, Christophe gathered his plants together, folded them into separate squares of linen, then stepped around her and departed without a backward glance.

As Rhiannyn watched him leave, she touched a hand to her abdomen. "Pray let it not be," she whispered, then went in search of something to distract her.

Chapter Twenty-two

Night came too soon, though the day should have dragged by, considering Rhiannyn's hands were idle without drink to pour. Although she was not Maxen's wife, he stood firm against her acting the serving wench any longer. Hence, she sat silent beside him throughout the meal, and when it was done, only then knew a brief reprieve in slipping away to the kitchens.

Upon returning to the hall, she was surprised to discover a knight had bedded down upon her bench—and was already well into the snores of sleep.

Should she awaken him and lay claim to her pallet, she wondered, or simply find herself a place upon the floor?

"Leave the man be," Maxen said at her back.

She spun around only to come up against his great chest. "I . . ." She faltered as his warmth enveloped her and his too-familiar hands curled around her upper arms. "'Tis my place he sleeps," she murmured.

"No longer," Maxen said, his voice a soft rumble heard just above the restless shifting of those sleep had yet to claim. "Your place is now with me. Come."

Then he again intended for her to occupy his bed throughout the entire night as if she were his wife and not his leman, Rhiannyn realized as she followed him across the hall. Though it was disconcerting, much more unsettling was the fact that Christophe had yet to deliver any herbal to her which might prevent pregnancy. If she had not conceived on the night past, she might do so this eve.

Reaching the chamber, Maxen released her and without hesitation, began unburdening himself of his clothes.

Although Rhiannyn's mind continued to turn frantically over how she was to keep Maxen from impregnating her, she stared as first his chest came bare, then his feet, legs, and lastly that below his waist. Her scheming halted, and in its place came a warming of her insides which boded no good for her.

"Methinks I would like to see you unclothed as well," Maxen said, jolting her back to the present she had momentarily strayed from.

Coloring, Rhiannyn dragged her gaze from him and looked down at her bliaut. Though she had given all of herself to him last eve, she felt awkward in complying. Aye, he had her virtue, but her modesty was still intact.

"Would you like me to assist?" he asked.

Worse yet. Shaking her head, she reached for her sash. "I can manage myself," she said.

As if sensing her embarrassment, Maxen turned and walked to the chair.

"I had not thought you would begin making clothes for me until you had first taken my measurements," he said, lifting her sewing from the arm of the chair where she had earlier left it.

"I used another of your tunics to gauge the size," she said, then pulled the bliaut off over her head.

"Clever," Maxen remarked, "if not for the fact that nearly all the tunics I possess were Thomas's—and quite ill fitting if you have not noticed."

Inwardly, Rhiannyn groaned. She had been so pleased with herself at coming upon this solution to avoid taking his measurements that she had forgotten he was larger than his brother. As Maxen guessed, it was one of Thomas's tunics she had used for a pattern. "I can make the seams smaller," she suggested.

His bare backside to her, Maxen held the tunic to him. "Perhaps," he said, "though I would not like them pulling on me."

Wearing only her chemise, Rhiannyn padded across the floor and reached around Maxen to take the pieced tunic from him.

He gave it to her, then turned to face her. "Ah," he breathed, his gaze drifting down her garment, "you have left something for me." A droll smile pulling at his lips, he laid a hand to her waist and urged her closer.

"Let me hold the tunic to your back that I might know whether or not I can make it fit," Rhiannyn said, desperate to bring his attention back to the garment. However, he was no longer interested in whether it would fit. Plucking it from her hands, he tossed it over his shoulder and began inching up the chemise that stood between his skin and hers.

Lord, but what was she to do? Rhiannyn wondered as her body started answering questions she would rather it did not. She had to stop him. Had to. . . . She groaned as his fingers slid up her thighs and over her hips.

"More, Rhiannyn?" he asked, trailing his fingers higher to the undercurve of her breasts, then to her straining nipples.

"More," she answered, breathless with the sudden need to shed this garment she had thought she wanted to retain.

Maxen complied. Lowering his head, through the thin material of her chemise he took the nipple of one breast between his lips and drew it into his mouth.

Rhiannyn convulsed, then unashamedly arched against him. "Aye, Maxen," she moaned. "More."

He loved her through her chemise for long, aching moments, then gave equal attention to her other breast.

Sharp pangs of need shot through her, culminating in that place between her thighs that she wanted him to come into again.

Sensing it, Maxen lifted his head, kissed her thoroughly, then swept her into his arms and carried her to the bed. Setting her upon the mattress, he spread her legs and knelt on the floor between them.

"Slowly," he said, meeting her gaze. "This time slowly."

And he did go slowly—excruciatingly slow. Trailing his hands up from her ankles, he pushed the chemise off her legs, and upon reaching the insides of her thighs, lowered his head and skimmed his tongue over her flesh in the wake of fingers that had caressed her to trembling.

However, whatever he intended when he reached that hidden place of hers grown sweet and aching with want, Rhiannyn was not to know that night, for she could wait no longer. Surging off the bed, she pushed a surprised Maxen onto his back and dropped a knee on either side of him. A moment later, she took all of him into her. She did not feel the scratch of the rushes beneath her knees, nor the ungiving floor. She felt only the splendor of two bodies made into one, and Maxen's guiding hands which gave her the rhythm without seizing the heading control from her. Gone was modesty, restraint, and all things proper, leaving only a drive as old as man and woman.

Ever faster Rhiannyn moved, aspiring to the gold that ultimately broke through and into the white. This time, though, when she cried out for all to hear her surrender, Maxen was ready. Pulling her down to him, he sealed his mouth over hers, took the cry from her, and as she spun downward, shared his own cry with her.

Her chemise damp between them, Rhiannyn sagged against Maxen and savored every one of the spasms that followed his own fall from the light. Then there was a stillness so complete it seemed the world had ceased to be.

Perfect, Rhiannyn thought. The end of everything and she lay in the arms of the man she loved—even if he did not know it, nor return that love. Nearly perfect.

However, virtual perfection passed into reality minutes later when Maxen spoke into her hair. "I have never had a woman so daring," he said. "You push me beyond myself, Rhiannyn."

Immediately, a flush of embarrassment supplanted her glow of fulfillment, and Rhiannyn wished for nothing more than to shrink into herself.

Maxen must have detected her withdrawal, for he clasped her tighter to him. "There is naught to be ashamed of. You please me mightily, little Saxon."

There was comfort in his words, but still Rhiannyn rued her rash behavior. She had not acted the lady, rather the whore. But that was what she was, after all. . . .

"Next time slowly, though," Maxen said, a smile in his voice. Then, emptying a regretful sigh, he turned with her onto his side and slowly withdrew. "Ah, sweet torment," he groaned as he rose up onto his knees. Gaining his feet, he stretched out a hand to her. "'Tis not a very restful place to make one's bed," he said, brushing the rushes from his back, buttocks, and legs.

Sitting up, Rhiannyn placed her hand in his and was easily drawn up beside him. Grateful for the fall of her chemise down her legs, she forced unwilling eyes to his. "You still wish me to stay?" she asked.

Maxen fleetingly pondered the foolishness of her question. For the love of God, he had said it, had he not? For answer, he lifted her into his arms, carried her to the bed, tossed back the covers, and gently laid her upon the mattress. After extinguishing the torch that was the only light in the chamber, he joined her and pulled her into the curve of his body.

"Cold?" he asked as he reached for the coverlet.

She shook her head.

Drawing his hand back empty, Maxen attempted to fill it with the soft curve of her belly, but there was too little of it. In time, though, the coming of his child would more than fill his hand—both his hands, he knew, then his arms. And when that happened . . .

What? he sharply asked himself. He had said he would not marry her, so what else was there? And why this desire to have her bear him a child?

"Maxen . . ." Her voice cut across his thoughts. "Why your gift of the Saxons to me? Was it payment?"

He frowned. "Payment?"

"For laying with you," she said, a miserable catch in her voice.

He shook his head. "Nay, Rhiannyn, not payment. I was trying to make things right with you." *And me*, he did not say, for that would require far too much explanation—both to her *and* to himself.

She turned in his arms and looked up at him. "Why?" she asked.

Thinking on the things she had told him the night before, he said, "You have been through much. I do not wish to see you hurt anymore."

Knowing there would be more questions he was neither willing nor prepared to answer, he put a decisive end to them before she had a chance to speak. "Sleep now," he said. "Morning is too soon upon us." Then he closed his eyes.

In the outer bailey before the portcullis that was being raised inch by creaking inch, Aethel stood tall and proud at the head of the four who were to leave Etcheverry with him. Though the figure of the great man was menacing by presence alone, he was doubly more so with the shock of wild beard and hair he had made no attempt to put order to. In fact, Rhiannyn thought he looked suspiciously like a bear she had seen skirting her village when she'd been little more than a fanciful, lighthearted child with only dreams to cloud her eyes.

When the portcullis squealed its last protest, a quiet fell over the entire bailey as knights and men-at-arms looked on. Too, the Saxons who had taken fealty to Maxen watched from the sidelines, grudging respect for what their new lord was about to do shining from their eyes. Throughout, the five prisoners moved not a jot, though their eyes seemed everywhere as if they suspected Norman trickery might descend upon them at any moment.

At last Maxen rended the awkward silence. Stepping forward, he met Aethel eye to eye and said, "Do you reach Edwin, I would have you deliver him a message from me."

"*Do* I reach him?" Aethel boomed. "And what makes you think I will not?"

"Tell him I will see him come spring," Maxen continued, ignoring the man's belligerence, "and that we will end this then."

Rhiannyn thought she glimpsed grudging respect in Aethel's eyes a moment before he shuttered them.

"I will tell him," he agreed, then looked past Maxen to Rhiannyn. "Have you also word for me to carry to Edwin?" he asked.

Disconcerted, she shook her head.

"Naught?" he pressed.

"Naught," she echoed, now wishing she had been less effective in persuading Maxen to allow her to attend this leave-taking.

Aethel considered her a long moment, then took an unexpected step past Maxen toward her.

In an instant Maxen wielded a dagger, its blade pressed against the Saxon's throat only a slash away from death. "Leave now, else you will leave not at all," he snarled.

Rhiannyn stared at the dagger. It was the same that had been put upon her tray to murder Maxen—that had murdered Thomas. It was Maxen's reminder to himself of the one he had yet to lay hands to.

"I mean her no harm," Aethel said, though he was careful not to twitch so much as a muscle.

"That is good," Maxen said, "for did you, I would disembowel you this instant."

Something about Aethel, familiar and at once welcoming, told Rhiannyn she had nothing to fear from him. She saw no more accusation in his eyes, nor felt the air of his suspicion. Nay, though he was not the same Aethel of her childhood, neither was he the Aethel she had feared during her visit to his cell.

"My hands are empty," Aethel reminded Maxen. "Surely a word with her will hurt naught."

" 'Tis all right," Rhiannyn said before Maxen could refuse him. Stepping forward, she placed herself alongside the two men. "What is it, Aethel?"

Aethel could barely bend his head to look down at her, for Maxen's blade still threatened the large vein along the side of his neck. "I wish to ask pardon of you," he said.

Then he no longer believed the lies about her? Did not think her a betrayer? Tears flooding her eyes, she swallowed hard to control her quick emotions. "You need not," she said.

"Aye, I do. I have misjudged you, and for that I ask your forgiveness."

What had brought about his change of heart? she wondered. Was it simply that she had asked for their release? Her ponderings useless, she nodded. "Given," she said.

Aethel smiled as best he was able to. "God be with you, Rhiannyn of Etcheverry," he said, then turned his regard upon the man who held his life at the edge of a blade. "God also be with you, Pendery. You will need Him."

Maxen accepted the threat without so much as a blink of an eye, then drew back his blade and pushed Aethel toward the freedom waiting for him beyond the walls. "Do not forget my message," he said.

The Saxon grinned, then motioned the others to follow him beneath the portcullis. With only the clothes on their backs, a single pouch of food each, and a skin of drink, the five passed out of the bailey and began a journey that might see them traipsing all of England in pursuit of their leader.

"I would like to go up to the wall-walk to see them off," Rhiannyn said, observing that Christophe had already gained the vantage for himself.

Maxen frowned, looked ready to refuse her, then nodded. "Very well," he said, returning the dagger to his belt.

"I will take you." He led her to the steps, and at the base, reached a hand behind him in silent beckoning for her to take hold of it.

Twining her fingers with his, Rhiannyn raised her skirts and followed him upward.

At the top, Maxen pulled her to the nearest notch in the wall—one left of Christophe's—and put her before him. "They certainly seem in little hurry to quit Etcheverry," he commented, staring over her head.

Aye, Aethel and those behind him treaded the cleared land with a stride that seemed not in the least bit hasty. Still, Rhiannyn was certain that if it were not Aethel who led, the four would be running for cover of the woods. The bear of a man refused to be intimidated.

She smiled. No matter the outcome of Edwin's battle and what role the Saxon played in it, there would be a place in her heart for Aethel forever.

The shrill sound of a loosed arrow split the air a moment before the Saxon making up the tail-end of the party plummeted to his knees. A darkly feathered shaft protruding from his upper back, he fell flat upon his face amid the long grasses.

Rhiannyn screamed, though the full horror of what she had seen had yet to be made sense of.

Maxen made quick sense of it—and just in time to throw himself and her down upon the wall-walk before an arrow meant for one or both of them made its mark. The missile struck the wall and clattered harmlessly to the stones.

His body shielding Rhiannyn, Maxen angrily spat, " 'Twould seem Ancel has decided it is time." A moment later he was on his feet, sword in hand, rushing toward the watchtower where the murdering knight had positioned himself atop the roof. "Christophe," Maxen called to the stunfaced youth as he passed him, "see Rhiannyn to the donjon."

Ancel had decided? Rhiannyn wondered past the anguish of the death she had just witnessed and the worry over whether the others had met the same fate in the seconds since the first had laid down his life. Amidst the clamor in the bailey below, she looked to the watchtower and saw Sir Ancel cross to the inner wall, all the while nocking another arrow to his bow. "Maxen!" she cried out in warning.

However, he was too fast a moving object for the arrow, which once again struck the wall and fell unbloodied to the walk.

"Rhiannyn," Christophe said urgently, kneeling beside her and gripping her arm, "make haste."

"Maxen," she gasped.

"He is a warrior," he reminded her.

Rhiannyn looked past him to where Maxen had reached the end of the walk and was now mounting the steps to the roof of the tower. Aye, she had to believe he would triumph. Had to. But what then of Aethel and the others? Had they also been killed? "And the other Saxons?" she asked as she rose with Christophe.

"I do not know," he said, "but come—"

"Nay, I need to know," she exclaimed. Jerking free of him, she swung around and leaned into the embrasure, urgently searching across the land below. At first she saw only the fifth man who lay motionless, but movement farther out pulled her gaze to the four who had abandoned their leisurely departure to run for their lives. Though with the distance Rhiannyn could not be certain whether her eyes told true, Aethel's peculiar gait gave evidence that he had also been struck, but perhaps not seriously.

"You have seen," Christophe said, taking her arm once again. "Now delay no more."

As Rhiannyn reluctantly turned with him, a voice rang out across the bailey. "The time has come to choose!" Sir Ancel shouted.

Both Rhiannyn and Christophe jerked their heads around to stare at the man who stood at the edge of the rooftop, his bow flung aside, his sword raised high above his head as he looked down upon those in the bailey who had paused in their flight to aid their lord. Maxen also paused, though not until he reached the roof and stood opposite Ancel.

The traitorous knight glanced once at his enemy, then composed a confident face and looked again to the upturned countenances of the knights and men-at-arms. "Let us draw the lines now," he called. "Those who stand with King William and me, there"—he pointed left—"and those who stand with the Saxons and Pendery, there."

A great uprising of voices sounded as Maxen's men pondered aloud the knight's unsettling words, for clearly none would wish to stand against their king. However, despite the indecision evident in the tumult below, only one separated himself from the others.

Pushing through the gathering, Guy made his way to the right of the bailey, where he stood conspicuously alone. "The side of right is King William *and* Maxen Pendery," he shouted. He threw his arm high and pointed to Ancel. "Not the traitor!"

"It is Maxen Pendery who is a traitor to the crown," Ancel cried. He leveled his sword upon Maxen, whose gaze was hard as he looked upon his men and waited to see with whom they stood. "He has released the enemy to do war upon our own."

"What are a handful of untrained Saxons to the greater Norman army?" Guy retorted. "Are you so weak to fear five men who know more of ploughs and scythes than ever they will know of swords and horses? Are you so short of memory to have forgotten our victory at Hastings?"

There was a stirring among the multitude as many eyes swept from Guy to Ancel to Maxen and back again, but naught else.

"'Tis your death with his do you not come to my side," Ancel called, a hint of desperation creeping into his voice. No longer did he speak with confidence that the knights and men-at-arms would turn from Maxen, that there would be enough division among the men to support his cause. Now there appeared not one among them willing to make such a decision.

"Mine is the only way," Ancel persisted.

Though their murmurs grew louder, the mass continued to hold.

"Do you—"

"Decide!" Maxen bellowed across Ancel's words.

Their vacillation at an abrupt end, the knights and men-at-arms stepped right, enclosing Guy at the heart of them.

Rhiannyn expelled a breath of relief.

"It is between you and me, then," she heard Maxen say.

As she watched, Maxen left his place near the steps and advanced upon Ancel.

"Fools! All of you!" the wretched knight cried, disbelief upon his face. "I will be the king's chosen, not he."

"Defend yourself," Maxen growled, now only paces from his quarry.

However, Ancel suddenly turned and ran toward the rooftop opening that led down into the bowels of the tower.

In the bailey below, Maxen's men fell silent, pressing back as one great body to better follow the contest that was about to begin.

With great alacrity, Maxen followed Ancel and overtook him before he reached his escape. "Come for me." Maxen beckoned his sword before him.

Having no other choice but to stay and fight for what he had claimed as his, Ancel stepped back, and in the next instant thrust his sword forward. The initial kiss of steel on steel knelled loudly in the expectant silence, and then grew steadily more deafening over the next minutes, as did the spew of curses, grunts, and groans of labored battle.

That it was an unmatched fight all must have realized as they watched in awe, their lord transformed into the celebrated Bloodlust Warrior. As if more beast than man, he drove Ancel farther and farther back until the knight remained standing only by the grace of a God who was very close to abandoning him.

The very thing that drove Maxen toward victory laid fear upon Rhiannyn as she watched this macabre contest of death. Maxen was completely ungiving, allowing neither his opponent nor himself a moment's rest. With each successive thrust, his great body bunched and strained, yet his strength seemed not to dwindle, but rather swell. Terrible sounds tore from his throat like the angry howls of a wolf, and when he took first blood he loosed such a shout that even the knights long tried in battle flinched from the horror of it.

"Come," Christophe said, a hand upon Rhiannyn, a trembling in his voice.

Shaking her head, she pulled out of his grasp. "Nay, I will stay," she said.

Immediately he stepped in front of her and blocked her view. "You should not see this."

Determinedly, she stepped around him. "I need to know."

"God, Rhiannyn," he gasped, "this is not the Maxen you love. Pray do not cloud your feelings for him with this."

Would her love for him wither after witnessing Ancel's slaughter? she wondered. Her eyes filled again with the conqueror and the defeated who still fought a battle already decided. Regardless, she had to watch, for this could be none other than Maxen's demon. To understand it, she must see it.

"I beseech thee, Rhiannyn," Christophe implored. "Come away now."

She shook her head, and to her relief, that seemed the end of the debate.

Showing signs that his arm had grown heavy and pained, Ancel clasped his other hand atop the first in a two-handed grip that allowed him to lift his dragging sword to counter Maxen's next blow. It was not enough, though, for Maxen's blade easily laid the other aside and slashed through Ancel's chest. With an anguished cry, Ancel dropped the point of his sword low, stumbled back, and slapped a hand to the gushing wound.

Although Maxen advanced no more, did not immediately finish with the knight as the Bloodlust Warrior would likely have done, he stood ready to end what the other had started.

"Devil's seed!" Ancel screeched. "Look what you have

done." Perhaps mad, perhaps in shock, perhaps a bit of both, he thrust his brightly stained hand before his opponent's stone-faced figure. "My blood," he wailed. "My blood."

Whatever Maxen's response, none but the speaker and the one spoken to could make it out. However, it would have been well-guessed that it was words of parting he uttered, for in the next instant he thrust his sword through the faithless knight, and Ancel was laid down as cleanly as the piteous Saxon who had been felled by Ancel's arrow.

A murmur rose to a roar as those of Maxen's men farthest back and able to see all that had transpired atop the watchtower spread the word that their lord was the victor. They had chosen well the one with whom to side.

"Have you seen enough?" Christophe asked, his voice harsh.

Swallowing hard, Rhiannyn tore her gaze from Maxen's back and turned it upon his brother. Though relief poured into her that Maxen was not the one lying in a spreading pool of blood, there was something deeper and older within her which nearly countered the good of what had happened. So many horrors she had seen these past years, but this reached out and touched her with fingers more chill than any she could remember.

Why? she wondered. Was Maxen not in the right to defend himself and his? After all, it was Ancel who had initiated it by murdering one of the Saxons, wounding another, and then aiming to put an arrow through Maxen. There was no other course Maxen could have taken other than the one he had. Why, then, this tumult of feelings?

Withholding the answer Christophe sought, she looked to Maxen again and saw that he continued to stand unmoving before the dead knight, his head bent, his broad shoulders seeming to carry the greatest of burdens upon them. Thinking that perhaps she understood this terrible feeling inside her, that it was Maxen's anguish, Rhiannyn said, "I must go to him." She raised her skirts, swept past Christophe, and began a swift negotiation of the wall-walk.

"Rhiannyn, you musn't!" Christophe cried after her. His bad leg preventing him from reaching her, in desperation he called out his warning. "Maxen!" he shouted above the din. "Rhiannyn comes!"

She had only put foot to the bottom step leading up to the roof when Maxen appeared at the top. Stern-faced, a thousand emotions hidden behind set jaw, flared nostrils, and darkened eyes, he began his descent.

Stepping back, Rhiannyn swept her gaze down his tunic to the spots of blood covering it—Ancel's blood—then to the hem of the garment where parallel streaks gave evidence that Maxen had wiped his blade clean upon it. Though she tried to keep her face impassive, she knew she had failed the moment he stepped down to the wall-walk, for a harsh guardedness entered his eyes.

"You were to have returned to the donjon," he said between clenched teeth. Giving her no time to defend herself, he clamped a hand around her arm and roughly pulled her after him.

"Maxen, I know you must feel—"

"Speak no more," he said shortly. "I am not of a mood to listen."

Then once they gained his chamber she would speak to him, she decided. Too, this really was not the place to address what had just transpired.

His stride unfaltering, he led her to a silent, watchful Christophe. "Now your Josa is avenged," he said.

Rhiannyn frowned in an effort to understand his words, but in the next instant a memory came to her of the Saxon healer who two years past had been murdered by Ancel, his only crime being compassion for the dying.

Christophe nodded.

"I will ask you again to deliver Rhiannyn to the donjon," Maxen added, his tone admonishing. He pushed her toward his brother.

" 'Tis not he to blame," Rhiannyn said, attempting to defend Christophe. However, Maxen did not linger to hear her.

Shoulders wide, stride strong, he descended to the bailey where a mass of men clamored to his side. Immediately, though, they were turned back with sharp words of rebuke. A path cleared for him, Maxen walked the bailey alone, his destination . . . the chapel.

Chapter Twenty-three

" 'Tis good," Christophe muttered as he watched his brother enter the building.

Rhiannyn looked up at him. "He goes to pray?" she asked.

"I believe so."

Aye, good, but still she could not help but think she ought to be with him.

"To the donjon," Christophe said, then motioned for her to follow him.

All the way down the steps Maxen had just tread Rhiannyn fought the impulse, but when she reached the bailey, she gave in to it. Ignoring Christophe's shout, she lifted her skirts and ran to the chapel as if she wore hose instead of woman's dress. At the great doors she paused, though only long enough to compose herself to go quietly into the sanctuary.

She found Maxen standing before the linen-covered altar, his head pressed to the forearm he rested upon it.

"What do you here, Rhiannyn?" he asked with her first footfall. He spoke not angrily, but with great weariness. Still, he did not turn to her.

As quietly as she had come in, how had he known he was no longer alone? she wondered. But more, that it was she? "I did not think you should be alone," she said.

"Is God not here?" he asked, the weariness in his voice straining.

"Aye, He is."

"Then I am not alone, am I?"

Steeling herself, Rhiannyn denied him an answer he did not expect, but neither did she leave. Continuing toward him, she was halfway down the aisle when she stepped on something she felt straight through her slipper—Maxen's sword still sheathed upon its belt. She had been too intent upon the man to notice he had carelessly cast his weapon on the floor. Unthinking, she bent and closed her hand over the belt.

"Leave it!" Maxen's harsh command rent the air.

Thinking he must have turned to have seen her reach for it, she looked up to discover he had not moved in the least. Straightening, she stepped over the sword, walked the last steps to him, and gently laid a hand upon his shoulder. "It had to be done," she said.

Immediately, the muscles beneath her fingers bunched as if he might pounce upon her. "You know naught, Rhiannyn. Now be gone."

"I know you are greatly burdened."

"I said be gone!"

". . . that there is much blood on your hands you would wish away."

Fury in every line of him, he pushed off the altar and swung around to face her. "Wish? *Pray* away, Rhiannyn," he corrected her, his face suffused with color, "though God knows I've done enough of that—and to no end. Hardly am I out of the monastery and already I have killed three, perhaps four men. And do not forget the Saxon who lies

dead—shot through with an arrow because I did not do
with Ancel what should have been done long ago. Nay,
God is not with me. He could not possibly be with me."

How she wanted to comfort him, to put her arms
around him and hold him as he'd held her when she had
spilled her misery upon him two nights past. But this was
a different kind of pain, the pain of guilt and self-
condemnation, whereas hers had been of loss. "You cannot
change Hastings," she said, "but you can change what happens now and in this place—and you have."

"Damnation!" he swore, stepping around her as if in
distancing himself he might gain control over his dangerous emotions. "Did you not yourself just witness a killing,
woman?"

"What other choice did you have?" She spoke to his
back. "For that matter, what choice had you at Hastings?
After all, 'twas for your liege you fought—to him you answered."

He was still a long moment before he turned back to
her. "You really believe that?" he asked, derision in his
tone.

"Is it not true?"

A haunting came upon his face, though his eyes remained flint-hard. He shook his head.

Rhiannyn's insides twisted. "What is the truth, then?"
she asked.

"The truth ..." He looked past her as if searching for
it himself. "The truth is that I more than earned the name
given me at Hastings. As a man who has been long without
food, I hungered for the blood of people who were not my
enemies—some of whom I grew up amongst and called
'friend.' "

Rhiannyn swallowed the lump in her throat. "Hastings
was a battle between two peoples." She sought to justify
what he had done, though never would she have believed
she would one day defend a Norman against a Saxon.
"You are Norman, Maxen, and your opponents were
Saxon. What else were you to do?"

He swept his gaze back to her. "But there is the lie," he said.

Not understanding, she frowned.

"By birth I am Norman, but I was reared in England among Saxons. I am more one of them than I am one of King William's."

"But he was your family's liege. It was your duty to fight at his side."

He shook his head. "But with such atrocity?"

Aye, so much that he bore a name which conjured visions of mass slaughter. Though she feared that to ask of it would take back whatever ground she'd gained, she said, "Why did you do it?"

Maxen stared at her—nay, through her—a long time before answering. "It was what I had trained for all my life," he said. "Nils, Thomas, and I always had to prove ourselves before our father. In fact, there is not a time I can remember ever having been without a weapon at hand. All that I learned, I learned from my father—not at his knee, but at the end of his sword." His expression one of disgust, he pushed his fingers through his hair. "Though I had killed before Hastings, it had ever been with just cause. However, William's battle was different, and I was eager— not to gain land as so many of his soldiers did, but to prove myself a warrior in every sense. To prove it to myself, my father, and William. And that I did."

It was difficult to listen to him speak of such things, especially when the faces of her father and brothers swelled upon her memory, but the Maxen he spoke of was not the one she knew. Not the one she loved. "But you repented," she said, taking a step toward him. "You entered the monastery and gave your life to God to atone for what you had done."

"And you think that is enough?" he snapped.

"In God's eyes it must surely be."

Looking as if he meant to charge her, his jaw set, eyes flashing, Maxen came toward her.

Although Rhiannyn's heart jumped with fear, she forced herself to stand brave. However, Maxen stepped around

her and a moment later pounded his fist upon the altar.
"Then why does He not take this haunting from me?" he
demanded. "Day and night it is with me, before my eyes
when they are open, and behind them when they are
closed." He shook his head. "You wished to know why I
released the Saxons, and I told you. But what I did not tell
you was that I also did it for myself."

More and more his pain became Rhiannyn's, tugging
her heart low. Though she knew she risked much, she went
to him again. This time, though, she gained his side and
put one hand to his shoulder, the other over his much
larger hand. "You have not forgiven yourself," she said
softly, trying to ignore the ripple of tension her touch
roused in him.

There was no welcome in his face when he turned it to
her. "How can I?" he asked. "Only after so many lay dead
did my sword run no more with blood. Only after I had
seen . . ."

"What?" she urged.

He considered her for what seemed hours—tormented,
yet unwilling to continue—then ground out, "Nils."

"Your brother."

"Aye."

"What happened?"

Though Maxen fought back the vision, it came as it
never had since he had first seen the reality. Lord, but he
should not speak of it, should not put the outrage of it
upon Rhiannyn, but her eyes . . . She needed to know—
even if it meant she might turn from him.

"I was wet through," he began, "not only with perspiration, but with the blood of Saxons, and though William's
victory was assured, still I raged with a need to slay
another . . . and yet another."

Maintaining as passive a face as she could, Rhiannyn
nodded for him to continue.

Very well, his eyes said, but you will wish I had not. "I
was strong with death, triumphant, and searching out the
next to die when I heard Nils. Thinking he meant to join
me in finishing the Saxons, I turned to him. But instead of

the powerful, invincible man he had been that morn, I saw a man barely alive, sprawled atop Saxons three deep, his chain mail being taken from him even as he groaned out the last of his life."

Rhiannyn's impassive expression fell against her determination to hold it, a shudder quaking mightily through her as her imagination showed her what Maxen had seen.

"Stripped of all things valuable by his own," he continued. "Aye, that's right, Rhiannyn," he said when he saw her surprise. "'Twas the Normans who robbed him, those very ones he had fought alongside. No glory. No honor."

She swayed under the weight of his haunting.

"Have you heard enough?" he demanded.

She gripped him tighter. "Are you finished?" she asked, praying that he was, but knowing she must hear if there was more.

"Are you?" he countered.

"Tell me."

His jaw shifted side to side. "Then I smelled it, saw it, even tasted it."

Though she really did not wish to know, she asked, "What?"

"The blood of William's conquering. Rivers of it. And when the Saxon women came upon the field to search out their dead, the hems of their skirts grew so heavy with blood they could hardly move. All those lives, Rhiannyn— all lost for naught but greed."

She closed her eyes. "I'm sorry."

There was no humor in the laughter he loosed. "*You* are sorry? You who are Saxon and lost your entire family to Normans? Has it not occurred to you that I might have been the one to slay your father? Your brothers?"

She forced her eyes open to stare at the fury in his. "It has," she admitted, "but no more of my life will I squander pondering their deaths, nor the deaths of all the others. And neither should you. You must forgive yourself, Maxen. Not only is the battle done with, but it was not of your making."

"In the beginning, but by the end I had made it mine."

"Perhaps then you had," she said. "Now it is in the past. 'Tis over."

He turned his whole body toward her. "Over? And who do you think the king will summon to put an end to Edwin Harwolfson come spring, Rhiannyn? Who?"

As if struck, she stumbled back a step. "Nay, Maxen, it cannot be."

"It will be, and then for *my liege* blood will once again stain all of me."

It would be so easy to give in to the despair rushing through her, but Rhiannyn was stronger than that. Had to be. "You will find a way," she said. "I know you will. That other part of you is no more."

"You think not?" he said scornfully. "Ah, but we will see, won't we?"

Determined, she shook her head. " 'Tis not what I think, but what I know."

He looked ready to refute what she knew, but in the next instant turned from her and strode to where his sword lay. As she watched, he picked up the weapon and belted it on. "You still think so?" he asked, spreading his hands to indicate the weapon finery he had donned.

Lord, how menacing he looked, she thought—how ready to do battle and scatter more of the blood he so loathed. "I do," she answered.

He shook his head. "So innocent."

"Nay, forgiving."

His eyes narrowed on her as if he searched for the lie behind her words. Then he beckoned her to him. "Come to me, Rhiannyn."

Stepping from the altar, she walked to where he stood. "Aye, my lord?"

Lifting a hand, he caught a lock of her hair between thumb and forefinger. "Have you really forgiven?" he asked, settling his gaze on hers.

"I try."

"Then you have not forgiven."

"Not all," she answered honestly, "but every day I forgive a bit more. So, too, must you."

He lowered his gaze and stared at the space between them. When he finally looked up, it was as if the vivid memories he had imprinted upon her mind had begun to ebb from his. "You give me hope," he said.

And love, she did not say; however, she offered him a tentative smile.

He returned the smile, then pulled her to him and pressed a kiss to her mouth. "I want you in my life, Rhiannyn," he said as he pulled back.

Her heart jumped with hope, but in the next instant she berated herself for foolishly thinking he might return some of her feelings. Christophe had to bring her something soon that would keep her barren.

Saying no more, Maxen turned her down the aisle and led her outside and past a group of Saxons, several of whom offered them hesitant smiles.

" 'Twould appear you have won them over," Rhiannyn said once they were out of earshot.

Maxen made no comment, but simply led her up the causeway toward the donjon.

Whether or not he acknowledged it, there was one thing Rhiannyn knew—even if Athel and the others believed the killing of one of them to be of Maxen's doing, these Saxons knew the truth of what had happened this day. And if only one good came of the bloodletting, it would be that Maxen had secured their loyalty by giving full justice to the Norman who had killed a Saxon without just cause. And that was very good.

"Maxen!" Christophe called as they mounted the steps to the donjon.

Rhiannyn and Maxen turned to watch as Christophe ran his lopsided gait up the steps.

"What is it?" Maxen asked.

Christophe took only a moment to draw a steadying breath, then rushed into his news. "The Saxon lives," he said excitedly. "Badly wounded, but methinks he will heal fine."

Looking up at Maxen, Rhiannyn glimpsed the relief

that shone from him before it was hidden beneath a stern face. "Then tend him," he said.

With a nod, Christophe swiveled and hurried away again.

"And you say God is not with you," Rhiannyn mused aloud.

Maxen shook his head. "Nay, but for certain He is with the Saxon."

Minutes later the bed was at Rhiannyn's back, all thought of turning away Maxen's seed flown out the window.

"I have prepared it exactly as Josa put down," Christophe said, referring to the notes the healer had left him.

Rhiannyn regarded the pouch he held out to her. It was well past a sennight since she had asked him for it, perhaps now too late, but she would know within five days when and if her menses came. Taking it from him, she said, "I am most grateful, Christophe."

"A pinch a day," he instructed her, "and that is all."

She nodded. "A pinch."

"For the first few days you might experience some nausea," he continued, "but after that you should feel yourself again."

"Thank you," she said, giving him her best smile.

He shrugged. "When you begin to run low, let me know and I will make you more."

She nodded. "What of the Saxon? Does he heal as you thought he would?"

"Aye, the worst is past. Hob should recover with naught but a scar to remind him of his fall."

"And when he is healed?"

"Maxen has said he may leave if he still wishes to—but I do not believe he will."

This was the first she had heard of it. "Why is that?"

"He seems well content with his surroundings. Having believed himself a dead man—of Pendery treachery—he now knows the treachery was not of Maxen's making and he begins to trust. Too, methinks he has his eye on your Meghan."

Proving that some things did come right. Rhiannyn smiled. "She assists you?" she asked.

"Aye, and quite good she is."

"Then what of Theta?"

Christophe scowled. "She complains far too much of her burden, especially since being given the added duty of serving drink at the meals. I could take it no more."

This explained Theta's recent behavior, Rhiannyn mused. She was more spiteful than ever, her looks more slaying, and her words more cutting. Except in the presence of Maxen, few were spared her, but what to do about the woman?

"Your choice of Meghan is a good one," she said to Christophe.

He nodded. "This I know."

Clutching the pouch of precious powder, Rhiannyn turned and headed toward the donjon. In the chamber she now shared with Maxen, she pinched an amount between thumb and forefinger, swallowed its bitterness dry, then hid the pouch where Maxen would never find it.

Chapter Twenty-four

The parchment fell from Maxen's fingers, and before it landed upon the floor, it had already rolled back upon itself.

Sensing the gravity of the missive that had been delivered only minutes earlier, Rhiannyn motioned for the scattered knights and servants to clear the hall. It was something she did without forethought, realizing only after they began withdrawing that she was acting the lady of the castle as Maxen had given her the privilege of doing. Though she had been slowly growing into the role, it still surprised her that the servants—and even Maxen's men—complied. But time enough to ponder it later, she told herself.

"What is it?" she asked Maxen once they were alone.

He did not answer her. Instead, he

stared straight ahead with eyes that had seen too much and now were seeing even more.

With great foreboding, Rhiannyn leaned down, retrieved the parchment, and attempted to decipher the heavily scrawled Norman French she had too little experience with to come anywhere near to understanding. In the end, frustration won out and she laid the missive aside.

"Tell me," she entreated.

Maxen closed his eyes a moment, then leaned back in his chair and met her gaze. "'Tis Edwin," he said, his voice like a sword to the man's heart.

Something terrible gripped Rhiannyn. "William has summoned you?" she asked, still unable to call the Norman by the title he had stolen from King Harold.

"Nay."

She blinked, completely flustered by his reaction to this letter that clearly was not what she expected it to be. "What, then?" she asked, growing more concerned as the color of wrath seeped up Maxen's neck into his face.

"Over a fortnight past, my sister, Elan, was caught outside the castle and set upon by a Saxon."

"She was hurt?"

The flush of color swept up Maxen's forehead and disappeared into his dark hair. "The bastard raped her," he growled.

The vile word was like a blow to Rhiannyn. Too much she knew of rape from the coming of the Normans to her village, though she had been spared personal knowledge of it. Hence, hearing that another—Maxen's sister—had suffered such terrible violation stirred the pain of a past she had no wish to relive. "I am sorry," she said.

"You are also blind," Maxen snarled. Leaping from his chair, he began pacing the dais.

"Blind?" Rhiannyn repeated.

He halted abruptly. "Aye, I spoke Edwin's name, then told of my sister's rape, and yet you draw no connection."

Rhiannyn's heart pounded as she saw the connection he made—one she would never have made on her own. "Ah, nay," she exclaimed, "it cannot be."

In an instant Maxen was before her, the savage in him lifting its head. "Edwin was in the area, Rhiannyn," he said, a muscle leaping in his jaw, "he is as Elan described him, and she says he called himself by that name."

Shaking her head, Rhiannyn backed away from Maxen, but could go no farther than the table she came up against. "Then either she lies, or someone posing as Edwin did the deed."

"Not so long ago you told me of the changed man Edwin had become after Hastings," he reminded her.

"But not in that way," she cried. "Never in that way."

Maxen stared hard at her, his seething visible in every line of his body and heard in every breath he drew. Although something eased in him as he looked at her, something that forced the savage back down, still, he was a menacing figure, not to be dealt with lightly. "How can you be certain?" he asked.

"I know Edwin, and I know he would never do such a thing. Never!"

"Then, as you say, my sister is either mistaken or a liar." He leaned nearer Rhiannyn. "And if she lies, what gain for her in doing so?"

Rhiannyn shook her head. "I do not know, but whatever happened to her, upon my soul Edwin did not rape her."

Maxen straightened. "And upon my soul, if it was he who did it, Rhiannyn, come spring he will pay for it with his life."

At least he conceded the possibility that Edwin was not responsible for what had befallen his sister, Rhiannyn comforted herself. "What of your sister?" she asked. "Was she not to wed soon?"

Dropping back into his chair, Maxen retrieved the missive and read the remainder of it. "My father has broken her betrothal," he answered a few minutes later.

There was more, Rhiannyn sensed. "And?" she prodded.

"And now he waits."

She frowned. "For?"

"Evidence of whether or not Elan's rape will produce a bastard."

"And if it does?"

"Then he will send her away until the child is born."

To a convent, Rhiannyn knew, where the bastard children of nobles were born and most often left behind when their mothers returned to their former lives, however much changed after their indiscretions.

But what of Maxen's father? she wondered. "And your father?" she asked. "Does he also intend to seek revenge against Edwin?"

Maxen smiled caustically. "There is no greater sport he enjoys than that of vengeance, no better thrill than blood upon his blade."

This was a perception of Maxen's father heretofore unspoken, and Rhiannyn was given further insight into the man she loved. Certainly Maxen and his father were not of the same ilk, but the man he had become at Hastings, and nearly again upon Ancel's death, was now better explained. "What will he do?" she asked.

"Bide his time."

"Then he will not seek William's ear?"

"You misunderstand, Rhiannyn. Likely the king was the first to receive news of Elan's spoiling. My father will think naught of casting further dishonor upon her by making known to all what happened. Aye, he will have his revenge, but with all cheering him on."

Rhiannyn made no attempt to suppress the shudder that shot through her. "I do not think your father is a man I would like to meet."

"If I can keep him from my walls, you will not have to," Maxen said.

Always there was something more to worry over, Rhiannyn thought. "Will you make me a vow, Maxen?" she asked.

"Ask."

"I would ask that you work no revenge upon Edwin until you know the truth of this thing that was done to your sister."

He sighed. "Rhiannyn, though I know it pains you to hear this, whether or not Edwin is responsible, his death will still be sought. 'Tis only the manner in which his life is taken that is in question."

True, for hardly a day went by without some word of Edwin's plunderings and raids. Only three days past, a messenger knight from the north had stopped at Etcheverry to rest his horse and replenish his food and drink. In the short time he had spent at Maxen's table, he had spoken angrily of his lord's wooden castle which Edwin and his ever-growing band of Saxons had attacked and set fire to—all of it burned to the ground. It was this news he had been dispatched to carry to King William, and a pleading for aid from the ruthless Saxon "wolf." Then yesterday, news had come that the king had raised the reward for the one who brought him Edwin's head—a purse of a staggering amount.

Aye, Edwin's death would be sought even were he known to be innocent of the rape, but Rhiannyn was not so certain his death would be gained—especially if she could prevent Maxen from being the one to confront Edwin. "Just promise me, Maxen," she said.

"Do I ever meet him again, I will afford him a chance to prove he was not the one."

Going up on tiptoe, she put her lips to his cheek. "I thank you," she said. "I know you do it for me."

"Do I?"

She pulled back. "Don't you?"

His smile was very near to being real. "Anything for you, Rhiannyn," he said. "Anything."

Her heart fluttering, her soul feeling one with his, she also smiled.

Another month passed, and fall fell into winter with the arrival of one who came without warning. Like a bluster of wind, a dozen horses and riders descended upon Etcheverry. Sitting at the center of this escort was a pretty young woman whose demeanor suggested shame, yet more than once Rhiannyn saw her raise her downcast eyes and look around with almost childlike excitement.

"You are most welcome at Etcheverry, sister," Maxen said as he lifted Elan from her mount.

Set upon her feet, she peeked up at him, then quickly cast her eyes down again. "I fear 'tis not good tidings I bring," she murmured.

"I guessed as much, but we will speak of it later."

"Elan," Christophe called as he pushed a way for himself toward her. A moment later his sister was squeezed into his embrace. "Years," he said.

"Too many," she answered.

Pulling back, Christophe looked at her from head to toe. "And look how you've grown!"

A quick smile lit her face, but in the next instant she put it away as if suddenly remembering it was not fitting. "As have you, Christophe," she said in a soft voice that did not seem to agree with the young woman Rhiannyn had caught a glimpse of.

Mayhap she was looking too hard, Rhiannyn thought—looking for something that simply wasn't there, in defense of Edwin against the accusations this woman had made. Lord, but it was not an easy thing to be fair to one she had come to resent these last weeks. As Maxen had predicted, his father had not thought twice about dishonoring his daughter by making public what had happened to her. Now the word was among knights, men-at-arms, and servants that Elan Pendery had been defiled by Edwin Harwolfson. But Rhiannyn was sure that it was simply not true.

Maxen motioned for his father's knights to dismount. "Wine and mead await you in the hall," he invited. "Come and warm yourselves."

It was a silent, expectant procession that ascended to the donjon, Rhiannyn walking behind Elan, who was flanked by both her brothers, the others following farther back. However, once within the hall, it was only a matter of minutes before voices began to rise, then clamor as the promised drink commenced to flowing.

At the high table, mantles removed and warmed wine

before them, those seated near Maxen trained their gazes upon the young woman who sat in their midst.

"Elan," Maxen said to her, "I would present Rhiannyn of Etcheverry to you."

Slowly rolling the goblet between her hands to take the chill from them, Elan looked up at her brother, then to the woman who sat beside him. There was probing in her eyes as she made an assessing sweep of Rhiannyn—almost as if she was searching for something just out of her reach. "Of Etcheverry?" she asked.

"Aye," Maxen said. "She was of this place ere it was Pendery."

"Ah, then she is Saxon."

"I am," Rhiannyn was quick to answer for herself.

Interest lit Elan's eyes, but again she veiled it by fluttering her lashes down over them. After a long moment spent composing herself, she lifted her lids. "And what does she here at your side, brother?" she asked.

An uncomfortable silence followed, then Maxen said, "She is the lady of the castle."

Elan's gaze flitted to Rhiannyn's bare hands. "Yet she possesses not your name, brother. To share a bed with a man most certainly does not make one a lady. Indeed, it makes one a . . ." A nervous laugh fluttered from her lips.

A spark lit a flame in Rhiannyn. "Ah, but I also share his bath," she quipped. From Maxen's stiffening she knew he was as angered by the callous tone of her claim as he was by Elan's spiteful bite.

At least there was one who found humor in Rhiannyn's frankness, one who had little to be gladdened by now that she had been given the added chore of serving drink— Theta. Snickering openly, the woman sloshed ale over a knight's hand as she poured for him. Whatever angry words the man retaliated with were lost beneath Maxen's.

"She is the lady, Elan," he said, his voice carefully even, "and while you are at Etcheverry, you will treat her with the respect accorded one of that station."

Looking none too pleased with her brother's pronouncement, Elan opened her mouth as if to protest.

"Elan, allow me to introduce to you Sir Guy Torquay," Christophe said, gesturing to the man beside him—an ill-disguised attempt to turn the conversation.

Elan snapped her mouth closed and turned to her younger brother.

Refusing to meet Maxen's gaze, Rhiannyn looked past him to Sir Guy, who, for the first time ever, appeared interested in something other than duty to his liege. Quickly, she glanced at Elan to gauge whether or not she returned Guy's interest. Perhaps, though it was difficult to be certain with her ever-shifting eyes and expression.

"Sir Guy," Elan repeated in acknowledgment. Then, pressing her lips together as if to prevent them from smiling, she looked back at Maxen. "I . . ." she began, then her voice trailed off into nothingness. A moment later, she swung her gaze to Rhiannyn. "I know who you are," she exclaimed. "You are the one Thomas wished to wed, are you not? The one who led him to his death."

It was a terrible thing for Rhiannyn to hear again, but there was no denying it. "It is true Thomas wished to wed me," she admitted.

"But you will not accept responsibility for his death?"

"As she is not the one responsible," Maxen said before Rhiannyn could even come near to formulating a reply, "she can hardly accept the burden of it."

Maxen's statement rooted Rhiannyn right to the bench; however, Elan, suffering no such ties, shot straight up from hers, causing many a head to turn to the high table. "And you," she said to Maxen, her eyes having lost their studied demureness and turned bright and flashing, "you, Thomas's brother, defend her."

"Sit down, Elan!" Maxen ordered. Everything about him—from his angry frown to his tense frame—warned that if she did not, she would suffer for her willful defiance.

Fortunately for Elan, she read her brother well. With great reluctance, she sank back down upon the bench.

"Now finish your drink," Maxen commanded, "then

you and I will talk of the reason you have come to Etcheverry."

"Surely you must already know," Elan said boldly, apparently unafraid to speak of it now and in the presence of so many.

"Later," Maxen growled.

Her lips twitched, but in this she was wise to push him no further.

Stunned by Maxen's revelation that she was not responsible for Thomas's death, Rhiannyn hardly noticed any of what followed thereafter. Was it true what he had said? she wondered. Or had he only said it to stem his sister's tirade? Perhaps. . . .

In contrast, Maxen was more than aware of what ensued during the next hour. Ignoring the pull of the woman beside him, he carefully watched his little sister. As thoroughly as possible, he assessed all she had become since last he had seen her well over two years past. She had been reckless then, quick and sharp of tongue, but the woman she was fast becoming—or perhaps not so fast becoming— had magnified every one of those not-so-desirable characteristics.

She was well acted, he realized as he watched and listened to the conversation she struck up with Guy and Christophe, having completely forgotten her earlier demeanor of meekness, mildness, and melancholy. Aye, quite adept at using every feminine device to lure men to her. He noticed Guy's peculiar response to her smiles, fluttering lashes, and husky words. Normally, the knight was unmoved by the advances of women, deciding for himself when and where he would better know one who caught his eye. With Elan, though, he appeared much moved, his usually serious face reflecting his interest in her.

For a moment, Maxen entertained the possibility that Rhiannyn was correct in defending Edwin and suggesting that Elan had lied about being raped. But why? Why?

"You are finished," he stated upon seeing his sister empty the last of her drink from her goblet.

Obviously wishing to delay the inevitable interview with

him, she said, "One more, Maxen," then raised the goblet for it to be refilled.

"Nay, you have had enough." Standing, he cupped her elbow in his palm and raised her from the bench.

She looked as if she might protest, but in the next instant lowered her eyes and nodded. "Very well," she said, once again the obedient one.

Maxen's first thought was to speak with her in the privacy of his chamber, but the second thought veered him far right of it to the storeroom instead. "Leave us, Aldwin," he ordered the butler, who, since being caught drunk the night Rhiannyn had slipped into the dungeons, had made an admirable effort to remain sober. The threat of being relegated to kitchen duty had worked well.

"The missive," Maxen said once he and his sister were alone. He held his hand out for it.

Grimacing, she removed the rolled parchment from the deep pouch at her waist and placed it in his palm.

Maxen turned it. "The seal has been broken," he said, more than a little irritated that Elan had taken it upon herself to discover the contents of their father's message.

For all her impudence, she actually looked a bit remorseful—or perhaps simply embarrassed. "As it concerns me," she said, "I saw no reason why I should not read it."

Maxen stared hard at her, then leaned back against a barrel and crossed his arms over his chest. "And what does it say?" he asked.

She shifted foot to foot before answering. "Why do you not read it yourself?"

"Save me the trouble."

She looked down, but when next she met his gaze, it was with long-suffering eyes. "As you know," she began, "I was . . ." She closed her eyes, squeezed them tight, and swallowed hard. Then, drawing a deep breath, she looked at him again. "I was raped." She spoke little above a whisper.

Though part of Maxen sensed that her pain was more

an act than something truly felt, another part of him stirred with compassion. "I have heard," he said.

Suddenly Elan was in his arms, her shoulders jumping and shaking as she sobbed into his tunic. "It was terrible," she mumbled. "The most awful thing."

Ah, Lord, Maxen inwardly groaned as the hardness in him began to dissolve. This was his sister who was hurting. He folded her more tightly against his chest. " 'Tis done with," he said soothingly, uncertain where the reassuring words came from. "No more can he harm you."

She shuddered long, then angled her head back to look up at him. "Is that a promise?" she asked.

He nodded. "Whoever did this to you will not go unpunished."

"Whoever? But it was the Saxon Harwolfson who did it," she said. "Did Father not write it to you?"

"He did."

"Then why do you not acknowledge it was he? Surely you believe me?" She looked almost desperate for him to believe her. "I do not lie in this."

He hoped not—or did he? Was it better his sister was truthful, or Rhiannyn correct in her estimation of Edwin? "I have not said you have lied," he said. " 'Tis just that Rhiannyn does not believe him capable of such an offense. She submits it may have been another disguising himself as Edwin."

"Rhiannyn!" Indignant, Elan withdrew from Maxen and began pacing the small room. "Ah, yes, she was once betrothed to the Saxon bastard, wasn't she?" she muttered. "Of course she would defend him."

"I also met Edwin," Maxen said, "and neither did he seem to me to be one who would do such a thing. A rebel, aye, but a rapist ... ?"

Elan swung around to face him. "Then you do not know him as I do," she snapped. A moment later, her face fell. "Obviously you do not know him as I do," she whispered. Her eyes fixed to some place in her memory, she pressed a hand to her belly.

"Are you pregnant, Elan?" Maxen asked, though he

was already certain of it from her rather theatrical performance. Aye, performance, he acknowledged after sharply
questioning the word that had come to mind. With each
passing minute, memories of the little girl he had occasionally seen about the castle while growing up returned to
him. She had been attention-grabbing and melodramatic
then, and the years since appeared to have matured none
of that out of her.

Dropping her hand, Elan thrust her chin high. "Aye, I
am pregnant."

Maxen considered her a long moment, then said, "You
seem not as disturbed by it as I would expect, sister."

She gasped in outrage. "What would you have me do?
Put a dagger to my wrists? Perhaps throw myself from a
cliff? A martyr? Me? Never. I will bear this misbegotten
child and then . . ."

"What?"

He saw the struggle in her eyes—the first real evidence
of a conscience. However, in the end, the indulgence of
youth that was so much a part of her firmly trampled the
responsibility of an adult. "Then I will give the babe to the
Church to raise as God wills."

"Easy as that, hmm?" Maxen remarked.

"Surely you are not suggesting I keep that—that rapist's
child?" she exclaimed.

"I am suggesting naught. I am simply asking. But tell
me, why have you come to Etcheverry rather than entering
a convent?"

" 'Tis addressed in the letter," she said.

Maxen tapped the parchment against his thigh, but still
did not unroll it.

Elan heaved a sigh. "Very well. Father would have sent
me to a convent, but I begged otherwise—that he send me
to you for the duration of the pregnancy."

"Why?"

"Ah, Maxen, can you imagine me in a convent?" She
made a face. "Either I would die of boredom or be flogged
to death for some little thing I said."

"And you do not think I will do the same?" he asked, purposely stern.

Feeling for his mood, she attempted to draw a smile from him with a coaxing one of her own, but when he remained unmoved, her eyes widened with misgiving. "Would you?" she breathed.

"If needs be."

She swallowed.

Maxen straightened. "You are welcome to stay, Elan, but do you intend to wreak havoc upon my household, I will put you over my knee myself, and then if you continue, I will pack you up and send you to the nearest convent."

She looked to be rethinking her plans, her gaze bouncing between him and the floor while her teeth vigorously worried her bottom lip.

"Do you still wish to remain at Etcheverry?" he asked.

She grimaced. "I am no longer certain which would be worse."

"Which is it?" he asked impatiently, long past done with the conversation—even if she wasn't.

"Etcheverry it is," she said, "for now."

Lord, but this was not going to be easy, Maxen thought. Already he had his hands full with one impetuous woman, but two? A wise man would never even begin to consider letting Elan pass her pregnancy under his roof, let alone actually allow her to do it. But in some things he was not wise. . . . Walking to his sister, he took her arm and led her to the steps.

"And now the rules," he said.

Elan groaned.

Maxen grinned. Then he began listing the things she would not be allowed, and those things that would be expected of her.

Chapter Twenty-five

Never had she thought she might become pregnant. Never. After all, she had more than once lain with Royden, a man-at-arms at her father's castle, before she had duped Edwin Harwolfson into taking the blame for her loss of chastity. Feeling sick right down to her toes for all that had gone awry, Elan turned on the pallet that had been overstuffed to accommodate her delicate condition, and stared at the shadowed ceiling above.

Ah, the lie of it, she lamented as she thought back to the day she had begun this ruse. Following her tryst with Edwin, she had ridden back to the castle with a few well-placed rips in her clothes and the smell of a man upon her. Thus, she had thrown herself at her father's feet, and as near hysterical as she could feign, had blubbered all of what had befallen her. Her sire had listened with growing rage that had eventually led to his shouts to the beams above and the heavens beyond.

Unfortunately, though she had made herself to look ravaged, Elan had forgotten one thing—to besmudge her skirts with what would have passed as the blood of broken virginity. Thus, harboring a faint hope that her virgin's flesh had not been rended, leaving her still pure enough to wed the man he had chosen for her, her father had summoned a physician to make the determination.

In the presence of Elan's mother, the physician had quickly concluded the examination. Elan shuddered to live again that terrible moment when the man had straightened and looked deeply into her eyes. For certain, he had known that the one she accused of raping her had not been the first to have her. However, perhaps because he was so staunchly Norman, he had not revealed her lie. Instead, he had muttered something hateful about visiting more death upon the barbarian Saxons if ever they were to be brought to heel.

How the hall had shaken when the physician confirmed to Elan's father that she was no longer a maiden. For hours thereafter, old man Pendery had raged. Elan had huddled against her mother's side and softly cried out a misery that became more real with each deafening curse and roar from her father. And then his anger had turned from the accursed Edwin Harwolfson to her. He had demanded answers, whipping her with his tongue for the foolishness of her unescorted ride outside the walls. There had been nothing affected about her tears then, for Elan had never been so harshly spoken to, nor so near to being struck by her father. Finally, though, his fury had subsided, and the watch was begun to see whether a Saxon bastard had been put in her. And so it was.

A shaky sob wrenched itself from Elan's throat. So much of her life had gone as she'd wished, but now for it to be ruined ere she'd even begun to live ... Angrily, she wiped the moisture from her cheeks. How she hated what tears did to her eyes—puffing them red and sore until she could only see through narrow slits.

No need to cry, she told herself. After all, did the child survive to birthing, she could wash her hands clean of it and be on her way again—providing she also survived. She slid her hands down her hips, wishing them just a bit wider than they were. Overall, she was not such a small thing, but the physician had warned that birthing a child would likely be difficult for her.

Another sob made its way to her lips. Damn Edwin Harwolfson for being so virile a man as to put her with child after only one encounter. Damn him for being so large, for likely his child would be of good size as well. If it had been Royden's child—

"Lady Elan, are you well?" a deep voice asked.

Startled, Elan swung her head to the side and found herself looking into the comely face of Sir Guy where he crouched beside her pallet. Whatever was he doing up from his bench? she wondered. Was it possible her sobs had awakened him?

"I am well," she said.

Though he did not touch her, his voice seemed to. "I heard you crying."

"Just a bit," she admitted.

"Why?"

She shrugged, but realizing he might not see the gesture, quickly answered, "'Tis just that I am sad."

"To have left Trionne?"

"That is some of it."

"And what is the rest of it?"

Something inside Elan shifted, took a peek, then began to blossom beneath the knight's concern. Ah, most wonderful, she thought. Better than Royden. "Has my brother not told you?" she asked.

Guy shook his head. "Nay, lady. I know not what you speak of."

He would soon enough, Elan thought, her hand drifting down to smooth her belly, which was still flat. After another moment's pondering, she sat up. "Let us speak elsewhere," she said, terribly aware of those she shared the hall's sleeping quarters with, even though it seemed they slept.

Sir Guy held out his hand. "I know a place."

The moment his fingers closed around hers, Elan was very certain of one thing—she liked the man's touch.

Gaining the seclusion of an alcove across the hall, Guy reluctantly gave up his hold on her. "Now what is it I do not know?" he asked.

Elan wished she still had his hand, for then she could have better gauged his reaction to what she was about to tell him. "I am with child," she said.

Surely her words must have shocked him, but it was too dark in the alcove to discern his expression. "I see," he said.

"Nay, you do not," she countered. "It is not just any bastard child I carry." Though she was prepared to pretend the shame of the admission to come, for some reason, her next words brought with them an embarrassment she had not experienced before. "It is the 'wolf's.'"

"As would be expected," Sir Guy said.

Of course, Elan thought. After all, her father had made certain that not just half of England knew of her rape by Edwin Harwolfson, but all of it. Still, she was mortified. Why? she wondered. How could this man make her feel so vile when she should not care what he thought of her? He was just another man. No different from Royden. "I understand your loathing, Sir Knight," she said, certain that condemnation hovered on his tongue. "And now I will return to my sleep."

Surprisingly, he did not accept the release she offered, but caught her arm and pulled her back from the step she had taken out of the alcove. "I do not loathe you, Lady Elan," he said, "for surely it is not you to blame for the babe."

No other, she thought, though she could not possibly tell him that. "Nay, I am not," she lied, perhaps her hundredth lie on the subject of the rape that had never been.

He nodded. "Harwolfson will pay for what he did to you," he said, his voice strong with resolve. "This I vow."

Guilt washed over her, though she tried to turn from it. Aye, it seemed likely that either by her father's hand, her brother's, or now this knight's, Edwin would pay a price he had never bargained for. And all because she had desperately needed to explain away her lack of virginity, which would have been found out on her wedding night had she not made the Saxon an accomplice to her self-serving plan. But nay, she could not think on that. Edwin Harwolfson had been a dead man long before she had given herself to him and named him a rapist. Regardless of her accusation, he would die for his rebellious war against the Normans. Thus, no real harm done.

Her conscience eased—or so she told herself—Elan asked, "And why would you take up my cause, Sir Guy?"

"Because, lady, I would be your friend if you would allow it."

Friend? That was all? she thought at once. But then, for shame, Elan Pendery, she scolded herself. Here you carry a bastard in your belly and already your mind turns to taking another man into your bed. "Then friends we will be," she said, oddly moved by his offer.

"Friends," he affirmed.

Her heart greatly lightened, Elan walked beside him to her pallet. "Good eve," she said, once settled beneath the blanket.

Reaching forward, he pushed a strand of her hair back from her brow—a stirring gesture for all its seeming innocence. "Good eve, lady," he said, then turned and crossed to his own pallet.

Until her lids grew so heavy their weight could not be held up any longer, Elan stared at where Sir Guy bedded down. Then, smiling to herself, she gave over to sleep and the dreams that followed.

"She is gone," Maxen said.

Rhiannyn turned from Lucilla, whom she'd put the question to, and looked to the man who strode into the hall. Leaving the vapor of his warm breath behind in the cold morning air, he pushed the door closed and continued toward her.

"You speak of Theta?" she asked, wondering if he simply made a statement about another, or had overheard her asking Lucilla as to Theta's whereabouts.

"Aye, Theta," Maxen said, coming to stand before her.

Bowing out of the conversation, Lucilla took herself off to the kitchens.

"I fear I do not understand," Rhiannyn said.

"I have sent her with my father's men. On their return to Trionne, they will drop her at Blackspur Castle."

"But why?"

Lifting her chin, Maxen pressed a kiss to her mouth. "She has plagued you long enough," he said when he pulled back, "and I will have no more of her lies filling the corners of Etcheverry."

Then he accepted that it was Theta who had lied about the Saxons revolting against him? "You believe me?" she asked.

He brushed a thumb across her bottom lip. "I do."

Rhiannyn smiled. The presence of Theta was a great burden to be lifted from her. No more would she have to stand against the woman's petty jealousies and nasty words. Still, another would eventually have to deal with her. "Does Sir Guy know you have sent her to Blackspur?"

Maxen drew his hand back and unfastened the brooch that held his mantle closed. "He knows," he said, "though as you have guessed, he is not pleased." He pulled the mantle from his shoulders and draped it over his arm. "As tempting as it was simply to turn Theta out and let her forage for herself, it seemed a cruel thing to do—even to her."

"Thank you, Maxen," Rhiannyn said, "both for removing her from Etcheverry and giving her another place to go."

"I fear she is not so grateful."

"She will be when the cold of winter seeps through her."

Maxen shrugged. "No matter. She is Guy's problem now."

• • •

A rapist.

He had kept his face impassive throughout the telling of the news of his latest atrocity, but now, alone with only the canopied sky, the trees, and lurking woodland creatures to witness his emotions, Edwin let it out.

"Jezebel," he hissed.

"Bitch," he growled.

"She-devil," he spat.

"Lying whore!" he shouted. Words. Only words. And not one could adequately express the rage inside him. To be called a knave, a miscreant, a pillager, even a savage, was one thing, for all he had earned himself, but now to be branded a rapist! Never had he taken a woman against her will, and most especially not the Norman bitch, Elan Pendery.

For days after she had given herself to him in the woods, he had knocked his mind senseless with pondering the woman's motive for spreading her legs for one she had known to be a great enemy of her people, but the answer had evaded him as surely as it did now. Worse, the mystery was further clouded by her having named him a rapist. Curse the lying whore! Damn her to—

"Hell," a graveled voice rasped.

Edwin swung around to discover old Dora directly behind him. How did she do it? he wondered. How was she, of bent and ravaged body, able to move so quietly over the obstacle-strewn floor of the wood? But more, how had she known what he'd been thinking?

She smiled, revealing a new gap in the top row of her teeth. "One day you will have to accept that I am who I am, Edwin," she said.

A sorceress? A witch? Nay, she saw and knew things others could not possibly, but because she was perceptive, that was all. "I do not believe in such things," he said harshly, wishing she would go and leave him be.

"After I put breath back into you when it was gone?" she tossed at him. "After I foretold you would be the one to lead your people back to an England free of Normans? After I showed you the truth of Rhiannyn and the truth was proven?"

Widening his stance and crossing his arms over his chest, Edwin stared hard at the old woman. "There was breath still in me when you pulled me from beneath the others," he explained with less patience than the dozen or more times he had previously done so.

"Nay, it was gone," she said, repeating what she had each time he denied her having worked sorcery to give him back his life.

"It has yet to be proven that under my direction the Normans will be vanquished," he continued as if she had not spoken, "and as for Rhiannyn ..." As for Rhiannyn, what? he asked himself. If Aethel and the others were to be believed, she had not turned from her people, but had only yielded when there was naught else for her to do. Yet what of the one lost to an arrow through his back when he had walked to what he believed was freedom? Had Rhiannyn known what Maxen Pendery had planned?

"She knew," Dora answered his churning thoughts.

Sharply, Edwin lifted his gaze back to her. "You read me well, Dora, and perhaps you are gifted with an unearthly sight, but that is all."

With a short laugh, she trod forward and placed herself less than a foot from him. "Sight, hmm?" she said. "Aye, I've that, though you know well that is not all I possess. I have the power. The power to—"

"Enough!" he barked. He would not be drawn any further into her web, for to do so would surely be to consort with the Devil's own. Why didn't he just send her away? he wondered for the third time in just this one day. How he wanted to, but each time he contemplated it, something kept him from doing so.

"She will bear you a son, Edwin," Dora said, her tone conspiratorial.

He frowned. "Rhiannyn?"

"Nay." Dora waved her hand side to side. " 'Tis the whore I speak of. Elan Pendery."

He was too taken aback by her announcement to remind her she had also named Rhiannyn a whore not so long ago. Was it possible one spilling of his seed had led to a child? he wondered, the thought not having crossed his mind before.

"A son," he murmured. Something about the possibility of his child coming into this world tugged at a part of him he had thought long ago sacrificed to hatred and revenge.

"Heed me well, Edwin," Dora said urgently. "He cannot be allowed to live."

"What?" he exclaimed. "Are you suggesting I murder my own child?"

"It matters not by whose hand, just that 'tis done."

"You go too far, old woman!" he growled, clenching and unclenching his fists. "Be gone ere I rid myself of you forever."

Her pink eyes widened. "The child will be Norman!"

"And Saxon."

"One drop of Norman blood is all it takes to foul the entire child."

Edwin had never found anything enjoyable about the killing of another, but at that moment the thought of snapping the old woman's neck appealed to nearly everything ill in him. "I will not tell you again," he said, then thrust her away from him.

Dora stumbled back, nearly tangling her feet in the trail of her mantle. "All I have done for you," she cried. "Deny it though you may, I gave you back your life! Not only at Hastings, but when Thomas Pendery . . ." She gulped back the remainder of her words.

In a breath, Edwin stood before her again. " 'Twas you, wasn't it?" he demanded. "You who did it."

She eyed him long, the pupils of her ghostly eyes widening and narrowing, then she said, "I killed him."

"You threw the dagger?"

"I did."

Lord, but mayhap she was a witch, Edwin pondered, for he could not believe that her withered, bony body had the strength to toss a stick ten feet, let alone aim and hurl a weapon twenty feet. "Why?" he asked.

Her tongue flicked between her teeth and wet her bottom lip. "He was going to kill you, and I could not have that happen—not after all I had given to put life back into you."

It was true that with the injury Thomas Pendery had dealt him, he would likely have died by the man's sword. But now, as then, Edwin could find no pleasure nor pride in his enemy's death.

"You are owing to me," Dora said.

Edwin broke free of his stare and focused upon her face. "I owe you naught, old woman, and most especially not the life of my son."

"Such a little thing, Edwin. 'Tis all I ask."

A rage building in him, he reached for her, his intent unquestionable.

Jumping back, she evaded him. "You have been warned," she shrieked, then spun about and ran from him.

Edwin stared after her, and when she was gone from sight, he closed his eyes and dropped his chin to his chest. Father, but he was weary. Weary of everything that had anything to do with blood and battle. Weary of running, pillaging, and wondering when William the Bastard would catch up with him. Weary of Dora's uncanny predictions. But more than anything, he was dead weary of the evil the old woman brought to his life.

Chapter Twenty-six

April, 1069

Winter melted into spring, and with the passing of Easter, word came of King William's triumph at York over rebel forces that had attacked the city and castle there. But Edwin Harwolfson and his insurgents were said not to be among those present at York—not among those who had fallen beneath the king's avenging fist. Indeed, Edwin had been strangely quiet for the past two months, and rumors about him abounded. It was said he had amassed worthy weapons not only by thievery, but through forging; that many of his men possessed horses upon which to ride into battle; that his followers numbered well in excess of a thousand; and that their training was merciless and patterned after that of the Normans. But what was true and what was not could only be guessed at . . . and worried over.

Though King William had yet to pull Maxen into his contest to keep England under his control, all knew the day approached, and that each day until then was only temporary reprieve.

Although winter was past, there were still many groaning bellies, but none at Etcheverry were unfed. The food was carefully rationed each day for every man, woman, and child, excepting only that Elan and her unborn babe received extra measure. Still, she might as well have had food rationed, too, for she partook little enough of it, almost as if she hoped to starve the growing child out of her. It would not be so easily cast away, though, pressing forward into the world until there was not one who did not know of Elan's pregnancy out of wedlock.

The young woman was an enigma to Rhiannyn, but one she steered well clear of—though mostly because Elan lied in her claim of being raped by Edwin, which no amount of wheedling would ever convince Rhiannyn of.

Maxen's sister could be pleasant enough when it suited her, but for all her quick wit and childlike charm, she soon became known for her bouts of moodiness and her ability to be at once fetching and offensive. Thus, she alienated many, although Sir Guy was not among them. Surprisingly, the knight was tolerant and understanding of her moods. A humor that few had known existed in him showed itself whenever Elan needed coaxing out of one of her low spirits, and if one looked closely enough, at just the right moment, one might even glimpse something akin to adoration in Guy's eyes, but Rhiannyn did not think any but she bothered to ponder it further.

As Elan grew rounder, her tirades worsened—even in the face of Sir Guy's support. Something was festering in her, of that there was no question. Still, it came as a surprise what passed in the hall on a cool spring day.

The nooning meal had only just been cleared when Elan thrust to her feet and turned angry eyes on all within the hall. "I hear you!" she shouted. "All of you—whispering about me behind your hands. And you . . ." She pointed to Meghan, who stood with pitcher poised above a waiting tankard. "You dare speak ill of me! You who would take a dog between your legs if there was no man to do it!"

"I would not!" Meghan exclaimed. Though it was no secret she had become intimately acquainted with a knight here and there, she had not the reputation of Theta, and took great offense at Elan's accusation.

"Lady Elan," Sir Guy called to her, hurriedly stepping from the hearth, where he and a dozen other knights had gathered.

"Ill fortune upon all your heads," Elan cursed as if she had not heard him. "A pox on all of you."

"Elan!" Maxen sharply commanded her to silence, but she ignored him as well.

"Think you I need your respect?" she continued. "I do not." She laid a hand to the evidence of her pregnancy. "It is true I carry a bastard, but I will not be ashamed of it when half of you are bastards yourselves. What have I to be ashamed of when my son is of the Saxon who will bring you all to your knees!"

Rhiannyn made it to Elan's side only a moment before Guy and Maxen. "You are tired," she said in a low voice. "Come and rest yourself upon your brother's bed." She was cautious in laying a hand to Elan's arm, and with good reason, for Elan immediately jerked her arm free and thrust her face into Rhiannyn's.

"And what of you?" she spat. "Why, you are more a whore—"

"Enough!" Maxen growled, pulling Elan back from Rhiannyn.

"I am not finished!" Elan shouted.

"My lord," Guy said, "if you would allow me, perhaps I can settle her."

"Settle me?" Elan snapped. "Think you I am a dog that can be rubbed, then set aside? I want no more of your understanding—none of it!"

The hurt upon Guy's face was fleeting, concealed a bare second later behind a tight-lipped mouth and hard eyes. "Then I am done with you, Elan Pendery," he said between clenched teeth. "Muck about in your self-pity all you like, but put no more of it upon me." All of him stiff, he pivoted and strode back toward the men he had left in coming to her aid.

"I have had enough myself," Maxen said, and pulled Elan toward his chamber.

Desperation freed her from his grip. "Guy," she cried high and miserable.

The knight halted, though he did not turn around.

It was enough for Elan. Shamelessly, she started after him.

Maxen caught her again. "To my chamber," he said, "and then to the convent."

She strained away, but a moment later was stumbling after Maxen to keep her feet beneath her.

Rhiannyn gazed into Elan's despairing face as the young woman vainly struggled to keep Sir Guy in view. Hastening after Maxen, Rhiannyn drew alongside him three quarters of the way across the hall. "My lord," she entreated, "what harm can there be in allowing the Lady Elan to talk with Sir Guy?"

"Harm?" he snapped without missing a step. "What good, I ask. He speaks to her every whim, indulges her when a hand to her backside is needed the more, and tries to understand what cannot be understood."

"Mayhap—"

"Mayhap naught! I am well and truly sick of all this coddling. It ends today."

Knowing she risked being trampled upon, Rhiannyn jumped in front of him. "I beseech, thee," she said when he was forced to halt. "Let Guy and Elan speak."

"Step aside," he said, hard-held control in his voice.

It would be so much easier to allow Elan to be the recipient—the rightful recipient—of his wrath, Rhiannyn thought, but one look at the young woman told her she must take the risk herself. "She needs him," she said.

Something in her voice must have reached Maxen, for the edges of his face softened. Then, frowning, he looked to Elan and stared into her woeful eyes.

"Please, Maxen," she begged, huge tears overflowing.

Considering her plea, he looked behind to where Guy stood unmoving. After another long moment, he heaved a sigh. "Sir Guy," he called, "bring yourself here."

The knight did not immediately comply, but in the end, swiveled around and strode over to them. "My lord?" he asked.

"My sister asks that you lend her an ear," he said. "Are you willing, man?"

Whether to punish or not, Guy made Elan wait on his answer, but at last conceded. "Very well."

Maxen passed Elan into Guy's care, but not before issuing a harsh warning. "End this, Elan, else 'tis the convent to which you will go on the morrow."

Although it was cool outside, it was there Guy and Elan sought their privacy, leaving Rhiannyn with nothing left to attend to but Maxen. Reluctantly, she looked back at him, but instead of anger, a lopsided smile appeared on his face.

"Only for you," he said. And there was no other truth about it, Maxen thought, for if not for her, he was certain he would have unleashed the angry words that had been building in him these last months, and which he had nearly shouted when Elan called Rhiannyn a whore. Aye, without waiting for a full day's light, he would likely have sent his sister on to the convent. Only for Rhiannyn.

"Come," he said, feeling a sudden burning in his loins that only her moisture could cool.

She smiled, then followed him around the screen and joined him on the bed. As was more common than not, their lovemaking was over with quickly, for the long years of Maxen's celibacy had yet to be offset. Still, every day they gained ground—though, it seemed, not in making a baby upon Rhiannyn. This was yet another reason for Maxen's growing frustration these past months.

Over and over again he had asserted he would never wed her, yet a need had grown within him to have her in all binding ways. He wanted this Saxon woman for his wife. He wanted her at his side for all the days to come, to make children upon her, and grow old with her. Thus, he impatiently waited for his child to fill her, for when that happened he would have an excuse to recind his refusal to wed her. Mayhap this would be the month. . . .

They lay on their sides facing each other, their limbs intertwined, the silence of satiation running its course before either spoke.

"Thank you, Maxen," she whispered.

"For my lady's desire," he murmured.

Playfully, she poked him. "'Tis not that I speak of, but Elan and Guy."

Maxen opened his eyes and stared into hers. "Elan," he groaned, wishing the subject had been allowed to lie just a bit longer. "What am I to do with her?"

"I would say that depends on Guy."

"And you think he can straighten what is bent in her?"

"If anyone can. . . ."

"Why do you care so much, Rhiannyn?" Maxen asked. "Why when before all she calls you a whore?" With his palm he felt the tensing in the small of her back, but a moment later it eased.

"I probably should not care," she said as she lightly pulled a hair upon his chest, "but something in me feels for her."

"Even though you believe she lies about Edwin."

She met his gaze. "She *does* lie."

Though Maxen did not say so, he was more inclined to believe Elan a liar than Edwin a rapist. "Spring is here now," he said, reminding her that before long he would likely face Edwin on the battlefield.

Again that tensing, though this time it did not ease. "It is," she said.

"There is something I need to ask you."

"Ask."

"About Edwin," he prefaced.

She lowered her gaze to his chest. "Of course."

"What would it take to make peace with him?"

Immediately, Rhiannyn sprang to sitting. "Peace? But even I have heard 'tis his death William seeks."

Maxen also sat up. "That is true, but methinks I may

be able to convince him otherwise—providing Edwin also agrees."

Confusion upon her face, Rhiannyn shook her head. "Why, Maxen? I thought you also sought his death."

"After all I have told you of Hastings?" For a moment, he slipped back in memory to the bloody meadow, but in the next instant dragged free of it. "Nay, if there is any chance of preventing further bloodshed, then that is the course I will seek."

"But is it your course William will follow?"

A very good question indeed. Only if the king still held him in as high regard as he had following Hastings was there even a remote possibility of turning back the man's vengeful quest. "Perhaps," he said, "but the question is, what will it take to satisfy Edwin to peace?"

Rhiannyn smiled, her eyes pooling with tears of happiness, then she leaned forward and put her arms around him. "I knew you were worthy of heart. I knew it."

Worthy of heart? Maxen wondered as he breathed in the warm scent of her. What, exactly, did she mean? That in attempting peace with Edwin he was not the savage he had proven he was when he'd told her of his role in William's conquering? How could she possibly forget or forgive that side of him when he could not himself? Still, he harbored a hope that if he could prevent this battle between Edwin and William, then at last God might forgive him his atrocities. A hope only, but one worth reaching for if it meant the unburdening of his soul. With that in mind, he asked again, "What price Edwin's peace, Rhiannyn?"

Tilting her head back, she met his gaze. "I do not know," she said. "It may already have gone too far for that."

"It was my understanding he sought to make Etcheverry his own."

"Aye, the land of his family, but now methinks only all of England will satisfy him. 'Tis likely that Etcheverry no longer figures in his rebellion—a small thing in the midst of a country so vast."

"Then I will have to think more on this."

"You had thought to offer him these lands to gain peace?"

"If that is what it took to end Edwin's uprising, I would relinquish Etcheverry to him, though I would first have to convince the king of the worthiness of such means."

Again, Rhiannyn smiled, something deep in her eyes pulling Maxen in and showing him what he had never thought possible. But was it possible? Was it truly love he saw there? Surely no brighter light had ever shone in a person than that which shone from her. Perhaps only gratitude. Nay, love, he told himself, needing badly to believe it. Rhiannyn loved him.

"I know you will do it," she said. "You will bring peace to England."

Her confident declaration yanked Maxen from further reflection on her feelings for him. He shook his head. "Though Edwin's following now numbers the greatest, there are others who seek to oust the Normans. Even if he can be put down, the fighting will not end. God willing it will lessen, but it will not end."

Rhiannyn's face fell, but then it lifted. "There can be no end without first a beginning," she said, "and that is what you will have if you can convince William and Edwin to lay aside their differences."

If. "There is something about Edwin I have long pondered," he said, steering away from the maddening "ifs" that had been plaguing him more and more of late. "Mayhap you can help me to understand it."

"What is that?"

"According to Saxon tradition, as a royal housecarle he should have died alongside his king, yet he did not. He survived the death of his lord and returned to Etcheverry to mount this rebellion of his."

"Aye, he returned, though 'tis said he should be among the dead, not the living."

"Dora," Maxen said.

Startled, Rhiannyn drew farther back. "You know, then."

He shrugged. "I know only the rumor that it was the

old woman who brought Edwin back to life when it was gone from him."

"Perhaps."

"Then you do not completely discount the possibility that he was truly dead?"

Uncomfortable with his questioning, she fidgeted a long moment before answering. "Edwin does not believe it," she said. "He has always said there must have been life in him when Dora pulled him from beneath the others."

Then Harwolfson was more God-fearing than pagan, Maxen concluded. That was good. "Was he badly wounded?"

She nodded emphatically. "He should have died for all that was laid upon his body, but Dora would not allow it—even when Edwin prayed for death that he might not suffer the disgrace of one who had survived his king on the battlefield."

"If that is so, then why did he not end it himself when he was able to?"

"I think he might have, but when he was well enough to walk the village and witness for himself all that the Normans had done, something greater came over him."

"Revenge."

Rhiannyn nodded. "Revenge."

Maxen studied her face and the sorrow in her eyes which had supplanted the love. "You have answered my questions well," he said, stroking the back of his hand down her jaw. "But now I would ask that you think no more on this."

Exasperation widened her eyes. "You think it is so easily done?"

"Nay, but you will try, hmm?"

Her smile came through. "I will try," she agreed, then lay back down.

Maxen followed, urged her onto her side, and pulled her back against him. Though he would more have liked to make love to her again, in the quiet that followed he found himself brooding over all he had just learned about Edwin Harwolfson. A man of honor, but also of revenge. Loyal to his own, but recklessly so. A Christian, yet one who kept a witch at his side. Stubborn, but bending ever so slightly when the occasion warranted.

For however long his mind spun with plotting and devising, Maxen lay awake in the great bed. Finally, though, he put his thoughts aside.

Turning the coverlet over Rhiannyn's sleeping figure, he clothed himself and went in search of Elan and Guy. However, it was Christophe he found before a game of chess he played with himself.

"I would call it love," Christophe said, then decisively moved a bishop across the board and captured one of the opposition's pieces.

Suddenly defensive, Maxen asked, "Love? What do you speak of?"

Standing, Christophe walked to the other side of the board and seated himself there. "Elan and Guy, of course," he said, his eyes never leaving the game. "Who else would I be speaking of?"

Wily youth, Maxen thought with irritation. Though Christophe's lips spoke of two others, his words carried another message. For certain, he saw what neither Maxen nor Rhiannyn would admit to, though he used the guise of Elan and Guy to prick him.

"If you have something to say to me, Christophe, then say it," Maxen demanded.

With great reluctance, Christophe looked up from his game, then leaned back in his chair. "I have said it," he said. "Sir Guy and our sister have taken a great liking to each other, and I think it goes beyond this friendship they would have all believe it to be."

Maxen stared hard at his brother, but the young man's face revealed no more than what he had said. With a disgruntled sigh, Maxen dropped into the chair Christophe had just vacated. "And what makes you think that?" he asked.

Christophe steepled his hands on his chest. "Perhaps it was the way they looked into each other's eyes . . . or the way they held hands." He shrugged, a smile tugging at one corner of his mouth as he watched Maxen tense. "But I would say what convinced me more than anything was when they kissed."

Maxen leaned forward in his chair. "Kissed?" he demanded.

"Aye, in the garden."

In the next instant, Maxen was on his feet, intending to seek out Guy. However Christophe, blocked his way.

"He is good for Elan," Christophe said. "Do not take from her the only thing that holds her together."

"And let her be ravaged more than she has already been?" Maxen growled, uncaring that others might hear.

"I assure you this ravaging she does not mind, Maxen—though a little kiss can hardly be called that, can it?"

"Unseemly is what it is," Maxen retorted.

"Only if he does not offer to wed her."

Realizing past his outrage that something was afoot, Maxen narrowed his eyes on his brother. "And you think he will offer?"

Christophe shook his head. "Nay, I do not think—I know."

"How?"

"Something I overheard."

"Out with it!"

"Sire Guy asked Elan if she would grant him permission to ask our father for her hand."

When Maxen did not immediately respond, Christophe added, "It would be a good match."

"And what makes you think that?"

"Do you so soon forget that our sister is an unwed woman with child? Who else do you think will offer for her once they know what happened to her? It will haunt her the rest of her days. Sir Guy is a knight above reproach—good, honorable, and worthy—but more, he cares for her in spite of another's child that grows in her belly."

Now Maxen understood, and grudgingly approved. "Methinks you are far wiser than I, little brother."

Christophe beamed, basking in his brother's compliment. Then, as if his mind had been half on his game even while he'd spoken, he picked up a chess piece and executed a move of pure genius. "I have won," he announced, proudly sweeping a hand above the board.

Maxen could not help but grin. "Then who lost?" he asked.

"My opponent, of course."

"But was not your opponent yourself?"

Christophe glanced at the vacant chair positioned before the losing side. "It only looked that way," he said, then chuckled. "One must make do with what one has."

In that moment, Maxen realized how lonely Christophe must be in this great castle. He was distanced from the others not only by his youth, but more, by the lameness of his body which made him more suited to books than weapons. Filled with a sudden need to be the brother he had never been to Christophe, he asked, "Are you up to another game?"

Christophe looked first surprised, then delighted. "Always," he said.

Rhiannyn awoke to laughter. She turned to curl her front to Maxen's, but found him long gone, the warmth of his body now a cold spot where he had lain.

Again, laughter from the hall pricked her ears. Laughter? she wondered. But what was so odd about that? The indoor games and conversations that had been of winter, though less so of spring, were not without their mirth, so why did this laughter seem out of place?

Rubbing her eyes, she sat up and cocked her head in anticipation of the next outburst. It came a moment later, though this time mixed with the laughter of others. It was Maxen and Christophe, she realized. Their joined laughter, a new sound to her, stood out against the voices of the others.

Hurriedly, she dressed and swept into the hall to discover the reason for this mirth that so surprisingly captured both brothers. There before the hearth she discovered a gathering of two dozen men whose heads were bent together toward some unseen sight.

"Pardon," Rhiannyn said as she shouldered her way into the group.

Maxen looked up at her as she emerged into the center of the throng. "Come see what my brother has done to me," he said, a wondrous smile bowing his lips.

Baffled, she looked from him to the chess game, then to Christophe's exultant face.

"I don't understand," she said.

Reaching for her hand, Maxen pulled her to his side. "Ah, but look at his cleverness," he invited, then began a thorough explanation of the moves Christophe had put upon him that had cornered Maxen's king.

Rhiannyn heard little of it, for she was too filled with the unaccustomed joy of seeing Maxen and Christophe treating each other as brothers rather than as distant acquaintances.

"I am thoroughly beaten," Maxen said good-humoredly.

Christophe grinned. "Another match?"

"That would see me on my knees yet again?" Maxen shook his head. "Not twice in one day, brother," he said, standing. "Perhaps tomorrow."

"Anyone else?" Christophe asked, looking to the others.

Shaking their heads, the men began withdrawing.

Maxen must have seen the disappointment that crossed Christophe's face, for he was quick to offer reassurance. "They fear you, 'tis all," he said.

Christophe shrugged it off. "I suppose they have reason to. After all—"

"Rhiannyn?" a soft, almost apologetic voice said from behind.

Turning, Rhiannyn came face to face with Elan. As it was the first time the young woman had addressed her without spite or anger, she was too surprised to respond.

"I would speak with you," Elan said.

Rhiannyn looked to Maxen, then Christophe, and saw that both appeared as surprised as she. "Now?" she asked, turning her gaze back to the young woman.

"If it is not a good time, mayhap later," Elan offered.

Wondering what she was up to, for it seemed highly unlikely that she was amiable for any other reason than personal gain, Rhiannyn said, "Nay, now is good."

"Come with me outside?"

Rhiannyn nodded. Casting a questioning look at Maxen, she followed his sister outside the donjon where there were none to overhear their conversation.

"I wish to apologize," Elan said.

"For?" Rhiannyn blurted in amazement.

"For how I have treated you these past months. I fear I have been most unkind."

"Forgive me if I seem a bit confused, but I had not thought you cared much for me."

"I don't really," Elan said, but was quick to add, "though I am beginning to."

Suspicious, Rhiannyn narrowed her eyes. "And how is that?"

"You convinced Maxen to allow me to speak with Sir Guy, for which I am greatly owing to you."

"And that is all?"

Elan frowned over the question. "Methinks you are not so bad. You perform fairly well the duties of the lady of the castle, even though you are not the lady, you lend an ear well to the servants when they bicker amongst themselves, and you seem to make my brother happy. Nay, not so bad."

Not so tactfully spoken either, but at least spoken, Rhiannyn thought. "Thank you," she murmured.

Elan looked well pleased with herself. "That is all," she said, "and now I go to nap."

As Elan passed her, Rhiannyn put a hand to her arm. "I hope we can one day be friends," she said.

"Friends?" Elan bit her bottom lip. "I suppose 'tis possible," she said, then hurried back into the hall.

Rhiannyn started to follow, but a voice hailed to her from the kitchens below. Lucilla. Likely something gone

amiss with the evening meal. With a sigh, Rhiannyn turned
and descended the steps.

"Though it would seem I am owing to you after that
game, I've a favor to ask of you, Christophe," Maxen said
when they had gained privacy.

"A favor?"

"Aye. You know well the herbs, don't you?"

"Far better than weapons."

As uncomfortable as he was with broaching the subject,
Maxen did not immediately rush into his request. For a
long moment he considered it, rewording it in his head,
but in the end he let it come out as it pleased. "Know you
of anything that might make a woman more fertile?"

"Whatever for?" Christophe asked, suspicion creeping
into his face.

Maxen had known he would have to tell him, though it
did not make it any easier. "Rhiannyn," he said. "In all
these months she has yet to miss her monthly time. Though
I would have my child grow in her, her body is not recep-
tive."

Such consternation crossed Christophe's face that
Maxen knew in an instant he was hiding something. "What
is it?" he demanded.

"Why do you wish her pregnant?" Christophe asked.
"After all, she is but your leman."

"Answer me," Maxen growled.

Looking uncertain, and a bit fearful, Christophe considered him before answering. "I . . ." He drew a deep breath,
stood taller, and pushed his shoulders back. "Rhiannyn
asked that I give her something to prevent her becoming
pregnant, and I did."

Damnation, the minx had gotten the better of him! To
contain his anger was a most difficult thing, especially
when it was already bursting before his eyes, but somehow
he managed to. "Why did you not tell me?" he asked.

"I did not think you would wish bastards upon her anymore than she wished them upon herself," Christophe answered. "I thought you would be grateful."

Arms crossed in front, Maxen rubbed at the tension building in his shoulders. "Bastards, nay," he said, "but legitimate children I do want."

"That cannot be without marriage," Christophe reminded him.

Maxen gauged his brother long and hard, then admitted what he'd told none other. " 'Tis exactly what I intend do I ever get her with child."

"You will marry her?" Christophe exclaimed.

"Aye."

"But you have said time and again . . ." A sudden knowing came over Christophe, leaving his words hanging in nothingness. "I see," he murmured.

"I'm sure you do," Maxen said, wishing he had not had to reveal so much of himself. As he stared at Christophe, it was almost as if he could see the turning of the youth's mind. And so it must have been, for when next Christophe spoke, he had a solution.

"Rhiannyn should soon be out of what I have given her," he said. "I could substitute something different when she comes to replenish it."

Maxen smiled. "I would be owing to you, brother."

" 'Tis done, then." Christophe turned to go, but came back around in the next moment.

What followed was as much a shock to Maxen as he had ever had. Unprepared, he stood rigid while Christophe pressed a quick hug on him, then watched blankly as his brother hurried across the hall.

Chapter Twenty-seven

Meghan smelled as a woman who had recently laid with a man. The pungent odor was near enough to make Rhiannyn retch. Skirting the other woman's path, she walked as steadily as she could manage to the chamber she shared with Maxen, and once around the screen, sat directly upon the floor and put her head between her knees.

"Nay," she groaned. Crossing an arm over her midsection, she began rocking herself. "Lord, let it not be." But it was. She had known it that morn when the fifth day had come and was now nearly past without bringing her monthly flux. She had to admit it. She was pregnant with Maxen Pendery's child.

The nausea was slow to pass—or at least seemed that way for all the twisting and turning of her insides—but finally it did. Wiping the moisture from her brow, she lifted her head and looked around the chamber. Would she be allowed to birth her child here? she wondered. Or would it be considered a defilement of the lord's chamber to bear his misbegotten child where one day a legitimate one might be born? That last thought hurt almost as much as loving a man who did not love her.

Attempting the impossible—not to think any more about the child growing in her—Rhiannyn teetered to her feet. As if with a mind of its own, her hand swept over her belly, feeling for evidence of the child. She could be no more than a month pregnant, she figured, her last menses having promptly come and gone. It was now June, so the child would be born midwinter did it come into the world in a timely manner.

Dropping her hand back to her side, Rhiannyn shook her head. Though the root had worked those first months, in the end it had failed her. Or perhaps it had never really worked. Perhaps she was simply slow to impregnate. Abruptly, she went back through her thoughts. It had worked the first few months, but not this past month. This past month when Christophe had replenished her supply. Had he prepared it differently? Forgotten something?

Dear Lord, what did it matter? she lamented. She was pregnant, and there was naught she could do to change that. Naught that she was willing to do, she clarified, as whispers of how one might terminate a pregnancy came back to her from the past. With a sudden surge of protectiveness, she wrapped both arms around her abdomen.

A squeal from beyond the screen caused Rhiannyn to jump. Elan, she realized when it came again, and then Sir Guy, answering her elation with a gruff laugh.

Having been oblivious to the goings-on in the hall these past minutes—or was it hours?—Rhiannyn hadn't a clue as to what might have happened. Curious, she left the lord's chamber and immediately located Elan and Guy standing before Maxen, who was seated at the high table. All the others who had been present in the hall when Rhiannyn had left were now conspicuously gone. Dismissed.

"What is it?" she asked as she drew even with Elan.

Her excitement causing her to forget propriety, Elan answered when it was her brother's place to do so. "He agrees," she said, pointing to the parchment Maxen held. "My father agrees to the marriage."

Though Rhiannyn and Elan still had their moments, the weeks since Rhiannyn had pleaded for Elan to be allowed to speak with Sir Guy had been tempered by an understanding and tolerance that had not previously been present. Not exactly a pleasant friendship, but definitely an improvement.

"I am most pleased for you," Rhiannyn said, looking from Elan's glowing face to Guy's. "Both of you."

Guy nodded and Elan glowed just a bit more.

"Then we will begin preparation for the ceremony," Maxen said.

"Nay!" Elan squawked. "Not while I am round as a pig."

Maxen stared at her a time, then asked, "What are you proposing, Elan? That the wedding be postponed until after the child is born?"

She nodded. "I will not be rushed into this, brother. I wish a proper wedding, a proper dress, and a proper figure to display it."

Maxen leaned forward. "Your vanity will only cast more ill upon this child than has already been," he said. Pointedly, he looked at her swollen belly. "Though it is too late for any to believe the babe is Guy's, if the ceremony is performed at once it can only help."

"But I am not going to keep it, Maxen," Elan reminded him.

"Even though you are now going to wed?"

"Of course not," she exclaimed. "It was ill-gotten on me, and I will not be made to suffer its upbringing—nor will I ask Guy to suffer it."

"You are its mother, Elan."

"Not by choice."

Maxen swung his gaze to Guy. "What think you?" he asked.

The knight seemed uncomfortable with the question,

and answered stiltedly, "If Elan wished to keep the ch
I would make it as good a father as I am capable of, but
is her decision."

"There, you see," Elan said. "My decision."

Perhaps it was only because Rhiannyn now carried a
child herself—a bastard, like Elan's—but she felt sudden
longing for the poor babe that would be cast away for no
other reason than its parentage. Mayhap the child could be
reared here with her own misbegotten child. . . .

Maxen also seemed disturbed by Elan's pronouncement, but conceded. "Very well, the wedding will be stayed
until after the child is born. And now, I have work to do."

Elan and Guy were quick to withdraw, but Rhiannyn
found herself unable to move. Maxen carried on as if she
had also gone, pulling a ledger before him and taking up
a quill. However, he had barely dipped ink when he noticed her. Questioningly, he raised his eyebrows.

Why *did* she continue to stand there? Rhiannyn wondered. Squashing the impulse to touch again that place
where their child grew, she clenched her hands into fists
and turned away.

"What is it, Rhiannyn?" Maxen asked.

She looked over her shoulder at him. "Naught," she
said. "I simply forgot to leave."

He smiled at her choice of words. "Forgot?"

She shrugged. "I am tired. That is all."

Something unreadable flitted across his face. "Is it that
you take too much upon yourself?"

"Nay, I . . . I have just not been sleeping well."

"I had not noticed."

" 'Tis nothing," she assured him, suddenly anxious to
be away from him lest he discover that she carried his
child. "Methinks I will go and lie down awhile." Stepping
down from the dais, she started across the hall.

So swift and sure did Maxen move that she did not
hear him until he was upon her. Closing firm hands over
her shoulders, he pulled her back against him. He lowered
his mouth to her ear and asked softly, "Are you with child,
Rhiannyn?"

...ad so shrewdly guessed the truth was nearly ...ng, but somehow Rhiannyn kept her startled sur- ...m bounding forth. Lord, but she was not ready to ...m. Not now. Not when this battle between William ...d Edwin loomed so large. Not when she had yet to come to terms with the pregnancy herself. Nay, now was not the time. . . .

Knowing that the longer her silence, the less Maxen was likely to believe her lie, she summoned her best face and turned in his arms. "Pregnant?" she repeated disbelievingly. "A woman must first miss her time of month ere that can be told."

"And you have not missed yours?"

"Nay."

"You are certain?"

"Of course I am. My flow was light this past month, but still it was there."

Inwardly, Maxen cursed his absence from Etcheverry during the time of Rhiannyn's last menses. Having been called to Blackspur Castle to settle a dispute between the master mason and the workers, he had no evidence as to whether what she spoke was true. Were his suspicions bound up in his wanting to believe her pregnant? he wondered. Or was it guilt he saw reflected in her eyes, and nervousness in the bob of her throat? God, but if she was lying to him again . . .

Reluctantly, he set her back from him. "Go to your rest then," he said.

Fearful of the doubt she saw on his face, Rhiannyn muttered, "Thank you, my lord," then quickly turned away. She was halfway across the hall and just beginning to think herself well escaped when Maxen halted her with an unsettling question.

"If you were to become pregnant, Rhiannyn, would you tell me?"

Words of reassurance on her lips, she turned around to him. However, something reflected in his face caused those words to flee, and out of her mouth came the pain of her heart. "Would you care?"

His marked hesitation told Rhiannyn that, at least for the time being, she was right in keeping from him knowledge of their child.

"I would," he finally answered.

"Then I would tell you," she said, justifying her falsehood with what she perceived to be his.

He stared at her for moments that caused her to ache, then turned on his heel and strode across the hall, outside into the thick mist of morning. Only when he was gone did Rhiannyn allow her shoulders to slump.

What to do? she wondered. Tell Maxen the truth and forever tie herself to being naught but his leman and bearer of his bastard children? Or mayhap she ought simply to disappear, go away from here and birth her misbegotten child in secret. Did she go far enough away, and claim to be recently widowed, the babe could escape the mark of bastardy. Of course, Maxen might follow. . . .

Refusing to be overwhelmed by the desperation threatening to choke her, Rhiannyn lifted her shoulders and chin, then raised her eyes heavenward. "What am I to do?" she asked the unseen.

The answering words were spoken not to her ears, but to her heart. The truth, they said.

She lowered her gaze, contemplated the rush-covered floor, then nodded. "I know," she muttered. She could not leave Maxen, and the lie must be revealed. Tomorrow, she vowed, then crossed to the chamber.

Chapter Twenty-eight

Once the castle had settled down to the routine of summer—the ripening of crops and fruit that, God willing, would make Etcheverry self-sufficient the next winter—Rhiannyn finally found time to take up her loom. Sitting with Meghan and three other women she'd enlisted to assist her in weaving new cloth—all Saxons—Rhiannyn found good conversation with them. They talked, laughed, from time to time fell silent, then talked again. There was talk of crops to be had, of the village being raised, and of the seasons past.

Though the winter and spring had not been easy on any, there was much to be thankful for, and it was confirmed to Rhiannyn while she sat with the women that the Saxons had invested all of themselves in their new lord. For certain, they were Maxen's now, and never again Edwin's.

Something about that was sad, she

thought, even if it was wrong to think it. With each of William's victories over the rebels, the era that had been the Anglo-Saxons' buried itself deeper and deeper in the past. Unless, of course, Edwin succeeded where no others had. . . .

"I've counted more than a dozen," one of the women said. "A busy winter 'twas." Her hearty chuckle was echoed by the others.

"A dozen?" Rhiannyn asked as she slipped back into the conversation she had drifted from.

"Aye, and there'll be more."

Rhiannyn met the woman's gaze. "More of what?"

"Why, women getting with child," she exclaimed. "Dreaming, are you?"

Rhiannyn smiled faintly, squelched the impulse to lay a hand to her belly that was yet flat, then took up her shuttle again. The tomorrow she had promised had yet to come, for she still had not told Maxen the truth. In fact, it was now well past a fortnight since he had asked if she was pregnant. She sighed, then resolved she would tell him that eve. Whatever his anger, she would deal with it.

Resigned to the impending confrontation, Rhiannyn rejoined the women's conversation only to be interrupted a short time later by a pert voice.

"Think you a crown of flowers would be too much?" Elan asked.

None had heard her approach, and in concert with her unexpected voice, two shuttles tripped from startled fingers and fell to the floor.

Bending forward to retrieve her shuttle, Rhiannyn silently talked down her flare of annoyance. "Would it be too much for what, Lady Elan?" she asked.

"My wedding, of course," she squeaked. "What else might I be speaking of?"

Aye, what else? Sighing, Rhiannyn leaned near her loom and traced down the warp thread she had last passed her shuttle over. "A crown of flowers would be lovely," she said somewhat absently as she began weaving again.

Stepping to the side, Elan placed her very pregnant figure alongside the loom so that Rhiannyn was forced to look at her. "You are not interested, are you?" she said accusingly, her bottom lip quivering.

Rhiannyn stifled a second sigh and sat back on her stool. "Of course I am. Now which flowers do you think you would like to make your crown of?"

She beamed. "I was thinking violets and columbines."

"Sounds lovely."

"Or roses."

"I like roses."

Elan scowled. "But which do you like better?"

"For me, violets and columbines," Rhiannyn said, "but with your coloring, roses might be better. What does your betrothed think?"

She shrugged. "I do not know. I was going to ask him, but he is nowhere to be found."

"He and Maxen are walking out the village."

"What do you mean 'walking out'?"

To Meghan's snicker, Rhiannyn shot a glaring look. "Laying its bounds," she explained.

"Dreary," Elan pronounced. "Most dreary."

"But necessary."

"If you say so."

At times—rare times—Elan seemed aged beyond her years, but most often she was the child she was today. What was it that made Sir Guy love her so? Rhiannyn wondered. Though Elan seemed different when in his presence, surely he saw how she was with others?

Love. Such a strange thing, she reflected, forgetting about Elan and Guy for the moment, and thinking instead of Maxen and the child growing in her. Love was indeed a strange thing—and painful.

Elan's voice intruded again. "I will need new cloth for my wedding dress." She skimmed her fingers over the hand's width of lavender cloth at the bottom of Rhiannyn's loom.

"And what color are you thinking?" Rhiannyn asked.

"I hadn't really," she said, "but this is lovely."

More snickering, though this time from one other than Meghan.

Ignoring it, Rhiannyn smiled at Elan. "Surely you know how to weave."

"I do, but I fear I am not as accomplished as you."

Though Rhiannyn knew it would be far easier if she simply offered what Elan was not so subtly asking, she also knew it would be better if the young woman did it herself—with a little help. "Then I will teach you," she said.

Elan looked at once dismayed and affronted. "If you have not noticed, I am pregnant," she declared.

"As if one could not notice!" Meghan said, unable to hold back any longer.

The other women laughed behind their hands.

"Why you . . . you . . ." Elan sputtered. "You ungrateful Saxon—"

"That is enough," Rhiannyn intervened. Jumping to her feet, she took Elan's elbow and pressed her down upon the stool. "Here," she said, pushing the shuttle into Elan's hand, "hold it like this."

Recovering, Elan started to rise; Rhiannyn gently urged her back down. "Now draw nearer," she said.

"I do not care to waste my time weaving," Elan protested.

"Do you not wish the most beautiful wedding gown?" Rhiannyn asked, hoping to play upon Elan's incessant vanity.

Elan opened her mouth to deny she had any such wish, but closed it in the next instant. After giving it some thought, she grudgingly nodded. "I *will* have the most beautiful gown," she said.

"Then there is no time to waste," Rhiannyn said. Taking advantage of the moment, she began instructing Elan in the art of weaving.

Though the other women resumed their own weaving, their attention was only half on it, for they were engrossed with what passed between Rhiannyn and Elan.

Amazingly, it was not a futile effort Rhiannyn undertook, for after a time Elan began to apply herself diligently. And later when the talk among the women resumed, Elan occasioned to join in, and even laughed when the others did. It seemed quite a miracle, but one which was cut short by Christophe's arrival in the hall.

"The king is come," he said, breathing so heavily from his run to the donjon that it took a moment for his audience to comprehend what he had said.

Rhiannyn was the first. Her heart pounding a terrible beat, she straightened and met Christophe's gaze. "Come?" she asked, fooling herself into believing she might have misunderstood.

Sharing her concern, Christophe nodded. "And with an entourage so great that 'tis all you can see from the wall to the wood. Soldiers, my lady. A thousand or more."

Maxen's time was come. With the passing of spring, Rhiannyn had harbored hope that he might not be summoned, but now he was. Although her short pregnancy had thus far been largely uneventful, she suddenly felt the faintness and nausea Elan had suffered in the early months. With only the loom to steady her, Rhiannyn curled her fingers around it and leaned as much of her weight on it as its frame would bear.

"Nay," she whispered. She squeezed her eyes closed and stared at the black on the backs of her eyelids.

"You should sit down," Christophe said, taking her arm lest she crumple to the ground.

Opening her eyes, Rhiannyn looked into his anxious face. Not realizing what she did until she saw her hand before her, she swept back the lock of hair that had straggled over his brow. "I am fine," she said, "just a bit . . ."

"You are frightened," Elan said. Lifting her ungainly body from the stool, she stepped alongside her brother and put a hand to Rhiannyn's shoulder.

The unexpected gesture brought tears to Rhiannyn's eyes. "Aye," she admitted, "I fear for Maxen."

"He does not need your fear, Rhiannyn," Christophe said wisely, though his own fear was visible for all to see. "He needs your strength."

"He will have it," Rhiannyn said as she determinedly drew herself up to every last bit of her height. "Now," she went on, looking to the expectant faces of the Saxon women, "there is much to be done ere Will—our king," she corrected with much effort, "comes into the hall.

"Clear the looms," she ordered one.

"Send word to Mildreth and Lucilla that we have visitors," she commanded another.

"Search out the menservants to position the tables," she directed the third.

"Fetch the linens and spread them upon the tables," she bid the fourth—Meghan.

And to a passing servant, she called, "Summon the butler to bring barrels of wine and ale into the hall, then begin filling pitchers."

"And what would you have me do?" Elan asked unexpectedly.

It was on Rhiannyn's tongue to decline her offer, but from the look upon Elan's face, she knew it would be the wrong course. "I've herbs you can scatter over the rushes," she said, wishing she'd had the floor covering replaced days earlier as she had planned. Always, there had been something more pressing.

Ah well, she inwardly sighed, if William did not turn his nose up at trodding the broken and bloodied bodies of men, then he could hardly take offense at rushes that smelled of mildew, and whatever else was trapped in them.

"Can you do that?" she asked Elan.

"Certainly," the younger woman answered.

Such an odd creature, Rhiannyn thought, at that moment liking her very much.

"I would offer to help as well," Christophe said, "but Maxen said I should return to him as soon as I had delivered the message."

Rhiannyn nodded. "You can assure him all will be ready for ... the king."

Christophe shot her an understanding smile, then hurried from the hall.

Telling herself she was not nervous, Rhiannyn dashed to

the lord's chamber, which that night might be occupied by England's king did he deign to stay over. The linens must be replaced, all surfaces dusted, the basin emptied, the tub wiped. . . .

So this was the bastard, Rhiannyn thought. William the Bastard. At the head of those coming into the hall he strode—the man who had claimed the crown of England and, in doing so, had caused vast quantities of Anglo-Saxon blood to soak the ground; so much so that Saxons still said the water carried up from wells tasted of blood.

Dragging herself from the horror conjured by that thought, Rhiannyn glanced at Elan, who stood alongside her. She saw the young woman's nervousness, then peered closer at the man who seemed the cause of it. Odd, but she had not imagined him with so human a face. Deceptively human, she sharply told herself.

"Ah, I see with mine own eyes the reason you have shut yourself up at Etcheverry," William said good-humoredly to Maxen, his appreciative gaze sweeping over Rhiannyn several times before settling upon her face.

"My liege, may I present Lady Rhiannyn of Etcheverry." Maxen attended to the formalities, though there was a chill in his voice.

William seemed not to notice. "Lady, hmm?"

"Aye," Maxen replied. "Lady Rhiannyn manages my household."

A flare of discomfort—that she was the mistress of Etcheverry, and yet not wed to the lord—shot through Rhiannyn. Although Maxen might name her a lady, the fact remained that she was but a leman with a lofty title. The king was not so coarse to say it, but his dancing eyes showed that he knew it.

"I am your king," he said to her. When she continued to stare at him, he glowered and more emphatically said, "King William of England."

The prideful Saxon in Rhiannyn pushed argument to her lips, but, with much determination, she sealed them.

Stealing a glance past the man dominating the space before her, she looked into Maxen's eyes and was comforted by the reassurance she saw there. There was something else, too, but William refused her time to interpret it.

"Have you no knees, woman?" he demanded as he looked down upon her from his great height, which was equalled by that of only two other men in the hall—Maxen and an older man who stood alongside him.

Ah, so that was the other thing she had seen in Maxen's eyes, she thought. Just as well the usurper had forced the issue, for she never would have thought of it on her own.

"Well?" William snapped, those behind him waiting in expectant silence to see what the punishment would be for her insolence.

Lord, but must she bend a knee to this monster? Rhiannyn wondered. She would much rather spit in his eye . . . smack the fury from his face . . . trod upon his grave . . . see him straight to the Devil—

Elan's elbow in her calf thrust her back to the present, and only then did she realize that the younger woman had already found her knees before her king. For Maxen, Rhiannyn told herself as she lifted her skirts out of the way. Only for him would she bend herself before this ungodly man. On her knees before William, she waited with bowed head for him to order her to stand again, but he did not.

Reaching forward, he caught her chin in his palm and lifted it. Towering as he did above her, he seemed to have grown twice the size, but she refused to fear him.

"A Saxon through and through," he said unexpectedly as he looked deeply into her eyes and picked out the loathing there.

Holding her breath that she might not release it upon his hand, she peeked at Maxen. He looked uneasy.

For him, she reminded herself. "Indeed a Saxon, your majesty," she forced past wooden lips, "but now a loyal subject."

William's face remained austere, his gaze as hard as stone. Then, without warning, his countenance cracked into a smile. "At least she respects one Norman," he said, looking around at Maxen. "You must please her mightily."

All the others joined in his laughter—except Maxen, who managed to summon a barely tolerant smile for his king.

Shamed straight down to her toes, Rhiannyn longed to yank her chin out of the bastard's hold, but knew dire consequences would surely follow such an action.

At the end of the laughter, William turned his regard upon her again. "You will come to respect me, Rhiannyn of Etcheverry. Perhaps even like me."

How was she to respond to that? she wondered. Fortunately, she did not have to, for with his next breath he ordered both women to rise.

Rhiannyn easily stood, but not so Elan. Seeing her struggle to lift her bulk from the floor, Rhiannyn reached to assist her. However, it was Maxen who pulled his sister to standing.

Trying to regain her dignity behind a belly so far gone with pregnancy that it looked as if she might topple headlong into the king, Elan smoothed her skirts and set her chin high. Then, taking a deep breath, she stepped around Maxen to the older man who stood beside her brother.

"Father," she addressed him.

"Daughter," he answered.

Rhiannyn nearly fell into the king herself. Blind was what she was. She had seen that the older man was the same height as Maxen, but had not noticed the marked resemblance between father and son. Both broad, both dark-haired—though the father's hair was liberally washed with silver—and both of strong countenance. Remove the twenty or more years from the father and before her would stand a man who might be Maxen's twin.

Ah, dread, Rhiannyn silently bemoaned. Not only William to deal with, but Maxen's father.

"Bring on the food," William ordered. Turning from Elan's reunion with her father, he strode toward the tables and a moment later was firmly settled in the high seat.

Though Rhiannyn knew that wherever the king went in

his realm, his place was the highest, resentment flared within her that he had taken what was Maxen's. Just as William had taken what had been King Harold's.

"I like this neck," Maxen murmured to her. He lightly trailed a finger down it to the hollow of her collarbone. "Pray do not press the king so hard that I will have to go to great lengths to save it."

Her black mood easing a little, she smiled at him.

"That is good," he said, "but can you hold onto that smile for my father?"

She glanced across at the man, and had only a moment to study him before he moved his gaze from Elan to her. Immediately, Rhiannyn became aware of his dislike, the accusation in his eyes. Aye, she realized, for certain he knew who she was. And hated her for it.

Maxen must have felt the hatred, too, but propriety had him pulling Rhiannyn forward to stand before the man. "Father, I present to you Rhiannyn of Etcheverry." He looked to her. "My father, Baron Pendery."

Stiffly, Rhiannyn forced a curtsy before the older man, but to no end. When she looked up, his face was as hard as before she had executed the gesture.

"I am not pleased," he said, shifting his gaze to his son.

"Then 'tis just as well your pleasure is not sought," Maxen said, seemingly undisturbed by his father's animosity. Placing Rhiannyn's hand on his arm, he turned with her and walked toward the high table where his king sat.

"Your father does not like me," Rhiannyn whispered as they rounded the table.

His gaze unwavering on the bench ahead of them, Maxen answered, "No longer does his approval matter to me. If he takes no liking to you, it changes naught between us."

Reassured, though still uneasy, Rhiannyn took her place beside him on the bench.

The meal that followed was an ordeal Rhiannyn likened to walking barefoot over nettles. Nay, not just nettles, but ... burning nettles. The odd thing was, that which made the meal such a strain was not what she would have expected. Along with the drink William downed, so did he lower his reserve and come fully into good humor. In the two hours that followed, time and again Rhiannyn felt herself being drawn to the accursed man's wit and charm. Resisting his pull was what made it all such a terrible trial.

However, come the end of the meal when all was being cleared away and the men gathered before their king to hear what he had thus far withheld from them, William donned the cap of business. No more waggery tumbled from his lips, no more jesting. He was once again the king, and all before him his loyal subjects.

As Rhiannyn had feared might happen, she and Elan were sent from the hall. Rhiannyn, with Elan tagging along behind her, chose to await summoning in the lord's chamber. Surprisingly, they gained it unopposed. Although she could not be before the king when he spoke, at least she would be able to hear much of what he said. Then she would know first-hand his reason for journeying to Etcheverry with a full army behind him—though she was woefully certain she already knew.

Rhiannyn was fully aware that it would appear unseemly to Elan for her to stand at the edge of the screen eavesdropping, but still she did it.

"I have had word that the weasel abides a day's ride north of Etcheverry," the king boomed.

"He speaks of Edwin?" Elan whispered.

Surprised to find her so near, Rhiannyn swung her head around and looked into Elan's questioning eyes. Naught to fear that Elan would think ill of her for what she did, for the young woman was as interested as she.

"Aye, I am sure 'tis Edwin he speaks of," she said. Though others might call him "the wolf," William did not grant the man so frightening a title. No doubt it made him feel superior to call his enemy a weasel.

"News was also brought me that he is readying for what he calls the final battle," William continued, "and that come a fortnight he intends to sneak an attack upon London."

There followed a murmur of men's voices.

"But 'tis I who will sneak an attack upon him," William went on with all confidence. "On the morrow we ride, and by the day after, his blood will flow the same as Harold's did."

Rhiannyn shuddered.

Elan wrinkled her pretty nose.

"Maxen Pendery, are you prepared to ride at my side?" William demanded.

What choice had he? Rhiannyn wondered, her stomach filled with unease, her mind with anxiety.

"I and my men," Maxen said. "When you ride, so too shall we, my liege."

"Guy?" Elan breathed. She shook Rhiannyn's arm until Rhiannyn looked over her shoulder at her. "Surely he cannot mean Guy as well," she pleaded, fear puckering her face.

As there was no comfort to be given, and a lie would only be found out on the morrow, Rhiannyn nodded. " 'Tis likely, Elan, for he is Maxen's first man. There is none held in higher regard." In the next instant, Rhiannyn was grasping at the young woman to keep her upright. "Elan," she called to her.

Her lashes fluttered and the whites of her eyes showed, then she slackened to a dead weight in Rhiannyn's arms.

"Ah, Elan," Rhiannyn groaned. "Do not do this to me." Knowing she could not long hold her up, Rhiannyn eased down to the floor with Elan, then pulled her head into her lap. "Elan," she called again.

A few minutes later, Elan's eyes opened, and this time there was more pupil than white to her eyes. "Say 'tis not so," she whispered.

"I am sorry," Rhiannyn said, "but I cannot."

If ever Elan showed genuine emotion, it was at this moment. Her eyes misting with tears, she said, "I never loved before Guy. I cannot lose him, Rhiannyn."

As she could not lose Maxen. "I know," she said, pushing the hair out of Elan's eyes. "But we must be strong—and believe."

"How can I? I am so weak with this child that there is

hardly strength in me to simply pass the day." She pressed a hand to her belly. "Ah, but to be rid of it."

"Do not speak so," Rhiannyn snapped. "'Tis not the fault of the babe for being."

Turning onto her side, Elan sat up and back on her heels. "You are right," she said unexpectedly. "It is my fault and no other's."

Sensing that revelation was upon Elan's tongue, Rhiannyn asked, "Not even Edwin's fault?"

Elan considered her, then withdrew into herself. "Of course it is his fault," she said, "but had I not been so foolish to ride alone into the wood, 'twould never have happened."

One day she would abandon her lie, of that Rhiannyn was certain, but not now. Issuing a long sigh, she stood and extended a hand to Elan.

Taking it, Elan staggered upright. "I know it is not what you wish to hear, Rhiannyn, but 'tis what befell me. Truly."

Knowing that to argue the matter would only prove futile and frustrating, Rhiannyn turned from her and focused again on the voices in the hall. They were a low murmur now, as if many had left. And so they had, she saw upon peeking around the screen. Where there had been all of a hundred men, there were now no more than a dozen.

What had transpired while she had tended to Elan's faint? she wondered with mounting exasperation. Had anything else of import been said? She skipped her gaze from Maxen to the king, settled it there a long moment, then looked to where Sir Guy and Maxen's father stood. Lastly, she looked at the others who surrounded the king. All of them spoke, though not at once and not loudly enough for their voices to carry to her.

"What are they saying?" Elan asked, leaning around Rhiannyn to look upon the gathering.

Rhiannyn pulled back. "Naught I can understand."

Elan also drew back into the chamber. "But what do you think they say?"

"They are planning. That is all I am certain of."

Her belly going well before her, Elan walked to the bed and leaned on it as she gingerly lowered herself to the floor. "I think I will pray," she said, steepling her hands before her face. "And you?"

Rhiannyn was too shocked to answer. A praying Elan? The best Elan she had ever known did not even come close to this. But that was love, wasn't it? It could change your life forever. "I will pray with you," she said at long last, then stepped forward and lowered herself beside Elan.

"We are close to being friends, you know," Elan said softly, then closed her eyes and began moving her lips to prayer.

Odd friends, Rhiannyn thought, but at least there was peace between them.

"What will happen?" Rhiannyn asked when Maxen returned from a night walk with his king.

Stretching out beside her on the straw pallet she had made for them in the hall, he pulled her against him. "What will happen, or what would I have happen?"

"The truth," she said.

"Far likely a battle, though I have given the king much to think about this night."

"And what is that?"

"Do you remember when I said I would give all of Etcheverry unto Edwin if it would bring peace?"

"Well I remember."

"It is that which I put to King William."

Rhiannyn's heart soared for this man she loved more and more each day. "And what did he say?" she asked.

"He berated me for a coward," Maxen said, his body tensing beside her.

Anger at William rushed through Rhiannyn. "He only goads you," she said.

"This I know, but when he said the Bloodlust Warrior was dead and that mayhap I ought to have remained at the monastery, I was overwhelmed with a need to prove him wrong."

"But that part of you *is* dead. You cannot possibly prove him wrong."

"Can I not?" He shook his head. "Though I pray it so, the frenzy is still with me. I felt it when I fought Ancel."

Rhiannyn was beset with the terrible memory of what Maxen had become when he met Ancel in battle. Though justified in the taking of the man's life, he had seemed inhuman—only a throw away from the beasts of the woods. Would it be the same if he confronted Edwin on the battlefield? At William's side, would he unthinkingly slaughter as he had at Hastings?

"Nay," she said, "there is a difference between slaying one worthy of death and one not so. Though you did not know it at Hastings, you know it now."

Maxen stroked a hand down her hip. "You keep me sane, my lovely Saxon," he murmured, clearly not wishing to speak any more about the confrontation to come.

"What will you do?" she asked, pressing him to tell more.

He sighed. "I will ride with him into battle and pray that the army Edwin confronts us with will be enough to make the king think more seriously on what I have proposed."

For William, it seemed, it was only a matter of whether Edwin came before him weak or strong, she thought. No concern at all for what was right and wrong. Fool of her even to think that might be a consideration. "Then you still believe there to be a chance of peace over bloodshed?" she asked.

"Slight," Maxen answered. "Although King William wearies of these constant uprisings, his power trebles with each victory. Thus, he may see the defeat of Harwolfson as his greatest triumph and one not to be denied him."

Rhiannyn pressed herself more tightly to him. "I fear for you, Maxen," she said.

"Put it from your mind. 'Tis of no benefit to worry on it."

He was right. As she had told Elan, she must be strong. Closing her eyes, Rhiannyn acknowledged that once again she was breaking the vow she had made to tell Maxen of his impending fatherhood. However, considering the day's events and the morrow's ride to battle, now was neither the time nor the place. After all, it was not simply a matter of telling Maxen of the child, but of admitting to a lie that would only arouse great anger in him. And that anger might see his sword arm unsteady when it was needed to protect his life. She could not risk it. Afterwards—and she had to believe there would be an afterwards—she would tell him.

Chapter Twenty-nine

"I do not wish to go!" Elan wailed. "How can you ask me to look again upon that man who did this to me?" She clapped her hands to her swollen belly.

"I am not asking," old man Pendery said gruffly, "I am telling. You will witness for yourself the bastard's death. This is your revenge."

" 'Tis enough for me that he dies," she countered.

"But not for me. Now gather your things and make ready to ride."

Maxen, Rhiannyn following, stepped out of the dark of early morn and into the hall. "She is too far into her pregnancy to risk the ride," Maxen said, having caught the gist of the loudly debated argument as he and Rhiannyn had mounted the steps to the donjon.

His father swung around to face him.

"You fear she might lose the bastard babe, eh?" he roared. "All the better, I say."

Maxen spoke no more until he stood directly before his father. "It is not only the child you risk, but Elan as well."

The old man's face, hard from too many years of being the soldier, grew brighter red with his growing anger. "Elan is of me," he said sharply. "Though she is but a daughter, she possesses my strength."

"She is a woman with child," Maxen pointed out, anger rising in his own voice. "She stays at Etcheverry."

His father stiffened, but in the next instant he thrust his face near his son's. "And I say she goes."

Heavenly Father, Rhiannyn thought. Were these two men of the same blood about to come to blows?

Maxen did not back down, but neither did he take the swing at his father that must have tempted his fists. He simply stared into the older man's eyes without flinching or faltering.

"She goes," Pendery said again.

"Stays," Maxen hissed.

"I am sorry, Maxen," King William said, coming out from behind the screen of the lord's chamber, "but I must side with your father."

Eyes like fire, Maxen swung around to face him. "Surely you can see how pregnant my sister is," he said, completely ignoring who it was he addressed and what punishment might be his for his lack of deference.

"I see as well as you, Maxen Pendery, and I see that the Lady Elan and her babe could prove quite useful if, as we discussed yestereve, it is necessary to proceed with your proposal."

Then he did not completely discount Maxen's recommendation of peace with Edwin? Rhiannyn thought. Part of her leapt with hope while another part worried for Elan's well-being.

"What proposal do you speak of, my liege?" old man Pendery asked.

William halted before father and son, then settled his cutting gaze upon Maxen. "As it is not likely to be exercised," he answered, "you need not worry about it. Need he, Maxen?"

"Regardless," Maxen said, "Elan should stay at Etcheverry."

"And your Saxon lady?" William asked, his gaze tripping to Rhiannyn where she stood to the side of Maxen, then dismissing her to alight again upon his man.

Maxen's guardedness multiplied tenfold. "What has she to do with it?"

"As she was once betrothed to the weasel, I have decided she should also accompany us."

Maxen's anger was most tangible. "For what purpose?" he asked, his jaws tight.

Displeasure lining his face, William leaned toward Maxen. "There are few I would allow to question me," he said, "and only because you once served me well am I going to allow it, but no more."

Clearly, there was more Maxen wished to say, but the warning he had just received was not empty. Rhiannyn only prayed he would not press William any further, for did he, death might be his well ahead of the battlefield.

The same thoughts were running through Maxen's mind. Although one-on-one he was certain he would be the victor of any match between himself and the king, it was not such a contest that faced him. But a word, and he would be at the mercy of William's soldiers—two dozen of whom stood against the walls awaiting orders. As rude as the truth was, he would gain naught in opposing the man. Neither Elan nor Rhiannyn would remain at Etcheverry, nor would his proposal come any nearer to seeing the light.

Though he did it grudgingly, Maxen backed away in the face of the king's consuming power. "I am your man, my liege. Your bidding will be done."

As if nothing had gone awry, the king's face brightened into a beaming smile. "You will serve me well again," he said, clapping a hand to Maxen's shoulder. "This I know." Then he turned and crossed the hall to the doors leading outside, his soldiers withdrawing with him.

There followed the silence of Pendery facing Pendery— the air of hostility between father and son.

Elan broke the quiet. "I do not wish to go!" she wailed again.

"Tell it to the king," her father snapped. A smug smile replacing his scowl, he turned and followed William. "A quarter hour, Elan," he said over his shoulder. "That is all I give you."

"I am sorry, Rhiannyn, Elan," Maxen said when they were without audience, "but it must be as the king commands."

"I will make ready," Rhiannyn said, somewhat gladdened that at least some good would come of it. She would be with Maxen during his time of trial.

Elan was not so agreeable. "I hope Edwin cuts William's heart out," she said. "Disembowels him. Severs his—"

"Elan!" Maxen reprimanded.

"I do," she retorted, tears overflowing her eyes. "How dare he do this to me. Who does he think he is? God?"

Aye, God, Rhiannyn silently agreed. Knowing there were yet many things Maxen had to attend to ere the ride from Etcheverry, she stepped forward and put an arm around Elan's shoulders. "I will help you collect your things," she said, exchanging a meaningful glance with Maxen, "and then you will assist me with mine."

"I ought to go naked," Elan mumbled past a sob, "then he would see that I am in no state to ride a horse."

"Wouldn't that be a sight!" Rhiannyn exclaimed as she ushered the young woman across the hall. "In fact, had I your courage, methinks I would join you."

His heart heavy, Maxen watched them go. Only when they were gone from sight did he make for the outer bailey that teemed with preparations for the coming encounter. *Be prepared, Edwin Harwolfson*, he silently mouthed to the sky above, *else you will be dead*.

As uncomfortable as the long ride had been for Rhiannyn, she knew it must have been miserable for Elan.

Whereas Rhiannyn had ridden with Maxen throughout the journey—excepting those times when William had commanded him to his side—Elan was too large to ride with Sir Guy. Thus, she had ridden at her betrothed's side, crying and complaining all the way.

Fortunately, the pace had not been as brutal as might have been expected, whether from consideration on the king's part, or arising naturally from his plans.

Dusk dusted the skies before the king called a halt to the procession, and on the ridge above a grassy field bordering a wood, camp was made. The place was named Darfield, and soon Rhiannyn learned that it was here on the morrow Norman would again meet Saxon in battle.

It was dark before Maxen returned from the king's tent. Throwing back the flap of the tent raised for him and Rhiannyn, he said, "He knows we are here."

Rhiannyn sat up from the bed she had made them. "Edwin?" The tent, lit behind by the many torches set about the camp, showed Maxen's shadowed figure as he moved toward her.

"Aye," he said, dropping down beside her. "He is in the wood, but tomorrow he and his followers will gather at the opposite end of the field to face William off."

Fear squeezed into her chest. "You are certain of that?"

"I am—as is King William."

She put a hand to Maxen's arm. "Mayhap Edwin will withdraw," she suggested hopefully.

"You think so?"

He did not believe it, and neither did she, so why deceive herself with such false hope? she chastised herself. Indeed, even if Edwin did turn away, the confrontation would simply come a day or so later. "Nay," she admitted, "I do not think so, but what of your proposal of peace without bloodshed?"

"As I have said, only if Edwin makes a fine show will William consider it. And mayhap not even then."

So many thoughts leapt to Rhiannyn's mind—questions whose answers would change naught, reflections that would only fill the silence, and pleadings that Maxen had already heard and done his best to answer—but knowing that this might be their last night together, that come day Maxen might lay down his life for his king, Rhiannyn pushed all aside. "Will you lie with me awhile?" she asked.

He pulled her into his arms and lay back upon the pallet with her. "Awhile," he said. And then he would go to William's side to do battle for the man.

Turning his palm to hers, Maxen wove their fingers together. "How is Elan?" he asked.

Rhiannyn drew a deep breath. "She complains of cramping and pangs. I am worried for her."

"Christophe is with her?"

She nodded. "And Sir Guy."

"What does Christophe say?"

"Unfortunately, for all his herbs and healing, he has had little experience with birthing. He is quite at a loss."

Maxen sat up. "Then the king's physician ought to be summoned," he said, disentangling himself as if he meant to go for him himself.

Rhiannyn put a staying hand to his arm. "He has been summoned, Maxen, and by now he is with her."

Maxen hesitated, then lay back down. "What if the babe should come now?" he asked.

The thought had occurred to Rhiannyn several times. "It is a month before it is due," she said, "but it is not entirely uncommon for a child to be delivered ere its nine months have passed."

"In good health?"

Some in good health, others not so. "I have seen it," she said, "though rarely with a child of less age than Elan's."

"Then you believe if she were to deliver early, her babe would fare well?"

" 'Tis possible."

"But not certain."

She shook her head. "I fear not, but it is for the physician to say, not I."

Though Maxen did not wish to worry Rhiannyn by speaking aloud his great anger with the king, he made himself a vow that did any harm come to his sister, and most especially to Rhiannyn, he would throw aside his quest to shed the cloak of the Bloodlust Warrior of Hastings and seek the king's death himself. So be it.

By the time night entered day, the king and all of his army stood to arms. As at Hastings, William had positioned his soldiers in three lines—archers in front, heavy infantry in the middle, and the cavalry of knights taking up the rear. In the midst of that cavalry he waited for Edwin Harwolfson to challenge him for the kingdom of England.

Her skirts billowing in the chill morning breeze, her mantle flapping at her back, Rhiannyn stood atop the ridge and looked down upon the great formation that might soon be broken did the miracle she prayed for not come.

How many did they number? she wondered, beginning a count for perhaps the dozenth time. Again she lost track when her gaze fell upon the papal banner that rose high and fluttering before the king. As it had been present at Hastings, so was it here, by presence alone proclaiming that William the Bastard was the favored son of the Holy Church, and bestowing upon him the papal blessing of conquest.

Shifting her gaze, Rhiannyn sought the figure of Maxen where he was mounted alongside his king. His mind heavy with the day ahead, he had not spoken a word to her when he had left her hours earlier. However, before he had departed he had taken her face between his hands and kissed her long and lingering. Then he had drawn back and touched his gaze over her shadowed features as if memorizing every one of them for eternity.

Her insides churning, Rhiannyn had watched him withdraw, and only when his shadow had melted into the dark had she attempted to deal with emotions so much at war, they nearly choked her. On the one hand she vehemently wished that the Bloodlust Warrior of Hastings would come again so that Maxen might survive the battle before him.

On the other, she prayed that he would forever purge the beast from his soul. But then he might die. . . .

No solution to her emotions, she had thrust them aside and put all her prayers into resolution through the peace Maxen had proposed to his king. A high order indeed, but nothing more worthy. Of course, William did not present the only obstacle to that path. One could not forget Maxen's avenging father.

Rhiannyn picked out the man who sat alongside his son. Aye, did the king come anywhere near to entertaining peace over bloodshed, most assuredly the old man would raise such an outcry, ears would be forever shattered by it. In which case, it could only be hoped that the elder Pendery held little or no sway over William. Hoped. Prayed.

So absorbed was she that Rhiannyn did not hear another's approach until he spoke. "Rhiannyn," Christophe said, his hand light upon her shoulder. "Elan calls for you. Will you come?"

A different concern filling her, she gave up the sight before her and turned to him. "Something is wrong?" she asked.

"She is in labor."

Rhiannyn gasped. "Since when?"

"Since the first hours of morning."

"And what says the physician?"

Christophe made a face. "That he must needs make ready to attend King William does injury befall him in battle."

Rhiannyn's heart thudded heavily in her breast. Then Elan would have her babe here, in the midst of what would most likely become a war? And without benefit of a physician? Lord, what hope was there?

"Will you come?" Christophe asked again.

"Of course," she said. There was only Christophe and herself now, the physician abandoning Elan for the possibility that he might be needed to tend the scrapes and scratches of his precious king. Rhiannyn caught one last desperate glimpse of Maxen, fixing the image of his broad-shouldered back upon her mind, then nodded for Christophe to lead the way. Far better a birth to wash her memories in than a death—hundreds upon hundreds of deaths—she told herself as she hurried after Christophe.

The physician was exiting Elan's tent when Rhiannyn and Christophe reached it. "I have given her something for the pain," he said in passing. "Now there is naught else to do but wait."

"Naught else but see her child safely into this world," Rhiannyn snapped at his back.

He halted, then looked over his shoulder at her. " 'Tis but a Saxon bastard," he said.

"You—"

Elan's cry snatched the remainder of Rhiannyn's heated retort from her. Snapping her teeth closed, she ducked through the flap Christophe held for her and stooped to accomodate the low-ceilinged tent.

"I am here, Elan," she said, hiding her startle at seeing the young woman in such a state. Her hair in tangled disarray, her skin flushed a glaring red and beaded with moisture, and her face contorted, Elan was quite a sight. Very little did she resemble the woman she had been the day before. Only her very large belly rising up beneath the blanket gave evidence that she was the same.

Grabbing Rhiannyn's hand and squeezing it with all her might, Elan whispered, "Dying. I am dying."

"Nay you are not," Rhiannyn attempted to soothe her. "You are simply having a baby."

"Simply!" Elan spat, anger taking the pain from her face. "Why don't you try it and see how simple 'tis."

"Mayhap I will," Rhiannyn said, "and then it will be you holding my hand and me bellowing at you."

Elan tried to hold onto her anger—mayhap it was easier to deal with than the pain—but it slipped from her face as laughter bubbled up from her throat. "Ha!" she grunted. "And then it will be my turn to tell you lies about how simple it is."

Smiling, Rhiannyn brushed the damp strands back from Elan's brow. "I'm sure you will."

Her convulsing womb easing, Elan slackened and sank more deeply into her straw mattress. She breathed a long sigh. "'Tis almost worth the pain to feel the peace of its lifting."

Forgotten by the two women, Christophe moved to Elan's feet and lifted the edge of the blanket. "I must look as the physician told me to," he warned his sister.

"Oh, do whatever you must," she grumbled. "Think you I care anymore?" To demonstrate, she grabbed the blanket and tossed it off her naked body.

It was as Rhiannyn's mother had once told her—modesty had no place in the birthing of children.

Fighting down his fluster, Christophe completed his exam, then pulled the blanket back over his sister. "The time is nearing," he said, then he shifted his gaze to Rhiannyn. "Once the head shows, I will need you to help me hold Elan up to squatting. Think you can do that?"

"Of course," Rhiannyn said.

"It will require great effort if the babe is long in coming."

"I can do it," she assured him.

A short time later, another contraction overwhelmed Elan. "It's killing me!" she shrieked.

"Find a good piece of wood to put between her teeth," Christophe ordered Rhiannyn.

It was no easy feat extracting her crushed hand from Elan's, but Rhiannyn managed it a finger at a time. "I will be back soon," she told Elan, though it was unlikely she was heard. Slipping out of the tent, her gaze lit first upon the morning sky, then fell to the throng of soldiers advancing upon the field where William sat ready to give them battle.

Fear burst through her. As Maxen had said he would, Edwin had come. And it appeared not to be a straggling army that marched with him, but an impressive array of Saxons come to change what Hastings had wrought. Dear God, Rhiannyn prayed, let this spectacle be enough to turn William from bloodletting to peace. Let him suffer enough uncertainty as to the outcome that he would do as Maxen had proposed. Heavenly Father—

Elan screamed.

Frantic, Rhiannyn dragged her gaze from the gripping scene and bent to find the piece of wood Christophe had asked for.

Keeping his emotions behind a face set to appear hard and unfeeling, Maxen stared straight ahead as Edwin's army marched toward William's. Although it might mean his death did he go into battle, he was pleased by all he saw.

In a formation identical to William's—archers, infantry, and cavalry—came Edwin's soldiers of a number that appeared equal to the Norman army. In fact, on closer examination, Maxen was certain they numbered more. All were armed with either a spear, a sword, the great two-handed battle-axe of the Saxons, or a bow and arrows. Some even wore chain mail. How Maxen had wished it so, but he had not thought it possible that Edwin could muster all that he had. Most admirable.

"By God, cavalry," William muttered disbelievingly.

Maxen knew exactly what the king was thinking. Much of the Norman victory at Hastings was owed to the fact that the Normans were accomplished at using horses in battle, whereas the Saxons had all fought on foot— obviously something Edwin Harwolfson intended to remedy this day.

"Look how he comes," William growled. "He configures his army to mine. He mocks me."

Likely the king had never been better matched, Maxen thought, than he was this day against an army of Saxon rebels. Still, though they looked the part, it did not mean they could fight the part.

"And weapons aplenty," William continued. "Never would I have believed it possible."

Holding his expression, Maxen looked across at him. "Then we do battle, my liege?" he asked.

"Of course we do battle!" Baron Pendery snapped. "I fear not a Saxon dog whose only accomplishment is the rape of innocent young women."

Certainly not Edwin's only accomplishment, Maxen thought, considering Harwolfson's plunderings these past months.

William's response was quick and crushing. "Do you think to tell me what I should do, Pendery?" he demanded.

Maxen's father hid his surprise well. "Of course not, my king. I but voice my opinion."

"Too loudly," William retorted.

Pendery bent his head in deference. "Forgiveness," he said.

William grunted, but said no more. Turning his gaze once again upon the adversary who came to challenge him, he waited through the clamor and clatter of Harwolfson's advance for the dead silence that always fell before the clash.

"God, I die," Elan panted. She hung limp between Rhiannyn and Christophe in the aftermath of a contraction that had brought the baby's head to crown.

Reaching behind her, Rhiannyn scooped a dripping cloth from the basin, squeezed the excess water from it, then patted it across Elan's brow. "Soon it will be over," she said, trying not to hear the movement of Edwin's army, the sound of which drifted up the ridge.

"And I will be dead," was Elan's oft-repeated rejoinder to any reassurance given her. However, this time the eyes she turned to Rhiannyn believed it to be true. "I must confess ere my last breath," she said.

"Nonsense," Christophe snapped. "You will live to rear this child as it ought to be."

"I must—"

Another contraction hit her, and when it was over she rolled her head on her neck and rested it upon Rhiannyn's shoulder. "Hear me?" she beseeched. "I must free myself of this burden."

Again Rhiannyn wiped her brow. "Don't talk, Elan. It only wastes your strength."

"I must needs ..." She swallowed the dryness of her mouth.

Rhiannyn dipped the cloth again, then tipped Elan's head back and wrung its wetness upon her tongue.

"It might make a difference," Elan said when she could speak again.

"A difference?" Rhiannyn had to ask.

Elan nodded. " 'Twas not rape. I—"

Both Rhiannyn and Christophe waited breathlessly through the next contraction to hear Elan's revelation.

"Knowing who Edwin was, I gave myself to him," she continued.

"I don't understand," Rhiannyn said.

Elan smiled bitterly. "Which would you rather present your father with—a rape you were incapable of preventing, or—" She moistened her lips. "Or discovery upon your wedding night that you were not a maiden?"

Then Edwin had been but a pawn in Elan's desperate plan to absolve herself of the responsibility of her loss of virginity. "I see," Rhiannyn said.

"My father should know," Elan said. The baby moved again to force its way into the world, and she became incapable of words. However, screaming was not beyond her, and she deafened Rhiannyn's ears with it.

Although Elan had previously refused it, this time she accepted the piece of wood Christophe put between her teeth. "Push," he commanded her, "and do not stop until I tell you so."

It seemed unlikely that Elan heard or understood any of what was said to her, but she found it in her to push until Christophe told her to cease.

How Rhiannyn wanted to think on Elan's disclosure, to find some use in it, but she knew now was not the time. She only prayed it would not be too late when the time came.

• • •

Underestimated. And that was as he had planned it to be, Edwin thought as he reined in his mount amid the cavalry. He and his followers had made themselves scarce these past months so that William the Bastard would misjudge their numbers and their strength, and the usurper had done exactly that. It was a formidable army the Norman had assembled, but certainly not as immense as it would have been had Edwin let be known the extent of his. Silence had served him well.

At this moment Edwin could not have been more pleased, unless, of course, his men were equal in training and skill to his adversary's. He had worked them hard and with severity for this confrontation, and though they could no longer be said to be simple men of the earth, that was what still lay in their hearts. Also in their hearts was revenge, and of no better service was it than in this present capacity.

As the remainder of Edwin's forces took position, he looked across the field to where his counterpart was mounted behind the papal banner. How like Hastings, he thought as memories swept over him. On that day, as this, the bastard had flaunted the Church's approval of his theft of another people's country, then he had slaughtered them nearly one and all. Would this day end as that day had?

"Nay," he said, not realizing he spoke aloud. God owed them this. Today the Saxons would triumph and their lands would be returned to them.

"Your mind is heavy with something," Aethel broke into his thoughts. "That other battle?"

Edwin looked down at the man who stood alongside him. "Aye," he admitted after a moment's reflection. "Almost I expect to see King Harold where you now stand."

As Aethel had been too awkward of size to make use of a horse, he had chosen to do battle on foot, and though he was of the infantry, he had marched to the field beside Edwin.

"What think you?" Aethel asked, jutting his bearded chin toward the enemy's army.

Edwin turned his gaze back upon them. " 'Tis the deciding battle," he said as he once again picked out William atop his mount. "Whatever happens this day will undoubtedly secure England's history."

Aethel fell silent.

Looking left of William, Edwin settled his eyes upon a large figure. Maxen Pendery. Of this he was certain, even though he could not make out the man's features.

Edwin's smile felt bitter. God willing, this day he would have his revenge tenfold. Not only would the Normans be purged from English soil, but he would know the satisfaction of repaying the man who had taken not only his lands, but also the woman who was to have been his wife. And if ever he got his hands on Elan Pendery . . .

Something pricked at the edges of Edwin's awareness. Snapping back to the present, he looked first to his adversary, saw nothing amiss, then turned his eyes upon his men. What was it about them? he wondered with sudden foreboding. Though silence prevailed, something unspoken coursed through a good many of them. Far too many.

He looked more closely, from one man to another, and then he knew. The eerie silence before the battle had sent unease through their ranks. Not the tense excitement of seasoned warriors about to perform their life's work, but the worry of men about to leap into something they doubted themselves capable of—mayhap were not capable of.

Dear God, why now? Edwin silently cursed. Why after all the times these men had proven themselves capable did they now doubt themselves? Many were the raids, pillaging, and assaults upon castles they had undertaken, and with unquestioned courage and daring. Why now?

The answer was the same as he had already determined. It was the silence. Though for Edwin it was as familiar as his sword, only a small number of his rebels had ever been confronted with it.

They would stand in good stead, he assured himself.

Once the battle commenced and the din of warfare filled the air, all they had been trained for would consume them and they would wield their weapons more sharply than ever.

A high-pitched wail split the silence—not the wail of trumpets or battle cries, but of . . . Edwin frowned. Could it be a baby?

Chapter Thirty

Though Edwin could not have known, the cry heralded the arrival of his son. Born early but in surprisingly good health, the infant let loose cry after lusty cry.

While Christophe tended to Elan, Rhiannyn held the baby against her chest and quickly cleansed the birthing from its pink skin that it might be swaddled in warmth once again. Only when that was done and the child comfortably wrapped did it quiet itself and nestle into the crook of her arm.

A peculiar joy overwhelmed Rhiannyn so much that for a few minutes she forgot what transpired on the field. "Would you like to see your son, my lady?" she asked, kneeling beside Elan.

Elan started to lift her weary head, but then she turned away. "Want naught . . . to do with it," she said.

It. Not him, but it. As if the baby had

not come from her. As if he was not even human. Had Elan not been ailing so, Rhiannyn would have shaken her, but that could wait until later. What could not wait was the battle that was swiftly approaching, and that might take everything dear from her. But what was she to do?

As if in answer, the babe squeaked and flailed a tiny fist free of the swaddling cloth.

"Ah, precious one," Rhiannyn began, stroking the backs of its fingers. And then she knew. As the child opened its hand and closed it around her finger, she hastened to the tent flap.

"Christophe, I will need your horse," she said over her shoulder.

"Whatever for?" he asked sharply. "And where do you think you are going?"

"To end this battle ere it begins," she said, and then she was outside. One quick glance over the ridge showed her the two armies that waited for the trumpets to sound the commencement of the deadly contest. She must reach Edwin before that happened. Loosing the reins of Christophe's horse, she stepped to its side to mount, but in the next instant realized the impossibility of doing so while cradling the babe.

"What do you intend?" Christophe asked.

Not realizing he'd followed her, she was surprised by his presence. "If ever there is a chance of ending this, it lies with this child," she said. "Edwin must see that he has a son."

"But—"

"Trust me in this," she interrupted, desperate to be off. "Take the babe, and when I am mounted, hand him up."

Christophe accepted the bundle pressed upon him, and when Rhiannyn had straddled the horse in the fashion of men, he passed the babe into her arms.

"It will end," she said, then urged the horse toward the sloping end of the ridge which marked the southernmost edge of William's army. The pace she set was one of urgency, yet safe enough for the baby. In fact, when she glanced down, Edwin's son had drifted off to sleep. The bump and bounce of the horse was a movement that seemed to suit him.

Although Rhiannyn had intended to skirt William's army before any might attempt to turn her back, she was noticed the moment she gained the field. However, surprise was her advantage, and while confusion spread as to what to do about her, she made it past the formation. Gone was the quiet as she guided her mount over the empty field that lay between William and Edwin, and in its place rose the clamor of voices and metal on metal. One of those voices was Maxen's, she knew, but she could not think on that now.

Pray let them not fire upon me, she beseeched the heavens. *Let them see that I am of no threat to them.* Sensing that Edwin would be among his cavalry, as William was with his own, she searched him out. It was not necessary, though, for as she neared, a path opened down the center of his army and he came toward her.

His eyes hard and steady upon her, he motioned his men to calm, then ordered in scathing tones, "Come no nearer."

Rhiannyn was well content with that. Reining her horse in, she turned it sideways that Edwin might see what she had brought with her.

"What have you come for?" he demanded as he approached. "More trickery?"

In answer, Rhiannyn pushed back the cloth and showed him the sleeping babe's face. "To present you your son, Edwin," she said.

His horse faltered with him, but was the first to recover. Carrying its master forward again, the animal was drawn to a halt less than five feet from where Rhiannyn waited.

"My son?" Edwin said, something of the past showing in his eyes.

Something within Rhiannyn told her of Maxen's coming, and one quick glance over her shoulder confirmed it. A single horseman—it had to be he—had broken from

William's formation and was galloping across the field toward her.

Edwin also saw him, a fire leaping into his eyes.

"Edwin, let him come," she said. "Surely you cannot fear one man with so many standing at your side."

"More Pendery trickery," he growled.

"Nay, he did not know I intended this. He only seeks to protect me."

"And what do you intend, Rhiannyn?"

"Peace," she said.

"Peace! Never can there be such a thing between Saxons and Normans."

"But there already is. If you would just—" The sounds of arrows being nocked to bows, then the hiss of strings being drawn taut, arrested the rest of Rhiannyn's words. Looking beyond Edwin, she saw that his archers had trained their weapons upon Maxen. "Edwin," she pleaded, "order them to stand down."

He dropped his gaze to the child she held, then raised it to her before turning in the saddle and calling for his men to lower their weapons.

Rhiannyn nearly slumped with relief.

" 'Tis of Elan Pendery," Edwin said, nodding to the child.

"Aye, just born."

Edwin's silence stretched, then he said, "He should have been of you and me, Rhiannyn."

What he spoke was true, but it could never be—was never meant to be. "In a different time and place," she said.

"But not this," he responded bitterly.

"Nay, not this."

"You love Pendery?"

The question was unexpected, but she answered it honestly. "Aye."

There was no more to be said on the matter, for suddenly Maxen was at her side, his hand closing around her arm. "Rhiannyn, what in God's name do you think you are doing?"

"Presenting me with my son," Edwin answered for her.

Maxen had never known such fear as when he saw the lone figure riding toward the enemy with a bundle in her arms. He had known immediately that it was Elan's baby Rhiannyn carried, and had not had to guess twice what she intended—unlike the king, who had roared anger at what he perceived to be treachery.

Thinking he might go mad before he was heard, but knowing that death would reach him before he reached Rhiannyn if he did not hold back his impatience, Maxen had waited for a break in William's cursing before putting forth an explanation for Rhiannyn's behavior. He had told the king that this was likely her way to peace—that in being shown his child, Edwin might finally submit to Norman domination. Surrender.

For once, Maxen's father had proven himself useful. His ravings gave the king the presence of mind to put aside his own anger and ponder the situation. Fortunately, he had not been too long in pondering, and had granted Maxen permission to ride across the field. Although Maxen would never have put Rhiannyn in such jeopardy, he knew that what she had done was good, for the trumpets had been about to sound when she had appeared. Now there was a chance.

He looked to the child cradled in her arms. "And what think you of your son, Harwolfson?" he asked.

Edwin flicked his gaze over the child, then settled it hard upon Maxen. "Born of rape, he can hardly be called mine."

"But he is yours," Rhiannyn said, "and it was not rape."

"How grand of you to believe me incapable of such appalling behavior," Edwin said, sneering, "but do not forget that the Pendery whore has accused me of getting her with child in such a manner."

"She recants," Rhiannyn said.

"What?" The question was spoken in unison by both Edwin and Maxen.

Rhiannyn nodded. "As she was birthing the child, she told both Christophe and me the truth—that she gave herself to you, Edwin, to hide from her father her loss of virginity to another man."

Maxen had not expected that scenario, having presumed that though it had not been rape that had brought Elan and Edwin together, she had been a virgin previous to their encounter.

"That may be," Edwin said, "but do you count the months, you will see that the babe comes too early to be mine."

That had also occurred to Rhiannyn, but she had been given proof otherwise as she had cleaned the infant. "He was born young," she said, "but he bears the Harwolfson blood." To prove her claim, she picked free the cloth covering the baby's feet and revealed the little one's left foot. "Four toes," she said, "as have you, Edwin."

While he stared in disbelief, Rhiannyn recalled her first encounter with Edwin at the river. Unabashedly, he had removed his boots to wade in the water while they'd talked, and she had noticed the absence of the smallest toe on his left foot. He had bantered about it, said that a hundred years earlier a witch had placed a curse on his family that all males born of the Harwolfsons would in this way be known for their treachery. When she had asked what treachery he spoke of, he had only smiled devilishly, then gone off on another topic.

"He is your son," Rhiannyn said, tucking the cloth around the baby's feet.

There was struggle in Edwin's eyes, and when he met Rhiannyn's gaze, he made no attempt to mask it. "And this is your peace?" he asked. "A son in exchange for all of England?" He threw his arms wide to encompass the land before him.

"England is William's," Maxen answered.

"Not after this day," Edwin barked.

"Aye," Maxen said, "even more so after this day do you fight a battle you cannot win." Having seen Edwin's men up close, and the uncertainty so many fought to hide, Maxen was convinced of it, though he would never tell William.

Edwin looked behind him, then back at Maxen. "My army outnumbers the bastard's," he said.

"Numbers only," Maxen harshly pointed out. "Of more importance is what each man brings to the battlefield. Experience in bloodletting, Edwin. Can you say that even half your men have that? One quarter of them? William will make but another example of you."

Edwin looked beyond Maxen to the king's army, and did not let go of the sight for long minutes. Then he focused on Maxen again. "Do we die here or in his prisons, it makes no difference," he said. "Here we have a chance to regain what is ours. Your way we lose everything."

"Not if you give William a reason to keep you and your followers alive."

Edwin tried to hide his interest, but some of it came through for Maxen to hang hope upon.

"What do you propose?" Edwin asked, his gaze drifting betrayingly to the child Rhiannyn held.

"Etcheverry," Maxen said. "Submit to the king, give him your fealty, and it is yours."

Disbelieving laughter erupted from Edwin. "And I am to believe that you would simply hand the castle and lands over to me?"

"If King William agrees, it will be done. My word to you."

"Your word? What of your word to Aethel and the others when you told them they could go from Etcheverry without harm? What of the man who died at the point of your arrow, Maxen Pendery?"

"Not my arrow," Maxen ground out, "and neither did he die."

"Shot in the back he was," Edwin spat.

"Edwin, 'tis true what Maxen speaks," Rhiannyn hurriedly broke in. "It was the knight Ancel Rogere who was responsible for Hob being shot, and now the knave is dead for it." She looked to Maxen. "And Hob lives."

"If that is true, then why has he not come to me?" Edwin asked.

"He has accepted Maxen as his lord."

"Not the Hob I knew."

"Aye," Rhiannyn conceded, "a different Hob, but of the same flesh."

While Edwin searched her face for the lie in what she said, Rhiannyn waited.

"Put an end to it, Edwin," Maxen urged. "You are the only one with the power to do it. Not William, but you."

It came as a surprise to both Rhiannyn and Maxen when Edwin wheeled his horse about, but naught else followed. He simply sat in his saddle before his men as if searching for the answer in their faces.

"Brave, my foolish Saxon," Maxen whispered in Rhiannyn's ear, "but do I live long enough to have you in my bed again, I will make you pay for every worry you have given me this day."

She smiled, knowing that his punishment would be of benefit to them both.

The minutes stretched taut until it was not a man who snapped it, but a babe less than a half hour old. The child began to cry heartily and to wriggle in Rhiannyn's arms.

When Edwin looked around, a frown upon his brow, Rhiannyn explained, "He needs his mother's breast."

Unexpectedly, Edwin nudged his horse alongside Rhiannyn's and peered down at the howling baby. "My son," he murmured, then reached forward and touched a finger to his bottom lip. The baby responded immediately, dropping his chin and sucking Edwin's finger into his mouth. "Indeed he is hungry," Edwin said with a mixture of wonder and shock. "I give you leave to take him to his mother." Drawing his hand back, he winced as the baby again took up a great howl. "Go, Rhiannyn. Pendery and I will finish this."

Wishing it would be finished that moment, that she might ride back to Elan and Christophe with good news to report, Rhiannyn glanced at Maxen, then prodded her mount.

"What have I to do?" Edwin asked when Rhiannyn was out of earshot.

The burden that had weighted Maxen's shoulders and

plagued his soul for more than two years shifted as if to ease, but did not lift—not yet. There was still much to be done. "Ask it," he answered.

"Very well. I will agree to what you have proposed, but would add my own terms to it."

"Which are?"

"Pardon for my men and a place for them."

"Of course," Maxen agreed. "'Twould be expected that a good many of them would follow you to Etcheverry. What else?"

"I want my son."

Considering Elan's intention of casting the child upon the Church, Maxen did not think it such a difficult request. "I will put it to the king," he said.

"And Elan."

Revenge. "That I cannot agree to," Maxen said. "Though my sister has done wrong, I will not allow you to do her any harm, Harwolfson."

One side of Edwin's mouth hitched into a caustic smile. "Harm? 'Tis true I despise her, but you are wrong about my intentions. As she bore my son, I would have her continue on as his mother. Thus, I will take her to wife."

Maxen could not have been more astounded had Edwin slid a dagger into his breast. "And what guarantee can you give me that you will not mistreat her?" he asked, the remembrance that Elan was already promised to Guy weighing most heavily upon him.

"My word," Edwin said. "The same as your word, Pendery."

"It may not be possible."

"But the battle is. Deliver me these things, and I will submit to the bastard. Deny me and . . ."

Maxen nodded. "I will take your proposal to the king."

"I will await his answer here."

Maxen turned his mount, but before he could dig his heels in, Edwin tossed a question at him. "Why is it so important to you, Pendery?"

Maxen looked over his shoulder at him. "Rhiannyn," he said, and that was enough. Though once he wished this peace only for the unburdening of his soul, now above all there was Rhiannyn.

The king was adamant. He had agreed to everything Edwin Harwolfson asked for—even Elan Pendery, in spite of the fit her father had thrown which had seen him dragged from the field—but not Etcheverry. Etcheverry was to remain Pendery, and nothing would move William on this all-important point. His explanation: it was too strategically placed for one he did not trust to command it.

Wondering if all had been for naught, Maxen returned to Edwin. "King William will permit you your son, Elan in marriage, and a demesne of a size to accommodate your people," he said.

"But?" Edwin asked.

Maxen stared into the man's knowing eyes. "But not Etcheverry."

Edwin's eyebrows inched high. "Is that right? Well you can tell your bastard liege that Etcheverry is not negotiable."

"What is negotiable?" Maxen asked.

After a moment's hesitation, Edwin said, "Though I do not wish my son to be named a bastard, I might be persuaded to give on wedding your sister."

Maxen was not surprised. "I regret the king will not agree," he said.

"Then I regret that we are where we were ere Rhiannyn brought the babe to me," Edwin pronounced. As if that were the end of it, he jerked the reins to turn his horse about.

Knowing the risk in what he did, Maxen grabbed Edwin's arm to stay him. Immediately, Edwin's soldiers reacted, the united clatter of their weapons echoed a moment later by that of William's soldiers.

"Think, man!" Maxen said. "Put aside your pride and think of your son growing up amongst the clergy. No mother. No father. A bastard. Think of the lives that will be spent for something that can never be. Can you live with it—likely die with it?"

All of Edwin's body tensed as he stared into Maxen's eyes, so much so that he began to tremble with the anger and indecision that coursed through him. Finally, he spoke. "Your problem, Pendery, is that you love. That makes you more a fool than I."

He loved. Lord, he had lied to himself at every turn of the heart, Maxen realized. He had refused to acknowledge it even when it had been near to bursting from him. But now he realized that what Edwin spoke was true. He loved Rhiannyn. "Nay, not a fool," he said. " 'Tis blessed that I am. But you'll never know that, will you?"

Edwin jerked his arm out of Maxen's hold. "What demesne does your bastard king offer?"

Maxen had just begun to accept that the chance for peace was lost, but now, miraculously, it appeared again. "Blackspur Castle," he answered, "and all its lands." What a mess, he thought as the words passed his lips. Blackspur was to have been Guy's, as was Elan. Now both might be snatched from his friend and ally.

"It does not even compare to Etcheverry," Edwin was quick to retort.

" 'Tis more land to settle upon for those who follow you. The castle is nearly completed. Water is there aplenty, and with hard work, the land will come to produce well."

"And I would be under your constant watch, wouldn't I?"

"The two lands border," Maxen agreed. " 'Tis natural that our goings-on would be seen by each other, but you would not answer to me. You would be vassal to the king, not to me."

"But if I should overstep my bounds, no doubt you would be there to rein me in, hmm?"

Sensing that Edwin had already accepted Blackspur, Maxen did not rise to the man's bait. It was too precarious a situation. "Do you accept, Edwin Harwolfson?"

Edwin's nostrils flared and his lips thinned until they

were more pale than the rest of him, but he nodded. "You can tell your king he has his peace."

Maxen's haunting of Hastings lifted from his shoulders, though still it hovered above his head. "And Elan?" he asked, praying that at least Guy would have something left of what he had been given.

As if he knew what havoc he wreaked, Edwin smiled. "I have surrendered Etcheverry," he said. "I will give no more."

It was heavens more than Maxen had believed possible when the trumpets had been called for that morn, but still he felt as if a stone lay in his belly. At least Guy would live, he attempted to console himself. Had the battle raged, the man might have lost even more than he already had. It was of little comfort, though.

"The bargain is struck, then," he said.

A distant look entered Edwin's eyes. "For as long as he keeps his end of it," he said, shifting his gaze to the man horsed behind the papal banner. Then he wheeled about and rode through the ranks of his men.

Forgiven, Maxen thought as he spurred his mount back across the field. It was as if the burden of a thousand years was lifted from him. Now his life with Rhiannyn could truly begin.

Chapter Thirty-one

It was gone the nooning hour before Maxen's role as intermediary was finally concluded. Body and soul spent from the stubborn haggling between Edwin and William, he guided his horse up the rise, and once atop it, paused to look out upon the field that might be ankle-deep in blood if not for the terrible risk Rhiannyn had taken.

Although both armies continued to stand opposite one another, few were the arms that had not been laid down, and rare was the soldier who continued to wear the stifling raiments of battle. It was over—though just for this day, Maxen reminded himself. Tomorrow, or the morrow after, there would come another uprising, though it was unlikely any would be as massive as Edwin's. The threat to William's crown was past. England was his.

Dragging free of matters he wanted

nothing more to do with, Maxen turned his horse toward the tents. In the next instant, though, he pulled the reins in. There, less than ten feet out, stood Rhiannyn. Her chin lifted high and hands splayed upon her hips in defense of the wrath she anticipated, she met his gaze.

Ah anger, Maxen thought ruefully. Why do you desert me now when 'tis over my knee I ought to put her? Wanting nothing more than to hold her, he beckoned her forward. "Come."

Uncertainty flashed across her face, but a moment later, her Saxon determination returned. " 'Twas right what I did." She spoke with unwavering conviction.

"Aye, it was. Now do you come to me or I to you?"

Clearly she was surprised that he conceded so easily, was even a bit suspicious. For a long moment, she considered him, then lifted her skirts and crossed to his side. "You are not angry?" she asked.

Reaching down, he caressed her cheek. "Mayhap tomorrow," he said, "but not today."

A hesitant smile reached her lips. "And of the morrow?" she asked.

Loving her as he did—every sparkle in her eye, every twitch of her nose, every tilt of her mouth—he could not help but smile. "I am most certain there are better ways to spend my displeasure than shouting it upon your head."

Her smile grew more certain. "Aye, there are."

He glided his thumb across her lower lip, then asked, "Will you come with me, Rhiannyn?"

She raised her arms to him.

Bracing his knees into the sides of his mount, Maxen lifted her slight figure up before him. "Let us find a soft place to lie down," he said.

"There is our tent."

He shook his head. "Nay, where none can interrupt us."

"I would like that," she said, and settled against him.

Such a place away from prying eyes was hard won, but finally Maxen and Rhiannyn found their peace in the wood. There they shared a loving free of the fetters of battle, and only when all that was in them was well and truly spent did they share words beyond their bodies.

"You are a seer unto my soul, Saxon witch," Maxen murmured into Rhiannyn's hair.

Liking the warmth of his breath upon her, she nestled more deeply into his shoulder and curved her body tightly against his side.

"I've a confession to make," he continued.

A confession. Rhiannyn was jolted back to the unpleasantness of her lie, which had yet to be revealed to him. If only it was already done with, she lamented, then this wonderful closeness they shared would not be shattered. But she must tell him. "I, too, have a confession," she said, her heart thudding so heavily she did not think it her own.

"Later," Maxen said, then tilted her chin up and captured her gaze with his. "I have worked a deception upon you, Rhiannyn—although it has yet to bear fruit."

She frowned. "Deception?"

Regret in his eyes, he nodded. "I enlisted Christophe's help that my seed might take and render you pregnant."

One moment Rhiannyn was curled against him, and in the next she had scrambled onto her knees. "What?" she exclaimed, uncaring that her only covering was her loosed hair about her shoulders.

Maxen raised himself to sitting. " 'Tis true," he said. "I asked Christophe to substitute another mixture for that which kept you barren."

"But why? Why would you wish a bastard upon me— upon you?"

He laid a callused hand against her heated cheek. "Can you not guess?"

She simply stared at him.

God's rood! Maxen silently cursed. Why was it so difficult to say? And why did he feel such a boy when he was now more than a dozen years a man? Finally, he struggled the words to the fore of his mouth. "It was to have been my excuse for wedding you," he admitted.

Stunned, she dropped back onto her heels, and though she opened her mouth to speak, she remained silent.

"What does it tell you, Rhiannyn?" he asked.

As if she did not even wish to ponder what it might mean, she mutely shook her head.

Then he would show her, Maxen decided. Rising onto his knees, he bent his head and covered her mouth with his. Rhiannyn was slow to respond, but when at last she did, it was with the dawning knowledge that he loved her.

With much regret, Maxen ended the kiss and drew back to search her face. Her confusion had cleared, and in its place he saw the mingling of disbelief and joy. "It cannot be," she said, her eyes awash with tears.

"It is," he assured her. "I love you, Rhiannyn."

Uncertainty pulled at her mouth, but then a smile, bright as a summer day, broke through. "I thought never to hear the words from you, though God knows I had ever hoped to."

"And now that you have heard them, can you tell me the same?"

Without hesitation, she declared, "I love you, Maxen. With all my mind, my body, and my soul." Throwing herself against him, she slid her arms up around his neck and clasped herself to him.

Something wonderful unfolding within him, Maxen pressed her head to his heart. "I would take you to wife that you might forevermore be known by my name," he said. "Rhiannyn Pendery."

How unlike Thomas he was, Rhiannyn thought as she basked in the love she had thought forbidden her. Although Thomas's obsession with her had caused him to declare his undying love for her at every turn, he had been naught but a shell of a man. Maxen was filled to brimming.

In the next instant, Rhiannyn unsuspectingly tripped over her love for Maxen and fell back to a time when she had known nothing of is existence. As she continued to hold to him, a day of rain and tears returned to her, and most loudly, Thomas's dying curses—curses she had accepted as his due. But she could no longer accept them. Not when there was Maxen and their child. . . .

Her thoughts trailed into the dust of a hundred misgivings. Not only Thomas, but the lie she had told Maxen regarding her pregnancy stood between them, and soon he would know the truth whether or not she spoke it. How he hated her lies, regardless of her reason for summoning them. Might this, then, be Thomas's curse realized? With her admission, would she lose Maxen's love? Rhiannyn fought the tremble that rose from deep inside her, but it shivered onto her bare skin.

"You are cold?" Maxen asked.

She had to tell him, she decided with fallen heart—all of it, from Thomas's death to the child they had made together. It could wait no longer. "Nay, only fearful," she said.

He pulled back. "Fearful?" he repeated, his gaze questioning. "I will make you a good husband, Rhiannyn. My vow to you."

"I know you will," she said. "That is, if you still wish to wed me after I have told you what I must."

His brows knit as he stared at her, then his mouth tightened. In a voice ragged with weariness, he asked, "More lies?"

She nodded. "One ... and some truths you may not wish to hear, but ought to."

His eyes closed briefly before opening again. "Have done with it," he said.

Risking all, Rhiannyn steadied her gaze on him. "About Thomas," she began.

"What of him?"

Seeing the suspicion that came upon his face, she was quick to remedy it. "Ah, nay," she said, " 'tis not what you think. I do not know who killed him. That truth remains."

"Then?"

She drew a deep breath. "When he lay dying in my arms, 'twas me he blamed for his death. Had I not run from him—"

"We have already discussed this," he said, relief shining out of his eyes, "and resolved it. You could not have known that he would be fool enough to chase after you without escort. His death is upon his own shoulders, not yours."

"But 'tis more than that, Maxen. I carry his curse."

"What nonsense do you speak?"

She closed her eyes as the words came so clearly to her, it was as if Thomas, and not Maxen, knelt before her. "A thousand times he cursed me," she said, lifting her lids to stare into Maxen's eyes. "To eternity."

"I do not believe in such foolery," he said, "and neither did my brother."

"But he spoke it."

"A man angry with his own death speaks many things when his passing comes slowly." As if his own words had struck him, he lapsed into thoughtful silence, then asked, "Was he in much pain?"

So easy to say Thomas had eased into death to prevent Maxen's wrath from unleashing itself upon her, but it would only be another lie. Rhiannyn steeled herself. "Aye."

He looked past her. "At least you are honest," he said, his voice tight with whatever emotion he fought to keep down.

Drawn to his pain, she laid a hand to his shoulder. "I am sorry, Maxen. So sorry."

Time passed like a bow drawing taut, then it sprang, though not as Rhiannyn had feared. "What is this curse you say you carry?" Maxen asked.

Rhiannyn grasped wildly to set aside her surprise. "That if I—if I would not belong to a Pendery, then I would belong to no man." *Your days and nights yawning pits of deepest despair*, she did not say, though those words were as much with her as the others.

"And that is all?"

She watched him closely. "He said that never again would I know the love of a man."

"The rest of it," he prompted.

"He called to you."

"To me?"

"Aye, to the heavens he called for his brother to avenge

him. At the time I thought he meant Christophe, but when you came to me in the dungeon, I knew it was you."

"The Bloodlust Warrior."

She nodded.

"And you believe Thomas's curse?"

"I ought not," she said, though a small part of her still believed in the traditions of her ancestors, "but I accepted it as his due—that I would have neither husband nor children."

"And still you accept it?"

She shook her head. "If 'tis true that you love me, I do not wish to accept it any longer."

Maxen touched her hand. "I do, Rhiannyn."

For a fleeting moment, she wondered if it was possible Dora had lifted the curse as she had proclaimed. Nay, she vehemently rejected the thought. If any was responsible for this love, it was God.

"Still," Maxen continued, "methinks that one part of Thomas's curse has been fulfilled."

She tipped her head to the side. "I do not understand."

"That if you would not belong to a Pendery, then you would belong to no man. Do you not belong to me, Rhiannyn?"

Strangely, she had not considered that, but he was right. She belonged to him—a Pendery. "Aye," she said, glorying in her happiness before reminding herself that there were still issues yet to be resolved between them. "What of your vengeance against the one who murdered Thomas?"

Maxen did not immediately respond, but the emotions of his thoughts shifted unguardedly across his face. "If ever I am to know who it was," he said finally, "then the answer must come to me. No longer will I seek it myself."

"Then you accept Thomas's death?"

"As much as I can."

Which was more than she had ever thought possible.

"Now the lie, Rhiannyn," he said, reminding her of the final test she must put his love to.

There was no way to soften it. Lowering her gaze, she

stared at the space between them which in a matter of months would be filled with her pregnancy. "There is something you are wrong about," she began.

"Which is?"

"That your deception upon me did not bear fruit." She swallowed the lump that rose in her throat. "I am with child, Maxen. It was a lie I spoke when I denied it." The truth finally said, she gathered all her courage and looked up to gauge his anger.

And there was anger—great and roiling within him. Maxen felt it almost as deeply as his love for this woman, but still it could not match that greater emotion. "Then 'twas not only yourself you placed in jeopardy when you rode to Edwin," he said, his words knit tight with tension. "You also risked our child."

Her anguish showing, she nodded. "I did, but it was a small risk I took. I knew Edwin would do me no harm, that even if I failed he would but send me back behind the field of battle."

"And what if one of William's men had shot you believing you to be a traitor?"

She acknowledged the possibility with a nod. "It had to be done, though, else it would not have been the blood of two, but of thousands. Please understand."

He did, though it stung that he might have lost her as well as their unborn child. He thrust a hand through his hair, rested it at the back of his head, then dropped his arm back to his side. "I understand, Rhiannyn," he said, then asked, "but why did you lie to me about the child? Why could you not have told me what you already knew to be true?"

"I was . . . uncertain. I did not think you loved me, and believed that the only future I and our child would have at Etcheverry was that of leman and bastard. I even considered running away from you that none would know how the babe was got."

"Yet you did not," Maxen said, sending thanks heavenward for keeping her with him.

"I couldn't. I loved you too much."

Maxen's anger dissolved like a morning mist gone to sun, and though he longed to drag Rhiannyn back into his arms, he continued to hold himself from her. There was one last thing he needed to know before all could be put behind them. "When you decided you would not run from me, why did you not tell me of the child?"

"I wanted to," she said, "but the time never seemed right. And when finally I decided it could wait no longer, William arrived. With his coming, it seemed best to delay telling you the truth until after the confrontation with Edwin."

"Why?"

"I feared that your anger with me might overshadow what you would face on the battlefield. I couldn't bear the thought of losing you to a lie." She waited for him to say something, and when he did not, asked, "Have I lost you, Maxen?"

He could hold out no longer. Pulling her against him, he folded her in his arms. "Nay, you've not lost me, Rhiannyn. You've found me . . . and I you."

She tipped her head back. "Then you forgive me?"

He brushed his lips across hers. "If you can forgive me for my deception upon which yours was built," he said, then laid his palm to her belly.

A shudder moved through Rhiannyn, followed by the easing of her tense body. "Naught to forgive," she murmured, then accepted his mouth more fully upon hers.

In a world turned timeless, they clung together—touching, tasting, and feeling each other's love—until daylight waned and the heat of their bodies was no longer enough to offset the chill of approaching night.

"No more lies, hmm?" Maxen said as he settled Rhiannyn's mantle about her shoulders.

"No more," she agreed. "The past is behind us."

He turned her to face him. "And now will you speak vows with me, Rhiannyn of Etcheverry?"

Lifting her hand, she laid it against his jaw and looked into eyes that had come unveiled for her. "Aye, Maxen, I will be your wife."

ABOUT THE AUTHOR

TAMARA LEIGH has a Master's Degree in Speech and Language Pathology. She lives in the small town of Gardnerville located at the base of the Sierra Nevada Mountains with her husband David, who is a former "Cosmopolitan Bachelor of the Month." Tamara says her husband is incredibly romantic, and is the inspiration for her writing. They have one child. You may write to her at: P.O. Box 1088, Gardnerville, NV 89410.

Enter the world of

TAMARA LEIGH

"Tamara Leigh writes fresh, exciting and wonderfully
sensual historical romance." —*New York Times*
bestselling author Amanda Quick

WARRIOR BRIDE
___56533-8 $5.50/$6.99 Canada

A beautiful woman skilled in the art of war falls prisoner to the
warrior who'd stolen her future . . . and even more than her
handsome captor she fears her own treacherous desires.

VIRGIN BRIDE
___56536-2 $5.50/$6.99

Lady Graeye Charwyck would give anything to avoid
being sent to a convent—even her virtue—but she never
suspects she'll also lose her heart.

PAGAN BRIDE
___56535-4 $5.50/$7.50

In exchange for his freedom, Lucien de Gautier pledges
to smuggle a young woman out of a harem—he couldn't
know the danger he'll face in the ravishing innocent
who would unleash his most sensual desires.

DON'T MISS THESE FABULOUS
BANTAM WOMEN'S FICTION TITLES

DON'T MISS THESE FABULOUS
BANTAM WOMEN'S FICTION TITLES

Bestselling Historical Women's Fiction

AMANDA QUICK

____28354-5 SEDUCTION .....$6.50/$8.99 in Canada
____28932-2 SCANDAL ....$5.99/$6.99
____28594-7 SURRENDER ....$6.50/$8.99
____29325-7 RENDEZVOUS ....$5.99/$6.99
____29315-X RECKLESS ....$6.50/$8.99
____29316-8 RAVISHED ....$6.50/$8.99
____29317-6 DANGEROUS ....$6.50/$8.99
____56506-0 DECEPTION ....$5.99/$7.50
____56153-7 DESIRE ....$6.50/$8.99
____56940-6 MISTRESS ....$5.99/$7.99
____09698-2 MYSTIQUE ....$21.95/$24.95

———

IRIS JOHANSEN

____29871-2 LAST BRIDGE HOME ......$4.50/$5.50
____29604-3 THE GOLDEN BARBARIAN ..$4.99/$5.99
____29244-7 REAP THE WIND ....$5.99/$7.50
____29032-0 STORM WINDS ....$4.99/$5.99
____28855-5 THE WIND DANCER ....$5.99/$6.99
____29968-9 THE TIGER PRINCE ......$5.99/$6.99
____29944-1 THE MAGNIFICENT ROGUE .$5.99/$6.99
____29945-X BELOVED SCOUNDREL ....$5.99/$6.99
____29946-8 MIDNIGHT WARRIOR .....$5.99/$6.99
____29947-6 DARK RIDER ....$5.99/$7.99

———

TERESA MEDEIROS

____29407-5 HEATHER AND VELVET ....$5.99/$7.50
____29409-1 ONCE AN ANGEL ....$5.99/$7.99
____29408-3 A WHISPER OF ROSES ......$5.50/$6.50
____56332-7 THIEF OF HEARTS ....$5.50/$6.99
____56333-5 FAIREST OF THEM ALL ....$5.99/$7.50

- - - - - - - - - - - - - - - - - - - -

Ask for these books at your local bookstore or use this page to order.

Please send me the books I have checked above. I am enclosing $_____(add $2.50 to cover postage and handling). Send check or money order, no cash or C.O.D.'s, please.

Name _____

Address _____

City/State/Zip _____

Send order to: Bantam Books, Dept. FN 16, 2451 S. Wolf Rd., Des Plaines, IL 60018
Allow four to six weeks for delivery.
Prices and availability subject to change without notice.   FN 16 3/96

THE VERY BEST IN CONTEMPORARY
WOMEN'S FICTION

SANDRA BROWN

___28951-9 Texas! Lucky $6.50/$8.99 in Canada
___28990-X Texas! Chase $6.50/$8.99
___29500-4 Texas! Sage $6.50/$8.99
___29085-1 22 Indigo Place $5.99/$6.99
___29783-X A Whole New Light $5.99/$6.99

___56768-3 Adam's Fall $4.99/$5.99
___56045-X Temperatures Rising $5.99/$6.99
___56274-6 Fanta C $5.50/$6.99
___56278-9 Long Time Coming $4.99/$5.99
___57157-5 Heaven's Price $5.50/$6.99

TAMI HOAG

___29534-9 Lucky's Lady $5.99/$7.50
___29053-3 Magic $5.99/$7.50
___56050-6 Sarah's Sin $4.99/$5.99

___29272-2 Still Waters $5.99/$7.50
___56160-X Cry Wolf $5.50/$6.50
___56161-8 Dark Paradise $5.99/$7.50

___09961-2 Night Sins $19.95/$23.95

NORA ROBERTS

___29078-9 Genuine Lies $5.99/$6.99
___28578-5 Public Secrets $5.99/$6.99
___26461-3 Hot Ice $5.99/$6.99
___26574-1 Sacred Sins $5.99/$6.99

___27859-2 Sweet Revenge $5.99/$6.99
___27283-7 Brazen Virtue $5.99/$6.99
___29597-7 Carnal Innocence $5.99/$6.99
___29490-3 Divine Evil $5.99/$6.99

DEBORAH SMITH

___29107-6 Miracle $5.50/$6.50
___29092-4 Follow the Sun $4.99/$5.99

___29690-6 Blue Willow $5.99/$7.99
___29689-2 Silk and Stone $5.99/$6.99

___28759-1 The Beloved Woman $4.50/$5.50

- -

Ask for these books at your local bookstore or use this page to order.

Please send me the books I have checked above. I am enclosing $_____ (add $2.50 to cover postage and handling). Send check or money order, no cash or C.O.D.'s, please.

Name _____

Address _____

City/State/Zip _____

Send order to: Bantam Books, Dept. FN 24, 2451 S. Wolf Rd., Des Plaines, IL 60018

Allow four to six weeks for delivery.

Prices and availability subject to change without notice.   FN 24 1/96

From *The New York Times* bestselling author

Amanda Quick

*stories of passion and romance
that will stir your heart*

Don't miss any of the sensuous
historical romances of

Susan Johnson